CONVINCED

CONVINCED

Book 2

of the

Paradigm Shift Trilogy

RAVEN H. PRICE

DEDICATION

To anyone who feels unlovable

Acknowledgements

First, I want to acknowledge my husband, Ralph W. Price III, again, who patiently puts up with my desire to write. Second, I want to acknowledge Shannon Hegwood Baker and Regina Hegwood for helping me proofread and edit my books. Third, I want to acknowledge my pastor, Stan Glass. His grace-and-love message has helped me see the truth in God's Word. Fourth, I'd like to thank Curry and Robin Bushnell for their makeup expertise and photography.

Disclaimer/Copyright

Convinced

This book is Christian Fiction and based on the author's imagination and faith. No one is slandered or libeled in this work; resemblance to other persons living or dead is purely coincidental in nature and places where events take place are fake to the author's knowledge. No portion of this book may be reproduced, stored in a retrieval system, or transmitted in any form or by any means electronic, mechanical, photocopy, recording, scanning, or other-except for brief quotations in critical reviews or articles, without the prior written permission of the author(s). No part of this book may be made into a movie without permission of the author(s). All rights reserved

Print history
First edition published April 2015
Second edition published November 2016

ISBN-13: 978-0692663141
ISBN-10: 978-0692663142
ASIN: B01CZ0IKSQ
Library of Congress Cataloguing-in-Publication Data

Contents

Prologue

In the spirit realm of the Most High God, the four generals of the angelic army accompany Jesus. Each general has command of angelic leagues sent to earth. The angels on earth, as in heaven, operate by rank. Everything in heaven and on earth follows God's specific order.

Earth must bow to God's will. Earthbound angels have orders from Jesus to reset the balance. Hidden in the spirit realm, these angels listen for the truth. Truth from the Holy Spirit's voice within God's children imbues them with power.

All over the world, the Holy Spirit continues to form the body of Christ, God's harvesting machine. Little by little, he finds candidates willing to be led. Once the Holy Spirit determines the person's ability, they are chosen by Jesus and assigned a heaven- bound general to watch over them.

The heaven-bound generals are known by their character. Characteristics empowered by Jesus Himself. These mighty angels have Jesus's spirit of insight, His spirit of justice, His healing ability, and His faith. Therefore, they are called Insight, Justice, Healer, and Faith.

On earth, the earthbound angels under the authority of Jesus's generals assist a chosen human candidate. Through the Holy Spirit's gifting, the chosen are empowered with a characteristic of Jesus and given a guardian angel. These angels assist, minister, and empower the chosen to do the will of the Father.

Once the balance is reset, heaven rejoices as a harvesting machine for souls is created. Even though the machine is complete in the spirit realm, on earth, the creation of such a mechanism takes time and patience.

~~~

In book two of The Paradigm Shift Trilogy, readers will learn how God's machine comes together.

Readers will also see how heaven and earth work with man to accomplish God's desire to gather souls.

In this segment, faith on earth is under attack. Until the battle is won in the earthly realm, the harvesting machine won't operate correctly. Satan targets mankind, forcing his images, his notions, and evil plots upon them, rendering them helpless. Death rules in the guise of life, giving people false hopes and dreams.

Jesus knows mankind needs childlike faith to overcome. Jesus also knows mankind needs help to let go and die to self-preservations. The faith of Jesus is twofold: childlike and sacrificial. This is why Faith has the face of a cherub in heaven, but Faith on earth has the face of the Ox. God sees Jesus's faith as a child in the spirit realm but as a beast on earth, willing to die for the chosen.

~~~

The Ox hears a joyful noise on earth. Heaven rejoices when a harvesting machine is operational again. Jesus has chosen a candidate. Ox can hardly wait for his orders to search for the chosen one he must serve. When the general's orders arrive, he is surprised. He is told to find two women this time. The Holy Spirit explains to him that in order to keep Satan confused, Jesus is using the Father's predetermined rule of seed-time harvest. Heaven's mystery was wrapped up within God's original plan. Jesus decides to use one woman with childlike faith to release joy from the word into another woman void of any knowledge of God.

Ox reveled in the knowledge that he would still get to work with someone he helped previously. He enjoyed the young-adult ministry, which allowed Him access; now he could look forward to being a part of it once again. The newly chosen candidate to become the reaper had a long journey, but with the help of Healer's human, Insight's human, and Justice's human, they could sway the reaper correctly.

Brent and Hope Arnold's young-adult ministry was the Lord's idea. Caylee Sellers, a needy young girl hungry for love, parental guidance, and approval, was guided to them. Caylee finds the Lord through the Arnold couple's personal witness. Their unconditional love helped the Ox develop within her childlike faith.

~~~

Joy from childlike faith can't be contained, and without knowledge, Caylee sows God's Word. God's Word as seed finds purchase in the heart of Gina Grimes, an unlearned and unprepared vessel, who is a perfect candidate to confound the wise.

Always lurking in the shadows, Satan watched as Hope and Brent Arnold worked for Jesus. While focusing on them, Satan didn't notice until it was too late that the Holy Spirit used one of the Arnolds' protégées. Before he could do anything to stop her, the young woman planted hope in an unbeliever. Furious, Satan screamed, "This cannot be!"

He has to steal that seed immediately! If he has to kill both girls in the process, hope must not grow.

Worried that his reign in the area is short, Satan risks everything and dispatches his demonic giants. He releases energy-feeding imps into the area. Earth is his!

My Merry-Go-Round

At twenty-three and recently out of college, I managed to free myself from the family home. For years, I longed to be released from Mom's controlling grasp and complaining. Her smothering attention would overwhelm me at times. Since my parents' divorce, Mom had been having issues. Her emotions ruled her. If life treated her good, I was her baby, which in turn caused her to smother me. If life treated her bad, she became overbearing, condemning, and complaining toward everyone.

Landing a job at a state Mental Health Center gave me the opportunity to change. I have money of my own now. I found a one-bedroom apartment and set up house. My new place isn't much, but it gives me the much-needed freedom I crave.

I had a comrade in my best friend from college. Angie Meadows, and I felt the same way; she hated being controlled by overbearing parents. We hated being condemned for our actions when we partied and flirted.

Angie and I thought about partying constantly. Our partying started every Friday at the local pool hall. There was no pressure, no judging parent breathing down my neck now that I live on my own

I thought my life was great until this new employee started working alongside me. Caylee Sellers, in her own sweet way, shared her religion with me each day. She made Christianity interesting and appealing. She talked about Jesus so much he became real to me. This God, who had come to earth, was a loving, accepting, and helpful person.

As Caylee talked about Jesus, she shared her dreams with me. She believed Jesus was bringing her a good life. She counted on that! What got my attention was how she thanked God for something she didn't have. She lived every day happy.

As I tentatively listened and watched her, I began to question myself. Was I truly experiencing a good life? No, I wasn't! I asked her how she coped. Her answer was enlightening: "I don't have to worry. God provides me with all I need."

Caylee's peace and joy overwhelmed me. Was this Jesus she professed my answer? I wanted the peace and joy I saw in her life. If believing what she said about Jesus was the answer, why not try?

She said he died for me. All I had to do was talk to Him, tell Him I sinned, ask for His forgiveness and help to change. If I did, I was guaranteed a better life.

I couldn't wait! Seated at my office desk, I decided I needed Jesus. I took a deep breath, closed my eyes, and bowed my head. "Jesus, if you are my answer, I need you. I've sinned and need forgiveness. Please help me change."

~~~

Jesus sang with joy as He threw out the robe of righteousness, His blood-soaked garment of divine love and protection. Heaven resounded with glee while ministering angels applied Gina's robe over her body. The time had come! God's kingdom could prepare for a harvest of souls! The Lord has chosen a candidate for Faith!

~~~

Satan was angry! Right before his eyes and at his playhouse of mental illness, Jesus's hope had been planted. Jesus had played a sick joke on him. Jesus would not have this girl. He would make sure the grain was plucked out immediately! That particular seed had to be aborted. He would use one of his mentally ill to destroy the seed. If he had to kill the girl, so be it!

Reaching into the past of this particular girl's life for ammunition to use against her, Satan saw she already had a self-absorbed party spirit. Friday night was the girl's usual playtime. He was about to have fun.

~~~

In heaven, a meeting with the generals was in session. Time ruled earth's growth cycle, and patience was man's weakest emotion. Patience had to be allowed perfect work. The earthbound angels had to have assistance, or Satan would use time to his advantage. To their advantage, they knew Satan understood that once Jesus established something, nothing could prevent it from manifesting. Now a war was on! Angels everywhere were geared for trials, tribulations, and persecutions.

~~~

Me, Gina Grimes, a born-again Christian! Who would have thought? I didn't feel any different; time would tell. I was new at this. I had to watch Caylee, see how it was done. She was a good example for me.

~~~

Inside the mental health facility, Ox smelled the scent of freshly plowed earth in the air. He'd found the other fledgling! No doubt, rocky hard soil had been plowed very recently. He smelled hope! He smelled the blood of Jesus, indicating a covenant robe had been given coming from within the facility. The scent was given, a newborn spirit was undeniable, the smell of life!

He was overjoyed the job could begin. Heaven immediately notified Ox of rough circumstances about to come against the mind and body of the newborn. His guardianship over the new believer was imperative. Inside the facility, Ox also noticed Caylee, the sower. She was unaware of what had happened. Seeking advice, he communed with the generals of heaven. Without their involvement, he was helpless. How could he split and guard two? Hearing Ox's pleas and seeing his dilemma, Jesus notified the generals that He would guard Caylee. Caylee had already died to self. Ox could focus on the other girl.

The generals assured Ox that Caylee had Jesus's favor. He must focus on the newborn. She, on the other hand, was without protection. He would need to stay close to her. This newborn hadn't experienced God's love yet. She didn't know He gave grace to count on for protection.

Encouraged by the news Caylee was provided for, Ox focused on influencing Gina's mind. Together with the Holy Spirit, they would render assistance to help Gina resist evil traditions until the Word could be planted deep.

Satan watched and listened to Ox as he placed desires in Gina's mind. He'd let him speak then counter with words of doubt. Satan thought the spiritual battle against the Holy Spirit was invigorating. This game was always fun. Ever since he fooled Eve into believing him, Satan used the same game against God's children. He loved watching them buckle.

~~~

Here I was, Gina Grimes, again habitually watching the clock on Friday afternoon with much anticipation. Each week when 5:00 p.m. rolled around, I would eagerly jump off the merry-go-round of work to seek some fun. My life consisted of working my butt off for five days to seek the elusive dream for the other two. Every weekend, I played at the extreme hunt.

My heart wasn't in the hunting game tonight. My mind was filled with what-if and why-not questions. *Why was I trapped in this hunt for the perfect mate, the perfect life, the perfect home, and family? Why did I have to pretend and flirt my way through life? I thought about Mom. Her life hadn't turned out so great. What made me think that my results would be any different the way I was going?*

Was Caylee wishing on a star? Did she believe in a true knight in shining armor? Would Jesus bring her a better life? Was I caught up in her fantasy? Was it a fantasy? What if it was true? I want to believe…I need to believe! Why shouldn't I have a charted life? Why couldn't I have a predetermined, prearranged, and satisfying life?

While pondering what if and why not, I went with my regular flow instead of staying home. The tradition of Friday-night fun with Angie had me committed. Angie depended on me. Not wanting to disappoint her, I painted my face and put on my most appealing attire.

What was I doing? Glamor and glitz weren't the answer. Although, it did help me pretend to be someone I wasn't. I didn't need this! Pretense attracts the opposite gender but doesn't provide the elusive. Then I thought, *don't we need to be positioned for wishes to come true?*

Satan laughed! This ping-pong game of right and wrong was fun! Gina's mind would be so confused shortly she'd have no choice but stay with what she knew to stay sane.

~~~

Even through this new confusion, my approach toward my dream was different tonight. I wanted a better life. I had a secret. I was trying to believe. I'd go out with Angie, but I would do something out of my norm. If my idea had any merit, it could change the course of my life.

Instead of being evasive and mysterious, why not be honest with myself? I'd go to let my hair down, totally relax, and dance. I'd be completely honest with everyone I encountered. Being fake wasn't fun anymore. Being dishonest only draws someone just as dishonest. I was tired of all the lies and hurts caused by relationships based on deception. I watched Mom and Dad's marriage fall apart from pretense. I'd been through more than one or two fake relationships myself. I couldn't wait to put my new plan into action.

~~~

Watching and listening to Gina, the Ox, and Holy Spirit were impressed. Their influence had given her determination and desire. Satan hadn't had much influence.

The Holy Spirit conveyed to Ox that they were operating within the season of growth. Space set apart for God's children to make appropriate decisions. Allowing her to find the way without interference was hard and unpleasant. Letting Satan have play was never easy.

One thing the Holy Spirit always counted on was Satan's inability not to set proper traps. His evil traps always backfired because it left him no choice but to attack life. When threats are made against the covenant robe of righteousness, the war is on. Vengeance is God's, and heaven's angels have permission to intervene.

Gina wore the robe. Even if she didn't know it existed yet, it was there and in plain sight for heaven to see.

~~~

As always, I met Angie at the pool hall. The place was large, electric, and appealing. On the weekends, it accommodated people who loved to play games of pool and darts, as well as those who loved to dance.

Satan tempted Gina's senses with flash and glam. He'd keep the flesh wanting.

Finding a table close to the dance floor, Angie and I parked our prettied bodies. That way, we could lure the opposite sex. In our glamor and glitz, we silently proclaimed, Look at us! We want to dance! We are available! Then if we caught a man's attention, we could judge if they were worthy. Most of our catches were not worth the trouble. We were very choosy. We didn't want to give just any man the idea he was the one. But sometimes we'd find a catch worthy of our time. We'd play him along and have a good time.

Ox touched Gina's mind while the Holy Spirit whispered, "You're better than this."

I hadn't been seated long before I realized I'd fallen back into the old pattern. It had emerged quickly. Hadn't I vowed to change? I wanted the deception to end. All I wanted to do was dance. I had no other agenda. I wasn't looking for a mate in this place. What did I want?

The Holy Spirit encouraged, *"Stay focused! Look and see the truth!"*

8

I ordered a cola instead of the normal glass of wine. My secret caused me to choose differently. Having wine didn't feel right. I wanted to stay sober. I didn't want my senses fogged anymore. My mind and body were in some kind of battle for me.

I just wanted to dance, but without alcohol, I was repulsed. My eyes were opened! Every available male in the place was a loser or a dishonest flirt wanting a dance between some sheets. I honestly assessed my feelings. I felt dirty and degraded. I had to leave.

I could see Angie was hooked in the drama. The loud music and lure of sex had her bound. I leaned in close so she could hear me speak after I got her attention. I tried to convince her to come, but she was too far gone. Giving up, I stated, "I'm going home! I don't want to be here!"

She wasn't too happy with me. She was having fun. She'd landed her guy for the night, so her reply was huffy and hurtful.

"Do what you want! I'm staying! It's not my fault you can't find someone. We'll see who has the most fun."

I was done! Totally insulted! My body was frozen, unable to move, stunned by Angie's words. My mind wasn't frozen, though. Determination for a better way of life poked and prodded me until I felt forced to leave. I wanted and needed to go home, take off the face paint. I had to put on my comfortable clothes and relax. Watch a good movie or dance alone to my CDs. Winding down from a week of hard work didn't mean getting drunk and ending with a sexual conquest.

"Good girl! I knew you were the one," the Holy Spirit sang. What was happening? I'd always loved to party and flirt. Was I being changed? My eyes were opened to the lie. This place was disgusting. This was not what I want. Caylee's words rang in my ears. She was waiting for her mate to appear. She didn't have to try and find him. She'd asked Jesus to send her soul mate. She was biding her time. Was this same supernatural belief causing me to think and act differently?

I wanted to be with Caylee. She'd asked me to go with her to a singles' group. She wasn't at church but some other place. Her singles' group sounded especially fun. Their activities sounded wholesome and respectful. I needed that, not the raunchy pool hall life. I'll seek it out next week.

The revelation awakened me and gave me strength. I did deserve better! Why was I still sitting in this stinky and nasty place? No one, not even Angie, was holding me here. I was free!

~~~

Satan was watching in the background. He knew how to destroy confidence. He'd send Dread and Fear to taunt this young believer. She'd be putty in their hands. Out in the parking lot, Satan was preparing a surprise for Gina. A mentally ill drug addict was being puppetted for service. He was going to have fun using the puppet so he could play with the luscious body before destroying the hope.

~~~

The dread of walking outside alone engulfed me. Fear of the unknown caused my chest to ache. I swallowed hard, gathered my courage, and proceeded anyway. I didn't need Angie's protection. I was a big girl.

Nerves caused my skin to prickle and my heart to pound. I was breaking a golden rule. I'd always made it a priority never to be alone in a place like this. I relied on the buddy system. Fear made me shake so badly, I almost went back inside. I had to face my fears! But what would I face in the dark? Could I get to my car unnoticed?

~~~

Satan's puppet was ready. Fear was doing a good job on Gina guiding her to him. It was time to spring the surprise. Satan loved scaring people and then tormenting them verbally and physically.

~~~

I was almost to my car when this obnoxious guy approached me. I could tell he was high or extremely drunk because of his rude remarks. Fear of his unwanted advances caused me to be overly mean verbally. Growling at him, I responded, "I'm not interested. I'm leaving. Go find a girlfriend inside."

He slurred. "Honey, I've found what I want. Don't be so hard to get. We can have fun out here. We don't need any music to get a groove on. The place doesn't matter; it's the type of action that's fun." I tried to sidestep around him, but my withdrawal made him mad, and he grabbed me. When I looked into his eyes, I noticed his face was pure evil. Using force, I pushed his hands away and yelled, "Get lost!"

Some guys don't understand the word no! No pulls a mental trigger enticing the opposite reaction. He grabbed my other arm and then pulled both of them behind me. Somehow, he'd trapped me against a car. He had fun groping and fondling while I screamed. But when he proceeded to unfasten his pants, I heard a loud voice in my head say, *Fight! Use self-defence!* I started squirming as hard as I could. I freed my arms and fought like a tiger, scratching his face and causing him to move back. Then I used my knee to attack his private area. That maneuver caused him to totally release me.

~~~

Ox hated standing there watching Satan use the man against Gina. The vision caused righteous anger to well inside him. He couldn't move against the man or Satan because he had orders to wait. The Holy Spirit wasn't moving against them either, but he did have compassion on the Ox's plight. He eased Ox's torment by voicing a command into the atmosphere for Gina to hear.

~~~

Angry that the Holy Spirit had foiled his plan, Satan released a giant of fear again to torment and kill.

~~~

Running to my car, I heard pounding sounds. I wasn't sure if the sounds were his footfalls or my heart. I was really spooked. Usually, this parking lot was crowded with people, but there wasn't a person in sight. I jumped in the car and quickly locked the doors. Wasting no time looking around, I cranked the motor and backed out of the parking space. When I did, a fist hit my windshield. The man was there! I'd barely missed hitting him. He was so close, I heard his threat: "I'll get you if I have to follow you home!"

I didn't stop; I kept going. Out of the corner of my eye, I glimpsed him get into an old truck. I needed to get away fast but couldn't. I had to make my way through the haphazardly parked cars. Once on the street, fear caused me to watch for the truck in my rear-view mirror. This diversion caused me to make a serious mistake. Number one rule for all drivers: focus on what's coming. Fear caused me to focus on what was behind. Everyone knows when you break a driving law, the predictable happens unnecessary accidents.

~~~

Satan laughed! He wanted to play with her body then yank hope out of her heart, but watching Fear at work was awesome. Fear had Gina trapped like a mouse. Fear was like a cat playing with his mouse before killing it.

~~~

Too late to correct my mistake, I ran a red light. The sound of horns made me look ahead. Instantly, lights blinded me as tires screeched. I couldn't do anything but brace myself. A large truck tried to stop but broadsided my car. The force from the impact shoved my car into a light pole. Like a slingshot, the pole bowed and hurled my car into the side of a brick building. As a passenger in the bouncing car, I had firsthand experience of life flashing before your eyes.

When the motion stopped, glass and my blood were everywhere. My arm felt weird, but I somehow managed to get my car door open. I couldn't move my legs, so I started screaming for help. That was when I saw the freak again. He wasn't there to help. He walked up and slapped me in the face, slurring. "Revenge is sweet! You got what you deserved."

~~~

Without realizing it, Satan's own trap sprung. What he had planned for evil backfired. Ox had watched as the giant of Fear tormented Gina. He saw Satan possess the drugged man's mind, ordering him to strike Gina. But when they tried to take her life, their game ended.

Already angry from watching the violence, Ox went berserk! He bowed his head low, doing what came natural and gored the demonic giant. He took the giant down alone. He justified the action by thinking; Justice would have pounced if he had been here.

Even though the giant was dead, Ox watched the druggie slither off only to be surrounded by many more giants. Proof Satan wasn't finished.

~~~

I remember someone hollering, "Get away from her!" It was the driver of the truck who crashed into me. He was trying to make sure I was all right. His soothing voice told me not to move. He had called 911 for help. The knowledge that help was coming relaxed my mind, then everything turned black.

~~~

The Holy Spirit commanded, "Call your comrades!" Ox bellowed loudly! Gina was in desperate need. The seed was in danger of dying before its time. First, he called out to Justice, the lion angel, "Gina has been violated! Justice has to prevail!" He bellowed a second time for Insight, the eagle angel, "Satan is on the prowl, I need help!" The third time he bellowed, it was for Healer. "Gina needs tending! I'm sending her your way."

~~~

Brent woke from a sound sleep wet with sweat. Had he dreamed that someone was in trouble? Not able to resume sleep, he got out of bed to keep from waking Hope. He needed to go in the other room and be alone with the Lord. Was his gift of justice being called into action?

He hadn't stepped too far from the bed when Hope sat straight up and screamed, "The Ox is in the ditch! He needs our help! Satan has found an innocent!"

"Brent! Where are you?" Hope screamed.

Puzzled because he was standing just a foot from her, he said, "Hope, honey, I'm right here."

"What is wrong? What do you see?" he asked.

Blinking, she regained her physical sight and focused on Brent. Then she asked, "Didn't you hear it?"

She went on. "I heard the Ox's cry! He sounded so pitiful. Right after I heard him, the Lord spoke to me, someone is in trouble. Someone is hurt because of Satan. He is after a newborn believer carrying hope from God's Word."

Brent replied, "I knew something was up! I didn't hear anything, but I woke up in a panic. I thought I was dreaming. Your reactions confirm my suspicions! My dream was from the Lord. Someone has been violated."

Hope asked, "Do you think we need to act or pray?"

"By all means, we need to pray first. We need the Lord to go before us. We can't handle this alone. We are helpless at this point."

Joining hands, they prayed in the spirit. Prayer assured them of his presence. Afterward, Brent said, "Hope, seek the Lord through your insight. He'll tell you what to do. I'll seek the word for wisdom until we know more about the matter."

~~~

The Lord heard their supplications in heaven. Requests were being made. He was being honored once again by the two of them working together. The Holy Spirit knew what to pray through them. Heaven's orders were being given for angels to hearken. Brent and Hope were releasing authority with their mouths.

~~~

Their assigned angels came alive. Assignments were issued. Heaven's generals watched over every action and request. Plans of an attack were made. An army was dispatched into service; the earthbound angels had assistance.

~~~

At the hospital, Mamie's hands started to burn, and her heart ached after hearing Ox's bellow. His bellow had been loud and frantic. Someone was coming who needed her gifts. It was his newborn whom Satan attacked. Immediately, she and the Holy Spirit started praying silently. She needed the Lord's help if her gift was called on for service.

Taking a much-needed break from her unit, Mamie ran to the Emergency Center. A young woman was being rolled inside on an ambulance gurney. Her heart ached. She knew instantly this girl was the one. She had to hurry; time was of the essence. She walked to the EMT hovering over the girl and asked him to stop the gurney. The Holy Spirit gave her favor, and he obliged. As fast as she could, she laid hands on the woman. It was up to the Holy Spirit to start the healing process. When the EMT asked what, she was doing, Mamie replied, "I thought this woman was someone I knew." He didn't have a clue what had just transpired. After Mamie delivered the Healer's ability, the Holy Spirit allowed her to see her teammate. Months earlier, Hope had shared with her the ability to see in the spirit, and with the gift, she briefly glimpsed Ox. Not having the full ability, Mamie wondered if what she was seeing was real. It looked like the cow was smiling. Not allowing doubt to be placed in her heart, she nodded to Ox, expressing that she was happy to help.

Where Am I?

Beep, beep, beep.

What is that sound? I thought.

When I opened my eyes, I was standing in a hospital room. Doctors and nurses were hovering around a woman, attaching monitors and IVs to her. Why was I in this room? I was just at the pool hall with Angie. Realization dawned! I was leaving the pool hall. I'd been in a serious car accident. Curiosity caused me to focus closely on the woman being assisted. Oh, my God! The woman was me!

Panicked, I needed to sit down before I fainted. I wanted to scream! What was this? Was I dead? What was happening?

I felt alive. I could see hands, feel my body, but my form was in two places. I had to know which was real. If I was lying in the bed, then who was I? There was one way to find out. I needed to see my reflection in a mirror. Every hospital room had a mirror. When I found it, I was anxious. What would I see? Would I have a reflection? Fearfully, I jumped in front of it quickly. Staring back at me was my reflection. Sighing happily, I turned around quickly to look at the person on the bed again. She was also me. This was weird!

The doctors and nurses left before I could talk with them. I went to the hospital door and peered out the window. Nurses were walking close by. Maybe I could get one's attention. I screamed and screamed, and no one heard me. I was stuck in this place. What was happening?

I went over to a chair to sit down only to fall through it to the floor. Confused, I sat there on the floor inside the chair until I calmed down. How could the floor hold me if a chair couldn't? I was going crazy trying to figure out what was happening.

I could do nothing. I had to wait. A nurse would come in eventually. I would have an audience soon. When a nurse came in, she didn't acknowledge me. I wanted her to know that I was standing next to her, not lying in the bed. She couldn't hear or see me. I tried talking to her! I screamed at her! I poked her to no avail. I was losing patience.

It really freaked me out when Mom and Dad came in the room together. They hated each other. Why were they so panicked? Mom held my body's hand and talked to my sleeping form while crying. Dad stood there silent, but his face was pinched with worry. I wanted to punch something. They didn't need to worry! I was fine! I was standing right beside them!

It made me mad seeing Mom talk to my body. I didn't need to hear her talking to it, telling it everything was going to be okay. No, it wasn't!

When Mom got frantic, she started shaking the body and imploring, "Gina, you need to wake up, honey! The doctors tell us that your coma is only temporary. Now wake up!" Dad just stood there!

I studied the body closely. This situation was not good. Definitely not okay. The leg was in a cast, and the head was encircled in bandages. It had stitches over one eye and cuts and bruises everywhere. I went back to the little mirror over the sink. I didn't have any cuts or bruises on this body, nor did I feel any pain. Was I truly okay? Was this what death felt like?

I gave up trying to get their attention. I sat on the floor again listening to Mom's moans and sobs. I really tried to wake the body but couldn't get its eyes open. I'd even tried poking it. I tried lying on it to see if my body would mold into the one on the bed. Nothing worked. Being two bodies was confusing and freaky. If I wasn't dead, I was having an out-of-body experience, and I couldn't tell anyone.

The next day, I watched Caylee visit the body. She sat on the chair beside my bed and talked to me. "Gina, I have only a few minutes. I lied to the nurses so I could see you. I told the nurses I was your sister. I'm afraid it won't be long before they figure out I'm not. Truth is, I feel you already are my sister in Christ.

God must have a plan for your life. If he didn't, you would not be here now, you'd be dead. Listen to me! While your body heals, let your heart search for the truth. Find Jesus! I know that God has been dealing with you lately. I sensed a change the other day. Satan also knows. That's obvious. He tried to take you away from us. Don't let Satan win! Come back to us whole."

She patted my hand and left me with amazing things to ponder. Was I a spirit being? I was peaceful, with no pain or worries. I agreed with her and admitted, "Okay, I'm a spirit, and the other 'me' on the bed is the body."

~~~

The Holy Spirit noticed a small opening for Him to operate. Gina was starting to believe in a spiritual existence. He would send her a messenger. It was too soon to introduce Himself, but an angelic captain would work nicely. Even though Ox was assigned, Healer's captains were perfect for this task. Healer looked like a man and had the ability to communicate with mankind. Ox's appearance would scare Gina badly.

Adrian, captain of Healer's army, was called. He was already in Georgia. Upon arriving at the hospital, the Holy Spirit instructed him to deliver a message. Adrian was to use one of God's promises designed specifically for Gina to capture her focus. First, Gina needed something to hold on to. She needed to have a desire renewed. Then the Holy Spirit could introduce Himself to her.

~~~

After I acknowledged to myself that I must be a spirit, something happened. The elements in the room blurred and vibrated then I heard a voice greeting me hello.

Someone else was in the room with me. Someone who could see me was saying hello. It scared me. What was I about to see? Slowly turning my head in the direction of the voice, I was astonished to see a large and beautiful man standing right beside me. He was glowing and majestic in radiant white. "Hello," I said back. Then I asked, "Who are you?"

"My name is Adrian," he said. "Are you real?" I asked

"Yes! I'm a guardian angel. A chief among millions," he answered.

"What?" I asked.

"I'm a guardian angel," he repeated.

My mind went into a panic. I thought an angel of death had come for me. I was sure of it. With that mindset, I knew I was about to leave with this angel soon. Suddenly, he snickered and said, "You're not going to heaven yet. You've been allowed to see me because you have finally accepted your spiritual existence."

Holy cow! He could read my mind, I thought.

Curiously, I inquired, "Then why are you here if I'm not dead?

Am I about to die?"

Softly answering, Adrian said, "No, you are not dead. God plans for you to live a long time. I've been assigned to give you a message then watch over you."

Not knowing how things worked in the spiritual place, I rapidly asked, "Is your message bad? Are you here to punish me?" "Stop worrying! God is love. He's sent me to assure you," he said soothingly.

"I have to admit, I'm a little bit freaked. Can you help me calm down?"

He began to laugh. The sound of his laughter reminded me of chimes. It was lovely.

Touching my shoulder, he said, "Relax!"

Every part of me calmed. I sank to the floor like melting butter. I was limp and refreshed at the same time.

Adrian continued to explain, "The message is from God. He loves you. He wants you to know he is very pleased with you. The decisions you made before all this happened showed us you were on the right track. For a long time, you were tricked by this world system into believing it had all you desired. I'm to show you part of your future. That is if you want it."

"How can I answer you? My mind is still trying hard to comprehend I'm spiritual. Nothing is factual to me now. What are desires in this form? I can't touch anything, I'm not substantial." Before replying, he laughed again. "Don't you remember what you were thinking and feeling the night of the accident? Thoughts are real. Thoughts produce fact from the spiritual. From the heart of your consciousness comes self-proclamation. From proclamation comes fact."

I didn't remember my thoughts and feelings. I remembered horror! I answered rudely, "No! I only remember running away from a potential rapist before I got broadsided."

"Would you like to travel back in time to see and hear yourself that night? That way, you can actually see what heaven was seeing," he calmly offered.

Freaked out by the offer, I asked, "I can do that... go back in time? Will it hurt?"

I wondered what he was thinking of me. He was staring and grinning, so he must think I'm stupid. He didn't answer me right away, so I felt shame from my questions.

He touched my shoulder again and said, "Your curiosity amazes me. You are not stupid. Don't let shame ever stop you from asking questions. Knowledge of heaven's power is always available to those who ask. Let me assure you again, God loves you, and wants you to know Him. I'm here to help you receive and learn. In the spirit realm, we are not limited by time or space.

Traveling through time will not hurt. The mental adjustment may be necessary, so questions are welcomed. Are you willing to try?" I was moved by his words of patience and assurance. My curiosity was wanted. I bravely answered, "I think I am. I'd really like to know what I did that caused all of this. Plus, I like to know what caused that." I pointed to the body lying helpless in the bed.

"Very good! Curiosity is powerful, isn't it?" Adrian quipped.

"If you say so! I'm still not convinced this traveling back in time is a good idea. You said God approves?" I probed.

Patiently, Adrian answered, "Let me assure you, little Gina, I can do nothing good or bad, for you or to you, without God's permission. We have His ultimate approval."

"What will happen to my body while I'm gone? What if it wants to wake up while I'm away?" I pressed.

"Your body was placed in the coma state to repair. It will not miss you while we are away. If our enemy tampers with your body, alarms will notify us. We will hear a cacophony of monitors giving warnings. The monitors have been programmed to beep loudly to notify your nurses. If your brain feels threatened or violated while we are away, we can return so you can resume your life in the physical. Once there, you may not be able to see or hear unless the Holy Spirit desires."

Okay! His answer was intense! It frightened me! "Why won't I be able to communicate with you after I re-enter my body? Who is this enemy?" I babbled.

With a serious voice, he shared, "Our enemy is Satan! He is out to harm God's people! He will try his best to keep you from believing or seeing the good God has in store for you. He is determined to keep you from knowing the Lord. Trust in God's Word to get you through life's journeys. His Word is the guide. Get to know the Lord on a personal level. Do it before Satan tries to stop you!"

What was I to do now? Go or stay? Read the Bible or go with the angel?

Seeing my mental struggle, Adrian helped by changing the subject. "God wants you to see His goodness. Are you ready now for your journey back in time?"

"Will you hold my hand and not let go?" I asked. Smiling, he said, "That's my plan."

Taking my hand in his, we were off in a flash.

~~~

Ox was pleased. The Lord knew what Gina needed. The messenger's encouraging work would help the seed of hope flourish and grow. With the seed's manifestation, blessings follow.

Revelation

We were traveling at such a fast speed; my mind could not wrap around the experience. Clouds were passing so fast; I was getting dizzy. Seeing my plight, Adrian suggested. "Don't focus on the speed or the clouds. Let your mind seek a time and place." "How will I know the right time and place to choose?" I asked. "You'll know. The Holy Spirit is leading you there. Trust in His urging," he replied.

I searched my mind until I remembered how all this started. I'd seen Caylee's peace the day of the accident. I'd believed in Jesus. We were in the break room at the mental health facility where we worked. She had just told me she was waiting for Jesus to bring her soul mate. Then we started talking about a singles' group she attended at church.

I kept my eyes tightly closed so I could focus on that moment. I was reopening them when I felt something solid under my feet. I was back in time experiencing a very weird sensation. It was like watching a television rerun. I knew the plot and words. Caylee had just invited me to the dinner party her singles' group had planned that night.

Adrian asked, "What are you thinking at this point?"

"What do you mean? What am I thinking now or what was I thinking then?" I questioned.

"What were you thinking then?" he corrected.

"I envied her happiness. I wanted what she had. She was honest, peaceful, and confident. She was content with herself. I needed that," I said.

"Good! You just established one of your desires. You want to be who you are without any pretense. You want to be confident," he gently remarked.

"Yes! I had just gotten off the phone with Angie after making plans to meet her again at the pool hall. I hated pretending. Caylee's description of the singles' group sounded wholesome. That is when I started envying her life.

Caylee said men and women attended her group and had fun. She said their shared beliefs kept them happy and that being truthful and loving drew the people together for the right reasons, bonded them. Some even married. I needed that," I shared.

Grinning, he informed, "You have another desire. You want a lasting, truthful relationship."

"Yeah. I've been searching for someone to share my life with for a long time now," I replied.

"What made you change?" he asked.

I knew he knew what changed me. He just wanted me to say it out loud. I complied. "Watching and listening to Caylee made me want what she had. When I asked how she coped, she told me God brought her everything she needed. She asked for a better life. So, I asked Jesus to help me. I asked for His forgiveness."

"Ah ha! You've got it!" he shouted. "Got what?" I queried.

"Sweet one, you've been given a new life. Your new life is struggling with the old. Don't you see?" he enlightened.

I didn't see! But he knew that too, the mind reader.

Then he said we had to revisit the incident at the club. I needed to see the struggle. I must watch how I acted; visually see when I came to certain conclusions. But I didn't want to experience that night again.

"Trust me, Gina. It's important," Adrian urged me.

Giving up, I held out my hand so we could go. The television rerun was playing again. This time, I saw my face when I realized the den of filth I was visiting. I saw clearly the type of people who were partying. The alcohol made me cringe. It no longer had an appeal. Angie wasn't a nice person. I was just her crutch until a guy came along. Nothing was what I thought it was.

"Gina, what are you thinking at this point?" Adrian asked.

"I was thinking how I loved to dance and move to good music but hated being groped by lust-driven men. I felt dirty. The revelation changed me. I wanted more for myself. I wanted respect," I said.

"Understand why the Lord was happy with you? You felt worthy of better," he explained.

~~~

Satan saw what was happening. This girl was being wooed. He wasn't stupid. Doubt was sent to speak into Gina's ear. Satan commanded, "Convince the girl that her God caused the accident."

~~~

Doubt rose in my mind. I was angry and couldn't resist asking, "If I'm so pleasing to the Lord, why did I have the accident? Why didn't he keep me from getting hurt?"

"Stop!" Adrian commanded. "The enemy is here! Doubt is trying to steal from you. He knows! He is trying to distract us."

The intensity grew, causing Adrian to hasten. "I have to proceed quickly with our journey. This conversation will be very fast. Try to stay focused! Trust in God's love. I will answer your question. From the moment, you called on Jesus, a very mighty angel was sent to you. He and the Lord knew an attack was going to happen, but they could not react until a threat upon life was made. Satan trapped himself by attacking you. Since then, many angels have become involved and are watching over your new life. Your body sustained injuries, but even the injuries will be used for good. God has a wonderful plan for you. He wants you to witness His goodness. He is allowing you a glimpse of things to come. His desire is to give you the yearnings of your heart, Gina."

Before I could ask more questions or inquire about Satan, Adrian grabbed my hand again, and we both returned to my hospital room. He had to check on my body. I looked at myself lying there and knew I really wanted to change. I loathed the pattern I'd been following. I got emotional and hugged Adrian hard. "Thank you for saving me from doubts," I said.

He abruptly pushed me away and sternly corrected me. "Gina, I only do what I am ordered to do. God saved you! You belong to Him. Please don't ever worship me. I only follow orders. Give your thanks to the Holy One."

My rebuke felt strange. I felt relief instead of shame. My heart was full of thankfulness. I needed to tell someone.

Reading my mind again, Adrian suggested, "Tell Jesus, Gina!"

"Thank you, Jesus!" I shouted.

"You're welcome," He answered.

Journey Unheard Of

"Did you hear that, Adrian?" I asked in amazement.

When I turned to see why he had not answered me, I was startled to find him almost face down on the floor. I realized he was praising and worshiping Jesus.

Then he looked at me with awe and said, "Gina, you've been honored."

"Huh? What do you mean?" I asked.

His hesitation confused me. What's the big deal? I heard you. "Gina, most people doubt Jesus is still alive. They only say they believe. It's an honor to serve you, young lady," Adrian said.

I still didn't understand why he was acting weird. I didn't have a clue what he meant, but I liked what he said. "Can I thank you now? I want to thank you for making me feel special," I asked.

"Thank you, Gina, for wanting to. I will accept your thanks on behalf of our Lord," he replied.

Adrian's expression got serious, and he faced the ceiling. He was communicating with someone I couldn't see or hear. I had to know what was going on. "What is it, Adrian?" I asked.

"Loshan has just informed me that our enemy is seeking ways to stop you. The coma time prescribed for your healing has to be shortened. I'll need to show you God's message quickly."

"Who is Loshan? What are you going to show me?" I asked. "Loshan is another angel sent to help. I'm to show you the elusive element you've secretly desired," he answered.

Taking my hand in his, Adrian looked up. In a flash, we were off on another journey. This time my mind was not leading me; it was my heart.

We stopped in a lovely place. People were preparing a picnic and having fun playing various games.

Adrian said, "Gina, our time is very short, stay focused. Remember details from what you've been given to see and hear. God wants you to remember each detail. Trust that it is His gift. This blessing is part of your future."

Again, I witnessed a show. Only this time, I watched myself not knowing what would be said or seen. This was my gift from God concerning my future. Wow!

In one specific scene, I stood at the edge of a beautiful lake, watching geese and ducks swim along. I had a sad expression on my face. I appeared to have been crying. Suddenly, a Frisbee hit me at the back of the head. Someone ran to me, asking if I was all right.

He was a very handsome man. I listened to his voice as he asked, "Are you hurt?"

"No, I was just startled," I heard myself reply. "Good! I thought the Frisbee cut you," he said.

"Forgive me," he said. "Let me introduce myself. I'm—beep! beep! beep!—Polk. What is your name?"

"Adrian, stop the beeps! I can't hear his name," my spirit shouted. "Gina, Satan is trying to block your hearing. Hurry! You must focus! Your body's monitors are sounding off. You'll have to re-enter consciousness shortly," he shouted.

I focused again seeing myself in another scene. This motion picture had been fast-forwarded. This time, I was riding on the back of a red motorcycle with my arms around the lovely man's waist. It felt like I'd been riding a bike with him all my life. I was so happy and enjoying the cool air as it played with my clothes.

Then the scene fast-forwarded again, and the two of us were all dressed up at Reo's. Reo's was a fancy dinner club in town. We were dancing. I loved to dance, and it seemed that he did too. Again, my heart was so full of joy and love.

Then I heard him say the most amazing thing. "Gina, will you spend the rest of your life with me as my wife?"

The movie fast-forwarded again. I was walking arm and arm with Dad down the aisle of a lovely church to meet this lovely man. I was getting married.

Beep! Beep! Beep!

The sound of the monitors was getting louder now in my head. "No! I need to see more," I shouted.

"Focus! You have a few more minutes yet," Adrian shouted.

Next, I was lying in a hospital bed giving birth. My husband was by my side. His beautiful green eyes were bright with tears and his smile so big. When the baby came, he cut the cord and brought our child over to me. I heard him say, "Gina, look at our daughter."

Beep! Beep! Beep!

The monitors were extremely loud and refused to stop. Then I heard my mom's voice. "Gina, honey, wake up now. It's time to come back to us."

"No! No! I want to see more!" I screamed at Adrian. "Remember, Gina, rely on God's Word. Don't forget what you've seen. Trust it! Satan will try to make you think it was a lie," he said. Then he faded away.

~~~

Satan was furious! He had a mess to clean up. No way was he allowing her to have a happy experience. Grabbing her by the throat, he shoved her hard back into her body, forcing her back into his reality.

~~~

Ox was furious! Nothing should touch a child of God. Satan will pay when the time was right.

~~~

Adrian had disappeared along with my movie. I had been grabbed out of my future and hurled back into the present. I was shoved, not gently placed, back into my body. I realized the force wasn't from Adrian but something sinister.

Consciousness came, and I felt my hand being squeezed. I felt the pressure of someone rubbing my arm and the colossal pain. I was in agony! "I might as well wake up," I told myself. I opened my eyes to see worried parents. I managed to say hi.

What were they doing here? They were together; this wasn't right. Nothing was right. I hurt all over and also felt broken hearted. Why?

~~~

Ox and Adrian talked. Adrian had encouraged Gina the best he could under the tight conditions. He'd been able to show her a few glimpses to provide hope. The wait was on. Time needed patience. Ox was ready for the fight. Satan knew as much as Gina. All that mattered was what the Holy Spirit wanted next.

~~~

The Reality

Wow! I really hurt! I grabbed my stomach, remembering the pain from having the baby. Didn't I just have a baby? Reaching to my aching head, I felt bandages and thought, *If I've just given birth, then why do I have bandages on my head and a cast on my leg?* I searched for my husband but only saw Mom sitting on the chair beside me.

"Mom? What's going on?" I agitatedly asked.

"Relax, honey! You've been in a very bad accident. You've awakened from a coma. Calm down!" she urged.

~~~

Satan slapped Gina's head. I'll give her back memories!

~~~

Like lightning, pain shot through my head. Instantly, memories came back. I wasn't married. I hadn't given birth. I wasn't happy. I was still on the merry-go-round. I started to sob uncontrollably. Confused and worried, Mom sought a nurse. She wouldn't understand. I'd just had my heart ripped out. Where was my family? My little girl and my husband?

I heard Mom call out the door, "Nurse! I think Gina is having problems. She is crying uncontrollably. She must be in pain!"

I thought to myself, *Mom, don't bother the nurse. I don't need meds. I need my family.*

Then I remembered Adrian. Was I truly with an angel? His words burned in my mind. "Don't forget what you were allowed to see."

I never prayed! I hadn't believed in such a thing until lately. I said a little prayer to the only supernatural being I knew. "Adrian, if you can hear me, please help me stay calm again. Help me keep them alive in my heart. I really want the life you allowed me to witness. I don't want it to vanish like dreams when we awake. I want to believe in God's gift. I was happy in my future."

~~~

Saddened that Gina hadn't called on the Lord, Ox submitted to facts. Gina didn't know how. To her, Jesus was God, not a real person who could relate.

~~~

A physician's assistant came in my room and said, "I've called Dr. Jones. His instructions were to check your vitals regularly and look for any signs of trauma. It's too soon to determine if you can have pain meds."

After a few minutes of being poked and prodded, his verdict was, "You look fine to me. There is no indication of swelling or bleeding. I'll let the nurse know that you need something."

Mom followed him out the door, pressuring him with hundreds of questions. Dad left after telling me he couldn't stay and watch Mom torment the staff. He kissed me on the forehead and told me to call if I needed him. He'd be back later when Mom wasn't around.

When Mom came in with a nurse in tow who was holding a syringe, I assumed what the nurse had were pain meds. I wanted to go back to sleep. I wanted to dream some more about my family. As the liquid fire rushed into my system, my body began to relax. I felt drunk instead of sleepy, numb, and disoriented.

Moaning because I still hurt and couldn't sleep, I inquired about the medicine, "What did the nurse give me? Why can't I sleep?"

Mom explained, "Gina, the PA told me you didn't need to go back to sleep this soon. The medicine is a relaxant. Your body was very tense. Try watching television. Let your brain readjust to normal sensations."

I lay on the uncomfortable bed staring at the TV as she flipped channels. When she got to a program about angels, I asked her to stop. If I couldn't dream about my angel, then maybe I could watch a program about others. The show was heart-warming and encouraging.

I knew Mom was being patient with me. She looked tired and exhausted. My brooding wasn't helping either of us. She had also been through a terrifying ordeal. After all, I was her baby, and she almost lost me. The revelation engulfed me! A feeling of loss took over. I wanted to cry! I wasn't with my family anymore. The mental anguish was worse than physical pain.

It was during the third show of Touched by an Angel. I noticed Mom sitting in a chair sound asleep. She had to be uncomfortable. She didn't need to stay any longer. I was fine. She needed to rest on her own bed.

Insistently, I asked, "Mom, aren't you uncomfortable over there?"

"I'm all right. Is there anything you need?" she groggily answered. "No, you're not! Mom, go home and rest in your own bed. It will be good for you. I'm fine. I'll be even more alert tomorrow," I assured.

To be truthful, I needed to be alone. Maybe I could talk with Adrian. I needed some sort of peace. Right now, I felt sucker-punched. I needed to hash out emotions. I certainly couldn't talk with Mom. She would think I was loony tunes. She didn't believe in religion. How could she understand my spiritual experience?

Mom agreed. "If you think you'll be okay, I could use some sleep. I'll go home for a few hours. I'm just a little anxious. Don't slip back into a coma."

"I know, Mom, don't worry. I'll be fine. If it will make you feel better, ask a nurse to call you if I flip out or something. I'm sure one would oblige," I joked.

Under the watchful eye of Nurse Ross, I was finally alone in my room. I liked this southern black lady. She had the wonderful way of making you feel special. Her voice alone soothed my mind. In her southern drawl, she asked, "Ms. Grimes, is there anything that I can do for you? Are you still in pain?"

"Something awful! Could I have something for the pain? I don't want muscle relaxants, they make me feel strange," I implored.

"Okay, honey! I'll see what the doctor has ordered for you. I'll be back in a few minutes," she said sweetly.

When she returned, she profusely apologized. "Orders say you need to remain alert for five more hours before we can administer anything stronger than a muscle relaxant. May I massage your muscles?"

"Yes, please! A massage would be wonderful," I agreed.

Her rubbing and kneading hands were better than any relaxant. Was she using a special lotion?

"What is that stuff you're rubbing on me?" I asked her.

She said, "Only love, child. People say Mamie has the healing touch."

"Nurse Ross, I'm hungry. Am allowed anything to eat?" I asked.

"Call me Mamie, Ms. Grimes. Let me check your record again. Give me a few minutes," she replied.

"Thanks, Mamie, and please call me Gina," I said.

She wasn't gone long. "Do you like Jell-O? That's all you can have until Dr. Jones sees you."

"Oh yes, please! I feel like I could eat a horse. What flavors do you have? Never mind, surprise me. I like Jell-O."

A few minutes later, I was savoring a cool lime-flavored treat. Before I knew it, I had eaten four cups. Surprisingly, the Jell-O filled my stomach. I wasn't hurting as bad either. Since I wasn't allowed to sleep, I decided to put my mind to work. Why not deal with the issues before me? Adrian said I needed to remember everything. I'll write down everything I remember.

I rolled over to look inside the bedside table. I found a pad and pen in the top drawer. I found a blue hardback as well. It was a Bible. Didn't Adrian say to seek God in this book?

Praying, I said, "Thanks, Adrian! You must have made sure I had this. Now help me remember everything. I want to write down what you showed me so I don't forget."

~~~

Ox stood in the corner of Gina's room accompanied by Adrian and Loshan. The three of them had to encourage Gina to seek out the Holy Spirit. The journey could wait. The Holy Spirit was more important. On each side of her, they sang, "Read the Word! Read the Word!" With their prompting, she picked it up and slowly began to read.

Ox stood close while Gina read. Reading the Word was important for her strength. Ox wanted to move things forward, but he had to wait for the Lord's signal. For the time being, he had to prevent Satan or his crew from tinkering with Gina's hope. Thanks to the Lord, Jesus had set boundaries by giving Gina a robe, preventing Satan access to her life. But the boundaries never stopped Satan before from trying to harm.

~~~

Satan made sure his little demons were everywhere. The little imps were useful. They were expendable and kept Jesus's angels busy. Hospitals were the perfect places for them to camp out. They could stay fat and strong from feeding off negative emotions.

One of the imps notified Satan that Gina was reading the Bible. He wasn't too worried. Hospitals had the Old English– language version, and it confused most of this generation.

~~~

On the other side of town, the spirit of Insight was restless! It had been three days, and no word from the Holy Spirit. Hope Arnold could sense a disturbance in the atmosphere. Her connection with Healer caused her to be increasingly restless with each minute. She started to question what was going on. Why had she and Brent been alerted in the middle of the night? Why was the Lord taking so long to fill her in on what was happening? Praying in the spirit eased her mind. She continued praying while she cooked dinner for Brent and Greg. In prayer mode, she inquired why she felt bound and helpless. Her spirit was being tugged. Why? What was the secret? She wanted to be useful. "Lord, I'm here at your service. Use me.

Release my restless spirit for service."

The Holy Spirit answered, "Hope, wait on Mamie! Healer is busy. Your time for service is coming. Don't be in such a rush to face the enemy. Communication with me is enough for now. The serpent knows we are aware of his schemes. Satan keeps a watchful eye on you. Since your last confrontation, he knows you rest in my name. That is why I haven't shared my plans with you. I'm not giving Satan a chance to scheme. Let him keep fearing you. Your time is coming soon. I will not leave you defenseless or without knowledge."

Nightmares

I stopped trying to remember my journey. The Bible was calling me. I put the pad and pen away and looked at the Bible. It was a King James Version written in very small print. My eyes had problems reading the tiny words. My mind couldn't wrap around the Old English. The book was very hard to comprehend. "Why do people love it so much?" I said aloud.

I read and reread passages. The harder I tried to comprehend, the fuzzier the print grew. My eyes burned. I fought sleep. I didn't want the doctor to think I was still traumatized. What was causing this dopey feeling? I had no choice but to put the book down. My eyes were just too heavy.

~~~

The devilish imp had caused Gina's plight. The moment he heard Gina complain about what she was reading, he started to feed. The results caused Gina's mind to fog and her eyes to burn. The imp giggled; he thought Gina's problem was funny. When Gina became weak from the emotional drain, fear came to torment. Through the imp's induced sleep, Satan would make Gina remember the horrors of reality. Reality would trump the visions Adrian gave her. Fact had more substance. Fact would erase the Holy Spirit's luring vision. Fact would replace hope with fear and worry.

~~~

Ox was no dummy. He was well aware of the imp. As soon as Gina closed her eyes, he had the imp by the neck. Then Ox growled, "Fool, didn't you know we were watching?" Afterward, he squashed it like a bug. Ox noticed Gina's mind struggling in the dream. He immediately set out to stop Satan. He alerted the Holy Spirit and called Healer. The Holy Spirit notified Mamie and warned her Gina was in trouble. Mamie had to be prepared for issues. Satan was allowing fear to trap Gina's mind.

~~~

I wasn't dreaming; I was remembering! My mind recalled that horrible night! I was unhappy and frustrated. I was fearful and dreaded the dark. I felt lousy and wanted to escape. Nothing at the pool hall appealed to me. Being alone was better.

I was leaving the pool hall without Angie. I didn't like leaving without a buddy with me. Alone and apprehensive, I faced my worst nightmare, a drunk and oppressive man with foul-smelling breath and nasty clothing. I remembered noticing how his hair was slick with oil and how everything about him stank. I was his prize. He thought he'd found a treat for the evening.

My mind and body wrestled with this memory. It caused me to thrash and shake on the bed. Could this actually be happening? I was reliving every detail. I didn't want to remember those things. Not only did I remember, but I watched myself being attacked again and again like the vision was stuck on rewind. The man kept grabbing me with his creepy, dirty hands. He caught my arms behind me somehow. When he pinned me against the car, he tried to rip away my clothes. He was trying hard to rape me. My heart was pumping wildly! I remember screaming, but no one heard me! I was helpless and trapped!

Words came from somewhere as forceful as a sonic boom: "Use self-defense training!" The words registered! I'd recently been trained to struggle, kick, bite, scratch until an assailant released you. I applied the moves until they worked.

Then I remembered running on shaking legs and frightened out of my wits. I knew he wasn't far behind. At my car, I fumbled through my bag for keys. First, I jammed the wrong one in the door. By then my hands were shaking badly. When I finally managed to open the car door, I jumped in and locked myself inside. I almost ran over the guy as I backed out. He hit my windshield, screaming, "I'll have you if I have to follow you home." I went from one fright to another. Two huge lights shone brightly on my face, a horn blasting before I could get out of the lane. Then in slow motion, I felt a jolt as metal pierced my leg. Then the metal twisted violently, breaking bones. Glass cut me in several places, and the airbag exploded on my face. I relived the spinning, the jolts, and the blows. I heard my bones crunch over and over. I felt like a twig, twisting and breaking.

After the car stopped moving, I noticed blood everywhere. My arms worked, and I managed to open the car door. To my horror, the first person I saw was that ugly man who tried to rape me. He didn't offer help! He hit me in the face! I heard stupid insulting comments. "Revenge is sweet. You got what you deserved, Ms. Goody Two-shoes."

Suddenly, I heard someone scream at my assailant, who quickly fled the scene. Then a nice man was looking down at me, commanding me to stop moving. He was there to help. He had called an ambulance.

Tossing fitfully in bed, I screamed, "He's trying to kill me! He tried to rape me! Help me!"

I felt a hand shaking me and heard Mamie's kind voice saying, "Gina, honey, wake up. You're having a nightmare. You are all right, child, wake up!"

Coiled and wanting to strike, I lashed out at her. Mamie was ready and prepared, so I didn't hurt her. I wanted to hurt something, though! Apologizing, I said, "Mamie? My God, I thought you were the rapist after me again. I'm sorry!"

"Drink some water, child! Mamie is here! No one is hurting you!" Mamie soothed me.

Breathing raggedly, I explained, "I wasn't having any old nightmare. I was remembering what actually happened. I may need protection. Don't leave me alone, I'm scared! What time is it? Can we call my mom? If you can't reach her, call my dad. I don't want to be alone anymore. Please!" I begged.

"Calm down, child. You really had a scare, didn't you? I don't think either would mind if I called them. I'll do it now. It's daylight anyway, and I'd like to speak to your mother before my shift ends," Mamie said.

"Please call them, Mamie! Let Mom know I'm okay physically. Both parents need to know what I remembered. I know why I was hurt!" I exclaimed.

Mamie didn't want to alarm Gina. She knew Gina had been attacked. Evidence presented itself the night of her accident. Mamie had stored the valuable information for when the time was right. The Holy Spirit had alerted her to look into the situation. He'd enabled her to see specific marks on Gina not made from being thrown around in a car accident. Some of Gina's bruises were made from hands. Gina had been forcefully manhandled.

Curiosity caused Mamie to study what Gina wore the night of the accident. Gina's blouse was cut from her body by the paramedics, but Mamie also noticed that buttons had been ripped away, more evidence of manhandling.

Now that Gina's recollection was vivid; Mamie knew Brent had to get involved. The time was right for Justice to come into play legally. First things first, Mamie needed to call Gina's parents, get them on the ball.

It was no surprise to Brent when Mamie called. He'd been notified the day before by the Holy Spirit. The Lord empowered His spirit of Justice to be on alert for action. Satan was playing dirty and up to one his favorite tricks. Brent knew instantly what Satan was doing. He was using a person to inflict injury.

Inquiring from the Holy Spirit, Brent was told a person under Satan's influence was still roaming free. The man's lust hadn't been satisfied, and he hungered to rape. Lust to rape, driven by Satan, was an extreme action, and a twisted, sick mind loved the power. Their physical need wasn't satisfied with sex freely offered. Satisfaction had to come through forcing sex on a helpless woman. When Mamie explained the reason for her early call, Brent knew what to do. The Lord's pre-empting assured him vindication would come, but it could be tricky. Being connected with the Lord was imperative for righteous justice. Brent knew if he judged wrongly, true innocence could be affected incorrectly. He also knew he had to spiritually fight for the twisted mind of the mentally ill man being used by Satan.

After his conversation with Mamie, Brent finished getting ready for work. Then he went to eat breakfast with Hope and told her who had called. When Brent shared that his gift of justice had been called upon, Hope's restless spirit was eased. Her time for service wouldn't be far behind.

At the office, Brent pondered over the information Mamie had given him. In order, not to forget, he made notes. Using his computer, he logged information about Gina Grimes and physical evidence Mamie had discovered. He was given spiritual knowledge, but the information Mamie gave could be used in a court of law. He didn't worry whether the violator would be caught. He knew the Lord would soon hand him over to authorities.

~~~

Ox, Healer, and Justice have teamed again on earth. Soon, the Holy Spirit would have Insight involved. Gina had more help than she could ever wish for. Man's strength was pitiful in comparison.

Police

Mamie fulfilled her promise and called Mr. and Mrs. Grimes. Mr. Grimes's emotions were steady; he agreed to come without question. Mrs. Grimes's emotions were uncontrollable. Mamie had a hard time calming her down. Mamie had to use Healer's strength because the call had badly frightened the woman. Mamie soothed Mrs. Grimes by stating that Gina was fine. She informed Mrs. Grimes that her daughter wanted her. Gina had a bad dream and missed her mom. Drawing upon Mrs. Grimes's motherly instincts, Mamie defeated the fear gripping the woman. With both parents, Mamie omitted why Gina needed them.

Gina must give them news of possible dangers. She would share her evidence when needed. Her job was to wait for the Holy Spirit to tell her when it was time.

Now that both of Gina's parents were on their way, she'd contacted Brent; Mamie didn't tarry. She quickly went back to Gina's room. Gina's emotional state needed comfort. Taking Gina's hand, Mamie let God's love flow from her. Mamie spoke comforting words into the girl's heart. "Gina, your parents are on the way. Sweetie, Mamie has other patients. I'll be only a moment away if you need me. I'll leave the door open so you can see me at my workstation, okay?"

"Thank you, Mamie. I'll be okay. Knowing you are close helps. Promise you won't let any man enter my room except my dad or the doctor," I requested.

Mamie agreed. "Okay, child, you can count on that! I promise you no man will enter. If one tries, they'll be facing this mother bear head-on."

I felt my body relax after Mamie's funny remark. While I waited, I tried to remember every detail so I could tell Mom and Dad. They needed a reason to call in the police and file a complaint.

I turned on the news while I waited for Mom and Dad. A lot changed, proving life goes on, in a few short days. According to the newscaster, the state mental health facility was moving into a new building this week. My work life was moving on without me. The information caused me to worry. What about my things? What about my job? Did anyone place me on family leave? It was too early to call the office. Waiting became frustrating. I had to wait for Mom and Dad. I had to wait for the office to open. Wait! Wait! Wait!

~~~

Satan laughed. Time was a jewel in disguise. Impatience and stress were his servants, so Satan called them into service. Gina was in the prime state of mind. Imps were waiting, licking their lips, hungry for the negative emotions to flow so they could feed.

~~~

Stress made my head and leg throb with pain. I wasn't going to ask for meds; I needed to stay focused. I was scared. There was a madman loose. He could hurt another person. He could be searching for me! I needed to stop this guy, but I wanted to sweep everything under the carpet and hide. The thought of losing my job was making me sick. *I'd lose my apartment. I'd have to move back home with Mom! What was I going to do?*

Lost in my own thoughts, I jumped violently when Dad spoke my name. "Dad! You spooked me!" I screeched. Then I burst into tears.

Mom came in shortly after and made a scene, fussing at Dad. "What did you do to her? She wants her mama! Why are you here?"

"Stop it!" I yelled. "I need both of you here!" Emotions overwhelmed me! Frantically, I tried to explain, but my Words were choked due to the impatience caused by panic and fear. It felt like my airway was being obstructed.

Dad said, "Gina, take a deep breath! We're listening! We can tell you are frightened, but for us to help and understand, you need to slow down."

I heeded his advice and took a slow and deep breath to release stress. Slowly my lungs relaxed, and my voice returned to normal. Starting over, I said, "I remember what happened the night of the accident. A man tried to rape me. I escaped from him, and while fleeing, I had the accident."

I had both parents' attention. They were equally concerned for my welfare.

Dad asked, "Are you sure about all of this, Gina? Mom and I have met the truck driver who broadsided your car. His name is Russ Jackson. He is a nice young man. He's been here a couple of times to check on you."

They were confused. I explained, "The truck driver wasn't my attacker. Another man tried to rape me. He was following me in an old truck, and because I wasn't paying attention, Russ hit me. I think he may be the man who ran the rapist away. I remember someone yelling 'get away from her' before I blacked out."

Mom said, "Honey, I'm confused. There were two men?" "Yes! After I tried to free myself from the wreckage, the same guy who tried to rape me was there. He hit me in the face before the other hollered to get away. The attacker swore he would find me at home! I'm scared he's still looking for me!" I exclaimed.

Convinced, Dad spoke with Mom, "Pam, we have to notify the police! Our daughter has been violated! I'm not waiting around for the creep to take another shot at her!"

Mom asked, "Gina, do you want us to report this?"

Exasperated, I blurted out, "Yes! That's the main reason I had you called. As much as I want to run and hide, I need to report this. The man needs to be stopped. He may try and hurt someone else. Will one of you call the police, or do I have to get Mamie to call them for me?"

Hearing and realizing I meant business, Dad left the room to find a phone. While I was alone with Mom, I asked her to help me bathe. I felt messy.

~~~

Mamie stood and prayed outside Gina's room. She asked the Holy Spirit to show her the right moment to talk with Gina's Mom. When Mr. Grimes left Gina's room door open, Mamie knew the time had come. When she overheard, Gina ask for a bath, Mamie knew she had the Lord's go-ahead to proceed.

As a nurse, Mamie entered Gina's room without invitation. When Mrs. Grimes started gathering items for Gina's bath, Mamie offered her assistance. While the bath proceeded, a conversation with Gina and Mrs. Grimes opened concerning the attack. Mamie politely brought Mrs. Grimes's attention to the evidence she had been harboring. Mamie showed Mrs. Grimes the attacker's hand marks made on Gina's body. With the marks disclosed, Mamie brought Gina's blouse from the closet to show how it looked.

After all was divulged, Mamie graciously gave Mrs. Grimes permission to use her testimony for the police records. Satisfied that God's work was finished, as well as the hospitals, Mamie went home to rest.

~~~

Dad had been waiting patiently for my bath to end. When Mamie left, he told us the police would arrive shortly. The daytime nurse, Mrs. Hamm, was also alerted. Seeing I'd been bathed, Nurse Hamm decided I needed my sheets changed quickly before the police arrived. It was evident she was more worried how the hospital room appeared than how I felt. The team she sent in jostled, poked, and prodded me, making the pain in my leg worse. I wanted to scream because the pain was so bad. I couldn't ask for meds because I had to stay focused.

When we were notified the police had arrived, Dad went to the lobby and escorted two middle-aged policemen into my room. They introduced themselves as Sergeant Harris and Deputy Rowe.

Their interest in what I had to say made it easy for me to answer questions. I didn't feel critically judged in any way. They sat attentively with pads and pens, taking precise notes of every detail.

After the interview, Sergeant Harris spoke with my parents. He informed them Russ Jackson's story checked out with mine. Russ had reported seeing a man strike me before running off. Then Sergeant Harris addressed me, "Do you think you could identify your attacker from a picture?"

"Yes, sir! I have his face etched in my mind. Why?" I asked. "We have a man in custody that fits your description. He was apprehended last night after a woman reported being raped. Police are with her in the emergency room, gathering evidence as we speak. If you verify the same man from this photo, then we will have two women accusing him," the sergeant answered.

"Do you want to proceed?" he asked. I emphatically said, "Please!"

"Show her the pictures, Joe," Sergeant Harris instructed the other policeman.

Deputy Rowe took a large photo from a bag and gave it to me. It wasn't a picture of one person; it was several pictures on one page. Mug shots of various men they already had in custody.

Looking intently at the faces, I recognized him instantly. "There!" I said, pointing out a specific face. "That's the man who attacked me."

Deputy Rowe smiled and said, "His name is Lyle Horne. He's a real sick puppy."

"Are you sure he is the one?" Sergeant Harris asked.

"Oh yes! He's the creep! I'd never forget that face," I exclaimed.

Sergeant Harris asked, "Ms. Grimes, do you want to press charges against him for attempted rape?"

"Yes, I want this man off the streets. If he is guilty of hurting other women, I definitely want him behind bars," I said.

"Are you aware you must face him in a court of law?" he asked.

"I don't care. I'll do what I have to when the time comes. I'm glad you were able to catch him before I was released from the hospital. Now I don't have to fear him staking out my house," I said.

When my reports were taken, the police informed us I'd soon be visited by the District Attorney's Office. After other questions from my parents were answered, they left. Mom, Dad, and I sat in silence for a while. It was nice being in a room with them without them fighting with each other.

~~~

At the District Attorney's Office, Brent waited for the case he was forewarned about. When the case file of Lyle Horne was handed to him, he knew instantly this was the man.

Justice roared over Brent's shoulder; he was ready to assist.

Innocent victims were violated.

Since connecting spiritually with Hope, Brent's abilities had been heightened. Before then, he would have had only physical facts to present to the Lord. Now he was aware there were other issues behind the physical facts that needed to be addressed.

After asking the Holy Spirit to attend, Brent called the jail and requested a visit with Lyle Horne. He wanted to see and hear what was behind this man.

Once Brent made the appointment to see Lyle Horne, Justice vocalized his agreement with a low-rumble, deep purr.

Tests and More Tests

Dr. Jones, a doctor who specialized in traumas, entered my room. He was a jolly older man who reminded me of Santa Claus. After he examined me, he made various statements and probed me with questions. "I hear you had an eventful night. Your memory came back full force, which is a good sign. You had a bad blow to the head. Do you feel pressure anywhere in your head? How are your sight and hearing?"

"I see, and I hear just fine. My head hurts a little," I answered. "I'd like to have new x-rays made. We need to see if there are any changes. Severe nightmares can be caused by various things.

I want to rule out any physical problems before prescribing pain meds for headaches," he instructed.

He continued, "After Dr. Carter checks your leg, I'll know more. We don't need to prescribe you something that interferes with your sleep. Some drugs help with pain but cause nightmares. Dr. Carter and I will collaborate and make proper decisions together. Do you have any questions before I go?"

"Can I eat something? My stomach is growling so loudly, they can hear it at the nurse's station," I said jokingly.

"I'll order you some soup. If your system tolerates it well, then we'll allow you heavier fare tomorrow," he said.

Mom sat on my bed and talked with me after Dad left to go to work. She was able to lift a huge weight from my mind by informing me that my office supervisor had placed me on proper leave status. I wouldn't lose any money or have my position jeopardized. It was good to know someone at work had my back. I was also informed that coma patients weren't allowed visitors other than family. No telephones either. Mom had to deal with friends and co-workers calling her house inquiring about me. She made sure my plants were watered, and my mail was put in my apartment. I had nothing to fret, just focus on getting better.

I was slurping soup for breakfast when Dr. Carter, the Orthopedist, came in to see me. He was the exact opposite of Dr. Jones. He was middle-aged, thin, and haughty. He hardly spoke to me while he examined my leg and kept referring to my chart. Blunt and to the point, he stated, "Ms. Grimes, you sustained several breaks in your left leg. We made sure all the bones and ligaments were properly adjusted. With therapy, you should heal nicely. It will be a long process. I see where Dr. Jones has recommended more x-rays. I'll order new x-rays of your leg as well. Prescribing the proper pain meds can be tricky. Until we have the test results, I'll allow only Tylenol. Do you have any questions?"

I replied, "Yes, sir. How long before I can have the cast removed?" "Six to eight weeks, followed by several months of physical therapy," he said.

"Any more questions?" he asked.

"Can I have this catheter taken out?" I asked.

"I'll have Nurse Hamm call Dr. Jones. He has to have the final say," he answered.

"Yes, sir," I agreed.

Thirty minutes later, Nurse Hamm came in with a sterile tray. I knew from her expression I was about to be freed from the urinary catheter. Before starting the procedure, she handed me a tiny cup with two pills inside and said, "Here is your Tylenol."

Soon after having the catheter removed, she informed me, "Your tests will begin soon. You're scheduled for an MRI in a few minutes, then right after, your leg will be x-rayed."

"How long do the tests take? I asked.

"I'd say you should be done in about an hour, max. Then you can take a nap before lunch," she assured me.

While waiting on the x-ray technicians, I remembered my warning. Oh, my God! I'd let the enemy distract me. This revelation really bummed me out. I hadn't thought once about the promise Adrian had given me. I'd totally forgotten my family. I'd allowed things to distract me. Then doubt arose, and I wondered. *Was Adrian real or a dream?* I was confused.

~~~

Ox was sad. Satan had won a small victory. Determined to show Gina God's love was real, Ox asked the Holy Spirit if Gina could be shown miracle working power. With approval, he set out to see what resources he had available. Gina didn't know the Word at all, causing his own abilities to be very limited. What he found available was the hospital's technology. Ox knew the Father owned everything. The Father even created technology for his children. He would use it to persuade her. When she was resting again in her room, he'd encourage her to read the Bible. He'd ask the Holy Spirit to highlight the Word, making it easier for her to understand.

~~~

I remembered reading a little blue Bible before the chaos started. Where was it? Before I could locate it, interns came in with a wheelchair. Their timing stank. I had to read it when I returned. Mom was still in the room, so I asked while being rolled out, "Will you please find the little blue Bible I had last night? I want to read it when I get back."

"Where?" she asked.

"Look under the bed," I instructed.

~~~

Ox followed Gina everywhere. He became instinctively aware of the demonic imps around. Imps were ordered to ruin things, feed on emotions, or pluck hope out of people before it ever had a chance to materialize. Gina was not going to be one of their victims.

Heaven had armed Ox with any means necessary to destroy imps. Adrian was also given the same power while he helped Ox. Adrian volunteered to hunt imps down so Ox could keep watch over Gina's emotions. Time was crucial, and they had to work together. Gina was easily distracted through the flesh.

With his sword drawn, Ox stood next to Gina, trying to calm her with encouraging words as he battled imps. Even though she could not hear or see him, his encouraging words had power. Doubt was also present. Satan had sent him to influence Gina's mind. Ox couldn't do much against the spirit of doubt unless Gina's mind had been renewed. But his words, filled with God's love, helped soothe her mind a little. Soon her mind would be freed from threats of any kind once God's Word got embedded in her heart.

Adrian's issues were equally problematic. He was continually destroying the imps set out to cause Gina physical pain. Satan had released hordes. There were so many Adrian needed a dozen eyes to locate all of them. On the way to x-ray, Adrian found a nest of imps under Gina's wheelchair, bug-like creatures ordered to hurt her broken leg. Others rode the air punching her in the head. Every time he'd kill one, two more would appear. Not only were they after Gina, they attacked the technician assigned to Gina. The attack confused the technician so badly, it made him walk away, leaving

Gina physically helpless and unattended. The unit was severely short-staffed, leaving little compassion for Gina's welfare. Stress was causing every employee in the unit to work with one interest: to finish their shift and get home.

Crying out, Adrian called upon heaven to Healer. "Please send me assistance!" Instantly, like a blanket, angels fell into the hospital corridor. Holy fire swept the area, destroying everything evil. God's love reigned!

~~~

The tests took forever. I tried to focus on the wonderful passages running through my mind. Words I wanted to trust and believe. As I waited, my patience wore thin. The pain in my leg increased and was excruciating. My head began to pound. Then the tech left me stranded. I had been left sitting too long unnoticed; something wasn't right. I cried out, "Hello! Is someone out there? Hello!"

My cry worked. A nurse came running, apologizing profusely. Another MRI tech showed up, also apologizing, stating they were short-staffed. When the MRI was finished, the new tech took me to have my leg x-rayed. Having my leg twisted and turned for pictures caused me to cry out, "God, please help me! This hurts so much!"

After the leg pictures were taken, my mental relief was shot down. Dr. Carter wanted x-rays of my hips and shoulder as well. That meant more manhandling. When I asked why, all I got was "they have been ordered."

~~~

Ox took control of the technology. Every piece of equipment responded to his touch. Even the technicians cooperated since no imps were around. Every time a picture was made, Ox placed his hand on the machine. He made sure the machine had power to capture where God touched Gina. Each test would show facts overridden by the healing hand of God. Ox left no excuse for any man to deny the miracles.

Hungry for the Truth

When the techs got me back in my room, a nurse was waiting to help me. She arranged for me to have a portable toilet in the room, so I used it before getting back in bed. Afterward, I was in unbearable pain. My dose of Tylenol had been two hours before, so I couldn't ask for more. Mom, seeing my agony, went to talk with Nurse Hamm. When Nurse Hamm came in my room, I burst into tears. I needed relief, and she was my lifeline.

"Ms. Grimes, you are experiencing pain from being out of bed too long. Moving around has caused your body to rebel. Give me a few minutes, and I'll phone the doctor. If he says it is okay, I'll give you more Tylenol," the nurse soothed.

Mom and I waited, then waited some more. All I wanted to do was roll into a fetal position and whimper. When a nurse returned, she carried a small cup indicating some relief was on its way.

After taking the pill, I asked Mom if she found the Bible. When she handed it to me, I held it close. I wasn't ready to read yet; my head hurt too badly. Just having the Bible in my hand calmed something inside. Gripping it tightly, I closed my eyes and tried to doze. Maybe a nap would turn off the distractions so my body could relax. Before I totally succumbed, Mom kissed my brow and said she needed to go home.

~~~

Ox couldn't relax. He stayed on high alert. Too many battles with Satan had trained him not to take quiet time for granted. After he and Adrian had soothed Gina's mind, Ox asked the Holy Spirit if it was all right for Adrian to insert visions from Gina's journey into her nap. Her hope had to be invigorated until the Holy Spirit decided to introduce Himself. When permission was granted, Adrian immediately opened Gina's memory bank. Instantly, Gina's mind released the memories he needed for her to revisit.

~~~

The ride was amazing! The power of the motorcycle was humming under me as I gripped my man tightly. The air smelled so good. Life was wonderful. Then I was dressed for a night out. My man and I had reservations at Reo's. To my surprise, he proposed. Seconds later, I was married too quickly giving birth to a daughter. My joy was overwhelming, and I was at such peace.

I was awakened from reveling in the dream by someone bringing in my lunch tray. With my mind, still enchanted, I fought to remain in the peaceful state. My growling stomach caused reality to take center stage. Hunger for food kicked in gear.

I had more soup. This time, it wasn't mainly broth; it was pureed butternut squash soup. It smelled good but tasted bland. The food was filling, but it left me wanting. Not even the Jell-O sent to be a dessert could soothe my soul.

What I really wanted, more than anything in the world, was the family trapped within my memories. I longed for assurance. The fact that the man I called mine existed. If I could find him, everything thing else would fall right into place.

I decided to try reading the little Bible again. Maybe this time I could focus better. Adrian had warned me prior to his departure to stay in the Word. I returned to a passage I read the night before. This time, when I read the scripture, words stood out clearly. The passage meshed with the words Adrian said to me earlier, "All things work together for good to those who love the Lord."

Was this what Adrian meant when he said even my injuries would be used for good? He said plainly that every word in the Bible was truth. What I was going through, all this pain and brokenness had to be for my good, according to this passage. I want my life to be good. I want to love the Lord. The doubt crept in my thoughts. *I hope God knows I'm trying.* I also remembered the incident when Adrian rebuked me for my doubts. From that memory, I purposely chose to believe God was seeing my efforts.

~~~

Jesus smiled. Gina's determination was sweet. Her trying to love was all He wanted.

~~~

I read and read, hoping other scriptures would stand out or be easy to comprehend. I got confused because all the thee and thou phrases didn't make sense. How could someone new to Christianity find help from this gibberish? Frustrated, I lay the Bible down then decided to do what I'd started to do last night: write down my memories.

~~~

Ox watched Gina closely. He was glad she had bulldog tenacity to hold on to her promises, but she needed to find Jesus in the scriptures. Without Him, front and center in her thoughts, the memories of her family would never manifest. He was the door for all promises to come through. The Word heard helped his ability get inside a person. Faith came by hearing. Using what was available again, he took control of Gina's television and remote.

~~~

Lying in bed bored and lonely, I decided to watch television. When I reached for the remote, it slipped out of my grasp. As it hit the floor, the TV instantly came to life. Since the 'call-nurse' button was also on the remote, I couldn't ask for assistance, so I decided to watch the program being broadcast. It was a Christian channel that hosted various preachers throughout the day. In no time, I was enthralled. It was like my mind was hungry. Each preacher's view was inspiring and encouraging. Time flew without pain, and before I knew it, late-afternoon doctor visits arrived.

Dr. Jones was all smiles when he came in and started right away giving me good news because of the MRI tests. "Gina, the tests show no signs of damage. All the bruising has disappeared. It's a miracle! People just don't recover this fast from as much trauma as you sustained."

I was shell-shocked from his statements. God had protected me! He is truly faithful!

I asked, "Dr. Jones, do many patients have life-altering experiences? Have some experienced an out-of-body episode? If I said I did, would you admit me to the psych ward?"

He laughed. "Many of my patients say they've had weird experiences after an accident, Gina. I've been doing this job long enough to know that God really does exist."

Then he pointed to the Bible lying on my lap and said, "I see you love His Word."

"Let's say I'm trying. But I can't understand it," I confessed. "You need a version written for this generation. Don't quit, keep reading it. God's Word has helped me many times," he informed. I thought to myself, *Good to know one of my doctors is a Christian.* Then he asked, "How is the pain?"

I honestly answered, "The morning ordeal caused a lot. After the Tylenol and nap, I feel better."

"Pain medication is important for proper healing, but when someone has many injuries, it is important to know what to give. I think Dr. Carter will agree your tolerance for pain is high. But you still need something to help your stress level subside. Stress from pain slows progress. After your evening meal, I'll have a nurse give you some Demerol," he said.

Before leaving, he asked, "Any more questions?" "No, sir," I said.

Thirty minutes later, Dr. Carter arrived. He instantly noticed the program on the television, and his face grimaced. As if frantic for change, he searched and found the remote and retrieved it from the floor, turning off the volume. Then his face became void of any emotion, and he turned to address me. His actions caused me concern. What would be his news?

With his cold, blunt demeanor, he said, "Ms. Grimes, your x-rays indicate you are healing nicely. I must admit I'm shocked. X-rays taken the night of the accident showed damage to your hip and left shoulder. I was expecting to see a slight change, but the photos show no damage either. What I thought were minor fractures were only bruising. You are a lucky lady."

"I'm just a miracle," I said seriously.

He snickered. "I wouldn't call it a miracle but amazing improvements."

I didn't trust him after that. Something inside me was repulsed. As was their custom, each doctor inquired if I had questions before they left. When Dr. Carter asked, I shook my head no. I didn't want to hear any negative replies from him. I sensed he fed on people's misery.

When dinner arrived, I was thrilled. I had turkey slices, mashed potatoes, green beans, and applesauce for dessert. I wolfed the food down to experience bliss from a full belly. Soon after the meal, I received the Demerol. The combination of turkey and pain meds caused me to doze off for a while.

Later that evening, Mamie came to see me, and she was all smiles. In her hand was a bag. Presenting it to me, she said, "Dr. Jones asked me to bring you this."

Inside the bag was a New American Standard Bible. Inside the book, Dr. Jones had written, "Enjoy! Better than any medicine I could prescribe. Get well, your friend, Dr. Jones."

Reading those words made me want to cry. He was a Santa Claus.

Mamie said, "Now, now, honey, are those tears of joy? Dr. Jones is a good ole soul. He knows how to heal from the inside out."

"Yes, ma'am. I've never known a doctor so sweet. You both are wonderful. I missed your company a lot," I exclaimed.

Joyfully, Mamie replied, "You're sweet. Girl, you're one of my favorites too. Let's stop all this sweet talk and get you settled in for the night. You need to go to the bathroom?"

Suddenly, my bladder felt like it was going to explode. Her question triggered an urgent need to pee. I wiggled to the side of the bed trying to maneuver the IV pole and my injured leg. Without hesitation, Mamie knelt and gathered me by the waist, hoisting me off the bed over to the portable toilet just in the nick of time.

"Whew! I almost didn't make it," I exclaimed.

Mamie laughed. "I was expecting you to give me a challenge.

Sweetie, you are a trip!"

When Mamie helped me back in bed, she informed me of tomorrow's scheduled events. I was going to be trained to use crutches properly. I couldn't wait!

Small Victories One Defeat

I slept through the night with no problems or bad dreams. Only sleeping didn't give me much time to talk with Mamie. She stepped in to check on me before she went home, though. During our conversation, she said I was allowed visitors and telephone calls today, and that the day nurse would install a phone in my room.

Who did I want to see? The only friend I really wanted to talk with was Caylee. I really needed to talk to her about my experience. Maybe she could guide me into my new Christian lifestyle.

I was anxious to get my day started. I adjusted my bed into a sitting position, preparing for the morning's activities. This simple action caused so much commotion. All the monitors and cords came loose from their sockets, causing the system to set off an alarm. The alarm was so loud, a panic started outside in the nurse's station. Three nurses came rushing in to see if I was in distress. I was very embarrassed. My attempt to be more self- sufficient only created more havoc.

The last thing I wanted was to be remembered as a problem patient. I apologized profusely for the confusion and assured everyone I was fine. Working at a mental health facility, I knew what it was like to have a panic alarm go off; adrenalin kicks into overdrive. I had just caused unnecessary chaos for these people.

Dad called and said he wouldn't visit until after work, but Mom came in early. I wish she would get on with her life as well. She needed to go back to her job. Making the suggestion, I said, "Mom, why don't you go back to work? I'm fine and on the mend."

She patted my hand. Then she smiled with tears in her eyes before replying, "Honey, I know. Humor your old mama just a little longer. Let me watch over my baby."

My heart broke. Something in her statement let me glimpse the horror she lived the last few days because of me. I had no choice. Mom needed reassurance that I would be all right, so I succumbed to her mothering.

When Dr. Jones walked in, I'd just finished breakfast. As always, he was jovial and all smiles. I opened my arms out wide and begged, "Come here, you!"

When he came over, I gave him the biggest hug. "Thanks for the Bible, you are the best!" I exclaimed.

"Gina, it does this old doctor good to know the younger generation wants to know the Word. I couldn't help myself. The gift shop beckoned me inside. Accept the gift and use it to mend your heart. You've been through a horrible ordeal," he urged.

Then Dr. Jones changed the subject. "I see you've had your breakfast. How was it?"

"Great! I ate like it was my last meal," I replied.

Laughing, he said, "You may feel famished for a few more days. Your system still thinks it is in starvation mode. Your cravings will stop soon."

Mom chimed in, "When can Gina go home?"

"If Dr. Carter agrees, Gina may get to go home this weekend," he answered.

I thought, *two more days, and I'll be free. I can begin my search.*

My man is waiting.

When Dr. Jones patted my leg, it jolted me out of my ponderings. "I'll have Nurse Hamm remove your IV this morning. You are doing well." Then he said before leaving, "See you this afternoon."

Nurse Hamm came into the room and removed the IV then she sent in an aide. Judy Knight was my aide's name. And bless her, she had a telephone! I was being set free, little by little.

Afterward, Judy set out to bathe me. She was a tiny thing! I couldn't fathom how she would be able to move patients around. But she sure fooled me; she was good. She had me bathed, and in a chair, in no time, so she could change the sheets.

Sitting in the lounge chair felt good with my legs stretched out. My back had better support. When I asked if I could sit for a while, Judy replied, "Sure! It will help with your circulation."

As if he had been watching and waiting, Dr. Carter showed up when Judy exited. Like before, he had no personality and was all business. If that was the way he was going to act, then I'll ask direct questions. "Dr. Carter, when can I start using crutches?"

"I'll need to check your shoulder and arm strength first," he said.

Removing the gown from my shoulder, he checked the bruising. Replacing my gown, he took my arm and started rotating it to see if the motion created any pain. Satisfied when I hadn't winced, he asked Nurse Hamm to get crutches. Lowering the lounge chair into a sitting position, he said, "Gina, move closer to the edge." Then he took my hands and helped me stand. When Nurse Hamm handed him the crutches, he placed one under each arm to see if they were properly adjusted for my height.

"Brace yourself on the crutches," he instructed. "Let your wrist carry the burden of weight, not your underarms. Let me know if anything hurts."

~~~

Ox watched while surveying the surroundings. He knew if imps could harm, this was a perfect time. He was equipped and ready for an attack. Satan always sent others. Hospitals were never empty of the foul creatures. If he weren't careful, one could sabotage Gina's recovery.

Just as Gina started to move, as if on cue, dozens of imps came out of nowhere. Two little devils grabbed her in the sensitive spot under the arm, but Ox thwarted their effort. Others focused on twisting Gina's wrists, so her weight couldn't be supported on the crutches, but their efforts were foiled as well. Ox's mighty sword swung and slashed until all were destroyed.

~~~

I pushed up with both wrists only to have one arm give way as I felt a shooting pain in my armpit. I started over, taking another step, and had success. I managed four or five moves hoping to satisfy Dr. Carter.

"Was there any pain?" he asked.

I answered, "Some under my arm."

I wasn't surprised when he blamed bruising. In addition, I was surprised to hear him order another drug. I watched as he reveled. He was excited that there was discomfort. I knew I had to prove myself. I was determined he would not receive a negative response from me. I didn't like this man. There was something off about him.

I listened with trepidation as he explained, "Your pain is still stemming from bruised tissue. The bones in your arms aren't giving you any trouble. I've prescribed something to reduce the inflammation. Stay off the crutches unless you just have to use them."

~~~

Ox was no dummy. He witnessed the doctor's elation. The enemy was using Dr. Carter. It was time to notify Healer and get the Holy Spirit involved. Doctors were harder to overthrow. Drastic measures were required to tip the balance back into Gina's favor. Jesus would have to convince this doctor to get his emotional kicks elsewhere.

~~~

When Dr. Carter left the room, Mom realized I wasn't in a good mood. She made a lame excuse to leave. Knowing her, she was off to buy candy for me. She always used sweets to calm down stressful situations.

I made use of the free time. I looked through my new Bible. This one I could understand. Mamie had made the suggestion to begin reading in the New Testament. She said I needed to know about Jesus. She also recommended the book of Psalms.

~~~

Ox sighed while Gina read. He loved hearing people read about his master. Soon Gina would understand the love available to her and for her. Soon, he and Gina would be able to work as a team. Her setback was minor.

Visitors

The book is amazing, I thought. The Psalms spoke to me. It wasn't until my lunch arrived that it registered to me I'd been reading a long time. I was surprised that the meds Dr. Carter prescribed hadn't made me sleepy. I was also surprised that Mom hadn't returned.

As I was eating lunch, Angie showed up. The first thing she said was, "Hey, you! Are you back from the dead?"

"Alive and almost kicking," I replied.

Our last words had been strained. I'd been hurt by her rejection. But I was still glad to see her. I wanted to share with her my new freedom. But before I could, she made a joke. "You'll be dancing with me again at the pool hall in no time."

Angie didn't have a clue. She wouldn't understand why even the thought of partying repulsed me. I'd changed, and I didn't want the party lifestyle any longer. Not to hurt Angie's feelings, I simply said, "Maybe not dancing, but I'll be moving to a new tune soon."

I could tell she was feeling guilt. She'd sat on the bed about to cry. Ashamed, she said, "I heard through the grapevine you left the pool hall mad. Someone saw your screeching tires. Were you mad at me? Did I cause this?"

"Angie, stop it! You had nothing to do with the wreck. I can't forgive you for something you didn't do. Stop feeling sorry for yourself and let's move on," I exclaimed.

"I was a little drunk and too engrossed in Rex to think of your safety. We'd never broken the buddy system before. Can you forgive me, Gina?" she begged.

"Please stop! I had a wreck because a man attacked me, it had nothing to do with you," I soothed.

She stopped blabbering after my admission. With shock on her face, she probed, "You were attacked?"

"Yeah! Some guy tried to rape me. I got away only to wind up here." I enlightened.

"OMG!" she screeched. "Thank the lucky stars you weren't killed!"

When she noticed the Bible, I'd been reading, she asked the oddest thing, "You don't have anything better to read?"

I was a little insulted. Angrily, I responded, "So far, it's the best book I've ever read. You should consider reading it yourself."

"No way! Those old stories wouldn't help me. They are designed to keep you bound up. I have enough guilt in my life without trying to find more," she answered.

"It doesn't make me feel guilty. I feel inspired and encouraged," I said.

Angie's attitude was as thick as a brick wall. My Words didn't faze her. She wanted no part of religion. Angie quickly changed the subject to her new boyfriend, Rex. Her apparent worry for me had ceased. All she wanted to talk about now were her excursions. I sat listening, struggling with myself not to hurt her feelings. I bit my tongue so I wouldn't say anything mean. The hour seemed to drag out; I just wanted this visit to be cut short. When she finally left, I was exhausted.

For years, I thought we were just alike. Our viewpoints on life were the reason she was my best friend. Now we had very little in common. Within a few days, I'd changed. My mind was being completely transformed. Was the Bible responsible? At that moment, I realized I needed to talk with someone who would understand. I needed someone I could share God's Word with. I picked up the telephone and called the office where I worked. I needed Caylee.

~~~

Ox sighed with relief. Finally, Gina understood! Light and darkness didn't mix. It signaled to him that the seed was growing. Gina was craving communion with like-minded people. She needed the one who started it all. Having Gina and Caylee together would make his mission easier. He also knew Satan would try to stop their union at all costs. Thank God! Jesus was watching over Caylee.

~~~

As soon as the receptionist heard my voice, she wanted to dominate the conversation. She was wishing me well, but it was keeping me from Caylee. Finally, I convinced Margie I was doing well so she'd transfer me to Caylee. She answered, "Caylee Sellers, how may I help you?"

"Hey, Caylee, it's Gina," I responded.

Shocked, she rattled, "Oh my God! You're able to talk, can I come over? When?"

"That's why I'm calling. I need you to come as soon as possible. I have something wonderful to share with you. Plus, I need my sister," I replied.

Gasping, she whispered, "Sister?"

"Yeah, I heard you call me that when I was in the coma," I told her.

"Oh boy! We really do need to talk. I lied to get in to see you!" she exclaimed.

I laughed and replied, "We'll talk all about it this evening when you come. Just get here soon. I'd like to tell you everything." "Okay! Look for me around 5:30 p.m. Is there anything I can bring you?" she asked.

"No! Just you!" I said.

~~~

Jesus and the Holy Spirit immediately dispatched an angel to cover Caylee's life. There weren't much the angels could do to stop the imps from hearing her plans, though. The mental health facility where she worked was also a breeding ground for the foul creatures.

Loshan, one of the earthbound angels, was called to watch over Caylee. Upon arriving with sword drawn, he was able to kill one eavesdropping imp but missed another because it slid under the door. Immediately informing the Holy Spirit, he said, "One of the devils escaped. It overheard their conversation. Mayhem is about to begin!"

The Holy Spirit replied, "I'll alert heaven. Ox will need reinforcements."

After the Holy Spirit met with the four generals' battalions, they were sent into service to watch over the hospital where Gina lay. Every corner of the building, even top, and bottom, were guarded. God's watchmen were everywhere.

~~~

I was really tired and didn't want to read or watch television. I focused on remembering as much as I could about my out-of- body experience. Maybe sharing it with Caylee would help me keep it alive in my heart. I'd do anything to keep from forgetting. I wanted my family badly. I needed the love and assurance from my future.

I referred to my notes. I jotted down what Adrian said. He had assured me that my husband and baby were as real as the people I love in the present. All I had to do was wait and rely on the Bible. I needed help understanding the Bible. Five-thirty p.m. couldn't get here fast enough.

~~~

Ox decided to help Gina use her imagination by giving her some of his ability. He released his huge wings to their full span and engulfed Gina within their safety. She wouldn't even know he was there. Within his wings, he could soothe her restless spirit and empower her with the ability to use her mind.

~~~

I closed my eyes and allowed my mind to drift so I could remember. Pleasant memories of a beautiful smile, beautiful green eyes, and wavy brown hair appeared. I remembered how my body responded to being held. I remembered the pain of labor. These were precious memories I couldn't and wouldn't let go of. I envisioned myself as a bulldog enjoying a tasty bone. The memories were my bone. I was selfish with my bone. I was ferocious and determined to keep it for myself. I stroked and I played with my bone. Then on purpose, I growled. *Don't mess with this bulldog or the bone!*

I woke to the telephone ringing. I must have fallen asleep. "Hello," I said.

"Hi, honey," I heard Mom say.

"I promised to call you before I came back to the hospital to see if you wanted anything."

Groggy, I said, "Let me wake up. I was taking a nap."

After a second or two, I asked, "Mom, are you close to a convenience store?"

"Yes, I'm parked at one now. I was just about to go in but decided to give you a call first. You want something?" she asked.

To make her feel wanted, I said, "You know what I need. I'd love some chocolate. How about it? Bring my favorites!"

I could almost hear her smiling as she replied, "Sure, I'll be there in a few minutes."

What time was it? Surely, it was close to being 5:30 p.m. Oh no! What had I done? I'd encouraged Mom to come back! I couldn't talk to Caylee in front of Mom. Mom would have me committed to the mental ward. I'd have to think of a way to make Mom go home.

Using my need to go to the bathroom as an excuse to find out what time it was, I called the nurse's station. When Judy came in to help, I asked her for the time.

"It's 3:00 p.m.," she said. "My shift is almost over."

I had two hours and thirty minutes before Caylee would be coming. How was I going to convince Mom to leave without her knowing why?

Smiling with bags of goodies, Mom said, "Boy, you look great! I was gone for just a few hours, what happened? You don't appear to be hurting at all."

"I hurt more than I'm letting on. I just want to get out of here, you know," I told her.

"Here is your candy. I bought all your favorites."

Tearing open a peanut-butter-cup wrapper, I said, "Thanks! I was having candy withdrawals. Candy is better than pain meds any day."

The joke gave me an idea. I knew instantly how I could get Mom to leave. Her desire to please me anyway possible would be her downfall. I'd get her cooking. I smiled and then baited. "You know what would be even better than this candy? I'll give you a hint. I'd love some of your German chocolate cake or maybe one of your cheesecakes. Could I twist your arm into making one for me tonight?"

Taking the bait, she said, "Sure! Which one?"

Answering slyly, I urged, "Both! I could share them with some of my favorite nurses. They deserve something special for taking good care of me."

"I'll be glad to bake them. You know it takes several hours for the cheesecake to set, don't you?" she exclaimed.

"Worth the wait!" I said.

She bit her lip and stated, "But I just got back, I wanted to visit."

"Why did you leave today?" I asked.

"I wanted to tell you about it tonight, but it can wait. If I'm going to bake for you and your friends, I need to get going," she replied.

Now my curiosity was heightened. "No! Tell me! I know you're about to pop with news. So, spill!" I demanded.

"It's about your car," she said.

Totally taken off guard, I inquired, "What about my car? Wasn't it totaled?"

Smiling from ear to ear, she replied, "Yes! But I don't want to mess up my plan."

The door to my room opened after a brief knock. Dr. Jones walked in, interrupting our conversation. "How's my girl?" he asked.

Showing him the bag of goodies, I said, "I'm doing great since Mom brought me some candy."

"Better than any pain meds in the place, huh, Gina?" He laughed. Patting his belly, he joked, "Chocolate does it for me too when I'm feeling low. Can't you tell?"

"How did you know I was feeling low?" I asked.

He informed sweetly, "I read where Dr. Carter placed you on a pain watch. When I walked in and saw you eating chocolate, I put two and two together and guessed. Appears your arm is causing you problems? Have you been taking your meds?"

"No, sir," I answered. "I was hoping if I didn't use them, I could improve on my own."

He sighed then said, "Gina, you need the meds, not only for pain but to remove the inflammation. We've got to monitor you. Work with us, and you'll go home sooner."

Before he left, he said, "I may have to go out of town tomorrow afternoon. Dr. Carter will take good care of you. Don't worry, you will be fine. You are my little miracle, and I'm very proud of you."

I wasn't happy about being left in the monster's care. But I gratefully responded to my Santa Claus, "Thanks, Dr. Jones. I'll save you a piece of cake. Mom is going to make me a German chocolate and a cheesecake. Which one is your favorite?"

"Save two pieces, one of each please," he said, smiling while he rubbed his belly.

I was hoping no one else would come. I didn't want any company but Caylee. But my hopes were dashed because my room became Grand Central Station. Mom was excited because my first visitor was John Harding, my insurance agent. Apparently, he and Mom had been working on my insurance needs earlier today. Mr. Harding said, "We have some good news. A junkyard in town bought your damaged car for scrap after I had declared it totaled on paper. Here is a check to help you get another car. When insurance issues clear, you should get more money. As of now, the tractor trailer company has agreed not to press charges.

Once the owner learned why you ran the red light, he didn't have the heart. Isn't that good news?"

I didn't know what to say. Mom had been busy. Sometimes she could be amazing. I thanked Mr. Harding then looked into Mom's eyes and gratefully said, "Thanks! Mom, I love you so much."

Then matchmaker Mom kicked in. Out of nowhere, she started talking about Russ Jackson. Mom said, "Remember us telling you about Russ Jackson? He's been helping us with everything. He told his boss what happened. He explained why it appeared that you were careless. He sent us to a friend of his that owned the junkyard. He is really a nice guy. I can't wait for you to meet him." I wasn't going to take the bait. I kept my cool and simply asked questions about things that interested me. "Was everything removed before they took it?" I asked.

"We went through it thoroughly, Gina. Everything is at my house when you want it," she assured me.

Then Mr. Harding chimed in, "Before I leave, Gina, I need your signature. It will finalize everything so you can start looking for a car in your budget."

Great - a new car and another monthly bill. There was no need for complaining; I needed a ride, and Mom wanted to make me happy. I just kept saying over and over in my mind, *all things work for good*. That phrase had to become my mantra, or I'd go nuts.

~~~

Ox smiled, thinking, "Good for you! Keep focusing on that passage and watch us help you succeed."

~~~

It had to be getting close to 5:30 p.m. Mr. Harding left, but Mom hadn't, and I was getting concerned. When a man walked in with a huge bouquet of flowers, I knew instantly what her holdup was. She'd encouraged this Russ Jackson person to visit me. Great!

Beaming, Mom invited him in. "Come on in, Russ. I'd like you to meet Gina."

"Hello, Ms. Grimes. I know you don't know me. I'm Russ Jackson, the truck driver who hit your car," he introduced himself.

Only to be polite, I greeted, "It's good to meet you. Thanks for everything, you've been great."

Any other time, a man like him would have caught my eye. He was tall, handsome, and very polite. But he wasn't my intended. His last name gave that away.

Then Russ remembered the flowers. "Oh! I brought you these. I hope you like carnations."

"Thanks! I love all flowers. These are lovely," I replied.

Seeing that he was nervous, I asked, "Would you like to have a seat?"

"No, ma'am, I can't stay. I had to see for myself that you were all right. I couldn't get any peace. My truck slammed you pretty hard. Your mom has been great. I called her every day to check on you. I have to get back to work, but if you need anything, have your mom call."

I was flattered by his statements, but I didn't want to encourage romantic notions. I simply would bid him farewell. "Thanks, Russ! I mean, thanks for everything."

"You're welcome. Oh! By the way! If you need me to testify about that man, call me," he volunteered before leaving.

When Russ left, I noticed the weather looked ominous out my hospital window. I had help from nature that would help me make Mom leave. She hated bad weather. I exclaimed, "Mom, look outside! We're about to have a storm. I think you should go, especially if you must stop at the store first. The thought of you stuck out in a storm frightens me. Please get moving."

"I'm out the door. I'll stop at the corner grocery next to the house. Don't worry, I'll be all right," she said.

With my mission accomplished, I settled back and watched television. As I waited for Caylee, I heard on the television that the weather was indeed horrible. Now I really was worried for Mom. Guilt overwhelmed me. I'd been mean and underhanded. *She would have been safe at the hospital,* I berated myself mentally. Then I thought about Caylee. She shouldn't drive in the storm to visit me. I started to call and ask her to wait until tomorrow but decided against it. She was a big girl. She'd make the right decisions.

I waited about thirty minutes and called Mom's home number. When she didn't answer right away, I started to panic. Concern for her safety was making me squirm. Where was she? All kinds of horrible visions played in my head. If something happened to Mom, I'd blame myself forever.

I called her cell, but it went to voice mail. I left a message for her to call me the moment she could. I was scared. Minutes turned into another half-hour. Still no – call back.

When the phone shrilled, I almost jumped out of bed. "Hello!" I shouted into the receiver.

"Gina, it's Mom. I'm home, baby. Stop worrying," she said.

"Where were you?" I asked.

"It was raining so hard after I finished shopping. I stayed and talked with the cashier for a few minutes. I didn't know you'd called because I'd turned the ringer of my cell phone off. I had it on vibrate while in the hospital. I'm sorry I startled you, honey."

~~~

Ox had a front-row seat to Gina's self-induced torment. She had been tricky and deserved the worry. Now it was time he calmed her down. Gently, he began to hum. Then he whispered into Gina's ear, "Read the Word. Feed your spirit."

Plans Backfired

Loshan watched and waited for an attack on Caylee. The air was ripe for threats. His only order was to protect life. Word had not been given for him to release any other kind of assistance.

~~~

Caylee rushed to get her work done while pondering on Gina's urgent request. *What was so important? Why did Gina want her to come as quickly as she could?*

Gina's "sister" statement had thrilled her. Caylee firmly believed in miracles and was hoping Gina wanted to share something wonderful. Unaware she was about to be assaulted, Caylee's curiosity was inflamed with a burning desire to get to Gina.

~~~

Loshan noticed Satan's demonic imps were not the only evil forces around. Their larger brothers had also been summoned. These demons had the ability to alter minds. Gremlins had also been set loose. Their specialty was to torment and cause havoc. Satan must be determined to keep these women apart; Caylee was surrounded.

~~~

In preparation to leave, Caylee retrieved her purse out of her desk drawer and set it on the floor. Her last duty before departure was turning off her workstation. As she reached to turn off her computer monitor, the telephone rang. This startled her, causing her to knock over a cola she had been drinking.

Ugh! What a mess. I should have been more careful, she berated *herself silently.*

As Caylee spoke into the phone, she attempted to mop up the mess. To her disbelief, no one was on the other end. The line was silent. Frustrated, she continued daubing the cola off the table and floor, unaware the sticky liquid had flowed freely into her purse.

Nestled in the bottom of Caylee's purse, the gremlin laughed. He was having fun destroying Caylee's cell phone. He enjoyed weaving the cola within the phone while listening to crackling and sizzling sounds frying the circuits. His job was to make sure nothing worked in the little instrument. When he was satisfied with his work, the gremlin left. He had to help set up the real problem that would make all this effort worthwhile.

~~~

Loshan sighed angrily that he couldn't stop the gremlin. He was frustrated! All he was allowed to do was watch! He wanted to fight! The Holy Spirit had to know. Something was about to happen. Loshan relied on the Lord knowing the smallest hidden details over what was presented, and this helped the Holy Spirit plan strategic operations. If Caylee's communication device was disarmed on purpose, his only recourse was to get prepared.

~~~

Caylee hated messes. Even though she wanted to leave, she had to make sure everything was wiped down and free from the sticky cola. When she was almost out the door, one of her coworkers stopped her and asked, "Aren't you planning to wait out the storm with us? The weather broadcast indicates it shouldn't last very long."

"No, I have plans to see Gina. Maybe if I hurry I can beat the worst part before I get to the hospital," she replied.

On cue, one of the mind-altering demons impressed upon the co-worker to give Gina bad advice. Then he touched Caylee's mind as well.

The co-worker suggested, "Don't take the bypass. It would be faster to go down Johnson Road. Too many people use the bypass. I've been trapped waiting too many times due to accidents from bad weather on the bypass. Traffic comes to a screeching halt."

Caylee knew Johnson Road was a shady part of town. The area was notorious for gang-related problems. Not many commuters travel that way anymore because of the crime. But Caylee wasn't planning to stop anywhere on the road. She agreed it would be faster, maybe not safer, but a quicker way out of the storm.

On the way, out, Caylee said, "Thanks for the advice."

When Caylee opened the door to leave the building, a blast of wind hit her hard in the face. The force alone should have been enough to frighten her. But the demon's evil touch had her mind clouded. She couldn't make good, safe decisions. The demon had fed her a lustful excitement to know a secret. He used Gina's request as the stronghold.

~~~

Outside in the elements, Loshan had bigger issues. Heavy rain and wind were becoming dangerous. Satan had demonic giants controlling the weather. One giant was determined to use the wind against Caylee. He'd watched it smack Caylee in her face then attack her car blow after blow. Loshan determined that the giant's focus was against life. Loshan could fight! One more threat from the wind and the war was on!

~~~

It was almost impossible to see. Heavy rain made driving slow a necessity, and with each blast of wind, Caylee almost lost control of her vehicle. Still, under the demon's evil suggestion, she fought the urge to pull over and stop on Johnson Road. She was afraid a gangster would approach her even in bad weather.

The giant fed on Caylee's fear. He threw blast after blast of wind at the small vehicle, relishing in the plan of making Caylee wreck. He was about to amp up the force when lightning split his head open. Loshan's sword of justice landed true. Afterward, Loshan exclaimed loudly, "You may have used the wind, but God gave me lightning!"

All around, angry giants roared! One of their mightiest had been slain.

With their angry cries heard in heaven, sirens started blaring. The general of Justice sprang to high alert. Strategic orders were given instantly. Jesus ordered heaven's gates to be opened for more angels to be released into action. Loshan would not be left unassisted, and Caylee would be guaranteed safety.

Within the earth's atmosphere, cloaked behind a spiritual veil, swords blazed and sliced, lighting up the night. As the mighty forces fought, smaller demons pursued Caylee. Without the giant of wind, their plans may fail. Then one of the smaller demons had an idea. "Use the battle!"

Climbing up a giant's body while he fought, the small demon reached the giant's ear. Divulging the plan, the giant agreed it may work. The little demons could throw trash at the angels; occasionally throw large limbs at them also. They could create a diversion. Then without warning, a giant could use his sword as a bat. They would disable or possibly kill Caylee before the angels could counter.

Loshan and his comrades laughed at the little demons attempting to fight. Trash! Come on! Then suddenly, a large limb was hurled at one of them. Dodging the limb, the angel ducked as a giant batted. The next thing Loshan witnessed was the huge limb heading toward Caylee's vehicle. It had been a strategic move on evil's part. No one could have stopped it. All they could do now was stop her vehicle from wrecking.

~~~

"Jesus! Don't let me die!" Caylee screamed as her car spun. The impact was horrible. The tire bursting was loud, but the uncontrollable spin was life-threatening.

~~~

Loshan and three other angels removed themselves from the battle. Controlling Caylee's vehicle was imperative. At the risk of their own demise, each one positioned themselves beside a tire. Grabbing the body of the car, the angels manipulated the car off the road, stopping it from overturning; otherwise, it would have plunged into a deep ditch.

~~~

Caylee was still screaming when the car came to an abrupt stop. With her heart in her throat, she knew she needed to get out of the vehicle. It was too close to the edge of a deep ditch, and water was filling it up fast. Shaking all over from the adrenalin rush,

Caylee talked to herself, "Get a grip! You're not dead! The Lord protected you! Get your cell and call for help!"

~~~

The air was filled with evil laughter. The demons thought the plan was funny until they saw rage coming their way. Abruptly, they vanished, leaving the scene. They'd let the giants battle their enemies. Caylee was in their part of town, alone and helpless. Their job was done. Too bad she didn't die, but at least she wasn't meeting the other girl tonight.

~~~

Reaching into her purse to retrieve the cell phone, Caylee's fingers felt the sticky cola. She had a feeling her phone was dead before she even attempted to call anyone. When the phone showed no signs of power, she took it apart and tried cleaning it, but nothing could revive the little thing. It was toast.

Caylee wanted to cry but knew that wouldn't help matters. She wasn't helpless; she knew how to change a flat tire. She could remedy her own problem. She'd watched others do it many times. With umbrella in hand, she got out to survey the damage and see what she was facing, hopeful until she saw the bigger picture. She'd come very close to being really hurt or killed. It was a miracle. Not only had her tire burst, the wheel mount was bent out of shape from the large limb. There was no way she could free her car from the limb's grasp. She was truly stranded in this bad area with no cell phone, dressed in business clothes and high-heel shoes. Walking was out of the question. She'd have to wait for someone to come along who would help.

She got back inside the car, turned on the emergency lights, and waited as she listened to the pouring rain. There wasn't a thing she could do to speed up her rescue, so she prayed. "Father, Your Word tells me You will never leave me or forsake me. I'm going to wait here with You until You send someone to help. I will not move into fear. Jesus asked You to protect us from the evil one. I know You heard Him make that request for me. I'm relying on You and staying strong. I know You love me. You'll provide what I need and who I need. I love You and will praise You always."

Now that she had released her worries, she started making her stay more comfortable. She turned up the heat in her car. She was cold from getting wet. She turned on the overhead light then sat back on her seat. Then she turned up her car radio. She continued listening to her favorite Christian station. She relaxed and sang along with the music. One of the songs was very appropriate for the situation. Some of the lyrics were, "I'll praise You in this storm." Time passed, and the rain came, and the night grew darker, but she enjoyed herself.

~~~

The Holy Spirit had already made arrangements for Caylee to have help. Russ Jackson was headed her way. He had encouraged him to go down Johnson Road. He was working a blessing into Caylee's bad situation. Jesus had shown Him days earlier that Russ would be part of Caylee's life—what better way to get them acquainted. Russ was a Samaritan through and through. He couldn't pass a stranded car on the road without seeing if the person needed help. Tonight, in the torrential rain, Caylee was about to be introduced to her lifelong mate. Her hope was being fulfilled. The outcome would be a true blessing.

~~~

Small World

Instead of fighting all the traffic in the heavy rain, Russ decided to go down Johnson Road back to work. To bide the time, he decided to listen to the radio instead of fumbling around for a CD. Finding a Christian radio channel, he decided to listen for a spell. In times of stress, he always found the music soothing and very relaxing.

As he drove slowly, he couldn't help but notice the storm damage all around. The area had been hit hard by heavy winds. Suddenly, blinking lights caught his attention! He slowed down to a crawl to inspect the situation when he saw a small car tilted dangerously off the road with emergency lights flashing. To his horror, the car was really banged up, and there was a person inside. Even in the rain, his conscience wouldn't allow him to pass by without seeing if he could assist.

Cautiously, he pulled alongside the vehicle and rolled down his window before approaching the person. He didn't know what to expect. The frightened person may pull a gun on him. After all, they are in a bad part of town, he thought.

Caylee also noticed the truck slowing down. Her heart started pounding from fear. But she cast that emotion down, reaffirming her commitment to remain unafraid. This was someone God had sent, so she started praising the Lord. Caylee watched as the driver rolled down his window then she did the same. Before any words were exchanged, she heard an awesome sound. He was listening to the same Christian radio station. "Thank you, Jesus!" she exclaimed aloud.

"I'm not Jesus, lady, but I may be able to help. Are you hurt?" he asked.

"No, sir! I'm just stranded," she replied.

Before exiting the truck, Russ asked, "Do you need my help?"

"Please!" Caylee screeched. "I don't have a cell phone."

"You can use mine. I'll bring it to you, I don't mind getting wet," he volunteered.

Caylee thought he was considerate and said, "Thank you!"

Russ parked his truck and jumped out. Caylee opened her car door and slid into the passenger seat, so Russ could get out of the rain. She noticed that even though he was a big man, he had a gentle, compassionate energy around him. She thought, *must be another sign from God.*

Then he confirmed her thoughts. "I sure wouldn't want my sister, if I had one, stuck on this street at night. I'm happy to help. By the way, my name is Russ Jackson."

"Thanks again! My name is Caylee Sellers. I haven't been stranded long. I was biding my time listening to music. When you rolled down your window, and I heard your radio station, I knew you were god sent."

Out of curiosity, Russ asked, "Why don't you have a cell phone?"

"Cola! Seems electronics and cola don't mix," she explained.

Laughing, he said, "Here is mine. Use it to call whoever you need."

"I don't know who to call first," Caylee said.

Trying to be helpful, Russ suggested, "I think you need to call the police. You know, report the accident. It may help with your insurance. Then call family. Deal with insurance agents later."

"You're right. I've never been in an accident before," Caylee replied.

After calling the police, Caylee called her father. After she'd assured her dad that all was well but that she needed him to pick her up, she handed the phone back to Russ.

"I'll be fine now," Caylee said. "Russ thanks so much for the help."

"No problem. If you don't mind, I'm going to wait with you until your father arrives. This is a creepy place," he stated.

"Oh! Gosh! I'd love the company," she replied.

Inside her small car, they talked. Caylee told Russ about the accident, the horror she experienced, why she decided to go that specific route. Then Caylee mentioned Gina's name. At that, Russ slapped his knee and shouted, "No way!"

Puzzled, she asked, "What?"

"I just left Gina Grimes," he explained. "I'm the guy who broadsided her car the other night. I'm why she's been in a coma for the last few days!"

"Wow! This is really a small world, isn't it?" she exclaimed. "How was she doing?" Caylee asked.

"Other than looking like she hit a Mac Truck with her face, she seemed okay," he said jokingly.

"I really need to call her. She may be worried about me," she told him.

Handing out his cell phone, he urged, "Here! Talk all you want."

"Cool! Thanks again," she said.

When the hospital service answered, Caylee asked for Gina's room. The phone barely rang before Gina answered, "Hello!"

Caylee said, "Hi, Gina. I'm not going to make it tonight. I've had an accident."

"Are you all right?" Gina asked.

"Yeah, I'm fine. I'm waiting for the police and wrecker service now," Caylee answered.

"I'm glad you called. I was worried, the weather is horrible," Gina said.

Caylee confessed, "Yeah! I should have called you and rescheduled. I'll come tomorrow."

"Great! See you tomorrow. Good night," Gina concluded.

When Caylee's father arrived, Russ felt awkward, so he said, "Caylee, I'm going to leave now. I enjoyed meeting you. Maybe we can catch up later?"

Caylee had the same thought. "Russ, can I repay you by cooking you a lovely dinner soon?"

"I'd love it!" he responded.

They exchanged numbers, and Caylee asked him to call so they could set a date.

Ponderings

I was very glad Caylee had not been hurt. But I was disappointed we couldn't visit. I'd worked myself up with excitement. I'd expected to share the bizarre events with someone who may understand. Now I felt like an emptied balloon—deflated.

~~~

Ox used the time to engulf Gina again with his wings. This time, he'd give her the ability to hear. Faith came by hearing. Plus, she needed to hear that her circumstance wasn't original.

~~~

I was bored and needed something to do to keep my mind busy. I turned on the television in my room and started flipping the channels until I came to a Christian network again. The television preacher was so cute and funny. His name was Jesse Duplantis from Louisiana. Right off, he got my attention. He was telling the audience about his heavenly experience after a car wreck. He even got to see Jesus.

A memory came back to me. I actually heard Jesus speak to me. This prompted me to take out my pad and again take notes. I had to write that down. Adrian said I had to remember everything I could. Listening to this preacher was good; it was refreshing my memories.

Jesse described every detail: what clothes were worn, sounds heard, and the smells. I needed to write down details like those as well.

~~~

Ox grinned and empowered Gina again, this time, with the ability to see from within the memories.

~~~

I focused hard and remembered the smell in the air. Remembered fall leaves. I also remembered my man's scent, earthy, not sweet like cologne. The smell of fresh bread at Reo's. I wrote everything down.

I looked at my notebook, happy with the information. I had a time frame! We were going to be together in the fall! It was already summertime. My excitement grew. This notebook and my Bible were two things I had to keep close. I kept listening to the pastor, hoping that something else he'd say would jog a memory. I wanted more pieces of the puzzle to mull over.

I was startled when my room door opened. I covered up my notebook and Bible quickly. I didn't know why. Maybe it was because they were too precious for anyone to know about? It was only the cafeteria lady with her dinner tray—no one to fear. Then I remembered Dr. Carter's reaction to the Christian program that morning. Maybe I was trying to hide my treasures from him. This protective instinct was puzzling.

~~~

Ox quickened her memory. Bulldog! Bone! Don't mess with the bone!

~~~

The lady said to me was, "Enjoy your meal." She was no threat.

I wasn't hungry at all. I'd been eating candy all afternoon, but I ate the food anyway. Then shortly after the tray was removed, a nurse came in with my evening meds. Obeying orders, I swallowed the pills as well.

Mom called after she got the cakes in the oven. She needed to chat. First, it was about the good news concerning my old car. Then about the beautiful flowers, Russ brought in. Then she began to probe me whether I thought Russ was cute or not. I didn't feel like making simple chatter or talking about men. I needed a believer to talk with. Where was Mamie? She would do nicely.

Ringing the desk, I asked, "Is Nurse Ross scheduled to work tonight?"

"Yes, Ms. Grimes. Do you need her?" the operator asked. "What time does she usually come in?" I asked.

Answering my question, the nurse conveyed, "Her shift doesn't start until eleven. Do you need anything?"

"No thanks! If Nurse Ross comes in beforehand, would you have her come in please," I replied?

I had four hours to wait. I lay everything aside and turned down the lights. Why not sleep until Mamie came? Sleep would come easy. I was feeling relaxed from the meds and full from the meal.

When Mamie came into work, I'd been asleep a little over three hours. Instinct woke me up minutes before she came in. I turned on my light again, making sure she knew I was awake; and when she opened my door, I was ready.

In her southern drawl, Mamie remarked, "Child, please! You're looking great! You have a glow all around you. A nurse at the station said you needed me. Care to tell old Mamie what's going on with you?"

"Mamie? How do you act like a Christian?" I ask tentatively.

She answered me proudly, "I just am! The Lord is all I have worth speaking about. Why?"

"Do you have time to talk awhile with me?" I asked.

"I am working, but I can spare a few extra minutes with one of my favorites. Honey, what is on your mind?" she asked.

~~~

Ox and Healer were ecstatic. Gina wanted interaction with Mamie. Mamie could soothe her spirit and calm her emotions. Two believers were connecting. Soon they'd be speaking the Word. When that happened, ministering angels could get busy, and guardians would have extra duties.

But hidden in the shadows was a devilish gremlin listening to Gina and Mamie's conversation. *This isn't good! What can I do?* I thought.

~~~

Gina asked, "Mamie, when you read your Bible, do you feel overwhelmed? Does your heart hurt? Why does my mind struggle with it?"

"At first, we all feel that way, child," Mamie shared. "What is happening to me, Mamie?" Gina asked.

Mamie was about to respond when an emergency Code Blue alert was announced.

Mamie stood up quickly and exclaimed, "I have to go! We will get back to this later."

~~~

Leaving Ox with Gina, Healer and Adrian flew into the room where the emergency was taking place. Inside they saw a gremlin pinching shut the patient's oxygen tube. The poor man wasn't able to breathe. He was turning blue and grabbing at his throat. The monitor on his machine was making so much noise; it added more stress and fear to his situation. The man's panic was in overdrive.

Healer assisted Mamie with the patient while Adrian dealt with the gremlin. When Adrian killed the devilish thing, monitors returned to normal instantly.

~~~

Mamie readjusted the patient's airflow and tried calming the patient's shattered nerves. But even with her abilities, the man still went into cardiac arrest. More nurses came in to assist. Everyone was on their toes. Hours went by until things got back to normal. Afterward, hospital regulations demanded that every issue had to be documented. Paperwork stole precious time from Mamie and Gina.

Mamie knew what happened. The ole devil had been shifty. He was to blame for tonight's interference. Her heart ached for Gina. God's spiritual healing had not been accomplished. Another's physical health had come first. Afterward, paperwork that came with physical help had to be done. It was a shame God's work had to take a backseat. Gina had to wait.

~~~

I lay on my bed helpless, listening to all the fuss down the hall. I could sense someone was dying. The whole ward was on alert, fighting for the person's life. My questions for Mamie seemed silly now in comparison to the person's life. After taking more pain meds, I was sleepy anyway. Mamie and I would have time to talk another night. Before I closed my eyes, I said a little prayer. "God, please help the patient down the hall and take away the nurses' stress."

~~~

When Mamie finished her paperwork, she checked on Gina. She didn't have the heart to wake her. Gina needed the rest to completely heal. When Mamie's shift was over, Gina was still asleep, so she went home uneasy because they hadn't finished their conversation.

At home, guilt took Mamie's sleep. Her thoughts lingered on the urgency of Gina's questions. The child needed guidance, and Satan had prevented her from helping. She lay in bed trying to catnap because deep sleep eluded her. Guilt kept berating her for leaving Gina in a lurch. Every accusation caused her to admit failure. Yes, she messed up and didn't wake Gina. Yes, she thought about getting home and resting before doing God's work. Her mind was in turmoil. Then realization struck! The enemy was messing with her rest. Jesus wasn't judging! He knew everything about flesh and the weakness that bound. Using her gift of healing on herself, she quit struggling and soothed her soul then asked the Lord for sweet sleep. She needed physical rest to do His work. Not much, but enough to function. Gina wasn't her problem. Gina was God's responsibility. If she couldn't help Gina, God would provide someone or something else.

With a new mindset, Mamie set her alarm clock for 1:00 p.m. By cutting her rest short, she could pay Gina a hospital visit that afternoon and do her part for the Lord. It was evident Gina needed to meet the Lord. Gina's spirit was screaming for help. Then Mamie thanked the Lord for giving her a special gift. She would use her personal time for Him and help Gina's spirit heal. With the plan of attack established, Mamie was granted the sweet sleep she requested.

Intervention

While Gina was asleep, Ox decided to hold a meeting. Time was of the essence, and he and his comrades—Healer, Justice, and Insight—had to work together as a team. "Come here!" he bellowed.

Instantly, his three comrades appeared, followed by their assistants: Adrian, Loshan, Trulan, and Navar.

As the four large angels huddled together, each extended their wings to touch. The touch connected their minds together as one being. Within the ring, the ground troops watched and listened to their leaders' conversations and only spoke when spoken to.

Each angel shared what his human was experiencing with the others. Justice assured everyone Brent was prepared. He had visited the attacker, Lyle Horne. Brent was aware Satan was using the man. Insight had helped Hope give Brent the gift of sight and hearing. He was equipped to watch the man spiritually during their interview. He witnessed Lyle being twisted and tortured mentally by an evil puppet master. Brent's compassion was in play. Nevertheless, Brent knew that subduing this person was necessary.

Brent realized the tricky part was how to prosecute someone under Satan's thumb. For now, all he could do was agree that Lyle had mental issues. Agreement with Lyle's defending attorney placed Lyle in county lockup to await hearings with his accusers.

Lyle was also placed under orders to receive mental health treatment while in custody.

Insight assured the team Hope was ready, waiting for the right moment. She'd been instructed by the Lord to wait on Mamie. Mamie was to hand-deliver the new convert into Hope's care.

Healer informed the team that Gina was mending nicely. Her own issue was her leg, but everything else was working properly. He also shared that spiritual health and mental soothing had commenced but had been interrupted. Plans were in place to continue in the afternoon.

Each assistant was asked individually how they were faring.

All stated the battle was intensifying.

On a happier note, the angels rejoiced when Loshan shared Caylee's news. The Holy Spirit had arranged for her to meet her life mate. Now, indeed, Caylee would have evidence for Gina that God did bring her someone.

Then heaven opened, and the Lord Himself was present. Following the Lord were his generals. The heavenly chiefs of God's armies - the ruling authorities of all angels declared loudly in everyone's presence, "Holy, holy, holy is the Lord!" Every knee bowed, and heads were lowered.

The Lord greeted all present and told them to be at ease. He said, "I have a special interest in what is happening with Gina Grimes, as well as Caylee Sellers. I've reinforced the canopy around both of them. Do whatever it takes to protect, minister, and assist their needs. Don't hold back! Satan knows his time is short in this location. From this point on, the Holy Spirit and I are taking charge of all strategic plans. You have my permission to do whatever it takes. I see many lives needing me here."

The air was electric; power surged everywhere. Jesus Himself had given direct orders. The mission was serious. He was taking Satan's attacks personally.

After Jesus left, returning to his temple, the Holy Spirit started giving ground troops more specific orders. Adrian was assigned as Gina's communicator with limited contact, no more face-to- face unless directed. He was to encourage her to reach out to the Holy Spirit. Ox will keep Gina centered and help Gina receive Him. Trulan is to watch outside the canopy for possible threats.

Then the Holy Spirit gave orders to Loshan. He was to defend and protect Caylee with Navar's help. Ox would assist Caylee when the time came for Gina to find other believers. Caylee had been down that road already. She would be used to help develop Gina's beliefs. No longer would precious time be wasted. They were to stay connected with the Holy Spirit at all times.

The last and final comment from the Holy Spirit before adjourning was, "The Lord has commanded that Gina's hospital stay end within twenty-four hours. She will not have any attacks to prevent her from leaving. Jesus has spoken His order directly into the earthly realm. A judgmental warning has gone forth. Satan cannot violate this order."

After the meeting adjourned, every angel noticed that they had been equipped with extra-abilities. They could all commune mentally without touching. Even their eyesight seemed to be more acute because everything was intensified. They'd been empowered! With this knowledge, their hearts burned with a zeal they'd never felt before.

Physical and Emotional Workouts

During the night, ministering angels prepared for Gina's release. Some overheard her desire for more food and provided the request. As Gina's guardian, Ox laughed. Gina hadn't wanted more food. She'd used her words deceptively against her mother. Now she was about to reap what she sowed.

~~~

I woke up thinking I had a new mercy. Then I thought, *what made me think that? What did it mean? Was the thought from something I read? I've never heard of having a new mercy before.* Physical demands cried for me to either get help or act. I decided to act. I was determined to get mobile, so I used the crutches and hobbled to the restroom. So, what if my arm hurt? I wanted to go home!

When I finished my business, I found my breakfast waiting for me on the bedside table. The amount of food lying there was staggering. It was enough to feed three people. Surely someone had made a mistake. There were six pancakes, four sausages, and four strips of bacon, four eggs over easy, a bowl of grits, and four slices of toast. I also had a large juice plus coffee to drink. Before touching any of the food, I reviewed the work order on the tray.

It had my name listed. *Could this be a mercy?* I thought. Someone must know I'm hungry.

The day was different. Dr. Carter came in while I was eating. He was all smiles and wasn't his usual grumpy self. He even seemed happy to see me.

The first words out of his mouth were, "I'm releasing you tomorrow morning. Will you miss me?"

I didn't want to speak the truth, so I just smiled. Then I asked hopefully, "Does this mean I won't be seeing you anymore?"

"Don't be silly, you'll need to follow up with me often. Even though I'm freeing you from this jail, I'm not finished with you yet. I have to make sure your leg mends," he joked.

I'm puzzled. *Is he on something? He must be high. He is acting weird. This must be mercy number two.*

~~~

Ox was encouraged Gina was seeing her blessings even though she mistakenly called them mercies. He could tell she wasn't used to having life fall into place. Events changed drastically after Jesus got involved. Since the intervention, the proclamation of His blessing had started to work. The words were unstoppable.

The enhancement of the new-believer canopy had also occurred. No evil knowingly would have the courage to violate Jesus's direct orders or go inside a reinforced canopy.

Gina was also going to be taught a lesson today. She would come to realize that dishonesty and manipulation came back to bite. Today's events were going to be interesting, and Ox knew he was going to enjoy watching both good and bad line up.

~~~

After the doctor left, I finished my breakfast and had to lay the bed down flat. I'd eaten so much I had to get prone. I felt like a beached whale. I was fat and happy.

I hadn't been lying in my happy state long when I heard a knock on my door. I extended the greeting to come in and was faced with a young man I'd never seen before. He chimed, "Good morning! I'm Chuck Armstrong, your physical therapist."

"Nice to meet you," I said.

Getting right to work, he said, "I see in your chart that you didn't experience any pain this morning. That's good news. I'm here to work with your arm and shoulder. I'll have to monitor your range of motion and strength. A lot of people have weak upper-body strength and can't manage crutches well."

"How do they get around then if they can't manage crutches?" I asked.

He informed, "Wheelchairs or walkers. If my tests determine you can bear weight, you can continue to use the crutches."

Moving over to my bedside, he raised my bed back into the seated position before proceeding with his test.

Noticing that my leg had a cast above the knee, he stated, "You are not going to be able to do my exercises sitting on the side of your bed. We'll need to compensate. Please sit up as straight as possible. The bed will support your legs."

Obeying, I sat up straight while Chuck lowered the bed as flat as it would go again. It wasn't long before the unsupported position started giving me trouble. The muscles in my back began to shake, but I refused to complain; I was determined to do the exercises. I'd promised myself earlier that, pain or no pain, I was going to get mobile.

My first test was to lift both arms out straight in front of me. I felt no pain. Then he said, "Good! Now, lower your arms and raise them out sideways from your body as high as you can."

Chuck analyzed my every move, plus he took notes. By watching him study me, I realized he was looking to see if the exercise caused me problems. Fear of failure gripped my mind. I hated being under a microscope. I didn't want to fail. Then all of a sudden, I felt a peace accompanied by a surge of energy, and I gritted my teeth and lifted my arms. I felt a slight twinge but nothing unbearable. I was free from pain. Mercy three.

~~~

Ox stared at the imp. Apparently, it hadn't received word of Jesus's order; apparently, the creature didn't know it had entered a no-evil zone. Without even lifting a finger, Ox watched the little thing burst into flame. Jesus Himself toasted it.

~~~

Then Chuck said, "Rotate your arms slowly."

This too I accomplished without any pain, just a slight twinge of discomfort.

"Good!" he said.

"The next test will be the hardest. Place your hands flat on each side of your hips and lift yourself up."

To stay focused, I looked directly at Chuck. I situated my hands like he asked then I pushed up and locked my elbows and wrists. I did it! I had my bottom raised about two inches from the mattress. Then my arms began to shake. I wanted to let go.

"Hold it," he ordered. Then he started counting.

I held out for thirty slow counts before my arms gave out. I dropped back down on the bed, proud of myself. I watched his expression for some sign, but Chuck mastered the poker face well. So, I asked, "How'd I do?"

"So far, you're doing well," he commented.

While Chuck jotted down notes, I asked, "Are we finished?" "No, ma'am! I have a few more tests. I'll be back shortly," he told me.

During his brief absence, I had to lie down. My back was hurting from the exertion. When Chuck came back, he noticed me lying down and giggled. He apologized, "I'm sorry! I should have told you to lie down. I had you in a very unnatural position.

Your stomach and back muscles took some punishment. I noticed they weren't very strong. I watched you shake, but in order to support your leg, there wasn't another way to perform the tests."

"I'm okay, just stuffed from breakfast," I lied.

"Just a few more tests, and please sit up, they won't take long, I promise," Chuck shared.

Standing at the foot of my bed, Chuck showed me an instrument that looked like a bow. He said the bow test required both of us. He held onto the bow part and told me to pull as hard as I could on the cord. A meter was set inside the bow, registering the force. Again, I watched Chuck's face as he gauged the meter. I pulled as hard as I could; confident I was passing the test.

"Very good!" he encouraged.

After he wrote down the results, he moved my bed from the wall and stood behind me. He put the bow over my head, placing me inside the instrument and lowered it down past my shoulders. "Gina, push the cord out straight as hard as you can," he instructed.

Once again, instead of pulling, now I pushed with all my might until I heard him comment, "Great! You can stop."

"Was there any pain?" he asked.

"No! Not even a little discomfort," I replied.

"You passed! I'm recommending you to stay with crutches. I think you'll be happier with them. Walkers are for old folks," he joked. "I'm going to let you rest now. It was good meeting you."

"You too! Thanks," I replied. Mercy four! I wasn't too weak.

I lay in bed completely exhausted, not to mention full. I was about to take my desired nap when I heard another tap on my door.

This time it was Caylee! "Can I come in?" she asked.

I exclaimed, "Please do! I've been eager to see you."

We hugged for a few seconds. Then I asked, "How did you get here? I thought you wrecked your car."

"I'm borrowing Dad's old truck. I had to see you first thing. Your news has excited me so much I could hardly rest wondering what it could be," she said.

Mercy five! I thought again.

I started crying. Emotions had built inside of me. I couldn't contain the emotional stress any longer. I was being freed but couldn't speak for crying.

~~~

With Caylee's arrival, Gina's room was crowded. Four huge angels were jammed in there as well, communing silently with each other. The joy they were experiencing was electric. Their two women were together at last as sisters. When two believing people come together, God was in the midst.

~~~

Puzzled, Caylee inquired, "Gina! What's wrong? Did I upset you? Why are you crying?"

I swallowed hard then confessed, "Nothing is wrong. I've just needed to talk with someone who may understand."

She apparently noticed that my room door was still open; she quietly turned and closed it. Then she turned to face me again and asked, "What's going on?"

"Caylee, my life has changed," I whimpered. "It started even before my accident."

"What are you talking about?" she asked.

"Do you remember our conversation that day at work? The one we had during lunch?" I asked. "You were sharing with me how God made life easier for you. How He knew your dreams. You said you were waiting for Him to bring them to you."

"Sure. Why?" she inquired.

"Well, right after that conversation, I asked Him to give me a better life. I needed peace and happiness. I asked for Him," I told her.

"You're born again! That's wonderful! You truly are my sister!" Caylee exclaimed.

I went on to share my secret. "That's not everything. Please don't think I'm crazy. I had a very weird experience afterward, so bear with me and be opened-minded."

"I'll do the best I can. But I can't promise. Just tell me, one step at a time," she encouraged.

With a deep breath, I started, "Here goes! That night while I was at the club, I began to feel dirty and disgusted. I started wishing I was with you instead of Angie. I knew I was in the wrong place and decided to leave. On the way to my car, I began to fear being alone. I should have gone back inside and asked for an escort, but I didn't. I was hardly out the door when a man attacked me. I got away, but in my stupidity, I caused the wreck."

"Oh, my God!" she exclaimed.

I said, "Wait! That's not what I wanted to share with you. Caylee, while I was lying in this bed, in the coma, I had an out- of-body experience. I watched people talk to me. That's how I knew you called me sister. But the most amazing thing was my supernatural visitor. I had an angel with me. His name is Adrian." "Get out! That's awesome! Don't stop, tell me more!" she implored.

Pausing to study her face, I could tell she believed. She was vibrating with anticipation for more of my story, but I couldn't continue until I knew what she was thinking.

"What are you thinking?" I asked.

"Are you kidding? I think I'm jealous! I'm awestruck!" she screeched. "If there is more, I want to know it."

Relieved, I continued, "Good. I was hoping you'd say that. Do you remember saying to me that I had a purpose? You said I would come to know the truth soon. It was after you left me that Adrian appeared. I'd been pondering over my predicament. He scared me so badly I could have fainted, but I wasn't able to. Spirits don't faint. He calmed me down, and we started talking." "Wow! Girl, I always knew they were real! We're never left alone," Caylee exclaimed.

Then I said, "Let me tell you something even more unbelievable. Adrian took me through time. We visited the past then he showed me some of my future."

Caylee couldn't control herself. "What? How? Get out!" "For real!" I declared.

"Don't stop! Share every detail! I want to know what it was like," she squealed.

"He introduced me to a man. Not just any man, Caylee. The man was my future husband. I was living in pure bliss until Satan started messing with my body," I said.

"What! You saw Satan?" Caylee was breathless.

"No! Thank goodness! Adrian told me. He said Satan could cause me physical problems. That is why he rushed me through my journey so fast. The monitors on my machines started beeping, and I wasn't able to hear. I missed hearing my husband's whole name. All I heard was his last name. But I saw his face very clearly. Caylee, prior to waking, I was forcibly shoved back inside my body. I felt pure evil around me. When I opened my eyes, Mom was standing over me, and my body hurt unbelievably. At first, I thought the pain was from childbirth. I was out of kilter, and my mind hadn't readjusted."

"Weird!" Caylee said.

Tears came flooding back; emotions spilled as I shared my intense recollection. "I didn't appreciate living at first! It's taken me awhile to come to grips that I'll have to wait. Grief keeps trying to overtake me. It's like my family is dead. It's getting harder to believe what is real. I want to trust in what I was shown, but I'm having problems believing in spiritual things. This is all very new to me. Help me! Please, Caylee, I need your help to understand!"

She sat on my bed and hugged me tight. Trying to soothe me, she said, "It's all right, Gina. You've been given such an awesome gift. Trust it! Once you are out of here, we'll talk with the pastor or Hope and Brent. Maybe they will be able to help you understand."

All the stress drained from me. I had an ally and friend in Caylee. I was free to feel normal. I didn't have to fear being a crazy person any longer. Then it dawned on me. Caylee had risked her life last evening in the storm. She had a wreck trying to come to me. I'd been wallowing in self-pity without any concern for my friend's condition.

Out of concern, I expressed, "Oh my God! Caylee, please forgive me! I've been absorbed with myself. I hadn't even bothered to ask you about your accident."

Caylee answered, "Oh stop it! There isn't anything to forgive. I'm fine now that we are finally together. I think my car is toast, though. After hearing your testimony, something is going on with both of us. It was a miracle my car didn't roll and flip in a ditch. What is even more bizarre is Russ Jackson stopped to help me. He let me use his cell phone and stayed with me until the police and Dad arrived. He is really a nice guy. Then I did something impulsive. I invited this stranger to dinner so I could repay his kindness. I hope I didn't come off sounding loose."

I laughed at her last statement. Caylee, loose? She was not even close to appearing or acting like any loose women I knew.

"Caylee, you're far from being loose. Tell you what, when I get out of here, why don't we both give a dinner party for Russ? I also owe him a lot," I volunteered.

She complied. "You've got an idea there. I'd feel more comfortable with the two of us giving the dinner."

I couldn't help myself. I had to poke fun. Jokingly, I nudged. "Nice guy, huh? Sounds like you like him."

"Yeah! We hit it off. He seemed genuine and compassionate, which helped me relax," she shared.

"How do you determine his character?" I asked quizzically. "Easy! I listen. I heard concern for my well-being within his statements. Plus, he was very concerned about you. He blamed himself for your condition," she said.

"Mom said he visited and called regularly," I said. "I hadn't met him until last night. I didn't overly encourage any conversation. I was too busy watching the clock wanting visitors to leave. I wanted to be alone with you."

Unity

Due to visitor regulations, Caylee had to leave, but she promised to return in a few hours. Mom came in shortly after Caylee with the two cakes I requested. She brought plates as well. She cut me a large slice of each and handed them to me. The thought of eating was nauseating; my breakfast hadn't digested yet. But to show Mom my appreciation, I managed to eat them. When Mom was appeased, she took both cakes to the nurse's station and left them in their refrigerator.

I told Mom about my release date, which made her happy. Then she excused herself, saying she had to arrange the house so I could move around unhindered with crutches. I didn't want to think about recuperating at Mom's, but I'd jump that hurdle later. Honestly, I was ecstatic; she wouldn't be hovering. My thoughts were racing, but all I could manage at that point was a nap. I was feeling sick.

~~~

Ox and Adrian laughed among themselves. Gina was paying for being deceptive. She would recover. This sick feeling was all her fault; Satan had nothing to do with it.

~~~

When lunch arrived, I almost gagged. The smell wasn't even pleasant. When I asked the nurse to take it away, she acted concerned until I explained why

~~~

At precisely 1:05 p.m., Mamie was up and moving. She had the Lord's mission on her mind. Gina needed spiritual guidance. The child sought her help. This mission wasn't her first rodeo; she knew what to do. Mamie knew their enemy would stop her any way he could. Before leaving her house, she prayed, "Lord, go before me. I'm on your mission. Prepare the way, so I'll have smooth travel."

Mamie stood steadfast on the word. She spoke in faith, relying on her predestined path. With God, beside her, she could rest assured. Love itself was her guide. Gina's guidance into God's family was imperative. God would show her just what to say. God would show her what to do.

~~~

Healer enjoyed healing a person's mind more than anything else. Without kingdom perspective, a new creature couldn't live in God's best. He was grateful this kindhearted woman was his helper, willing to be used for the Lord.

~~~

I was thankful for my little rest. It was just enough to ease my discomfort. Without being able to move around, it took longer for my food to digest. I must not overeat again.

I was getting back in bed after a short rest in the lounge chair when Caylee returned. She was all smiles and holding a bag. Once I was completely situated, she said, "I bought you something. You're going to need it now."

Pulling out all the tissue paper from the bag, I noticed a good-sized box. It was the largest Bible I'd ever seen. Compared to the little blue one, this thing was four or five times bigger. I looked at her puzzled and asked, "Thanks. Why such a big one?"

Caylee beamed. "It's my favorite study Bible. I carry a smaller one with me in my car. If you are going to learn God's ways, you'll need to understand what you've read. I love mine."

In less than twelve hours, I'd been given two Bibles. Was this a sign? I flipped through the one she bought and noticed it had four different translations in one. When I leaned over to put the bag on the floor, I heard something rattle inside. Quizzically, I asked, "You bought me two things?"

"Yeah! I study with a highlighter in my hand. If I find a verse that speaks to my heart or warns me of something, I highlight it. I study God's Word more than any book I've ever had. It helps me when times get hard. It gives me promises to rely on and share with others. That's why I wanted you to have it. Man will pass away, but God's Word never dies. I'll be your study buddy, but if I should fail or disappoint you, remember that God will never let you down," she said, pointing to the book.

I shared, "I've been reading a King James translation, but I couldn't relate. My doctor gave me a Bible too; it is a New American Standard. I think God is trying to tell me something. I enjoy reading the scriptures, but my mind is confused. I don't know how to use what I've read. I was going to talk with a nurse friend the other night about God when all hell broke out down the hall."

Caylee squeaked, "Gina! Think about it! Your angel was right. Satan knows something is up. He stopped you from learning about the Lord."

Out of curiosity, Caylee wondered. *Could it be Mamie?* She had to know, so she asked, "Who have you met in the hospital? Does this person make your heart feel safe?"

I answered, "The head nurse on the midnight shift. Why?"

Caylee got all mysterious and commented, "It just occurred to me that God may have placed a spiritual protector in this place for you. Kind of like a covert agent or undercover operative. Who is she?"

I snickered at her funny description and replied, "Her name is Mamie Ross."

"No way!" Caylee exclaimed. "What?" I asked, concerned.

"Mamie is the greatest! I was hoping she was your nurse. She is one of my mentors at church. She is awesome! Mamie mothers everybody, young and old, in the place. She keeps us in line and encourages us when we're down."

Caylee reminisced before confessing, "I don't know what I would have done without Mamie. It was through her that I came to know God. I was still rebellious, though. It was a lot later that the knowledge of God drew me back to church. She took me back in and loved me. She and Hope helped me understand myself."

They were discussing Mamie when the lady herself walked in the room. "What do we have here?" Mamie said when she saw Caylee.

Caylee squealed, "Mamie! We were just talking about you!" "You'd better get over here now and give this old woman a hug," Mamie ordered.

"I'm so glad to see you. I didn't know the two of you knew each other until just a few minutes ago, What a blessing!" Caylee exclaimed.

Mamie then focused on Gina. "How are you doing, child? You've been on my heart since last night. I couldn't sleep until I asked the Lord to put me under. That old trickster caused me a problem. I hope you know I wanted to help you, but Satan disabled me from doing God's work. Then he tried to make me feel miserable about not helping you."

"I'm fine, Mamie. I was just lonely and had some questions concerning something I'd read in the Bible. I didn't know where to begin, and I thought you could help me. I'm sorry I made you worry," I conveyed.

~~~

Ox and Healer stood together. Gina's training had begun!

~~~

Mamie knew Gina was struggling but failed to understand why. Gina's statement about her heart hurting construed Mamie's thoughts. Assuming the Holy Spirit was in Gina's heart; Mamie took the big Bible off the bedside table and opened it. "Here is how I fellowship with the Lord. I ask Him to direct my studies. Every day we get a new mercy, and we get help in a time of need through His Word."

My eyes flew open. Mamie had my attention by using the word mercy. God was definitely trying to tell me something.

Mamie continued slowly, "Jesus and this Word are one and the same. I rest my mind and listen. Sometimes He tells me in a soft voice where to read, other times, He lets me choose when I need clarification on a message I heard. Just trust your inner voice. Your inner voice is God speaking. He will never lead you wrong when focused on what He says. This is having a personal relationship."

"Personal relationship with God? How?" I asked.

Patiently, Mamie continued, "Talk with Him as you read. Believe He is right beside you. If you don't understand, He will guide you to other scriptures. He wants you to understand. He won't leave you confused. You show Him you want to live for Him when you start believing what you've read. You act on what you've read as if it has already happened. Talk positive about your promise even if it doesn't seem like it will happen. Do you want to know why?"

I was still confused, but not wanting to appear stupid, I said, "Sure!"

"In God's eyes, your future has already happened. When you find a promise that strikes your fancy, you've bonded with His Son, Jesus. It's like a seed planted in the ground. The more you speak the promise aloud, the faster it grows," she explained.

It was evident Caylee understood. She chanted loudly, "I told you she is great! Didn't I? She makes it easy for you to understand."

Then the conversation changed. Caylee burst with excitement, urging, "Tell her, Gina! Tell her!" "Tell me what?" Mamie asked.

"Gina's had an angel visit," Caylee blurted out.

I was just about to share my experience when Chuck came in again. He said, "I'm sorry, ladies, but visitors need to wait outside for a while. Ms. Grimes and I must talk."

Mamie and Caylee gracefully left the room and went to the waiting area, leaving me alone with Chuck. I was confused about why he had returned.

"Gina, I contacted Dr. Carter and shared your tests results. He has informed me to start your physical therapy this afternoon. After you've been released, you will follow up with therapy at our center next door. Dr. Carter feels you are ready."

Mobility, here I come! I was ready to get started. Without even being prompted, I swung my body to the side of the bed and put my good foot on the floor. "What do we do?" I excitedly asked.

"Whoa, Nellie! Get back in bed," Chuck ordered.

It was about that time a nurse pushed in a machine. "What's that?" I asked.

"It's a bone-growth stimulator. Once you are hooked to it, energy flows through your leg, stimulating the nerves as it increases blood flow," Chuck explained.

I was amazed. "I don't have to move?"

"No! The machine actually helps speed up bone recovery. Hopefully, you can have the cast taken off in about six weeks. That's when strenuous therapy begins," Chuck said.

~~~

In the waiting-room area, Mamie and Caylee had time to chat. Mamie, being the more mature, took control guiding Caylee. Caylee needed to slow down and think. Mamie reminded her how it felt to be a newborn. Gina needed time. Mamie also asked Caylee to let Gina share at her own speed. Gina must desire to share her experiences and feelings, not be forced into sharing. They had to protect Gina's heart. She needed to feel secure and safe above their desire to know her experiences.

Feeling an urge to get somewhere quiet, Mamie excused herself from Caylee and went into a restroom. Within the small room, Mamie sensed the Holy Spirit. "Lord, what is it?" she asked.

The Lord said, "Gina doesn't have me. She's still confused.

Don't force the Word. I'll enter her soon."

Repenting instantly, Mamie begged, "Oh! Lord! I'm sorry! I just assumed. Forgive me for not communing with you first."

"Don't fret! Your teachings whet Gina's appetite. She's curious now," he said gently.

"Thanks, Lord! What should I do?" Mamie inquired. "Lead!" he directed.

Continuing, he instructed, "Also, don't frustrate Caylee. Caylee and Gina are connected. Listen to both their hearts. A farmer is always rushing the crop, impatient for a harvest. Caylee is the one who planted the seed for a good life inside of Gina. Be gentle with the sower. The reaper will endure the change. Caylee's life will be the anchor for Gina to hang on to. Gina will be watching Caylee. Watching Caylee's reactions will help Gina endure her fight. Teach both, guide both, and comfort both. Gina's angel called you into the battle; he is seeking your assistance with Caylee as well. I've also called on Hope and Brent with their angels."

"I see, Lord. I knew Gina was special. Now I understand why Caylee is involved. That is why Caylee's excitement for Gina to share makes perfect sense. Thank you for informing me. Continue to go before me. Be my guide and show me what to do. Then work through this body and mouth," she prayed.

~~~

I sensed something was different when Mamie and Caylee came back in the room. I was sure they'd been talking about me, and I was uneasy. Had Caylee shared my secret? Did Mamie think I was crazy? I couldn't determine by their mannerisms. I noticed Caylee wasn't as excited for me to tell Mamie my story. Before they had walked out of my room, she couldn't wait for me to share. I took their quiet manner as a clue not to bring up the matter. There would be a time when everything would fall into place, but right this minute, I didn't feel comfortable.

Guidance

Remembering my cakes, I offered, "Guys, Mom brought me a German chocolate and cheesecake this morning. She took them to the nurse's station so they could be refrigerated. You are welcome to a slice if there is any left."

Caylee exclaimed, "Yum! I'd love a piece of German chocolate." "I'll go fetch us a slice," Mamie offered.

Before leaving the room, Mamie turned and asked, "Gina, what do you want?"

"None for me, thanks. I overate at breakfast then I had to eat a piece of both to appease Mom," I replied.

Confused, Caylee asked, "How could you overeat here? Most hospitals don't give you much, and what you get isn't good."

I laughed before replying, "Trust me, when you haven't eaten in a while, anything tastes good. This morning, my tray had enough food for an army. There were pancakes, toast, bacon, grits, and eggs with juice and coffee. I ate most of it. Then I ate two pieces of cake. I had to. I felt guilty for making Mom make them. I couldn't hurt her feelings, so I stuffed them down. Now the thought of food makes me want to puke."

Mamie overheard before going after their cake, and she and Caylee cackled with laughter.

Mamie spoke up, "The cafeteria must have made a mistake and given you the wrong order, Gina. It doesn't sound right. Most patients are eased back into eating after a fast. I'm going to check on this. You could have hurt yourself with food."

"There was a ticket on the tray with my name on it, so I assumed all was legal, and I pigged out," I said.

"Maybe human error, child. Things happen that aren't planned," she answered.

While Mamie was away, I asked Caylee, "Did you tell Mamie?" "No. She said it wasn't my place and stopped me. She explained to me that you'd tell her when you wanted, not at my insistence," she concluded.

"Good. For some reason, I feel uneasy about her knowing," I said.

"Huh? I don't know why. I tell Mamie everything. She's the mother I never had," she explained.

Sadly, I asked, "You don't have a mother?"

Caylee explained, "No. My mother died when I was young. I was raised by my dad. I met Mamie when I was fourteen. Our housekeeper encouraged me to go to church with her one night, and Mamie was the youth teacher. She took me under her wing that first night. It was crowded under there because she had about a hundred more. The lady loves kids. When I got, older and had boyfriend problems, Mamie introduced me to Hope and Brent Arnold. When I was bad, they all jerked a few knots in me."

Mamie overheard the last part of Caylee's testimony when entering the room and said, "You were rotten. For months, you gave me problems. I thank God someone was able to get through to you."

Mamie handed Caylee her slice of cake, and as they ate, Caylee shared her escapades. She had been a terror and a notorious flirt, not the sweet little angel I'd made her out to be at all.

Then out of nowhere, Caylee stopped the conversation and exclaimed, "Mamie, I think Satan tried to kill me last night."

"What are you saying, child?" Mamie asked, worried.

~~~

Ox had prompted Caylee to share. Gina needed to see how love and compassion worked among believers. Gina had to learn how to trust. Caylee could get a point across without feeling judged. Her childlike demeanor had to be expressed for Gina to grasp.

~~~

As Mamie lovingly listened, Caylee shared every detail of her accident. Not only was I shocked to hear what Caylee faced, I witnessed a love I'd never seen before. Mamie's concern was all about Caylee. I never heard a reprimand or judging statement. My mom and dad would have berated me for being stupid. Caylee's car had been destroyed because she wasn't being smart, but that didn't matter to Mamie. Mamie was more concerned with Caylee's emotional state, as well as her health. I also noticed Mamie's protective instincts deepen as Caylee told us how she endured problems in a terrible neighborhood after realizing her cell phone wasn't working.

Something inside me changed. I wanted a protective mother bear, not an overbearing judge. I saw how Mamie reacted when Caylee stated Satan tried to kill her. I had the same enemy! Had I unleashed him on her? Tears rolled down my face as I listened to them talk. Mamie saw things differently and helped Caylee understand. I needed some of that insight. I was worried Satan had attacked Caylee because of me. She had endured so much fright. Mamie saw my tears and stopped Caylee in midsentence. "Gina, what is wrong, child? Please tell old Mamie," she encouraged.

My throat was choked with emotion. I had to trust! I broke and blurted, "I'm scared! Mamie, Satan is after me too! I asked Caylee to come last night. I think Satan attacked her because of me. Help me understand what is happening! Please! What have I started?"

Without saying a word in response, Mamie knew what to do. She would lead the horse to water. It was up to the horse to drink.

Mamie reached for my new Bible and turned the pages until she found what she needed. Then she gave me the Bible and said, "Read John 10:10."

> *The thief comes only in order to steal and kill and destroy. I came that they may have and enjoy life, and have it in abundance (to the full, till it overflows). (John 10:10, amp)*

After reading this verse over and over, my mind finally understood. I reasoned that it was because I'd asked Jesus to come in my life that I now have an enemy who wants to steal from me and kill and destroy me if possible.

Then she took the book again and found another scripture for me. Then she said, "Now read 1 Peter 5:8."

> *Be well balanced (temperate, sober of mind), be vigilant and cautious at all times; for that enemy of yours, the devil, roams around like a lion roaring [in fierce hunger], seeking someone to seize upon and devour. (1 Pet. 5:8, amp)*

This scripture didn't give me peace at all. If anything, it caused me to worry more, and I confessed, "Mamie, this scares me. I don't know how to be balanced and vigilant."

"You'll learn, child. Once you are out of here, Caylee and I will introduce you to people who can help you learn. That's what church is all about, a bunch of people learning how to stomp the devil. We love each other, support each other, and help each other. Being a Christian is not easy, but it is very rewarding. I've learned to trust my Jesus. I rely on what He asked the Father to do in John 17 verse 15. That scripture helps me daily," she said lovingly.

Then she took the Bible again and turned directly to the scripture for me to read. It said,

> *I do not ask that you will take them out of the world, but that you will keep and protect them from the evil one. (John 17:15, amp)*

"Honey, Jesus asked God to keep and protect us from Satan. Who better than the Creator Himself to watch over and protect us? Knowing He is watching helps a lot, even when times are hard," Mamie said with a smile.

Our conversation was interrupted by none other than Dr. Jones. He was back from his short trip and was holding a plate with two pieces of cake.

He commented, "Thanks for the sweets. The nurses had sliced me these two with my name on the plate. They said your mom threatened to shoot them if I didn't have a slice of each. How are you feeling today?"

"I don't hurt much. But I did make myself sick by overeating. I haven't wanted anything since I ate cake on a full stomach," I replied.

Mamie asked, "Dr. Jones, did you order Gina a full menu? She said she had an army-sized breakfast this morning."

"My orders were she was to be given a regular meal," he conveyed.

Giggling, he asked, "Did you eat it all?"

"I tried. I was so happy to have real food, I couldn't help myself," I confessed.

"If you don't want dinner when it arrives, ask the nurse to save your tray. Don't send it back to the cafeteria. One of the nurses can heat it up for you in the lounge microwave if you get hungry. Try to eat something so you won't be too hungry when breakfast comes. You may be tempted to overeat again if you don't," he advised.

Changing the subject, he said, "I hear Dr. Carter has released you to go home tomorrow. That's good news. Have they taught you how to walk on stilts yet?"

"Yes, sir. They're no fun, but at least I can get around," I answered.

Before leaving, he said, "I'm going to make an appointment for you to see me in a few days. I'm happy you're doing better. Thanks again for the cake, they were both delicious."

Meeting Justice

Standing at the door of my room, waiting for the doctor to finish his visit, was a tall, very distinguished man. I didn't know him, but something about him made me relax. I asked, "Can I help you?"

When he approached, Mamie smiled, and Caylee squeaked with delight, "Brent!"

Inside the tiny room, the earthbound angels bowed when the third commander entered with his human. To allow the commanders complete access, the lesser angels backed out of the room where they could continue to listen.

In the room, Healer stood to Ox's right, and Justice stationed himself to Ox's left. Even though Insight was absent, the three still had to touch. The proximity created a magnet effect when they were standing at ease, which made the atmosphere around them electric and clean.

Brent hugged Caylee, saying, "Hi there, cutie!" Then he greeted Mamie.

I lay there confused. Who was this person?

Extending his hand, he introduced himself, "Hi, I'm Brent Arnold, Assistant District Attorney."

I was thoroughly confused. Who was this man? Why would a District Attorney make Caylee squeal with delight and Mamie smile?

I offered my hand then said, "I'm Gina Grimes. Are you here to visit Caylee?"

"No! Ms. Grimes, I'm here to visit you. Our office is representing you in your suit against Lyle Horne. Do you mind if I ask you a few questions?" he answered.

I'd forgotten all about Dad pressing charges for me. I was about to tell the man I didn't want to proceed when I felt a struggle in my mind.

~~~

The Lion used his influence on Gina and gave her courage. Then he whispered in her ear to encourage her to press charges.

~~~

Seconds passed after his question. Then boldness rose in my mind. I wanted revenge, or was it vindication? "No, sir! I want men like him off the streets," I answered.

"Very well then!" he replied.

Brent directed his gaze toward Mamie and Caylee then said, "Ladies, I'm here on official business. You need to let me have a private conversation with Ms. Grimes. Mind waiting outside for a few minutes? I'll call you back shortly then we can chat."

"Aw! I wanted to tell Gina about our group," Caylee said.

"In a few minutes, cricket, I'm not all fun and games. I have to work for my dinner," Brent said.

Mamie took Caylee by the shoulders. "Come on, busybody! We've been ordered out. Let's go to the café and get a drink, my treat. Brent is in attorney mode and doesn't need our input."

Winking at Brent, Mamie let him know indirectly she was aware why he came. There was more to just getting answers. The spirit realm was busy; she sensed it with every fiber of her being.

~~~

When Mamie left the room, Healer followed her but left his subordinate, Adrian, in his place to assist Brent. In the room with the Holy Spirit, the other angels were given knowledge. Brent had asked the Holy Spirit for help. Brent had failed to obtain information from Lyle Horne's last victim. Susan Hall was no longer interested in prosecuting. Somehow Satan had frightened the woman from testifying. Brent didn't want that to be the case with Gina. Brent asked specifically for Gina's mindset to be strengthened and for her words to be salted and preserved for later use and for proof to back up what she said. With that in mind, the angels got busy assisting Brent to obtain the request.

~~~

Brent sat on a chair and opened his briefcase. Removing a file and small tape recorder, he asked, "Ms. Grimes, do you mind if I record our conversation? It helps me remember."

I agreed, "I don't mind. Please, call me Gina."

"Good! For the record, is your name Gina Louise Grimes?" Brent asked.

"Yes," I answered.

"On August 24, 2014, were you attacked by Lyle Horne?" Brent asked.

"Yes," I answered.

Handing her a picture of Mr. Horne, Brent asked, "Is this a picture of Mr. Horne?" Brent asked.

"Yes," I agreed

Then he encouraged, "In detail, please outline for me what happened on August 24. Try to remember what was said as well as done."

~~~

Ox knew Gina was struggling with the request. The nightmare had to be relived again. This knowledge was impressed to the other two, and the three of them enveloped Gina within their wings. Ox lowered his head and whispered, "This will pass. Innocence must be protected. Lend your strength by sharing your knowledge." With the simple request, power drained from him to Gina.

~~~

I was terrified. Sweat popped out of me. I didn't want to talk about that night. I swallowed hard and took a deep breath. In my heart, I knew I had to do the right thing. Someone else might get hurt or maimed if the man was set free. I closed my eyes and felt a peace come over me. I lay my fears aside and accepted the challenge. The statement took about ten minutes to divulge. I told Brent every horrid detail.

After my statement, Brent asked, "Do you have any evidence proving Mr. Horne touched or violated you?"

"I do! I have bruises and scratches, and my blouse is torn," I said.

"Do you mind if I get a few pictures of your marks? I'll have Mamie take the photos," he said.

"I don't mind, you'll need them," I answered.

~~~

Brent stepped out of Gina's room so he could fetch Mamie. When the three returned from the café, Brent explained to Mamie what he needed, and then he stayed with Caylee.

Out in the corridor, Caylee excitedly shared the events with Brent, unaware he suspected she was part of a puzzle God was putting together. He and Hope had been alerted one of their pupils was the one responsible for planting hope in Gina. When he saw Caylee in

Gina's room, the puzzle piece fit, so he stood listening to the little songbird give vital information. Issues he could take to the Lord through intercession.

~~~

When Mamie finished taking photos, Brent laid business aside to do God's work. Reentering Gina's room, he introduced himself to her again as the young-adults' leader at their church. "Gina, I'd like you to come with Caylee to one of our gatherings. My wife, Hope, and I would love to have you join."

I relayed, "Caylee has shared how much fun it is."

"We've created a wholesome environment where young people can meet and enjoy life without the world's harsh distractions. Caylee can verify we provide support to friends when they need us. Mamie is a part. She can tell you. We stay busy, but we enjoy every minute. Would you be interested?" he asked.

"I can't wait! When is your next get-together?" I asked excitedly. "Tomorrow night. Maybe you can make it to the next one," he replied.

"You're right. Mom won't let me out of her sight for a while.

I'll be there as soon as I can," I promised.

Brent stood up and extended his hand. "We'll look forward to you being with us. God's plan for us is grand. All we must do is walk it out. Stay with Caylee, she's a good kid."

Since Caylee wanted to stay longer, Mamie got her a permission slip from the nurse's station. Then Mamie said good-bye to us and walked out with Brent. When Caylee and I were alone, she couldn't stop talking about Brent and his wife, Hope. Those two people were very special to her. They were responsible for getting her through a very emotional point in her life. To Caylee, Hope was super special. The woman had an uncanny ability to see what was affecting people. I was awed. I couldn't wait to be a part. A week ago, I would have thought Caylee to be insane, but not now. Maybe this Hope person could help me find my way. Maybe she could help me find my mate.

Hello Again

When Mom visited, she insisted I eat when the dinner tray arrived. Like a little kid, I was guilt-tripped into obliging. Her constant nagging was insufferable. Caylee saw firsthand what I dealt with. Not to cause me further embarrassment, she excused herself and went home. When Caylee left, the air became oppressive, making it hard to breathe. Alone with my own mother, I had a panicky feeling when I should have had peace.

All she would talk about was how she was going to take care of me. She could dote on me like a baby again. Every fiber of my being was screaming no!

The only way I could get her to leave was to trick her once again. This time, I suggested she go to my apartment and pack a suitcase with my belongings so she wouldn't have to do so tomorrow. That way, we wouldn't waste time after my dismissal and could go straight to her house.

When I was sure she had gone, I sighed with relief. The last thing I wanted was to be trapped in my old house with Mom dictating my every move.

Frustrated, I prayed, "Adrian, I wish you were here to talk with." Before I finished my last word, I heard, "Hello, Gina."

It was Adrian! I was sure of it! I asked, "Where are you? I don't see you."

"I've only been given permission to talk with you. It is good to converse once again," he said.

"Is there a reason why we can't see each other?" I asked.

"I can see you, but my orders were explicit not to appear before you. You'll have to settle for only my voice," he explained.

"Why?" I asked.

He answered, "That's simple. Your focus needs to be on the Lord, not me. The desire to see Him more than your desire to see me." "I do! Every time I'm alone, I seek for Him in my Bible. Ever since you encouraged me to read the Word, I haven't stopped seeking," I declared.

Jesus was thrilled. Adrian had drawn a confession out of Gina. Instantly, He shared with the angel a method to meet Him. Gina needed Insight!

Honoring Jesus's mental request, Adrian gave a suggestion. "Gina, we understand you need help. There is a person who can help you find the path. Ask for her help."

Forgetting he was a mind reader, I asked, "What? How did you know? I only thought about her help."

Adrian urged, "Hope is one of ours. She's dedicated her life to the Lord. She will be able to help you understand our ways. She lives life mainly in the spirit realm, so what may seem to be fantasy is her reality. She is God's choice of educator for you."

Eagerly, I asked, "How can I get her help?"

"Through Mamie. Mamie will return shortly. Ask her to contact Hope for you tonight. Hope will come," he shared.

"Mamie won't be back for hours. Her shift doesn't start until 11:00 p.m. Are you sure she's coming back?" I asked.

"Yes, she walked out of your room without her cell phone. It's under your bed. She didn't notice when it fell out of her bag. She'll remember having it in here. When she comes in, ask her to call Hope," he said.

"Cell phones? Why would cell phones be tampered with? Caylee had one destroyed yesterday," I inquired.

"Wasn't by us, and can't say the same for Mamie's though." He laughed.

"Okay…" I muttered.

As if on cue, Mamie was back. Adrian was right! She came back!

I greeted her. "Hi, there! You're back!"

"I'm sorry to disturb you, Gina. I think I left my cell phone in here. I'm tied to technology as much as the younger generation since I don't have a landline anymore. I'll only be a minute. It has to be in here or in the nurse's station," she insisted.

"Mamie? I'm really glad you came back. I need to talk with Hope Arnold. Tonight, if possible!" I blurted out.

Stunned, Mamie asked, "What's the matter, child? Maybe I can help."

It was at that moment when I felt an urgency to share with Mamie. I told her almost everything I'd shared with Caylee about my out-of-body experience, except for my future husband. I even told her I knew she was coming back for her cell phone because of my angel.

Mamie also listened to me without judging. She agreed wholeheartedly that I needed to talk with Hope as soon as possible.

At that, I told her she could find her cell under my bed. Hope was called at once, but all Mamie got was her voice mail.

~~~

Brent found his home empty after work that afternoon. It meant one thing if Hope wasn't home: she was at the Boys' Home. Thursday nights were her dedicated time to be a house mother for a few hours. She and Greg loved their weekly visits.

Changing clothes, he decided to meet up with his family. Something special must be going on over there, or Hope and Greg would be home by now. Hope's life had changed. She no longer needed employment, so she divided her life in four ways for the Lord: First and foremost, Hope was a wife for Brent and mother to Greg. Then she gave her heart to the other boys at the home, followed by being a guidance counselor for the young adults' group. Plus, she was an intricate part of their church's intercessory group.

On the drive, over to the home, Brent reflected on married life. He and Hope were about to celebrate their first year together. He was a happy man. Life was good. Hope was a good wife and a terrific mother. Their adopted son, Greg, was flourishing. Together they had purchased a beautiful home with a large yard. This way, Hope could plant a garden, and Greg could play. Whenever he came home and found the place abandoned, it meant one thing the Lord persuaded Hope to stay or go to one of her other ministries, taking Greg with her.

Pulling into his usual parking spot at the home, Brent noticed a red motorcycle parked next to the barn. The bike indicated a childhood friend was visiting. The friend's visit explained why Hope and Greg had stayed over.

Walking toward the barn, he heard shouts and cheers coming from inside. But before he reached the barn door, he felt small hands grabbing his legs. Looking down to see who was pulling on his pants, he noticed it was Greg. His son was excitedly trying to get his attention. Brent asked, "Why are you outside unattended? Where is Mom?"

"I saw you come up and ran to meet you! Daddy! Mama is beating Uncle Carl's ass!" Greg whooped.

Stunned by Greg's choice of words, Brent said, "What, buddy?"

Exasperated, Greg repeated, "Mama is beating up Uncle Carl in the rink. She's stomping his ass!"

Trying not to laugh, Brent stifled the emotion and corrected Greg. "Greg, it isn't nice to say ass. Mama will get you for it if she hears you say it."

"Okay...I'm sorry," Greg responded. "But Mama is winning, come see!"

Greg was right! Hope was beating Carl's, ugh—butt! He was glad to see it. Fear for Hope's safety was one less worry for him. Hope had gotten proficient in martial arts. Ever since her ordeal with Sam, she was determined to be strong in body, as well as spirit. Carl had trained her well. Tonight's combat was pure entertainment. They wanted to encourage the boys, as well as train them with their friend Wade Polk's help as an umpire.

Everyone noticed when Brent came in the room with Greg. They also noticed when the match took a different turn. Brent's presence caused Hope to lose focus, giving Carl an advantage. Not wanting to hurt Hope, even though he could, Carl swiped her feet from under her instead. Down she went hard. Wade called the match. "Tied!"

Helping his wife to her feet, Brent hugged Hope close then commented, "You did great. You gave Carl a run for his money." Then he stuck out his right hand toward his old friend. "Good to see you. What brought you our way?"

Wade responded, "Needed some bike time. Thought I'd ride over to see you guys. It was good seeing Hope defend herself. I enjoyed watching Carl get his ass beat."

Brent exclaimed, "So you're the culprit. Greg has been around you, my friend, and picked up a few words."

Wade looked confused and asked, "What words?"

Hope's motherly antennas went up, and she asked, "Yeah... what words?"

"Whoops!" Brent muttered.

Looking at Hope apologetically, he said, "That was supposed to be between Greg and me. I didn't mean for you to know, but since I've let the cat out of the bag, Greg bragged by telling me you were beating Uncle Carl's ass."

Hope couldn't help laughing. Rather than confuse the guys, she said, "My baby is growing up. He is all boy and a large sponge. Wade, you had no way of knowing this, but Greg is really enthralled by you. His Uncle Carl was his hero until you came along. Why do you think I asked Carl for a match? He watched the two of you spar with amazement, so I wanted to show him women could be strong too. That way Greg would never underestimate the power of a woman."

It was getting late, and the boys had school the next day, so the games stopped. Mr. Elder herded all the guys back to the main house where preparations for the next day could be made before bedtime.

The other four adults, with Greg in tow, walked to their respective vehicles. Not wanting Wade to leave, Brent asked, "Have any of you eaten dinner? I'm hungry."

Carl agreed. "Yeah, I'm hungry. Let's go get a burger and talk. Wade, I'll treat."

Being the only female, Hope felt like a third wheel. She preferred taking Greg home and preparing him for pre-K the next day. If she were absent, the men could bond. Before she had a chance to bow out, she heard a faint beeping sound coming from her purse. She had a voice mail. Deep within her spirit, Hope knew who it was. Her time had arrived. She was about to join forces with the others. Listening to the voice message, Mamie was requesting Hope's presence at the hospital because Gina Grimes had asked to meet her.

Taking Brent aside, Hope shared, "My time has come. Mamie has called me to meet the young woman."

Excited about the news, Brent exclaimed, "Good! Mamie and I sense God is up to something."

Remembering her son, Hope stooped down to Greg's level and said, "Honey, you get to be with the big guys tonight. Promise me you'll be good. I'll tuck you in when I get home."

Greg beamed, happy he was able to stay with the men. He hugged Hope's neck and said, "I'll be good."

~~~

When Hope left the men, Brent set to reacquaint himself with his childhood friend. It had been a very long time since he and Wade could visit. Brent learned Wade had served in Iraq as a US marine and been to school. He'd wisely used his military scholarship and acquired a doctorate in physical therapy. Brent was happy his friend had settled down. Wade was a rough character as a teen. The military time had changed Wade for the better. The harsh service had given Wade a compassionate nature. He was apparently content helping the disabled as was evident through his speech. He talked excitedly about the new technology designed to help his patients.

After Wade finished telling Carl and Brent about his career, Brent asked Wade about his church life. Wade's reply was that the family went to his mother's church. Joking, he said, "If Mama wasn't happy, no one was happy." Then he tried to explain, "Mama hounds us and makes our lives miserable if we don't attend."

Brent knew by Wade's tone that his friend wasn't receiving good spiritual food. If he was, he wouldn't be complaining about attending his mom's church. He would have to intercede on his friend's behalf. Wade needed God's help.

Relief

It was 8:00 p.m. Hope returned Mamie's call. "I'm on my way. Don't leave. I have specific instructions from the Lord to be introduced to Gina by you."

Hope conversed with the Holy Spirit while driving to the hospital. "Lord, what are we facing? What is this urgency concerning Gina Grimes?"

Without hesitation, he answered, "Gina is very important to our plan. Hope, she is like you, she's been equipped with a specific power. We gave you spiritual sight and hearing, but she received the power from Faith without her knowledge. Faith went into her when she heard Caylee's joy. From the moment, Gina wanted our life, we saw a desire in her only, and empowered faith could bring it out into the open."

"I thought everyone received a measure of faith," Hope said, puzzled.

"They do. Most fail to use the faith. We see a strong determination ingrained in Gina. Faith's ability can use this determination for good. There is a coming time when you, Brent, Mamie, and Gina will be intricate vessels needful for a great harvest of souls. The four of you will join forces with Pastor Reed to bring me the lost, the hurt, and deceived. Gina's ability will act as a shield during this stage, but until she comes to trust me, the shield is inoperative.

After Satan tried to destroy Gina's life, Jesus had to put her in a reinforced canopy to keep her heart protected. Gina has no biblical training and needs you to assure her she isn't crazy or confused. Encourage her to share. Comfort her the way we comforted you. Help her receive me."

"Do you want me to share my gifts with Gina?" Hope asked. "No! Not yet. Gina is coming through a fantasy mindset. Until she discerns truth from fiction, she can't receive the shared gifts. Once she allows me access, I'll guide her through the Word. I'll let you know when and where to enhance her. Brent and Mamie were well established in the Word before I allowed the shared gifting to happen," He counseled. "Are we in a war?" Hope inquired.

Again, without hesitation, He replied, "Yes!"

~~~

Sneaking around under the guise of darkness, Satan came around the corner of the hospital just in time to hear the Holy Spirit warn Hope about a war. After hissing, Satan retracted deeper in the darkness where he could listen to their plans. He hated this woman the Lord used. She had become one of his archenemies. Hope was the Lord's pet who foiled his plans too many times lately.

~~~

Hope knew it was armor time. Her covenant robe would not be enough. Some of heaven's worst battles were fought in hospitals. She wanted the Lord to proceed.

After parking her SUV, Hope sat inside looking at the building for a few minutes. Using her spiritual sight, the place looked ominous. She knew that within the huge building, good and evil fought violent battles for the souls of people. It had been over a year since she'd been cared for within the building. She had received excellent care from Jesus there. Hope wondered how Gina was faring. She knew the girl was under Mamie's care, but what about spiritual care? What was the girl thinking?

Hope quieted her mind and spiritually stepped into her Lord. With her spiritual sight, she watched the red armor cover her body. The blood of Jesus made its appearance known. With it in place, Hope was ready to face evil. Hope was safe. Even her own breath was encapsulated inside of Him. It was like breathing with a hand over your mouth and nose, the warmth of the air came back to the face. Within the protective armor, Hope moved swiftly with a proper mindset. Jesus's appearance would ward off evil. Evil would see Him and flee. If they didn't flee, oh well! Hope knew from experience what would happen.

~~~

Satan threw a fit! Screaming at his demonic horde, Satan blamed them for allowing his enemy time to get fully dressed in Jesus. Why hadn't they kept up with Hope's every move? Why hadn't they distracted her? Now, what was she up to? Satan could see that Hope was headed toward the newborn within his haven. Panic gripped him. Who was this girl his enemy sought? Why did Jesus have the young girl trapped within a super energized barrier? Was the girl about to become another threat to him?

~~~

Demons and giants were everywhere inside the hospital. To Hope's surprise, there were also just as many angels in all sizes. Even within the armor, Hope heard deafening screams. They were so loud; she wanted to cover her ears. The Lord's presence apparently terrified the evil creatures. As demons scattered, the angels followed curiously, seeking who the Lord was visiting. Hope knew her angel always followed her closely, but even he couldn't outshine who she was wearing at that moment.

From the time, Hope stepped into the building, she and Mamie immediately connected spiritually. Healer and Insight were being drawn together like magnets. With spiritual sight in operation, Hope purposefully walked through each area. Before she even got near Gina's room, she saw the grandeur of the enhanced canopy. The transparent film was beautiful. It was like a super energized robe. She couldn't wait to see what was inside the room. When Hope entered Gina's small room, it amazed her how full it was of heaven's helpers. Of course, Healer was present because of Mamie, but there were several other angels there as well. Then Hope found Ox standing next to Gina. The angel was enormous! Large, kind, and expressive eyes in a cow's face were overcome by joy before it bowed. Joy also overwhelmed Healer, and he bowed. Even Mamie was glowing.

Hope felt relief. She had expected a fight, not joy. Then she remembered the Lord's presence. Hope knew why the angels bowed. It certainly wasn't because of her or Insight. Honor began to engulf Hope like a physical force. The respect was wonderfully pleasant. She loved the feeling. It was addictive, but this honor wasn't for her. To gain balance, Hope immediately refused to receive the emotion anymore. The awe, that kind of love and respect, was His alone. Mentally she exited the armor so the Holy Spirit could receive what was His. Afterward, she joined forces with the others in agreement. Holy was her Lord.

Peace filled the room. Hope watched as the Holy Spirit and Ox communicated. When Ox relaxed, Hope focused quickly on Gina. The young woman definitely belonged to God's household. Gina's eyes were full of light, evidence of her newborn status. Then Hope laughed to herself after she spotted Gina's robe lying on the floor beneath the bed.

~~~

When Hope walked in my room, Mamie went straight to her. She wasn't anything like I had envisioned. Even dressed in jeans and a T-shirt, Hope radiated confidence. For some reason, I expected her to be dressed in a business suit, wearing glasses, and having an air of dominance. I watched her take in the surroundings and witnessed a humble expression take control of her features. Love seemed to shine from within her. Then her gaze fell on me.

Mamie gripped Hope's hand and then directed Hope closer to my bed. Mamie introduced us. "Hope, this is Gina Grimes. Gina, meet Hope. Since you two have much to discuss, I'm going to get out of your way and let you talk. Gina, I'll check on you again around 11:00 p.m."

Scared, I asked, "Mamie, do you have to leave?"

Her warm reply was, "Yes, child, you're in good hands. Hope can answer a lot of your questions. I'll be back soon."

~~~

Hope watched Healer leave with Mamie, but in his place, was another angel just like him. Healer's representative and Ox stood close and were humming strangely.

Seeing the question within Hope's mind, the Holy Spirit urged her to speak. "Breach the gap! Break the silence! Ask Gina about her messenger."

~~~

Hope and I were left alone staring at each other. I didn't know this woman. What was I going to say? Unexpectedly, Hope blurted out, "Tell me about your messenger."

Stunned by her request, I asked, "Who told you I had a messenger? I've only shared that information with Caylee and Mamie."

Hope grinned. "The Holy Spirit told me. He urged me to ask you about Him."

I didn't trust easily. I didn't know what to say. I did know Hope was here to help. To calm down, I stared into Hope's lovely eyes. When my mouth finally opened, I whispered, "Please sit down, this may take a while."

After Hope pulled a chair closer to the bed, she reached for my hand. The touch sent waves of comfort through me. Her touch was very similar to Mamie's. The sensation was more confirmation that I was in the company of another caring and nonjudgmental person. The knowledge freed me to speak without fear.

I told Hope about Adrian. I shared with her how we went on journeys. Then I told her how I was coping. I also expressed my fears. I was afraid of the unknown as well as Lyle Horne.

Hope knew exactly what to say. She took each phase and helped me understand. Then she assured me, saying, "Gina, I can personally vouch for you. You aren't imagining things. Angels are all around us. I see them all the time."

"You really see them?" I asked.

"Yes! Your Adrian just greeted me. Let me prove it. He is about six feet tall, has olive-toned skin, brown hair with golden highlights, and lovely green eyes."

"Yes! Yes! It's him!" I shouted.

Squeezing my hand, Hope said, "You and I aren't the only ones. Many people see into the spirit realm."

~~~

The Holy Spirit had a plan. He gave Adrian permission to appear before Gina. He'd fill Hope in later.

~~~

I wasn't in a dream state or in a coma, and Adrian appeared without an invitation. Then he greeted us. "Hello, ladies." I was so happy to see him again that tears came freely. God showed me I wasn't crazy.

I was entranced. When I snapped out of it, Hope was saying, "Gina, Adrian is wonderful, but there is one here who is greater. He wants you to know Him." I didn't want to look away from Adrian. He was my only connection to my future. Then Hope shook me. She addressed Adrian, "Adrian, would you mind leaving? Gina and I need to talk." Instantly and without a word, my guardian disappeared.

Hope got what she wanted. Adrian's disappearance did it. I gave her my angry attention. "Why did you order him to leave? He is my guardian angel, not your servant."

The Holy Spirit warned Hope, "Go slow! Be gentle! I told Adrian to appear. I will fill you in later. His presence is necessary. Don't be offended, trust me."

Hope gently responded to Gina's angry question, "Adrian is not your source. He was sent to you by the Lord. Wouldn't you rather know the one who sent your angel?"

I apologized for my angry tone. I was very new to all of this. God hadn't appeared to me, but Adrian had. How was I supposed to react? Hope waited patiently for my answer. She wasn't being mean. She was eager to help, but I didn't know what I needed.

"Hope, I don't know what I need. I've sought the Lord. I've been reading the Bible when I can. I know I need to read it, but I can't understand it very well. What more can I do?" I asked.

Hope smiled. "Simple! Ask the Holy Spirit to come into your heart. Stop trying to shove Him in your head. He's already forgiven you and given you a new life. Let Him fill you up. Then what you read will come alive. Promises show up when you have Him living inside of you."

I was confused and said, "I thought I already did that. I received salvation the day of my accident. Caylee and Mamie said that was why I was attacked."

"You received God's forgiveness from sin. You became a new creature, but you are still empty. Mamie and Caylee are right, you were attacked by Satan, but it wasn't because you accepted Christ, it was because of your desire. Do you still want to have your God-given life? He wants you to have Him. If you do, the two of you can share all good things. He'll even fight your battles," Hope explained.

~~~

The Holy Spirit alerted Ox. "Get ready! Your ability is needed." This time, not only did Ox engulf Gina, he lowered his head to touch hers. The mind-meld would give Gina the strength she needed to die to self.

~~~

"**W**ill he be visible to me like Adrian?" I asked.

Remembering her bathroom experiences, Hope laughed. "Yes! You'll definitely know He's around. Take it from me, you can't go anywhere without Him."

I submitted. "What do I need to do?"

"Just give me a few minutes Gina," Hope requested.

~~~

Hope knew what to do. But she took a few minutes to commune with the Lord. With her face turned away from Gina, Hope asked, "Lord, how will we do this? Will this be a personal experience with You and Gina or am I expected to participate?"

"Pray her through. Invite me in, and I'll do the rest. Let her know I'm coming as love. Ox and I will be giving her visions that will help her understand. We are showing her the canopy but in the form of a cocoon. The process has already begun. She has given her cares over to you. Patiently wait and answer questions if she has any. She has very little understanding. Until recently, Gina has feared Christianity. She had no knowledge of me. I'm ready to bond with her," He proclaimed.

Introduction

When Hope finished praying, she left her chair and eased down beside me on the bed. Gently, she took my hands in hers again and asked, "Gina, do you trust me?"

I bowed my head, closed my eyes, and nodded.

Hope guided me. "I'm going to pray and ask the Lord to baptize you with the Holy Spirit. After that, I'm going to ask Him to show Himself to you. When He does, don't be alarmed. He is awesome! He is pure love and wants you to know this."

I mentally gave this woman all my emotions. My heart was in her hands. I wanted something better.

As Hope prayed, I agreed with everything she said. When Hope asked the Lord to fill my heart, I said, "Please!"

With my eyes tightly shut, I began to see something in my mind. I saw myself trapped in a cocoon. The proximity was terrifying. Inside the transparent bubble, I squirmed, thrashed, screamed, and cried. I was naked and cold. In the vision, it was evident to me that I was dying in the cocoon because I had no air, no water, and no food. I was fighting for my life. I was straining against an invisible foe and losing miserably.

Then I heard a command. "Stop struggling! Rest! The harder you fight, the longer this will take!"

I fell against the cocoon and lay still. I felt peace. I gave myself over to death. But I hadn't really died. I'd just watched myself die.

Suddenly, the air changed! I heard a rushing wind come in the hospital room. Astonished by the sound, I opened my eyes, awakening from the vision, and was confronted by a bright light coming toward me. The closer it got, the brighter the light became. It wasn't a normal light; it was more like fire. As the flame positioned itself above my head, I heard a soft whisper, "Hello, my love, I'm here to abide in you. Welcome to my life."

The flame touched my head and love entered my mind. The feeling was incredible! Then Hope cooed, "Gina! Welcome to the family. The Holy Spirit now lives inside of you. You'll never be the same."

After that, I looked at Hope differently. I saw her through eyes of love. The feeling I had inside of me for this woman was overwhelming. Alarmed, and thinking Hope would answer, I asked, "What is happening?"

Instead, I heard the Whisperer say, "You are seeing Hope through my eyes. I love this woman dearly. I love you just as much. Listen to your sister. She can guide you through the supernatural. She's been there with me. I've shown her how to see the truth. She'll teach you how to see me."

"Hope! Did you hear that?" I asked.

"Yes. I've been allowed to hear Him speak to you," Hope replied.

I inquired further, "What do I say?"

Hope laughed. "Gina, the Holy Spirit is a person. He is just a spiritual one. Talk to Him. Ask Him questions. He's your best friend, and the good part about Him is He will never leave you."

"What do I call Him?" I inquired.

"Huh? What is He to you?" Hope quizzed.

I thought for a moment. *Was He my master? Is He the great and powerful one?* I didn't have a clue, so to answer her questions, I said, "Tell me! I don't know."

Hope asked, "Where is the Bible you've been reading?"

I didn't know. I'd had them until Brent visited. I looked around until the big one caught my eye. "They are on the window ledge near the flowers." I showed Hope.

"Good! You have a New American Standard. It will have a concordance in the back. Look up the words Holy Spirit. The concordance will give you every scripture. Find Him in the Word. Now that you hear His voice, ask Him questions. Let Him lead you and tell you the truth," Hope shared.

As Gina looked up the words, Hope and the Holy Spirit conversed. "Leave her with me. You've shown her what she needs." I found so many verses. I didn't know where to start. I inquired,

"Hope, where do I start? Which one do I read?"

"Gina, just read. Talk with the Lord. I'm going to leave you with Him. My family is waiting for me. I'll leave you my cell phone number. If you need me, call. Trust me, the Lord loves you and wants to be your friend," Hope urged.

I didn't want Hope to go. I had hundreds of questions. I wanted to know if she could help me find my mate. When I started to ask her to stay, my throat locked up. For some reason, I just couldn't bring myself to beg. I bid her farewell instead.

~~~

Before Hope exited Gina's room, she reentered the armor. She knew she would be confronting unhappy evil forces. Five huge giants met her growling and snarling. Then she heard an evil voice from behind the giants say, "I heard everything. You will not win! People are weak!" Here again, she had to remind herself that voice lied. His threats were against the Lord, not her. Plus, the giants' growls were focusing on who she wore. This time, their threats didn't affect her so badly. In fact, she took the reproach proudly, happy that evil hated and feared her Lord.

Inside the SUV, Hope continued to wear the Lord's armor. She didn't take it off until she arrived home and when the Holy Spirit had finished sharing His plan with her. She made sure Satan couldn't hear anything.

"Remember your lessons. You were difficult even with knowledge instilled from youth. Gina doesn't have any training, so teaching her to trust me will be more challenging. Adrian will assist. His healing abilities combined with Mamie's will be very useful. Use him when you need help with Gina. Don't be offended if Gina calls out to Adrian from time to time. I'll eventually become her main focus."

"Why Adrian and not Ox? Isn't Ox Gina's angel?" Hope inquired.

"I knew you would question. Until Gina becomes kingdom-minded, anything other than a human face will terrify her. Ox is around. He is not leaving. Commune with him also. Both angels want to help," He told her.

~~~

I sat on the hospital bed stunned. Before me were words describing who lived inside of me. He is my Comforter, Counselor, Helper, Intercessor, Advocate, Strengthener, and Standby given to me by the Father.

I was thoroughly confused. I wondered *Who is the Father? Is He God? What is the difference?*

The Whisperer said, "Ask me, Gina. I'm your Counselor, and I will help you."

The voice shocked my system. I wasn't used to having an inner voice respond to my every thought. I'd asked for this. If I was going to change, I needed to adhere. I must learn. I timidly decided to converse. "Sir, I'm scared of you. Are you God?"

"Don't be afraid. You are safe. I love you, and yes, I am the Father, the Son, and the Holy Spirit. We are separate but also three in one," he answered.

"Do you treat all believers the same? Why is this happening to me?" I asked.

Sighing, the Holy Spirit said, "We want to treat all believers the same. We would love to teach, comfort, and help them all, but most can't or won't allow it. They believe in us but don't live through us."

I asked, "What does live in you mean?"

"Very good question! Do you remember your vision? Do you remember the command?" He asked.

I had several visions come to mind. But I knew He meant the last one, so I inquired, "When I died?"

"You weren't dead. You quit struggling and rested. The invisible bubble is my life. As a new creation, you can thrive within its walls," He enlightened me.

"Why was I naked? Why was I cold? I had no air, food, or water! I thought I was dying! That is why I was struggling to get out!" I exclaimed.

The Spirit laughed. "Love, your spirit man doesn't need air, water, or food. I am all it needs. What you saw was not your body but the real you within me. Remember how you operated outside of your body with Adrian?"

I did! I didn't hurt, nor was I hungry. I didn't remember needing air, but I remembered having on a hospital gown. There was a lot I remembered about myself, and it was all good. I wanted more!

"Sir? Please tell me more. My experience with Adrian was the best of my life," I said.

"Find out through my Word. Use the method Hope gave you," He answered.

I spent the next hour looking up various references from the concordance then reading each passage in the three different versions. I was amazed how much I understood. I was very involved when I heard a rap on my door and saw Mamie walk in.

"Studying? That's a good sign," Mamie chirped. "Yes, ma'am! I have a new hunger," I answered.

Smiling, she shouted, "You have Him! Girl! You will never be the same. I'm going to let you continue. There isn't anything like feasting on the Word."

Before Mamie could leave, I had to tell her something. I must let this lovely woman know what she meant to me. "Wait! Mamie, don't leave," I begged.

"What is it, child?" she asked soothingly.

"Mamie, I love you! Can I call on you after I leave here? Will we see each other often? I need you! I need a motherly person in my life. My mom doesn't have a clue. She won't be much help with my new life. I'm leaving in the morning, and I'm scared," I confessed.

Bear-like arms wrapped me tight. Against a large bosom, I felt Mamie's love. "Sweetie, I love you too. I don't think we are going to lose touch. Caylee has big plans for you. The two of you will be under my feet soon enough. Give me a pen and paper, and I'll write my cell number down for you. Call ole Mamie anytime," she exclaimed.

After we exchanged numbers and Mamie left to go to work, I laid my books aside and whispered to my new friend, "Lord, I'm happy. You've sent me some amazing new friends. I'm looking forward to all of us getting to know each other."

Sleep came swiftly with dreams about the fire. As the fire followed me around, it was warm but didn't burn my skin. The fire would not go away or go out. I tested it to see if it would leave me. I threw water on it. I threw a blanket over it, but nothing changed the intensity. Even through the blanket, the light glowed. When I was convinced the fire was good and not evil, I decided to walk into it to see how it reacted. It proved to be my friend, whispering and welcoming me inside. I was comfortable and secure living and breathing in the fire. When I exited, I felt cold and threatened. Even the air was foul. It didn't take long for me to ask the fire if I could return to its safety.

Discharged

I woke to the sound of someone entering my room. It was Mamie, "Good morning, sunshine! Did you sleep well?"

"Uh huh! Never better," I said sleepily.

Mamie probed, "My shift is over, and I wanted to tell you bye. If you feel like it, I'll come to get you Sunday morning and take you to church. You interested?"

I sat straight up in bed. "Would you, please!" Then I inquired, "Do you think I could go to group tonight?"

"No! The first day or so, you need to get used to the crutches. Find out what you can do. See if you can clean and dress," Mamie exclaimed.

I hadn't thought of that. I hadn't needed clothes. All I needed here was a hospital gown. How was I supposed to put on panties? "Mamie? How will I completely dress? How do I put on panties with my leg like it is?" I inquired.

Mamie cackled! "I recommend you sit on the edge of a chair and put your bad leg through first and pull it up. Then maneuver the other foot in and pull it up. Practice or go without. You'll figure it out, I need to go home. I've been up a long time. I'll call you later and check up on you."

After breakfast, my not-so-favorite doctor visited. Dr. Carter commended me on my progress and told me that before I could go home, I had to have stitches removed. I was totally confused. What stitches? Where? When I asked, he looked at me as if I were the craziest person on the planet. He answered with a cold, "Your stitches are on your head and left leg. Don't you remember I had to operate to put your leg together? For the stitches to be removed from your leg, an orthopedic technician has to remove your cast."

The news excited me. Maybe I could get another cast that wasn't so stiff. Rather than ask this mean-spirited doctor anything else, I'd wait and ask the tech.

Dr. Carter continued giving me strict instructions that required a follow-up appointment within the next week. He had to be convinced that I could take care of my needs properly and move easily before agreeing I could go back to work. His excuse was again my leg issue. Having a leg broken in several places was a problem even for the very strong. He said he was concerned about me traveling. That was hard to believe.

The countdown was on! After my stitches were out, I could call someone to come get me. The hospital should be finished with my release papers by noon.

I called Mom's house, but she didn't answer. I called the place she worked, and the receptionist said she'd taken the day off. A little anxious, I called her cell to make sure she would be available for me. When she finally answered, she said she was shopping. When I asked why, she said she was on an errand for me. I was not to ask any more questions, just wait and see.

To kill time, I decided to sponge-bathe. I gathered clean towels and tucked them under my right arm; then I hobbled over to the small bathroom using my crutches and stood at the sink. I was determined to learn how to take care of my needs. After filling the sink with warm water, I propped the crutches against the wall and stood on my good leg, and I sponged most of my body with soapy water. After rinsing, I sat on the toilet and sponged off my right leg then leaned over and wiped off my left toes. Fortunately, I had a toothbrush and a hairbrush already in the bathroom so I stood again so I could look in the mirror and combed my hair and brushed my teeth. By the time, I was finished, I was exhausted. I slipped on a clean hospital gown and exited the bathroom to find a cute tech waiting with a two-wheeled chariot to take me to the Orthopedic Center.

On the way, over to the center, the tech introduced himself as Shawn Davis. He informed me the procedure shouldn't take more than an hour, depending on what kind of cast I needed. The statement prompted me to inquire, "Do you think it would be possible to have a different kind of cast? Maybe one that I could open and shut periodically? The one I wore made my leg itch horribly."

Shawn sweetly informed, "You are itching because the stitches need to come out. But I'll ask and see what we can use."

The smell coming from me would make a buzzard vomit. The dried blood, the dead skin, and fumes from the plaster being removed caused me to gag. Concern for me caused Shawn to stop what he was doing to get me a puke bucket. I was so embarrassed and apologized profusely.

Shawn smiled and then said, "It is okay. Most people hate the smell. I'm used to it."

Thank goodness, the smell didn't linger. As soon as Shawn removed the plaster from the room, the odor left too. The air on my skin felt heavenly, but the sight of my leg scared me. Not only was I bruised, but I had a two-foot-long suture made of staples running along my inner leg.

I didn't have to wonder for how long Shawn would remove the metal from my leg. He had a staple remover the size of my hand. With each snip and pull, I had to grit my teeth. Each removal burned and stung, making tears flow down my cheeks. When he was finished, Shawn rubbed my leg down with a disinfectant, and I wanted to shout for joy. The burning and itching were gone!

After the procedure, Shawn disappeared for a long time. Afraid to move, I lay patiently waiting and wondering what was going on. When the door opened, a hand protruded holding a large black nylon-looking boot. Was this my new cast? Shawn hopped around the door, grinning from ear-to-ear to say, "You hit the jackpot, ma'dear! Dr. Carter agreed to let you try a boot. You can't remove it, but you can loosen it so your leg can breathe as long as you keep your leg perfectly straight."

God is being good to me! I thought. I felt like a new person. My new boot was light compared to the cast. Maneuvering wouldn't be as hard.

I was back in my room and resting in bed when Mom arrived. When she wrestled in with several bags, I was puzzled. Didn't she know I was leaving? What possessed her to bring gifts here instead of keeping them for me at the house?

Urging me to open the bags, she said, "Blame Mamie! The woman called the house and said she couldn't sleep until she told me where to buy you some special panties. She was worried you would fall and hurt yourself trying to get regular ones over your cast. Since you are coming home today, I went and purchased a few pair. Then I got carried away buying other things."

I opened the first bag she handed me to see three pairs of white granny panties. They looked like normal underwear until I noticed the left side had snapped. Then I opened another bag to see a slip, a bra, and a pretty draw-stringed skirt and a matching blouse. My last bag contained a cute pair of slip-on shoes.

My heart melted. Mom had gone out of her way for me. Then I heard Him again. The Whisperer commented, "She loves you! Receive the love."

Any other time, I would have felt smothered and unappreciative because she was running my life, but not today. Why?

The Whisperer spoke again, "You are seeing her through my eyes and understanding her actions. Remember how you viewed Hope last night?"

This voice was hard to get used too. He could hear my every thought. He was like Adrian. No! Better than Adrian.

Then the Whisperer replied to my thoughts of Adrian, "I created Adrian to serve. I'm here to love."

"Gina! Snap out of it, honey!" Mom said.

I'd been lost in a conversation with the Holy Spirit and blocked Mom out totally. This was weird.

"I'm sorry, Mom! I was lost in thought. I can't get over all the gifts," I confessed.

"Do you like everything?" Mom asked.

"Everything is great! Help me get dressed so I can get out of here," I exclaimed.

Mom quickly closed the door to my room to give me privacy. The hospital gown was off in a flash. With catlike grace, I had my good leg in the new panties and had snapped the left leg in place. Mamie had come through for me again. Next, I tried on the bra. It fit perfectly. Everything else was just window dressing. The skirt and blouse were cute. They gave me a new attitude. The style was gypsy-like, which made me feel free-spirited. Mom's idea was right on target. I needed the inspiration because I was being set free.

A wave of bittersweet emotion flooded me. This room had been my cocoon. I was safe here, well taken care of. All my needs were met. New friends had come to me here. I'd received Adrian, Mamie, Dr. Jones, Brent, and Hope. Then I remembered last night. I'd also found the fire. He was in me. He had come to me here. My dream vividly came to mind. I was happy in the fire, welcomed. This made me wonder: what would I face outside?

The wonder came to a halt when a wheelchair arrived. Papers were signed. Doctor appointments and prescriptions were given. Then I was wheeled outdoors by an orderly to wait for a ride home. As Mom retrieved her car, I felt the heat from the sun on my skin. It was warm and pleasant at first; then it became too hot, causing me to sweat and my skin to burn. This fire wasn't welcoming. Suddenly, I wanted back inside the small, cramped hospital room where I felt safe.

The panic made me silently cry out, *Lord! Help me!*

"Don't fear, Gina! I'm here! Stop struggling. All is well, I'm not leaving you. Your new life in me is just beginning," the Comforter replied.

The Whisperer's voice soothed me a great deal. The calming effect made me realize the new life I desired had begun.

~~~

The demonic watchdogs assigned to Gina were jumping for joy and shouting, "She's out! She's ours again. It's time to cause her grief."

~~~

Trulan and other angels quickly alerted the Holy Spirit of possible attacks only to be told, "It's all under control. Ox and I are with Gina. She's cried out to the Lord. We wanted her to experience the difference between our love and the world's hate. The demonic horde will not destroy. Gina must understand love's safety. She must remember how secure she was within the canopy of her cocoon to understand she has that available at all times."

~~~

Mom's compact car was not designed for the physically disabled. I hurt myself sliding in backward behind the driver's seat. To keep my leg extended, I had to scoot backward along the backseat over to the passenger's window to properly support my leg. If this was an indication of how I had to travel, I was not going to be happy. My skirt didn't cooperate, my back ached from not being properly supported, and the pain in my leg grew. It hadn't given me problems in a long time, but it screamed with pain.

Gina's chariot, the compact car, was a perfect place to start torment. One gremlin made her hit her head while another held on to her skirt, preventing her smooth movement inside the car. Another tormentor twisted her injured leg. All the anguish they caused Gina made her emotions decline a negative path, which in turn lured the demonic imps to swarm as they eagerly fed off Gina's pain, dread, fear, and anxiety.

I was conflicted. I wanted to go home but also wanted to go back to my comfort zone. My leg and head pleaded for the pain to subside. To have relief from the pain, I needed a prescription filled, which meant more time cooped up in the small car. Why was I experiencing pain? I hadn't had any in a while. To suddenly have it levied upon me now caused me to wonder what lay ahead. I remembered my dream again. I was safe in the fire.

"Mom, please stop at the pharmacy. My leg is giving me a fit," I begged.

Willing to please, she stopped. Before going inside, she asked, "Want anything else?"

I sure did! I needed the one thing that soothed emotional strain for me. I boldly asserted, "Chocolate! Lots of it, please!"

On the road again, I took my pain medication and washed it down with cola. Then I fed my misery with chocolate. My mind reflected again on the visions given me. I was trapped in a bubble. I loved living in fire. What did they mean? I also reflected on reality. Free from the confines of the hospital room, the outdoor exposure was too intense, and the sunshine burned. What was real?

When we arrived home, getting out of Mom's car was just as frustrating as getting into it. My skirt didn't grip this time to keep me from scooting; it caused me to slip out of the car too quickly. The silky fabric propelled me like I was on a waterslide. To keep from landing on my rump, I grabbed the front seat, but not in time to prevent injury. My good foot dug into the ground to stop the momentum, but my effort didn't prevent my injured foot from hitting the pavement hard. The jolt caused tears to flood my eyes; the pain was awful.

~~~

In the atmosphere, evil snickers and laughs flooded the neighborhood. Their plaything wasn't having a good day, which was good news to them. The more they made her complain, the better. Complaints were food for all to get fat from.

~~~

Ox laughed. He and the Holy Spirit were about to torment the tormentors. They were about to put the demonic imps on a fast. Gina wouldn't be complaining. Soon she would be happy and excited. Little did Gina know, but her request for a better life also involved her whole family. Angels were at work restoring something that had been broken.

~~~

Mom wasn't any help. She was afraid of hurting me, so she let me maneuver at my own pace. When I finally managed to get inside the house, I was amazed. She'd been busy. Furniture had been rearranged. Paths had been widened. My old room was even changed. Mom had moved the bed to one side of the room and taken out an end table, making the room wider for me to move around.

"Mom! How did you do all this?" I asked.

Her answer amazed me more than the rearranged house. She said, "Your father came to help me."

Stunned by what she said, I questioned, "What? Dad, came here? How did you manage that?"

"We've been talking. The relationship is still strained, but since your accident, we sort of lean on each other. When I told him you were staying with me, he wanted to help make your stay more comfortable," she explained.

"Huh! So, it took nearly dying for the two of you to talk civilly to each other again. Imagine that!" I chirped.

She timidly shared, "Waiting for you to wake up from the coma left us without anything to do but talk with each other. We had one thing in common, and that was you. We both love you. We both weren't leaving the hospital. When we thought you were dying, we came to realize we meant something to each other once. Our marriage brought us both mostly happiness and gave us you. Stupid and hurtful circumstances tore us apart. Like I said, old memories haunt, making a strained relationship, but we're trying."

I didn't know how to respond. I wanted to be happy. Having them back together would be wonderful, but I remembered the fights, the accusations, and the threats. Could this work? Do I want to relive their quarrels? Tentatively, I asked, "Mom, have things improved or are you hopeful?"

"He says he misses us. He's been lonely. I want to trust. Gina, I don't think I've ever been good enough for him, what should I do?" she asked.

One thing came to my mind. One suggestion I was no longer afraid to share. Mom needed a new life. We could to this thing together. "Have you prayed for a change?" I asked boldly.

She shrugged and said, "No! Maybe I should, it couldn't hurt. God hears prayers. My prayers were answered when I prayed for your life. Maybe the Lord would help bring Dad home."

My jaw almost hit the floor. I couldn't believe what she said. My mom had prayed. There was hope for her after all. Hallelujah! Now I was crying for joy!

~~~

Hating the circumstances, a gremlin spun Gina's equilibrium out of control, causing her to become dizzy. If he couldn't make her complain, then he would put her to sleep.

~~~

All of a sudden, I had to sit. The room seemed to be moving. My body had to be responding to the pain medication. I hadn't needed any in a while, and now this new one was making me dizzy and very sleepy. Maybe I should have eaten a meal. I'd only had candy. I needed to lie down. I stretched out on the bed and promptly went to sleep.

Dad's voice woke me a few hours later. Overhearing him and Mom talk was sweet and comforting. It was at that moment I knew I wanted my parents back together. I prayed too. "Lord, help them find love again. They deserve a good life. I'd love for both of them to be Christians with me. Help them find you. Amen."

My stomach growled; I was starving. I hadn't eaten food since breakfast. I hobbled into the kitchen to see what was available. Mom was cooking one of my favorite meals, chicken, and dumplings. The smell made my mouth water. But it was something other than food that made me happy. I'd interrupted Dad's flirtations. He'd been pinching Mom playfully, causing her to squeal like a kid. They were acting like lovesick teenagers.

"Hey, you two! Straighten up! You're giving me a mental picture I can't believe," I blurted joyfully.

Dad came over to hug me but found it hard to get close due to my crutches, so he settled for a kiss on my forehead instead. Then he inquired, "Mom and I together is a strange sight, isn't it? Do you mind if I eat with the two of you?"

What was he thinking? I wanted him to eat with us every meal. I wanted Daddy home. I wanted to be home! What was happening? Things were wonderful.

I exclaimed, "Please, Dad! I love having you here. Seeing you two together is better than medicine."

A Sign

It was group night. A time set apart for young adults in the community to come together in a wholesome environment and enjoy each other's company. Caylee was looking forward to the fun. She had invited a friend and was pacing on the porch of the community center waiting for him to arrive.

While Caylee waited for her friend, her mind took her back to the previous day where she reflected on last evening's conversation with Russ. She hadn't been home from visiting Gina long when her landline telephone rang. She remembered how taken aback she was when she answered, and the caller was Russ Jackson. She had been thoroughly caught off guard and surprised that Russ had wanted to get in touch with her so quickly. It surprised her even further when he asked her to go on a date the next evening. Not expecting Russ's invitation, she politely refused. Not because she didn't want to date Russ, but because Friday nights were group night, her special time to be with church family and friends. When he questioned why Caylee wouldn't go out, she stated honestly that she went to a young-adults' group every Friday evening. Then, to her amazement, Russ asked if he could join her. Caylee was thrilled!

As she reminisced further about their conversation, Caylee realized something else: a pressure had been taken off her shoulders. She wouldn't need to make good on her invitation to have Russ over for dinner before they could get to know each other better. The strain of appearing too flirtatious had been removed. Russ had freed her; she could stop worrying about her overzealous invitation because he had taken the reins into his own hands and been first to advance their relationship past an acquaintance.

Coming to herself on the porch, she realized she was pacing back and forth, acting like an overeager teenager waiting for a boyfriend to arrive. Now she had a different strain. Not wanting to appear too eager, she stopped for a moment to analyze the situation. Should she go inside and wait? Would waiting outside give Russ the wrong signal? Here again, she worried. She really liked the man and didn't want to appear flirtatious and loose. In her past, her overzealous nature scared boys away. At other times, the same zealous nature drew in the wrong kind of men who wanted to use her for their pleasures.

Caylee's mind raced and raced. She had come a long way in her relationship with Christ. She was happy and confident that Jesus was bringing her a soul mate. Now here was Russ. He was the first man she had met in nearly a year who was interested in her since her dedication to Jesus to live a better life for Him. What was she to do?

Quieting her mind, Caylee took another moment and prayed, "Lord, I'm scared. You know my past. I don't want to go back there. I asked You to bring me someone and then I promised to wait. Russ came to me in a time of need. I believed You sent him… did You send him to be my mate? Lord, I don't want to break my promise to You if he isn't. Please give me a sign. I'm throwing out a fleece just like Gideon. I can't trust my own emotions. Here goes! If Russ brings me a flower, I'll know you sent him. If Russ doesn't bring a flower, I'll be nice to him this evening, but I'll stop encouraging a relationship."

~~~

Jesus heard Caylee's sweet prayer. The sign wouldn't be a problem; she deserved to know.

~~~

Russ drove up and down the wrong street wondering why he couldn't find the church. When he realized, he was traveling down Cooper Street instead of Cooper Lane, he wanted to scream. He was going to be late! It would take fifteen minutes to drive to the other side of town. Caylee told him to be there before their movie started at 7:00 p.m. and it was already 6:45. So much for good impressions; Caylee was going to think he stood her up. He hated knowing she would be disappointed in him. He banged the steering wheel with his fists, wondering what had made him drive to Cooper Street. He knew the church was on Cooper Lane; he'd driven by it dozens of times.

Determined to be a gentleman, Russ turned his truck around, making the decision to show up late. He would somehow find a way to apologize for his tardiness.

~~~

Caylee felt sick. She had really hoped Russ was different. It was a good thing she had prayed and asked God for a sign. God had answered her, but it wasn't the way she expected. She had to be thankful anyway. Apparently, God intervened. Not only had Russ neglected to bring a flower, but—he hadn't shown up at all. At least this way, she thought, she wouldn't have to suffer through an evening being nice to the person God hadn't intended for her. She submitted and went inside the community center. It was already 6:50 p.m. and she had specifically told Russ that their movie started at 7:00 p.m. Wanting to feed her misery, Caylee went to retrieve a bag of popcorn before finding a seat to watch the movie. She was looking forward to watching the movie; she'd heard it was great. She would enjoy the company of her friends and continue to wait for God's best to find her.

At the popcorn stand, Hope stood talking to other members about the summer picnic at the Boys' Home when Caylee walked up to them. She could tell the girl was wrestling with an issue. It was very apparent because Caylee never frowned.

Curiously, Hope inquired, "Caylee, are you all right?"

Caylee shared, "Yeah. I'm just disappointed. I was expecting this guy to come tonight, but he stood me up."

"Do you want to talk about it?" Hope pressed.

Not wanting to cry, Caylee shook her head and whispered, "Not now. I'm going to get some popcorn then go watch the movie. I'll be fine."

Caylee had her back turned from the community hall entrance as she gathered her snack, preventing her from seeing who came inside the building. When Hope spotted a new face, she knew this was the young man that had caused Caylee's sadness. He hadn't jilted Caylee. Happily, Hope exclaimed, "Caylee, I think the young man is here. I see a new face, and he looks lost."

Caylee turned around quickly to see Russ. Trying not to appear overjoyed, she walked slowly over to him to confess, "I thought you weren't coming."

Russ expressed, "I knew you were going to think I lied! I just went down the wrong street, causing me to be late."

"It's okay," Caylee answered.

Holding out his hand to Caylee, Russ offered a gift, pleading, "No, it's not. I saw these pretty wildflowers along the side of the road where I parked, and I picked them for you. Please take them as a peace offering."

Caylee started shaking then she burst out crying. God was handing her two gifts that night! The man she had asked Him for and flowers. Her heart was full of emotion. Words just would not come. Knowing within her heart that all would be well, she acted naturally, freed to be herself, and hugged Russ. This man would not think she was a loose, overzealous woman. This man would cherish her. This man was God's pick. Someone suited for her personality and disposition.

Shocked by Caylee's response, Russ hugged her in return and stated, "If wildflowers bring you tears of joy and get me hugs, I'll bring them to you often."

Quickly introducing Russ to Hope and retrieving two bags of popcorn, Caylee ushered Russ into the movie room. Like two lovebirds, they ate their popcorn, watched the movie, and eventually held hands. When the movie was over, Caylee joyously introduced Russ to her other friends. Then she took over the room, enlightening everyone on how Russ had saved her two nights before. She'd been very scared. The whole crowd was captivated by her story as she beamed, describing every detail. But deep within her heart, Caylee held a secret. Russ may not have God's special knowledge of their future. She also knew she needed to get to know Russ better, as well as her friends. But without a doubt, she knew he would be wonderful. Getting a grip on her exuberant emotions, Caylee slowed down and rested in the knowledge that God had her future under control.

Russ walked Caylee to her car, not wanting their night to end. Making sure she knew how much he enjoyed her company, he said, "I had a good time tonight. Your friends are terrific."

"Yeah! Everyone is great. We're like family," Caylee confessed.

Russ shyly asked, "Can I see you again?"

"Yes! I'd love it," Caylee replied.

Without anything else to say before saying goodnight, Russ slowly moved closer to gently hug and sweetly kiss Caylee. He kept from kissing her passionately because he felt she wouldn't approve.

~~~

Satan wanted to gag. The sight of love nauseated him. As he quickly left the scene, he knew he needed to put a kink in the mix. He couldn't allow this to develop. True love between two believers created more kids for Jesus. What could he do? The shield Jesus had around Caylee was too strong. Maybe he could mess with the guy?

Satan played with Russ's mind as he rode with him in the truck. Seeing from within Russ's old memories, Satan saw what had usually attracted Russ. Russ liked the look of curvy blondes with big breasts. This gave Satan an idea. He could deceive. Lure the man away from the goody-two-shoes with someone more sexually appealing. He would bring Russ one of his girls, one willing to comply. One who was just the ticket and soft and just as sweet.

~~~

Russ wasn't tired. He was wired. The night had been invigorating and exciting. Everyone he'd met was extremely nice and welcoming. The young-adults' group had it going on. He could see why Caylee loved it. The atmosphere there was clean and honest without pretense.

Deciding to get some coffee and maybe a late-night snack, Russ stopped at a diner on the edge of town. He hadn't sat long before a very pretty blonde edged into the seat across from him and asked if he'd like her company. At first glance, the woman appeared to be a knockout, extremely beautiful and smelling lovely. Another time Russ may have wanted her company, but not tonight, especially not after leaving Caylee.

Taking a moment, Russ compared Caylee to the strange but lovely woman. Caylee was nothing like this lady who was bold and flirtatious. Caylee was beautiful, but her true beauty came from inside. She had a personality that was energetic but a little shy. Caylee was sweet and gentle, which made him crave more of her. The woman in front of him had thrown herself at him. She had a needy and desperate hunger for him that was repellent. Then he studied her face closer and noticed she really wasn't beautiful; she was plastic and fake. He knew immediately he didn't want her company. Russ sweetly asked the lady to move on, stating that he was already a taken man.

~~~

Caylee hated not having her car or cell phone. Otherwise, she would be chatting up the evening's events with Gina while she drove home. Gina had to know what happened. Caylee could hardly wait to get to her landline phone and give Gina a call. She had proof! She was on a mission. Gina needed hope to keep her vision alive. If God came through for her, Caylee knew Gina wouldn't be disappointed either. Her man would come.

Meat on the Bone

Ox watched Gina's face while she chatted with Caylee. He didn't like what he was seeing. Her every expression was pinched and strained. Needing to understand why Gina was distraught, Ox used his supernatural hearing to enter their conversation. What he heard was good news. Caylee was sharing her blessing. She was giving Gina hope.

Still needing to know why Gina wasn't happy, Ox entered deeper into Gina's thoughts where he could see what she was thinking. What he found inside her mind was a seed of doubt brought about by the lack of understanding. She was wondering why she was going through all the stress. She wondered why she had to believe for a specific person as a mate. Caylee didn't know who her mate was until this evening. *Why couldn't she be like Caylee and get surprised? Why was she given a face and partial name to search for? What was the point?*

Ox knew Satan was involved again. The evil angel loved planting seeds of doubt and deception. No matter. The seeds wouldn't take hold; they were about to be uprooted. God had a plan for this woman. The Holy Spirit was with Gina now. He would release Gina from this doubt. When Gina knew God's plan, Ox would be able to rip Satan's seed from the ground. God was always on time. With this in mind, Ox gave Gina the assistance she needed. She could pull from his strength.

In the realm of the spirit where Ox worked, he moved closer to Gina. When he was close enough, he gently embraced Gina tightly within his wings. Ox gave of himself, allowing Gina to draw from his strength. That was his sole purpose. With his strength, Gina could face the challenge. She must have his strength to die to self again.

Ox knew how to rest inside the realm of God. Once Gina knew the Holy Spirit, he rested in the large bubble knowing the Lord oversaw Gina in the earthly realm. He knew for sure heaven's plan would be fulfilled. He'd wait for the Holy Spirit's directive. Then he would assist Gina with his power to enter into the rest. Ox also rested in the fact that any assistance he rendered would not affect Gina's will. God already had her will. That is why she was chosen for the task.

Her will had been submitted moments before she professed Jesus and hours before her earthly issues began to unfold. Heavenly authority was already granted. Ox had the grace to give Gina thoughts and ideas that applied to heaven's plan. He could also influence Gina's thinking, giving her questions to ask of the Holy Spirit. He loved his purpose!

~~~

This helplessness was the pits! I hated crutches! I was either tripping or getting tangled when I used the stupid things. It was much easier if I just hopped around on my good foot inside Mom's small house. I had the walls to brace myself against or chairs to grab on to so I wouldn't fall, and I had lights inside so I could see where I was going. But outside in the dark, I had no walls or lights, and what I needed was in Mom's car.

Standing at the kitchen door, I peered out into the darkness thinking about what Caylee said. She had asked God for a sign because she didn't have a face or name to look for. God answered and gave her proof that Russ was the chosen man for her. Why was I taken on a mysterious journey? Why was I given mental pictures and the last name? What I had as proof was written down in my notes. It wasn't a photograph; it was a written reminder for me. What I had wasn't a flower; it was a piece of paper. I wanted to study the proof again, but it (along with my Bibles) was in Mom's car.

Until my conversation with Caylee, I hadn't even thought about my notes or my Bibles. I was too caught up in my physical pain. Then I became focused on Mom and Dad's new relationship. What was going on with my life? I kept wondering what the point was of me going through all this stress. Why was it so important to Caylee that I strived to believe in a vision I had? The more I thought about all this, the more I realized the visions were fading from my mind. I needed my notes! I need to re-examine every detail I wrote down when the visions were fresh in my head. Maybe then the faces and details from the memories would become clear again.

Standing between me and my notes were my own weaknesses, not the darkness. I could see Mom's car plainly because the moon was shining brightly, so I didn't need any extra light. My heart wanted to take the chance, but my mind convinced me to wait. I reasoned with myself because I knew I must not risk hurting myself. I could not afford to suffer a setback. My other option was to wake up Mom. I reasoned again, and reason won over emotions. I would not wake Mom for a piece of paper, no matter how important it was to me. Mom needed her rest.

I stared at the moon's beauty, seeking comfort when I remembered who made the moon. "Lord, my heart is in your hands. I'm so confused," I cried.

"Gina! I am your hope and future. Inquire of me, and I will answer. Require from me, and I will give," the Whisperer beckoned. I was jolted out of my melancholy. The fire was here! I hadn't left it at the hospital; it was here! Then I remembered reading from scripture that the Holy Spirit was my Comforter. Could I take a chance and ask Him questions? I had to know why. I had to know what to do.

In my mind, I laid my heart on an altar submitting all my concerns to the One who should know everything. I thought for a moment for the right words to use to ask my questions. In my humbled state, I knew what I needed more than the manifestation of my visions. I had to know the reasons why the Lord gave me the visions. What made me so special? Why was I was given an angel to show me wonders upon wonders? I didn't understand why He made Caylee wait, and why I was just given a face to vaguely recollect.

While I stood at the window, I looked up at the beautiful moon God created. God created it to give light in darkness. Why did God create me? Did I have a purpose?

I closed my eyes and prayed, "Lord, as I stated earlier, I am confused. I'm inquiring like You asked. Why did You single me out? Why did You show me wonderful things to hope for? I'm a nobody. I'm helpless. I don't know anything about You. Why me?" Behind my closed eyelids appeared a glimmer of light. When I saw it, I focused as hard as I could. Light could be fire. I wanted it to be fire. As I sought the flame, I noticed a man walking in firelight. He was coming to me. I determined to keep focus. I clamped my eyes tighter. I wanted to know this man who walked within the fire. Between me and the man was the door my body was pressing against. I could remedy that. I wanted to touch him. I fumbled for the latch until I received a light rebuke.

"Stop! Don't do that. Material objects can't come between us," He whispered.

With my eyes still tightly closed, I pushed away from the door to let him enter. I sought with my hands for something to grasp hold of before hopping only to be grabbed by very strong hands. I almost opened my eyes to see who had me when I noticed I was being stabilized by the man in flames. I gasped! Still refusing to open my eyes! I would not lose this sight!

"I am your Comforter. I am your Standby. I will support you forever. I've come to give you the answers you seek. Trust me and follow," He offered.

"Yes, Lord! I will," I sputtered.

"Gina, I love you. I've loved you before you were created. Do you believe me?" He asked.

I nodded my head, yes, knowing he could read my mind. Then He continued, *"You were created to give others hope. Deep within you, I planted the ability to believe. This ability is called faith. When you use the ability I've given you, nothing can stop my plan."*

"Lord, may I know what the plan is?" I asked shyly.

"Yes! That is why I'm here. You desired to know my will more than what I can give you," He answered.

I did! I needed to know why I had been given the visions. What was the reason? I certainly didn't deserve that much happiness. I couldn't fathom why.

"What is my purpose? Do I have to earn the visions?" I asked.

"No! You do not have to earn anything. I freely give to all who believe in me. It is, for this reason, I chose you, you have the ability to believe. That is your purpose. I've chosen you to be an example. That is the reason why I gave you a piece of your future. Now you have something to hope for. Use your gift! Believe for what was shown you. Stand firm against threats. Learn how you can believe through my Word. I'll always be with you to help you understand what is written or what is said in my name," He replied.

I had to know the difference between me and Caylee, so I asked, "Why didn't you give Caylee a mental picture? She didn't have a clue what to hope for."

"Yes, she did! She saw what she wanted in my Word. It was a specific characteristic in a man. She found something she liked from what I said. Afterward, she formed a mental picture of my Words and used her gift," He answered.

"What is her gift?" I inquired.

"Any other time I wouldn't say, but in this instance, you need to know. Caylee has the gift of patience mixed with faith. She has the will to wait on me," He said.

"I'm confused," I confessed.

"Gina, you have determination and grit. You can hold on to what I gave you. You don't have to wait; you just have to hold. I gave you a face, now go and find the characteristics you desire within my Word," He enlightened.

What He just told me wasn't very hard to grasp. I had a gift of faith mixed with determination; something God thought was strong enough to help others. What I had problems with was that God wanted me to be a leader. I could hardly find my own way. I would definitely need His help that was a certainty. The only way to make sure that would happen was to ask if He would. I understood I needed to know more about His Word. I could focus more on that. But I was losing sight of an important item. I was losing sight of what my future family looked like.

"Will you please re-enforce me? I need help. My vision has faded," I confessed.

"Yes!" He replied.

Behind my eyelids, God instantly gave me another vision within this vision. I watched the Lord point His finger out into the darkness, which directed my focus outside, past the kitchen door. I saw another light coming. It too was a fire. Within that firelight was a man on a red motorcycle coming toward me. He was wearing a black helmet decorated with flames. He stopped out in our driveway and removed his helmet. When he did, I whimpered. It was the face I loved! The beautiful face! He too lived in the fire. I was overjoyed! I wanted a man who knew the Lord.

"Lord? Is he the same man from my visions? I see fire all around him. Is he living in the fire with us?" I asked.

"Yes! He is from me. He is one of my brothers. Now, believe for your future! I know you can do this!" He encouraged.

The bulldog in me started drooling. I danced and spun for joy! My bone was back! My bone was back! I hadn't lost it! It was the same bone, but this time, it had a little fresh meat around it!

My visions ended, and both men were gone. I was left again in reality with nothing to beg and dance for. I opened my eyes to a room bright with electric light. My body slumped from exhaustion. It felt like I'd been standing for hours in the same position. When I looked at the clock shining on Mom's stove, the time was 12:30 a.m. I'd only been dreaming for thirty minutes. I was weary, and I needed sleep. My mind was full and somewhat amazed at the task God had laid before me.

I hopped along the corridor to my room, turning off every light as I went, remembering to divide truth from reality. I knew the truth lay within the visions just shown to me; it was within the firelight in my heart and behind my eyes.

As I lay on my bed, I pondered on the word gifted. God had a plan for me, and it depended on this gift. All I had to do was believe. I could do that! I wanted to believe. I wanted the promise within the vision. At that moment, my body groaned; it was too tired to believe tonight. I would give my body the rest it craved and let my mind do the believing and run free in my dreams.

~~~

In the shadows, Satan saw and heard everything. He loved working in dreams. Since Gina was out from under that reinforced shield at the hospital, he could steal the vision from her. Snatch it away and destroy her hope. He'd kill the man within the vision; slay him in front of her dreaming eyes. He would show her who was the boss in the land of the living.

~~~

Deeper in the shadows, the Holy Spirit and Ox laughed. Satan had taken the bait. They could always count on his stupidity. Satan thought he would face a weakling. Little did he know, inside Gina's dream, what he was going to face was a mean, vicious bulldog. Satan thought he could take and kill the man, but this man wasn't the dog's bone. He was in for a surprise! Gina was a bulldog equipped with faith. A bulldog empowered by determination and a spiritual purpose. Both the Holy Spirit and Ox knew Gina would be taught a valuable example through this dream-fight tonight. When faced with the same type of attack in her reality, Gina would know what to do. She wouldn't have to fight tooth and nail.

~~~

In my dreams, the bulldog in me came alive again. I had my bone! I loved my bone! My bone still had meat on it, and it was juicy. All of a sudden, I felt a jab then another. Something was trying to run me away from my bone. The tormentor struck me again and hollered for me to leave. The mean creature stomped and kicked at me, but I refused to relinquish my bone. Another mean creature came. This time, I had two trying to touch my bone. Something in me broke! All training to be loving and nice ceased! I bared my teeth with a hateful warning growl. I scratched in the dirt, sharpening my claws, and I foamed at the mouth and growled. I acted insanely. Straddling the bone, I dared the tormentors to touch my love, but more tormentors came. This time, they beat me with rods of iron. I was bloody and bruised, but I didn't give up. I snapped at their hands and feet with my fierce teeth. I bit, scratched, and tore at their flesh. Still, more tormentors came. By this time, I was weak and tired. I could hardly fight anymore. At this point, all I could do was lie on my bone for protection, trying to hide it with my body. I'd give up my life before I gave these tormentors my bone.

Then I remembered who gave me the bone. I realized I wasn't going to die. I remembered why I was given the bone. I would be showing others how to keep theirs. Why had I worried? In what I thought was my darkest hour, weak and frail from the physical beating, I gave up the fear of losing my bone. I gave up even trying to fight for it. Lying on my bone, I whined and whimpered like a baby crying. Calling out to the Lord, I mentally declared, I give the tormentors to you, Lord. They can't stop Your plan. The problem is all Yours. Then I rested on the bone, watching and waiting for help. I knew any second help would come to me. Even though the tormentors kept beating and kicking me, I simply didn't care. I relaxed in knowing they were about to get their punishment.

Fire came down from heaven with a thunderous clap! My Comforter did not let me down! Standing there beside me was my maker, the One who gave me a purpose. I rolled over to show Him my bone. I had not lost what He had given me. He was my friend! My standby! My Master! With Him was a mighty army, my loved ones; Mamie, Hope, and Brent were also with me, ready and willing to join my Master's fight. Awesome creatures accompanied my loved ones. They were creatures with animal faces and wings, so they had to be angels. One of the angels looked familiar. It was Adrian! Or was it Adrian? This Adrian was much larger. Hovering over me with an expression of love was a very large ox.

The angelic army had my tormentors trapped. They didn't have a prayer. Fire and lightning came from every direction, and every one of them perished. When the judgment was over, I was lovingly ministered to by my spiritual cohorts and their angels. I had my cuts and bruises soothed, and my feelings calmed by the ox. I was nice again, and right beside me was my bone. Only this time, my bone wasn't bare. It was hidden within flesh. Not a small piece of meat either. My bone was fully covered.

Game Changer

I woke from my dreams when I smelled bacon cooking. I loved bacon! After taking care of a more immediate need, I hopped to the kitchen to indulge in one of my favorite meats. When I entered the room, I noticed that Mom was deep in thought. To get her attention, I greeted her. "Good morning. You have the place smelling divine."

Mom jumped like I'd hit her. "Gina! I didn't hear you come in!" "Evidently, you were staring into the frying pan like it was a magic cauldron," I joked.

Mom sighed and confessed, "I have a lot to think about. When I'm worried, I cook. It is a good thing you're here to eat."

Laying jokes aside, I asked, "Why are you worried? You looked happy enough last night. You and Dad seem to be getting along great."

"That's just it! I feel like a kid again, but Gina, it has been almost twelve years since your dad and I divorced. I'm not the same. I know I've complained about being lonely, but to be truthful, I love my independence. I have to work hard to keep my lifestyle, but I love what I do. I was just thinking about my transformation. It took getting divorced to make me stronger. I was a wimp when we were married. I depended on your father for everything. I also understood that I leaned on you too hard," she confided.

I knew it was time, to be honest. If things were going to change among all of us, honesty had to be foremost. I blurted, "Yes, you did! I felt smothered or judged. It drove me crazy."

Mom had tears in her eyes. I'd hurt her feelings, but she needed to know how I felt in order for things to really change. I declared, "From here out, my life and all involved will live by honest and uplifting means. We will stop holding grudges and start building a new relationship. Agreed?"

Mom nodded her head and said, "I promise. I don't want us ever to feel harsh with each other again."

After the declarations, she sat a plate in front of me full of good things. I had toast, eggs, bacon, and hash-browned potatoes. I looked at the food with gratitude and thought about something else I wanted to start doing. I asked Mom if she would put her fork down for a minute. I took her hand, then lowered my head and prayed, "Thank you, Lord, for what you are doing. Thank you again for this food. Bless us today. Amen!"

Mom looked at me shocked. I could tell she wanted to ask me a question. I decided to tell her what was going on with me. "Mom, I've accepted Jesus. I'm starting a new chapter in my life. I'll be living a better lifestyle from here on. The party scene is over. I'm about to become a churchgoer. Would you like to join me?" I encouraged her.

Excitedly, she chirped, "Sure! Where?"

"To be honest, I don't know where or even the name of the church. My first visit will be with Mamie. She promised to come after me in the morning, so I'll soon find out. I'd love for you to come," I said.

"That would be great. I really like Mamie. She will be a fun person to hang out with," Mom agreed.

With that settled, I began to eat. Mom ate breakfast differently than most people; she liked sandwiches. I watched her make a breakfast sandwich with the toast, eggs, and bacon like I'd seen her do hundreds of other times; but this time, seeing her make a sandwich jolted me. She was building something she liked. It was the same food I was eating; only she preferred it in a sandwich form. I pondered why I was fascinated. Then it came to me. *Build*! I was supposed to be building my man's characteristics from the Word.

Before Mom had even had the first bite of her sandwich, I screeched, "Mom! I need my Bibles and my notebook from the car!" My hunger for bacon was gone. I was starving for another kind of meat.

Mom was totally caught off guard. "Do you need them this instant?" she asked.

I'd just promised to live honestly. I'd just declared to have a better relationship with my mother, so I took a deep breath and tearfully shared, "Mom, my Bibles, and my notebook are my lifelines to a better life. At this very minute, I need them more than air."

~~~

Jesus was very proud of Gina. Love had changed the young woman. With her new commitment, Gina had put in motion a change without even trying. Angels were at work restoring Gina's relationship with her mother.

~~~

Mom pushed back from the table and took off running to her car. When she returned, she was panting from the exertion. Her eyes were bright with excitement, and when she deposited the books on the table beside me, she inquired, "Can you share with me? Is it something I need to know too?"

I had to stop and think for a moment before saying anything. I didn't want to share my secret, but Mom could also build herself a better life. I'd answer truthfully but vaguely in terms she could understand. "I heard that to have a better life, you need to find what you want from these scriptures. It's like desiring a specific cake. You find the recipe from the Bible, and you jot it down for future reference. You give the recipe to God and let Him make the cake," I explained.

"Okay then! Show me how while we finish eating breakfast," she begged.

To appease Mom, I slowly ate some of my breakfast as I showed her how to use the concordance in the back of my New American Standard Bible. Together, we thought of words then looked to see if the words were in the concordance. If we found a reference, we'd look at the scripture pertaining to the word. We were having loads of fun. It was like playing a game where we laughed and enjoyed the other's company very much.

One of the words we looked for was build, and the scripture that got our attention pertained to the builder. It clearly said if "God didn't build the house we labor in vain." It verified what I said to Mom earlier. We find the recipe, and he builds (or makes) the cake.

We had fun for a while until Mom's phobia over dirty dishes plagued her thoughts. I tried to convince her that the dishes weren't going anywhere, but she couldn't rest. She loved everything clean and tidy. Everything had to be in its proper place, or she'd freak out.

While Mom washed dishes, I focused on finding my own recipe. I flipped through the concordance searching without a clue, but the Lord knew. If He could build, He could direct me to the blueprints and supplies. He'd promised to guide me. I closed my eyes and asked, "Lord, will you give me a clue? Show me a word?"

Behind my eyelids, He showed me bones. There it was - my clue! I opened my eyes and flipped hurriedly through the concordance to find the word bones. I found many references, but only one caught my attention. The reference led me to the book of Ezekiel, chapter 37. I read the whole chapter.

It referred to bones coming alive. Suddenly I visualized myself in the book. I was the person walking upon the bones, the person the Lord was speaking with. God's command was directed at me. The words ordered me to speak to the bones. I was to tell them to hear, breathe, and receive flesh. My heart began to pound. I began to perceive that the scriptures were pertaining to the dream God gave me the night before. I was given a vision of my mate. I perceived my mate as being my bone. Would speaking to my bone give it flesh? Was this why I had these scriptures? Everything in my mind told me I had to do it quickly.

~~~

Ox set out to correct Gina's thinking. He would gently remind her to let the Lord build and stop her from thinking she had to do something, but the Holy Spirit stopped him. Ox turned to face the Lord after his rebuke but immediately relaxed when he saw the Holy Spirit smiling. Then the Holy Spirit directed, "Trust me, my friend. I know she thinks I'm telling her to speak into her future for a mate. Watch and see what she does."

~~~

I didn't have a bone, but I had my notes. I tore the page out my notebook and rolled it in my hand. To keep from appearing crazy in the kitchen speaking to the paper, I excused myself and hopped to the bathroom. I shut the door behind me and propped in front of the bathroom sink then looked into the mirror. I held up my hand, looked into my eyes, and spoke the words given to me from scripture. I stared at my face and spoke to the bone. When I finished, I sat on the toilet seat and cried.

~~~

Ox was still confused. His heart was breaking. Gina was distraught, and the Lord had not explained. Pleadingly, he required direction from the Lord. Bowing his head, he reverently submitted, resting in the higher purpose.

Compassionately, the Holy Spirit enlightened him. *"Gina unknowingly spoke to herself. She looked into her own eyes and declared my Words. Before she was born, we programmed a purpose within her. It wasn't her fault she never received training about me.*

Her parents never took her to church. She never felt the need to go. Circumstances of her life, combined with her lack of knowledge, caused the purpose we programmed to lie dormant. She just woke it up. She is the first of many. Others will follow her example."

Ox pondered over what he heard. He remembered how his counterpart in heaven, the cherub, faced angel of faith, how he felt and acted after Caylee lassoed him. Cherub moved freely in heaven working to bring Caylee a good life. They were tied together like horse and chariot. But Ox didn't feel the same as Cherub; it wasn't the same on earth. He felt different! Heavier! Then he realized what Gina had done. Her declaration had placed a heavy yoke on him. Gina didn't have a lasso; she owned a harvesting machine. She'd freed herself from the yoke of iron and stopped tugging and gave him the job. It was what he wanted all along. His power could bring Gina through difficulties. He was used to being the power before a plow. He'd assisted other humans through this before. He used to be like Cherub, free to work. Now he could. Only this time, he pulled a combine and not a plow.

The Holy Spirit laughed when He realized Ox almost understood. "Ox, my friend, your power has been energized by Gina's grit and determination. Together, the two of you have made for me a machine with teeth. Just another prophesy come to pass," He said.

Ox wanted to shout with glee. When he opened his mouth to bellow, he barked instead. Then he noticed his mouth was different. He had fangs. Sharp teeth! He had threshing teeth. He was like Gina's bulldog.

~~~

I gathered my wits and decided while I was in the restroom to take a sponge bath. What I would give to be able to sit in a tub of hot bubbling water soaking my stress away. I put the piece of paper in my robe pocket for safe keeping and went about the task. After washing, I hopped to my old room. Mom had brought clothes from my apartment and had them put away. I had things hung in the closet and in the dresser. I found a pair of new panties and adjusted them to me quickly. My bras and blouses weren't a problem. The only problem was that there weren't any skirts. I had one alternative: wear the one I had on yesterday. We could retrieve some more skirts from my place later.

I put the piece of paper in my bra so that it would be close to my heart. Then I finished dressing and applying makeup. I felt better. I felt strong. I felt like I had accomplished something God told me to do. I was sure the bones I cared about were coming together. All I had to do was wait. God was building the house.

Mom was studying the Bibles when I hopped back in the kitchen. She was diligently jotting down notes. Apparently, she was gathering ingredients. It was a beautiful sight. I wasn't about to suggest she stop for me. I could wait for clothes. I wanted her to keep focusing and continue to gather what she needed for God to build her life.

Creating the Agenda

Every Saturday, Hope followed a pattern: clean the house and do weekly shopping while communing with the Lord. It was a habit she held dearly. It was her special time alone with Jesus. She'd learned the hard way that if she didn't keep things balanced, her life could fall apart quickly. Saturday was their day; the rest of the week she allowed intercessory needs and other issues to keep her prayer life busy. Of course, she included Brent and Greg in her special time with Jesus. She treated them extra special on Saturdays, remembering who and what they represented in honor of Jesus. In Hope's mind, Brent was Jesus's brother, assigned as her mate and earthly companion, who represented the head of the Lord's body. Greg was her child, God's gift. The three of them were a single unit inside the family of God.

While Hope cleaned, she thanked the Lord and bragged on her family. It was when she was sharing how proud she was of Greg when the Lord stopped her midsentence. "Hope! Gina needs you," he commanded.

"Lord, it's Saturday, our day! I don't want to disappoint you ever again," she objected.

"Every day is our day. You formed the tradition when you worked for a living. Today I have a request. Armor up! I need you covered," He insisted!

Battle mode gripped Hope's heart. She laid the vacuum cleaner down and mentally suited up. "What is it, Lord! What is here?" Hope inquired.

Responding, the Lord said, *"Satan, or one of his hordes, is always around. I need you suited within me so our enemy cannot hear our conversation. When dressed for battle, Satan flees, but when you are dressed in your robes, he hovers around waiting and hoping you will slip up and let your guard down."*

Hope relaxed. There wasn't going to be a battle. The Holy Spirit wanted to give strategic orders. Now she was excited! This meant He was about to enlighten her on something wonderful. She took a deep breath and said, "I'm ready, Lord."

"I promised to inform you about Gina Grimes. As you are now aware, Gina has a special gift. You have also met her guardian, Ox.

She is bound to you in the spirit as part of my four characteristics. Gina has been the missing link of faith needed to create a harvesting machine in this area. She is in a sensitive spot. Until today, her faith lay dormant. Gina had it from birth, but it was never developed. When Caylee entered Gina's life, a seed of hope was planted, and things for Gina changed. Caylee's sweet disposition and kind heart convinced Gina she needed me, thereby creating her born-again spirit. That's when Satan tried to kill her."

"Mamie quickly laid hands on Gina when the EMTs brought her to the hospital, here again, giving me access to Gina where I placed her in a coma state. I needed a place where she could be influenced. That is why I sent Adrian to her in the first place. I knew she could not accept Ox. Adrian was assigned to show Gina her future and give her something to hope for. Unlike Caylee, Gina was given faith sight first. Caylee was given hearing faith first, and then she had to find what she wanted in my Word. Gina has a strong determination to mix with faith to fight. Caylee has the patience to wait. Both have yoked their angels," He said.

Hope interrupted the explanation. She was confused. Past experience prompted her to inquire when she didn't understand. She knew the Lord would be gracious and patient until she had knowledge. Eagerly she sought Him. "Lord, I don't understand about the two angels. I haven't seen one follow Caylee."

The Lord chuckled. *"Caylee's angel is in heaven. You won't see him. Caylee's faith causes her to inquire of me. Now her angel is gathering wisdom from what has already been created in heaven to give Caylee in the earthly realm. Now Gina has harnessed Ox with her heavy burden Gina's faith requires of me. Ox's job is to force Gina's requirements to manifest on earth. He trudges through Satan's worldly dominion and hordes, with me, to furnish any of Gina's needs. Gina has bound Ox to her with grit and determination. In order for Gina to require of me, she must hear what to believe She already knows what faith in her future looks like."*

"Both types of faith will always please the Father. It doesn't matter if faith is applied through inquiry or demand. Since Ox has been yoked, my harvesting machine is running idle. Gina must learn more about me in order to know what to require. I've directed your pastor to preach what she needs. With each sermon, Gina will hear the Word directive, clamp down on it, and grit her teeth. She needs

to understand spiritual living. That is where your testimony will come into play. Use every one of your testimonies to encourage this girl's faith. Share your visions with her. Tell her about your manifestations, but allow the pastor's message to direct you when and what to share. Keep Gina under your wing," He responded.

"Does Satan know about this?" Hope asked.

"Not the whole story. That is why I had you suit up. The reason I have two people moving through Faith is because I'm purposefully confusing my enemy. Satan knows Caylee is mine. He met dire opposition the other night when he came against her. He suspects that Gina is valuable, but he doesn't know how much. He is focused on trying to destroy her and her hope at every turn. But if Satan finds out what Gina's gift is, he will try to use it to destroy my plan instead of destroying her. He fought against Gina's will last night, so he is angry. Be watchful, nurture and help develop Gina's soul strength. She has the mind, will, and emotions of a feisty bulldog."

"It's time to enlighten Justice. Bring Brent here with me so we can tell him how to be watchful for Gina. He and Justice must be continually given spiritual insight. Brent must keep track of Lyle Horne. Satan uses that man. He may use him again to come after Gina's integrity. Mamie has already been directed to watch over Gina's spiritual and physical well-being," He finished.

Hope quickly put away the vacuum so she could locate Brent. She was ordered to keep him in the loop. When she found him, he and Greg were cuddled in front of the television watching cartoons on the family-room sofa. She loved her gentle giant. He was a perfect representation of her Lord. She wanted to gaze at the beautiful sight of father and son, but she knew the Lord's mission was more important.

"Brent! May I speak with you?" Hope inquired.

When Brent looked up to inquire, he saw that Hope was shining. If Hope radiated light, it meant that she was fully engaged within the spirit realm. Questions would be answered in private, so he quickly rose from the sofa and went to his wife.

"Come with me," Hope beckoned.

Directing her next words toward her son, Hope cooed, "Greg, honey! Mama and Daddy will be back. Watch your programs, okay."

Alone in their bedroom, Hope took Brent's face in her hands. Brent knew instantly Hope wanted to share something spiritual.

She'd shared her gift with him once before on their honeymoon night where traces of her gift still lingered with him. Bracing himself, he leaned into Hope's touch and waited.

Same as before, Brent's sight and hearing increased supernaturally. But this time, something was constricting. "Hope? What's going on?" he asked.

Hope responded by saying, "I've brought you into one of my secret places. You are inside the Lord's armor with us where Satan can't hear our conversation."

Brent looked around inside the tight space for another person, but it was only he and Hope. Then he noticed that they were naked and stuck together. Nothing, not even air, could come between them. When the Lord spoke, Brent realized that the two of them were with the Lord as one unit. They were there, each as one and together as one, to receive their agenda from the Lord, allowing Him to direct their steps.

As they exited the armor after their meeting, Brent and Hope snickered. Both had the same thought: *communing with Jesus together was better than sex.* Both felt giddy, relaxed, and fully energized, not physically drained.

Hope broke the mood by declaring she had to find Gina. Asking Brent to babysit Greg, Hope set about to find Caylee's phone number.

Hope knew just how to include Caylee in the agenda. She would make it seem like she and Caylee were involved in a planned covert operation for the Lord. She would convince Caylee they had to protect Gina.

When Hope had Caylee on the phone, she told her about the covert plan. Then she clued her in by suggesting they be responsible for getting Gina to and from work and to doctor appointments during the week. Then Hope continued the conversation by telling Caylee she planned to include Mamie in their scheme. Someone had to help get Gina to church. Between the three of them, Gina would be corralled, hemmed in, and protected from past relationships. Their mission was to bring Gina into the sheepfold of Christ, keep her from being lured back into her former traditions.

Caylee loved the secret plan, and she was in full agreement. She wanted to get started. "Hope? Can we visit Gina today?" she asked.

Hope planned to call Gina before the afternoon and wondered why Caylee wanted to visit. *Had the Lord prompted her?* Curiously, she inquired, "Why?"

Caylee excitedly shared, "Gina's Mom gets on her nerves. She may need a distraction from a bad influence at home. I tried to encourage her last night after group, but she was depressed. I told Gina about Russ, hoping my good news would give her strength. It didn't. I'm worried she may be having problems at home."

Remembering for a moment Caylee's issues with men, the mother hen in Hope started asking Caylee to enlighten her about Russ when the Holy Spirit said, "Stop! Don't pry. She will share in time. Caylee is not the same young woman. She took Brent's advice to wait patiently."

"Caylee, please call Gina and ask if she would like company today. If she does want our company, call me back." Hope consented not to let Caylee know, but she had full intention of barging in on Gina regardless of approval.

Hope reminisced while she waited for Caylee to call her back. She remembered the early days when she was in training. After her divorce from Sam, she had loving parents and friends to encourage her along, followed by the Holy Spirit. But even with all their help and encouragement, she had been depressed and afraid, on top of being lonely. Hope knew firsthand the Lord was in Gina, but she wondered why she was still depressed. Gina must have deeper issues. She sympathized and hurt for this girl.

Two Mothers

Instead of waiting any longer for Caylee's call, Hope started changing clothes. Even if Gina didn't want company, she had to go into town anyway. Why not get ready?

In the process of dressing, Hope had a few questions she needed to be answered. Armoring up mentally again, she asked, "Lord, it just occurred to me that you said you wanted me to take Gina under my wing. Do you mean like a mother or just as a friend?"

Laughing, the Lord replied, *"Motherly, of course! You are good at it. Remember how you helped Amber?"*

"Yeah, but Amber wasn't gifted. Amber was foolish and misguided. Gina has been chosen for a specific purpose. I'm going to need help," Hope conveyed.

"Go to the Father," the Lord directed.

Hope was sitting on the edge of her bed, bent over, tying her running shoes when she heard the directive. The suggestion caused her to gasp and sit up straight. She had never gone to the Father. Not on purpose—alone.

"I always come to you. I rely on you for everything. Doesn't the Father know we talk?" Hope inquired.

"Abba knows we talk. He appreciates the fact we are close. But sometimes, when issues are too great for you, you must seek Him as your Father, He is not just mine. We are spiritually married. You are his child as much as I am. Didn't He prove His love for you when you needed help the most? He personally defeated your natural enemy," the Lord reminded.

"How do I go about this?" Hope asked.

"That, I can answer! Put on the crown and royal robes He gave you. It pleases Him immensely when you know who you are. Then boldly go to the throne of grace and obtain," He instructed.

Hope flashed back to that horrible yet amazing day when the Father came down personally from heaven and helped her. She remembered fearing for her life and asking Jesus for His armor when He directed her to remember 'the name.' Instantly she had mentally dressed in robes and crown. With no warning, as to what would happen, Hope watched God come down from heaven Himself and end Sam's life quickly and without mercy. Yes! She could honestly say, "Abba loves her!"

With a surge of love, Hope no longer feared her Abba. She wanted to talk with Him. Mentally she changed from wearing mental armor to donning her gold-woven gown and slippers, red-velvet robe, and heavily jeweled crown. Then she entered her bedroom closet and bolted the door from inside. The large closet was specifically designed for her intercessory prayer time alone with Jesus. Brent had installed a lock on the inside to keep everyone out, even himself when she needed privacy. Also inside the room was a lovely handcrafted chair fit for a queen. When Hope sat on it, she was all Jesus's. This time, she would sit at the feet of her Father on the floor, in front of the lovely chair, and humbly ask for help.

Taking a deep breath, Hope then visualized herself walking the long aisle toward the throne. Then suddenly, she was there actually making the journey. The realm of heaven opened to her, and she was granted entrance. The long aisle was lined on both sides with angels bowed reverently. She wanted to object but mentally had to correct her thinking. After all, she was the bride of Christ and must remain in that mindset in God's presence.

At the foot of the platform, Hope bowed her head and stopped to curtsy before her address. "Hello, Father. May I come forward?"

Suddenly the air smelled of freshly baked goods, all kinds of scents. There were aromas of roasted meat, savory vegetables, sweet, ripe fruit, pies, and cakes. I smiled at the lovely gesture. My Father had prepared a table just for me.

"Come eat beside me, my daughter, and tell me what is on your mind. I'm always happy to see you," He beckoned.

Confidently, Hope accepted. "Thank you, Father. I've come to you for advice. Jesus has asked me to mother Gina Grimes, and I'm not sure what is expected of me. Would You be so kind to give me suggestions?"

"Do what comes naturally for you. Why is this so hard? I'll be there to back you," He encouraged.

"I was concerned Gina may need special guidance," Hope confessed.

"No more than Greg. Do you remember some of his first statements to you?" God asked.

Hope thought hard trying to grasp old memories. It had been a while, and all she could remember was why she went to the Boys' Home. She went to mother the little ones. But she couldn't remember Greg's words.

Seeing her struggle, God said, *"He said you looked like his mother."*

God's statement brought memories flooding back. She thought her little guy was delusional. Hope thought Greg's comments were from his being traumatized, not because his mother had looked like her.

"Yes! I remember him saying that. I thought he was suffering. He was so sweet, and it made me want to know what his mother looked like. I was shocked when I saw the woman's picture. She was a drug addict who didn't resemble me at all," Hope said.

"Greg wasn't delusional, Hope. To ease his conscience, I gave him a vision of his true mother. That is why he treated you special. He knew who you were, he just didn't know how to tell anyone," God explained.

Hope was stunned. Her baby knew about their relationship even before she did. Tears welled in her eyes. God loved her family before it was even created. With a choked voice, Hope said, "Thank you, Father. I love you so much!"

Rising to leave, Hope knew what to do. Gina was to be her spiritually adopted daughter. On the way back to reality, Hope heard a roar. The sound came from within her spirit. Then she remembered Justice, the part of Brent that he shared with her on their honeymoon. Her lioness nature was now awakened, and it was powerful. She was a new lioness, one with a newborn cub. Now Hope knew how Brent felt. Hope knew why Brent always radiated with a protective air and why he acted like he was always thirsty for justice. Hope wanted justice, but not for herself. Hope wanted her cub to have what was rightfully hers, a father.

Hope unbolted the closet door and entered her empty bedroom. She wondered how long she had been away and worried that Caylee may have tried to reach her. The bedside clock read 11:30 a.m., so she hadn't been gone long. She'd entered the closet at 11:00 a.m. fully dressed and ready to go, Hope entered the living room to be greeted by her son. Greg had her cell phone in hand. Seeing the little guy caused her to tear up again. Grabbing Greg in a hard embrace,

Hope whispered to him, "I love you, baby. You're my gift from heaven."

"I love you too, Mama. Your cell phone buzzed a few minutes ago, I wanted to take it to you, but Daddy wouldn't let me in your closet." He beamed.

"Thanks, sweetie!" Hope responded.

It had been Caylee. She had left a text after being unable to speak with Hope on the phone. The text read, "Gina is excited we want to visit. She wants us to come around 1:30 p.m. If you are game for lunch, I'll pick you up at noon. If not, call."

Hope quickly called Caylee. When she answered, Hope replied, "I'd love lunch! I have a ravenous appetite. I'll see you in a few minutes."

While Hope waited for her ride, she loved her family, and it gave her an opportunity to share with Brent what had occurred during her time in the closet. When she finished, Brent laughed out loud then he said, "Now you know why I'm hungry all the time. A justice-driven nature makes a lion crazy for meat. Also, could it be that your belly may be reacting because you denied it food? I bet you didn't eat what was laid before you at the Lord's table."

"No, I didn't eat. I was on a mission," Hope said.

During lunch, Hope studied Caylee. The young girl was truly a delight. She didn't have to spiritually adopt her. According to Caylee, Mamie had already beat Hope to it. But the girl needed a friend, and Hope was there for that. During the short lunch, Caylee couldn't stop talking about Russ; she didn't leave any details of their relationship hidden. Caylee even shared with Hope how she inquired of the Father. She had thrown out a fleece request and had it answered. The story was lovely. That was when Hope realized it had been a good thing the Lord stopped her from reprimanding earlier. Hope wasn't ready to accept things on Caylee's level. She needed her own experiences with the Father to help her appreciate the sentiment. Otherwise, she may have been harsh and reprimanding. Hope was still learning how to be a guide. She had good intentions because she wanted the best for her young-adult members. Caylee's situation would remind her to step back and listen more with spiritual understanding. Hope needed to use the hearing gift as much as her supernatural sight. From listening intently, she knew Caylee was on target. She wouldn't have to worry any longer about Caylee being too exuberant. Russ was Caylee's gift from God.

As Caylee drove, Hope quietly prayed in the spirit. But mentally she stayed robed in authority instead of the armor, refusing to let her guard down and bracing herself for a possible confrontation. Who knew what Satan planned? What would she and Caylee face? Was Satan in control of Mrs. Grimes? Were they about to face a lunatic, bound by a vicious master? Even if Satan didn't have control, what kind of mother did Gina have? Would the woman be welcoming? Was the woman willing to let Christians invade her home? The woman was certainly not a churchgoer. Not in God's armor, Hope continued to reason, allowing her mind to remember what Satan could do to a person. Would she have to fight? After all, she had been appointed to be Gina's motherly influence, who or what could come against heaven's order. If she must fight, then she was ready. Carl had taught her well. She had nothing to fear.

The Lord sighed; He could see that Hope was still bound in fear. Even with all her evidence of love, she continued to remember her past torment and judge everything from that standpoint. He had to wake her up, make her realize she had a problem, gently touch her heart and make her see before the problem grew.

~~~

Satan followed at a distance; he knew better than to approach someone dressed in royal garb. He knew that anyone dressed that way was under God's protection. But he couldn't help wonder what Hope was up to. He kept thinking, *why would his archenemy be dressed so fine if she weren't trying to hide something?*

He knew something was developing, and it concerned the two young women he'd come against recently. Both women were heavily protected. Why? He needed a small opening, a crack in the atmosphere where he could hear without being detected. Suddenly, he had a clue: he could converse with his old friend, the giant called Rejection, also known as Low Self-Esteem, who hovered over the Grimes's home. Satan planned to use the visitation to stir up emotion. Rejection could inflict panic on the older Grimes woman. Maybe through her fear, Rejection, or his demonic horde of imps, could possibly learn of Jesus's plan before they began feasting off her raw emotions. He knew there would be severe casualties, but he didn't care. He needed information if it meant sacrificing thousands of imps and possibly one giant, but better them than himself.

Skirmish

Ox knew the moment he arrived with Gina inside her mother's kitchen that Rejection was near. The evil giant always made himself known. He loved to torture people, making them feel useless and worthless. Ox hated the oversized egotistical beast, but unless he personally touched Gina, he had to tolerate Rejection's company.

After Caylee's call, Ox knew Rejection had Mrs. Grimes in a tizzy. She muttered to herself as she frantically dusted, swept, and mopped. Then once the house was clean, she started baking cookies. When the house suddenly began to stink, Ox realized how bad Mrs. Grimes's emotions were. She had unknowingly summoned thousands of slimy, negative-emotion-eating demons. The life-sucking demons were everywhere. Every room was full of them. (They were worse than flies; at least people could see flies) Ox spread his wings then wrapped Gina inside them. Gina was his priority; at least within his wings, she was protected. But Mrs. Grimes was vulnerable, and Ox worried she would be mentally tormented. Not able to bellow for help any longer, he barked, hoping other comrades would come and assist.

~~~

Mom's demeanor changed drastically when I informed her that my friends from church were about to visit. It appeared as if she'd lost confidence. She started dusting, then began to sweep while constantly complaining, "I can't believe you invited church folks to the house! I'm so embarrassed! This place is a mess!"

Mom always kept the house immaculately. I didn't understand what the fuss was about. After she mopped the kitchen and bathroom, she went about making cookies. Mom was a whirling dervish; she couldn't relax.

I didn't know what to say. Now I felt bad about inviting my friends. I felt lousy because I couldn't help her clean. I tried to soothe her by saying, "Mom, it's just Caylee and a friend of hers. What's the problem?"

Mom broke and started crying. Then she sat with me on the sofa and started wringing her hands before she confessed, "I don't know what my problem is! I'm nervous and scared! I'd want to make a good impression. I don't want to give anyone a reason to talk. Don't church folks judge you by how clean you are? Don't they believe that cleanliness is next to godliness? If I'm going to start going to church with you, I don't want them to say we live in a nasty house."

I sighed. "I think you are mistaken. I don't think this church is that strict," I said soothingly.

"I don't care! I'm still concerned about appearances," Mom exclaimed.

Then she ran to her room where I heard dresser drawers being opened and shut and things being banged around. "What are you doing?" I yelled.

"Trying to find something to wear that doesn't need ironing," she replied.

There wasn't anything I could say or do to ease Mom's self-inflicted torment, so I turned on the television and waited.

~~~

When Loshan and Navar appeared and started terminating imps, Ox relaxed; their presence meant Caylee was near. Before the doorbell rang, God ordered Insight to step into the room first because Hope was operating in fear. Ox thought Insight entered to signify Hope's presence. It wasn't until Mrs. Grimes opened the door that Ox realized why Insight acted so formal; Hope was in royal attire. Her attire meant God's spirit was with her, so Ox instantly bowed his head in reverence.

~~~

Hope smelled the stench before the front door of the Grimes's home opened; she knew creepy imps were inside. Steadying herself for a spiritual confrontation, she swallowed hard and tensed for a fight. When Pam Grimes opened her front door, Hope didn't just see imps, she was face to face with a giant. The ugly tormentor was in control of Gina's Mom, and he bore through Hope with eyes filled with hatred. Mrs. Grimes's eyes were blank and dark, signifying demonic control, but at least she acted sanely. Hope calmed when Mrs. Grimes's words were sweet and inviting. There wouldn't be a fight, and Hope felt shame for even entertaining the thought.

~~~

At first, Rejection felt in control. He thought he could frighten the woman who had the powerful escort. But when Rejection realized God's spirit had entered with her and witnessed his dirty work, he freaked. He immediately knew Satan had victimized him. He tried to repair the damage by giving back Pam's mind before escaping in hopes his life would be spared, but it was too late. Rejection's life ended when God blinked. His body burst into flames.

Meanwhile, Loshan and Navar continued to swat and mash imps without worrying what they were up to; these were mindless creatures with only one purpose. Little did they know some stronger imps had another agenda. These were bound by strict orders not to feed until they gathered knowledge, so they hid under the carpet, in drapes, and beneath chairs where they could listen.

~~~

When Caylee and Hope entered our house, it felt like I was greeting family. The love I had for them was as strong as my love for Mom. When Hope came to me, I was compelled to stand so we could hug. When we touched, something within me changed. I threw my arms around her and held on as if my life depended on her strength. I no longer worried whether I was accepted, and I no longer feared. I lost every ounce of trepidation. I trusted this woman with my heart. Hope was special to me. I didn't even trust my own mother with my heart.

~~~

While the women embraced, Insight and Ox enjoyed the hug. It gave them an opportunity to connect with each other. They reveled in knowing that the fledgling was experiencing power from the energy exchanged. It also allowed Insight the opportunity to enlighten Ox on Hope's and Gina's new spiritual relationship.

~~~

Hope whispered to Gina, "You have become my daughter in Christ. If there is anything I can help you with, I'm here."

Before breaking their embrace, Hope thought she saw something. Panic rose in her again so she enhanced her vision. When fully engaged, she spotted a creepy imp hiding under a chair, drooling. The thing wasn't hovering; it was hiding, intent on mischief. Aware she needed to be discreet, Hope selected that particular chair to sit on. But before she sat, she stomped her foot and patted the side of the chair, hoping it would notify the angels that a demon was hiding. Fearful that more skirmishes were about to take place, Hope focused on her friends. She wasn't there to rant and rave at imps; she was there to love and help a spiritual daughter.

Hope's actions did alert Loshan that an imp was hiding. When he dispatched it, they looked for other hiders. He and Navar searched behind and under everything; they even patted down the carpet. When they finished, the air became clean and smelled of pine, the way Mrs. Grimes wanted it to smell.

Hope witnessed the giant's death and immediately noticed the change in Pam Grimes. The woman had a sweet demeanor and loved entertaining. Again, Hope chided herself for thinking the lady would be evil and hurtful. Compassion for her gave Hope the energy she needed to befriend the woman, instead of pushing her out of fellowship as she had intended.

After Mom retrieved the warm cookies and drinks, I noticed she wasn't frantic any longer. She was relaxed and appeared to be enjoying the company. To my joy, she and Hope were becoming fast friends. I was very excited. Mom seemed very interested in the church and the church's outreaches. When Hope invited her to attend the next service, my heart leaped for joy. It confirmed to me my prayers were being answered. My parents would be drawn into Christianity with me.

When Caylee asked me what I had to wear in front of Mom and Hope, it dawned on me I didn't have clothes for church at Mom's house, and I couldn't see wearing my new skirt for the third day. I knew Mom heard, and if I didn't say something, Mom would feel obligated to retrieve the rest of my things. I studied her before I spoke: she looked pale and tired from her self-induced stress this morning. To keep from hurting her feelings, I had no alternative but to reverse psychology. I focused my comments on her appearance letting her know I respected her health in order for her to relinquish my issue. I began by saying, "Mom, I need clothes to wear to church. You look tired. Wouldn't you rather Caylee and Hope take me to my apartment so you can rest a while?"

Mom looked as if a heavy weight was lifted off her shoulders. I could see my plan worked. She relaxed then looked in Hope's direction before asking, "Would you mind? I could definitely use a few minutes."

Hope took the bait graciously. "Caylee and I would love this opportunity to take care of Gina. We've been planning to help her get mobile anyway. We can call this our pilot run," Hope chirped. I hopped to my room, slipped on a shoe, and gathered my handbag and crutches. Like Hope said, this was how things were going to be, so I'd better get used to the challenges. I couldn't stay stagnate, pinned-up, in Mom's house. I had places to go and a man to find.

I was expecting to ride in a car and was flabbergasted to see an extended cab truck parked outside. Then I remembered Caylee was driving her Dad's truck after her accident. The truck was high off the ground. How was I going to get inside? I watched Caylee place a blanket on the backseat before I even approached. I thought it was because the seat was dirty. Both women braced me as I supported myself on the crutches. I placed my good foot on the truck's runner, and they both hoisted me upward. Slowly I turned, being ever mindful how small the runner was. When I felt secure enough holding onto the door frame, I slowly sat on the blanket. Once I sat, Caylee told me to wait and not to move. I didn't have a clue why until she ran to the other side of the truck, opened the door, grabbed the blanket, and pulled me in. The chick was smart! Her trick kept me from having to wrestle with my skirt. That was when it occurred to me they truly meant what they said earlier. They came prepared to get me mobile. My needs had already been figured out. These women were amazing!

~~~

During the drive to Gina's apartment, Hope stared out the window. She tried to listen to the two women chatter about work and other nonsense, but when she realized she wasn't interested in their conversation, she allowed her mind to drift. She had an important issue she needed to deal with, a problem. She was still living in fear. Even with the Lord by her side, she had experienced panic in the house and tensed her muscles to fight. She had to take this issue to the Lord and not let a crumb of fear linger. If the thought of small skirmishes frightened her, how would she handle an actual battle? Her body was strong, and she could fight, but God wanted her to live in joy, not fear and anger. She wasn't drawing from His love correctly.

It dawned on Hope she may still be suffering from the effects of her kidnapping and torture. Grief grabbed her heart. Disappointment in herself made her very ashamed, but Hope knew she had to deal with it quickly and allow external help. Addressing the Father, as well as her Lord, Hope humbly confessed, "I know the two of You witnessed the same thing I did. I am sinning. I'm not resting in how much You love me. I've allowed myself to live in fear. Please forgive me. I'm so tired of worrying. I know it isn't Your will for me to be like this. I want to use my gifts to help people, not fight and look for evil all the time. May I please be released from this so I can rest in Your love and enjoy my assignment?"

"We've been waiting for you to realize and deal with this! We never expected you to fight for yourself. You just need to stand in the strength of who you are. It is not a sin to be strong. Your strength can be used to help others. You may find rest in my love! Your angel now carries your burden, so watch him work," the Lord instructed soothingly.

~~~

To follow Hope and Gina, Insight, and Ox both rode on top of the truck. Both were present when they heard Jesus speak to Hope. A split second after the Lord's order, Insight's eyes bulged, and he squawked loudly. Something heavy had been placed around his neck. Ox knew what happened. He couldn't help but grin when he heard Insight squawk. Then he remarked, "Feels good, doesn't it? Our time has finally come!"

The joy Insight felt was amazing! He had to fly. Standing on the hood of the truck, he released his wings to their full expansion and narrowed his eyes before taking flight to search for demons. His fast was over; he was finally going to feed. He could kill and eat whatever evil he found. God had given him permission. Now nothing could stop him!

As Insight flew, he grabbed the imps who had followed with both of his talons, killing and eating them quickly. The substance gave his body strength. When he arrived at Gina's apartment, he was fully energized and twice his former size. Then he had the pleasure of showing Hope that he could deal with any giant. What would usually be a harsh battle was just a small skirmish. Insight's newly acquired strength allowed him to rip a giant's head off without issues. When finished, he reveled in the knowledge that he no longer had to wait for Hope to be attacked. He could go before her and clear the way instead of following from behind. Any spiritual bloodbath from this day on would be from him. He anticipated the fight; battles meant more food.

Hope purposely allowed her spiritual sight to enhance. Seeing evidence of her angel work would be how she could heal. Jesus told her to watch and rely on the angel's works. Now, her eagle-faced angel just flew around the truck, and he was flying almost too fast for her to see. But what Hope saw each time he passed by her window was that his body mass had grown. When Caylee parked the truck at Gina's apartment, Hope spotted a giant immediately. It was huge and powerful, and he was one of Satan's most useful. Refusing to react to fear, Hope searched for the eagle like Jesus recommended. Then quicker than lightning, Insight was on top of the giant, and with one twist of his wrist, Insight had the giant's head in his talon, severed from the body. Squawking loudly, Insight threw the head away, honored the Lord, and then bowed in Hope's direction.

~~~

Satan was furious! Over and over his plans failed. Now he had to recruit two more giants to replace Rejection and Dread. Plus, he had to be mindful now that God had released a hunter, one who was faster than lightning and could see and hear anything that moved in the spirit realm.

Out with the Old

Caylee and I had talked nonstop the whole ride to my apartment. When we arrived, I had a deep sense of dread engulf me. What could be the matter? Then I heard my Whisperer.

"I sense your anxiety. Relax, Gina, and enjoy your family. Let them show you a good time," He said gently.

I immediately relaxed. The fire was with me.

Caylee opened the passenger door and motioned for me to be still. "Don't move, Gina. Let Hope and I pull you out with the blanket. Just be mindful to keep your bad foot and leg clear of obstacles," she instructed.

Hope joined her, and they both tugged at the blanket until my bottom reached the end of the seat. After standing on the running board with my good foot, they held on to me while I jumped to the ground. The team effort was great; now I wasn't afraid.

When we entered my apartment, I apologized for the mess. I hadn't cleaned the week before the accident. Sundays were usually my downtime days, so I shopped for groceries, washed clothes, and cleaned the apartment. Then I remembered the old motto Angie and I had: "Flaunt it when you can and clean it when you can't flaunt." Things have really changed in a week. I have no desire to flaunt at all.

Remembering Angie made me sad. She hadn't called or anything since the day she saw me reading God's Word. It made me curious to know why. I wondered if maybe Caylee or Hope could enlighten me.

"Hope, I have a question. If someone who didn't believe in the Bible saw you reading it, does it usually change their opinion of you?" I inquired.

"Sometimes," she replied. "Why?" I asked.

Hope sighed. "Oil and water don't mix. Darkness can't remain in light. There are many examples, but the truth is, when ideals and morals change, judgment starts, and arguments sometimes arise. Has this happened to you?"

"I think it may have. My best friend and running buddy came to visit me in the hospital while I was reading the Bible. She reacted as if my reading offended her, and I haven't heard from her since," I shared.

Hope asked, "Do you still want a friendship with her?"

The question caused me to pause and think. I didn't know how to answer. I hadn't thought of Angie either. It wasn't until I came to the apartment and remembered our motto that she even came to mind. Honestly, I hadn't missed her at all. But I felt remorse. Sort of like when someone you knew died.

"I don't want our old friendship to continue," I stated. "Explain," Hope said.

I led them to my bedroom so we could pack my clothes. While there, I began to explain how Angie and I became friends. While I was talking, it occurred to me Angie and I weren't truly friends; we used each other. There wasn't a sisterly bond at all. When I finished speaking, Hope said, "Pray for her. One day she'll come around and be a good friend. Just be patient."

Afterward, I thought about the statement. Angie would be hard to change, but I'd pray for her salvation. In the meantime, I was happy I had these people in my life. Caylee was a lovely woman who doted on me and wanted to be my friend, and Hope was more motherly than a friend. I needed them both and wanted them around. Angie was quickly becoming a faded memory.

Hope changed the subject and walked over to my media center. Then she asked, "What kind of music do you have? Let's rock while we work."

I couldn't believe my ears. Hope wanted to dance; she wasn't frumpy and stiff as I assumed she'd be.

As we listened to music, Caylee and Hope searched through my closet. I could tell by their expressions that my clothes were inappropriate. Now I know why Mom retrieved my work pantsuits and jeans because every dress I owned was too sexy. Even my skirts were short and most blouses too revealing. It made me wonder who I was, really. Evidence pointed out I was definitely a tease. Super flirt! Man-eater! I was mortified.

I didn't know what to say. I bit my lower lip in anguish, silently hoping they would find something I could wear while worrying what they thought of me.

Hope realized Gina was struggling. Gina's eyes were filled with tears, and her lower lip swollen from her chewing. She knew what she had to do. Jesus had directed she use every testimony she had to encourage the girl. Hope wouldn't have to wait on Pastor Reed's message as a guide today.

Hope sat on the bed beside Gina and motioned for Caylee to have a seat. She then proceeded to dredge up memories. "Girls, it is time I came clean. Not too long ago, I loved to go to nightclubs. I liked to flirt and entice men. I found my second husband in a nightclub."

I couldn't help myself, I had to ask. Hope just released a bomb, and it floored me. I had to know. "You've been married three times?" I blurted out.

My enthusiasm and frankness caused Hope to burst out laughing. When she composed herself, she answered, "Yeah. That's what I'm trying to tell you two. I wasn't always like I am now. My first two marriages failed because I relied on self-effort. I thought I had to promote how I looked, set a trap for the eye. I didn't have problems meeting men. I had problems afterward."

"How did you find Brent?" Caylee asked. "I'm getting to that," Hope responded.

Hope started over. "I was raised in a Christian family. We went to church every Wednesday and Sunday, so I had a good foundation. I met my first husband at college. I baited him with sexy attire and flirtatious moves because that was how my friends met guys. After we married, I changed. Due to my wholesome upbringing, I turned into a homemaker. I wanted a family, but that wasn't what he craved. He liked sexy women who loved to party, and one day, I found him with someone else. That led to our divorce.

"Because I was lonely, I started hanging out with people who liked the nightclubs. Again, I thought I had to present an appealing package, or I wouldn't get attention. I got attention all right. I met my second husband, who was an alcoholic and accused me at every turn of having an affair. Jealousy caused him to go insane. One thing led to another, and we had to divorce.

"My parents and my best friends encouraged me after that to return to church. It saved my life. At first, I was apprehensive. I felt judged for my actions. Then I found peace from the Holy Spirit. He led me to Brent. At first, I resisted. I didn't want to have a relationship again. Brent persisted until Jesus intervened. My Lord opened my eyes. He showed me Brent was his representative specifically designed just for me. I submitted. Mind you, I liked

Brent from the first day we met, but all I wanted was a friend. Jesus had to show me that my friendship with Brent had grown into love. I grabbed hold of Brent with both hands. I can be myself. I can do what I like. We are buddies and lovers.

I guess what I'm trying to say is don't put me on a pedestal. I'm like you, just a little older. Gina, if I hadn't found sexy and revealing clothes, I would have been more surprised. Don't feel ashamed."

Caylee chirped, "I wasn't all sweet and nice either. Hope can vouch for that."

I loved these women. I looked forward to our friendship growing. They made me feel accepted and weren't judgmental. But I still had an issue. I didn't have clothes I could wear to church.

I remarked, "I feel better now. I knew you weren't approving of my clothes. I guess we need to go shopping for a few pieces, and I mean few! Money is tight."

"No problem!" Hope exclaimed. "We are going to my house."
"Why?" I asked.

Hope said, "I have bags of clothes you may be interested in. I'd planned to give them to charity but hadn't gotten to it yet. You are welcomed to all of it."

"But you are smaller than I am," I replied.

"Trust me, they will fit. I haven't always been as fit as I am today," Hope confessed.

I looked at the pile of clothes laid across my bed. Clothes I never wanted to see again. My nightclubbing was over. "What can we do with these?" I asked, pointing at the mess.

Caylee offered, "I'll bag them, and we'll dump them off at one of the charity sites."

While I watched my old things being bagged, I thought again of Angie. Was I throwing our friendship away as well? I hoped not. She needed to know what true friendship was.

I prayed softly. "Lord, help Angie find you. Send someone she will listen to like you did for me. Amen."

Prepped

As we rode to the Arnold house, I sat quietly in the backseat and listened as Caylee drilled Hope for details. Caylee had the poor woman under a microscope, hungry for every juicy detail of her romance with Brent. I can't say their conversation was boring; in fact, it was interesting. I learned a valuable bit of information in the process. Hope played hard to get. From her explanation, I didn't think she intended to play at all. She wanted to be friends with Brent, but the fact that she resisted caused Brent to pursue her relentlessly. It had to be very flattering.

After all my conquests, I felt cheap. Now I know why. I gave away part of myself for a little male attention. But now my man would be someone like Brent, as my Whisperer promised. It seemed men like a love mystery and would be put off by a woman willing to give herself away freely. I learned through listening to these two ladies that Hope wasn't seductive; she stayed demure and chaste. That was how I wanted to be. I was through being pretentious.

I remembered wanting to be free from pretention the night of my accident. If I had listened to my heart and stayed home, things would be very different. I shuddered from a realization that I remembered questioning Adrian about why God allowed my accident. I also remembered how he acted. He was horrified that I had questioned God. Now I see why. If I hadn't been in the accident, I wouldn't have these wonderful people in my life. Nor would I have a lovely picture in my mind pertaining to my future. The Lord truly turned something horrible into a wonderful thing, and He did it just for me. He loved me before I even desired to know Him. This knowledge overwhelmed me, and I wanted to cry. I probably would be a sobbing fool, but arriving at Hope's changed my focus.

When Caylee opened the door, I prepared myself again for the blanket slide and hop out of the truck. This time was easier. When I landed on the ground, I yelled out, "Thank you, Lord!" I screamed out for more than one reason. I hope He knew what I meant. The holler was my way of acknowledging Him and being appreciative of my blessings. I now had friends who were like family. I had provisions offered freely. I was happy.

The Arnold house was lovely. It was every girl's dream. It caused me to pause and wonder, *Would I have a place like this too*? What would my man's occupation be? Brent was an attorney, so, of course, he had money. This was something I had to talk to Whisperer about. I immediately chided myself; I had to stop thinking of my Lord as the Whisperer. He was the Almighty.

"Why?" He asked. *"I like my nickname. It's sweet, and it lets me know I don't have to yell at you."*

I almost jumped out of my skin when I heard His voice. I didn't want to appear crazy by responding out loud, so I talked with Him mentally. *You scared me! Again! I'm not used to you being around and responding to my thoughts. Did you hear me earlier? Thanks for everything. I can't wait to get home so we can talk.*

"Looking forward to it and you are welcome," He replied, snickering.

Caylee and I followed Hope through the laundry room into the kitchen. The interior of her house was also fabulous. When we approached her dining table, she motioned for us to have a seat and then she called out to Brent. When he entered, I almost gasped. I knew he was a big man when he visited me at the hospital and nothing struck me as enticing but dressed in cut-off jeans and no shirt, the man resembled a bodybuilder. He was powerful-looking. Unwillingly, my eyes indulged. He was a beauty to behold. How did Hope remain chaste before marriage? She had to be superwoman. I see now why Caylee was enthralled and was hungry for details.

Silently, I prayed. *Lord, help! He isn't mine, and I don't want him. Keep me from making a fool of myself.*

"Don't worry! Brent will make it easier for you," He said.

As promised, when Brent realized they had company, he politely excused himself to put on more clothes. When he returned, he had on jeans and a polo shirt. He looked casual, and I had more control over my eyes. Again, I chided myself. What possessed me to stare? I don't want Brent!

"Stop torturing yourself! We'll deal with this. Most humans have this flesh issue. It takes time and persistence to change. Love yourself. Respect yourself. You have someone just a wonderful coming," He encouraged.

Thanks! I'm trying to remember, I answered.

Thank goodness Brent didn't hover around. He politely greeted us, got a cola, and joined a little boy who was playing outside. Afterward, Hope offered Caylee and me cola and snacks before she ventured off to another room. While she was away, I asked Caylee, "Do you have a lustful eye? I just did."

She giggled and confessed, "Brent is dreamy, isn't he? Every woman in this county thinks so. Some have thrown themselves at him. He is a gentleman about it though. He's faithful. Hope doesn't have to worry. He only has eyes for her. You'll see, the more you are around them, the more you'll crave someone like him for yourself, and I'm not talking about his body. He is a wonderful person."

~~~

While playing catch with Greg, Brent's mind wasn't in the game. He couldn't help wondering how Gina's integrity could be threatened. The Holy Spirit mentioned Lyle would use her past as a tactic against her in his court hearing. What did the man have on Gina? He had to inquire. Should he be doing research now? The woman was here. Should he interrupt Hope's assignment with her?

When Greg's wild pitch caught Brent in the chest, causing him to lose his breath, Brent knew God helped him decide. His mind wasn't with Greg. God wanted him to focus on his assignment. Prepare for an attack on Gina.

Before walking away from his son, Brent motioned for Greg to come near. Grabbing Greg in a bear hug, Brent said, "You didn't mean to hurt Dad. The bad pitch will not be why I'm quitting. Dad has something to do for Jesus. Can we play this again later?" "Sure, Daddy! Can I play video games instead?" Greg begged.

"Okay, sport! None of the rough stuff," Brent agreed.

When he and Greg entered the house, Brent noticed some of Hope's old clothes spread across the table and chairs in their dining room, and he had a feeling Hope was sharing them with the girls. When he spotted one dress, he knew exactly what to say. He also knew Hope would follow his lead.

Directing his question toward Hope, Brent said, "Plan to give away the power dress?"

Hope replied, "I'm giving these clothes to Gina. She needs dresses and skirts to wear because she can't wear pants right now. The red dress is too big for me. Even though I have fond memories of it,

Gina needs it. It is doing no one any good lying in a sack on the bottom of our closet floor."

Brent then directed his comment toward Gina. "Wear it next Thursday at the court hearing."

"What? No one has said anything about a hearing so soon," Gina said, surprised.

Brent explained, "I planned to visit you personally on Monday so we could prep for the hearing, but if you don't mind, I'd like to ask a few questions now."

"I don't see why not. I trust you guys," I complied.

"The questions I ask may seem personal," Brent said, "but, Gina, I need to know everything. A defense attorney will try to destroy your credibility and make you appear as the one at fault. No matter how embarrassing the answers may be, it is best to have everything out in the open."

Gina was confused and questioned, "Why would I be the one faulted?"

"A good defense attorney will try to sway the people into believing you lured a sick person into doing what he did. He couldn't help himself," Brent answered.

"But I'm innocent!" Gina exclaimed.

"I know you are. Everyone in this room knows you are. But will the masses believe you are not the same person you were a week ago?" Brent enlightened.

Gina had, to be honest. Who would? No one. Gina had lived a fast and furious lifestyle. She had to confess. "I see what you mean."

Brent recommended they play a game. Pretend they were in a courtroom surrounded by people who were bound to judge legally between her and a criminal. He would play the part of Mr. Horne's defense attorney, and she would play herself. He made her promise she would not get upset with him because he would be using every trick he knew to make her fold under pressure.

She had to prepare herself. She would be testifying in court next week unless she dropped all charges.

They began by Gina laying her right hand on a Bible and repeating, "I promise, to tell the truth, the whole truth, so help me God."

She was bound by God through the statement! She had no other choice but, to be honest. Even in the world system, to lie was perjury and subject to criminal charges. She was more afraid after her statement of what her Lord would think.

"I know everything about you already," the Lord said. *"I will not be surprised. Tell the truth. Allow Brent to know everything. It will help you in more than one area."*

She was ready. She had the Lord's support to sustain her.

What could she lose?

Brent's first question was harmless. He asked, "Do you regularly visit the pool hall where you were attacked?"

Gina answered, "Yes."

The second question was, "Do you normally indulge in alcoholic beverages?"

She answered, "Yes."

Then he asked, "How about recreational drugs? Do you indulge in them?"

Gina hesitated. She took a deep breath and answered, "Sometimes."

Then Brent's questions became demanding. "Can you honestly say, Ms. Grimes, that you have never entertained Mr. Horne?"

The question made her pause. Brent warned her he would be tricky, but being bound by God's Word, to be honest, she had to be truthful. On occasions, she got extremely drunk, and sometimes she got high. Gina's answer had to be, "I can't say for sure."

Tears started forming behind her eyes. Shame began its dirty trick.

Brent's next question was even more personal. "Do you openly and publicly flirt and engage men with displays of affection?"

Gina didn't understand how to answer. She honestly confessed, "I don't understand."

"Ms. Grimes, have you kissed men in public? Have you allowed men to touch your private areas in public view? Have you had sex with any of these men?" Brent demanded.

Here again, honesty had to come out. Gina was mortified. She blurted out, "Yes! But I was usually drunk!"

Brent's voice got loud, and he started demeaning her. "You mean to say in front of these witnesses that you have sex with men you meet at the bar after getting drunk on alcohol or high on drugs each weekend. So, drunk or high in fact, you don't even know who you are allowing to touch you? Didn't you honestly say you couldn't remember if you'd entertained Mr. Horne?"

By this time, Gina was sobbing. Her creditability could not stand. Her past had caught up with her.

Brent came to her. "Gina, I apologize for hurting your feelings. But you had to be aware of what may happen. If we had not played this game, I would not know how to defend your claim. Get yourself together and let's start over. This time I'll be directing questions at you and not a defense attorney. With the information that was just uncovered, I can lead to focus away from your past. I may even be able to stop the defense from making you appear at fault. Are you willing to proceed?" he asked. Gina took a few minutes, drank some cola, and gathered her composure. Brent was her friend; he was not the enemy. Gina felt she had come this far, and most of the dirty laundry was out in the open. The Lord wanted her to proceed. Why would he say "be honest" otherwise?

She motioned to Brent that she was ready for phase two.

He began, "Gina, on the night in question, had you been indulging in alcohol or drugs?"

"No," she answered.

"How long were you at the pool hall before you decided to leave?" Brent queried.

"Less than an hour," Gina stated.

"Did you entertain any men?" Brent questioned. "No," Gina said.

Brent asked, "Is it possible you may have been friendly with Mr. Horne in the past?"

"Maybe," Gina stated.

"Let me rephrase my question. Would you willingly entertain Mr. Horne if you were not under the influence of alcohol or recreational drugs?" Brent asked.

"No, sir!" Gina stated.

"Why?" Brent asked.

"I hate dirty, smelly men. Even when I've been under the influence of alcohol, men with foul body odor and rotten teeth turn me off," I proclaimed.

Brent sighed. "We have what we need! Gina, see, truth always comes out. You just have to know what to ask."

Gina didn't know what he meant. What could be causing his relief? "What did I say?" Gina asked.

"Gina, subconsciously you stated a fact. You let me know what repulses you. When first questioned, you honestly said you couldn't remember having entertained Mr. Horne. Truth is, no one would have remembered someone they brushed off. But when I asked to explain why you normally wouldn't entertain someone like Mr. Horne, you stated a truth. You gave the people a mental picture of a man you would reject, no matter what," Brent explained.

Again, Gina sobbed. This time, for joy. Hope and Caylee both hugged her and said she did great. Afterward, Hope said, "You definitely need to wear the power dress. I wore it when I needed the Lord and Brent's help. Red signifies the blood of Jesus. It will help you remember you are covered in His love and power."

~~~

Three large angels huddled and watched while their humans interacted. As always, when they were together, they touched each other's wings. They loved being connected; it made them one. This time, the connection was making Insight's and Ox's body vibrate strangely. The sensation was soothing but odd, and it made both angels look at each other puzzled. It was when they heard Justice purring deeply that they understood why. Justice's contentment made a rumble from within his body, and everything that touched him vibrated with joy. Justice was content because Brent was happy.

The Mystery Begins

With Brent's mock hearing behind me, I shamefully wanted to explain my life. I barely had a few words out when Hope kindly stated, "What happened in the past needs to stay in the past." She even had a scripture reference to back her comment with. She asked, "Have you ever read or heard about Lot's wife?"

I could honestly say I hadn't. I came to find out the lady referenced loved her past, but being married to a godly man, she was ordered to leave everything behind. The reason was that God wanted to destroy the city they lived in, but before he could, they had to leave. In their haste, she turned back to look at the city and was frozen in a pillar of salt.

The story was strange to me. I wasn't taught the Bible properly, so I asked Hope if she minded explaining. When she smiled, I knew I was in for a treat. Hope must love teaching.

Her story began, "The Bible has many symbolisms, but one of my favorites is the reference to salt. Salt is a preservative; it is today, and it was thousands of years ago. Lot's wife was turned into a pillar of salt. She was frozen in it for eternity because she loved her past more than what God wanted for her. Apparently, she wondered what would happen if she stayed. What I'm trying to tell you is this, don't look back. Learn from my mistake. I fell into that trap just today. I looked back at what happened to me, and fear overwhelmed me, and I froze. When you wonder about the what-ifs, it freezes you somehow where you physically can't function. When God has changed your direction, be happy because He is with you and has given you a different course. Everyone here could care less what you did. You are not that same person. We know you've been placed on a different course, and we are here to help you stay focused."

After the speech, Hope changed the subject. The ladies began choosing from the enormous bundle of clothes what would be easy for me to wear. By the time they finished mixing and matching items, it was almost dinnertime. I didn't want Mom to be worried about me. Knowing her, Mom may have cooked a huge dinner again.

I phoned the house, and when Mom answered, I was surprised to hear she had company. When asked if it was Dad, she kindly said no. She told me Mamie had dropped in, and they were having a wonderful conversation. I shared this information with Hope and Caylee, and they just looked at each other. I wasn't stupid. I knew a conspiracy was going on.

Being comfortable with my new family, I demanded, "Spill the beans. What are you ladies up to?"

Caylee was a pushover. Her face turned red, totally giving her away. Hope's mouth twitched.

"Come on, ladies, out with it!" I urged.

Hope laughed then she shared, "We are making sure you don't get side-tracked. Like I said earlier, we are here to keep you focused. It is really easy to get back into old customs. We felt if we stayed with you long enough, you'd love us and what God has in store for you more than your old lifestyle."

"Get real! I already love you guys more than my past. I didn't have many friends. Angie was the only girl I hung out with. I'm hoping she comes around to our view soon," I proclaimed.

"Give her time. We'll pray for her. Without you in her life, she may want to make a change soon. It seems like you were her crutch anyway," Hope said. "But for now, while you are convalescing, we want to help. When you are able to go back to work, Caylee will see that you have a ride. When you have doctor appointments or court hearings, I'll be available. Do you have a problem with our help?"

"Of course, I don't have a problem with you helping me," I said. "I love it. But I have a question. Why is Mamie so interested in my mom? She has called her a few times lately using me as an excuse."

"Can we be honest?" Hope asked. "Please!" I cried.

"Caylee shared something with me this morning. She believes you have issues with your mom. She told me your mom stresses you out at times. If Mamie has picked up on this, knowing her as I do, she will be determined to iron out the wrinkles. She'll focus on your mom and bring her into the sheepfold and teach her how to love. Mamie is our church's mother bear. She wants all women to be empowered with love. Trust me, your mom is in very good company," Hope said with a smile.

I wanted to shout, "Praise God!"

"Hope, since our first visit, I've felt differently toward my mom. No, let me rephrase this. Since I met the Holy Spirit, I've felt different, period. I now give Mom credit for wanting to help, and I'm more sympathetic toward her feelings. My stress was self-imposed, I know this now. Mom is really a good person. She needs a friend like Mamie," I confessed.

At home, I found Mom in a serene peace of mind. Mamie had apparently worked her magic. After showing her all the beautiful things Hope had given me, we had a lovely dinner together with plans to get to bed early so we could go to church the next morning. This way of life would be different for both of us. For me, I usually didn't get out of bed on Sundays until 10:00 or 11:00 a.m. The new me will rise and shine at 7:00 a.m.; I had a continuous date with my Lord to feast at His table. I snickered at the thought. Who would have thought I'd be a churchgoer?

By 9:00 p.m., I was thoroughly exhausted. I had overworked myself. Every muscle ached. What I would give to be able to soak in a hot bubble bath. When I went to the bathroom to brush my teeth and bathe in preparation for bed, the sight peering back through the mirror frightened me. My underarms were blue. I'd bruised them using my crutches. No wonder my arms and shoulders hurt.

Hopping back to my room, I called Mamie. She would know what to do. Mamie informed me to use ice packs after I bathed. Apparently, I had inflamed tissue. The ice would soothe and help the bruising. I cringed, worrying about tomorrow. How much pain would I be in? No matter! I would go to church if I had to leave the crutches at home. I would hop every step if needed.

~~~

Ox watched Gina closely. When Gina undressed completely for bed, Ox made sure he saw where she placed her treasure. He had to see what was written on the piece of paper she carried close to her heart. Adrian had encouraged her after their journey to write down her dreams and make them plain. Those words were written down as instructions for him. He was to make sure they were carried out completely.

When Ox noticed Gina's pain, he called out to Healer, and instantly Adrian appeared beside him. Gently, Adrian lovingly ministered healing to Gina while she sponged down her body. After the bath, he soothed the inflamed tissue while Gina administered ice. Between the two, Gina's arms would be able to sustain more weight tomorrow. After all, she had a date with God's minister. She would get to hear about her Heavenly Father. Ox unfolded the paper when he was certain Gina was sound asleep. It had been so long since he last studied anything. Since the yoke was on him, he could work again so each detail had to be precisely created. The words written on the paper were precious. They were orders from God written from Gina's memories. This was now a burden given to him to resolve. Promises that weren't God's intentions were too heavy for mankind to carry or bring into manifestation. God had created him from the dawn of time to bring things to fruition by a person's faith. Now he was able to do this once again. Together with the Holy Spirit, Ox was bringing God's plan out in the open. He was happy. While Gina rested, he could work.

~~~

Ox and Adrian weren't the only angels watching Gina. In deep shadow, Satan watched closely because he knew the woman was being groomed for something. The new girl was too much like the one who thought she was queen bee. Apparently, heaven saw something special in the girl. It was evident because she had a guardian. Satan knew guardians were very similar to his giants. He also knew they were specifically assigned to follow around specific humans.

He also waited for Gina to fall asleep. But he had another agenda. He wanted to watch her guardian, so he could determine what may be happening. When he heard Gina's deep breathing to indicate she was asleep, he moved in for a closer look at the beast. He was intimidated by this guardian. He didn't look threatening like Hope's. But when he focused harder, he faltered and stumbled back. Concern plagued his mind. It could not be! He thought. The beast was his old enemy, the beast of burden, the one he had stolen the power from.

Once Satan composed himself, he peered closer so he could see what the creature was doing, only to be startled out of his wits again. The beast wore the golden torque! He had God's power again! That meant one thing! The heavy yoke he'd placed on man had been removed, and the beast worked because he didn't know of his authority yet. Hissing from the realization, Satan knew his time was severely threatened and may be limited. He looked at the girl again with hatred. No wonder she was highly protected. She held a key! Somehow, she'd set herself free.

Satan could only think of one alternative: use whatever the beast was studying and twist, ruin, or destroy it. But when he recognized what the words on the paper meant, he became infuriated. He remembered the experience he had from Gina's dream the other night. Heaven was protecting the woman and a man. He wondered who the man was. *No matter*, he thought. *Humans are easy prey, especially weak men.* Satan set out, determined to watch the beast and ruin God's plan. Whatever the beast did, he would counterfeit and lure either the man or woman down the wrong path.

~~~

The first thing Ox did was assign protection for Gina so he could visit the Polk family. Following leads gleaned from his union with Justice, Ox was determined to set up changes so Gina and Mr. Polk could meet. From the mind-meld with his comrade, Ox understood how Mother Polk's influence had the whole family bound. So, his first task was to change her mind.

~~~

Gazing at Ox, Satan knew the beast's actions weren't proper. The beast was very rusty. Ox was forgetting protocol, leaving his human behind. Satan could use this error. The misguided steps would give him an opportunity to mess up God's plans. Before leaving the scene, Satan used a second of time to order chaos into Gina's room then followed his enemy.

~~~

When Ox arrived at the Polk home, he overheard Wade and his mother discussing Pastor Reed's church. Somehow, Wade was doing the groundwork for him and was making progress. Mrs. Polk was finally beginning to understand the need for their family to be in a church environment, which had people of all ages. Wade had convinced his mother that her church only catered to older people, and it didn't show growth. Listening closely, Ox heard Wade use Joe and Olivia Arnold's name and mentioned how they loved their church. He appealed to her by saying his two childhood friends Carl and Brent loved the church as well. Ox was elated! Justice was involved. Ox's job would be simple. He could sway Mrs. Polk's motherly instincts and make her see Wade's need. Then through her willingness, their whole family would be part of this marvelous church body, and it wouldn't be long before a stage could be set for Wade and Gina to meet.

~~~

Satan snickered under his breath. It was interesting that Ox was focused on Mother Polk. He knew what he had to do. The lady was up in years; he could tamper with her body and change the Polk vision altogether. He would make the Polk family's focus be the preservation of Mama instead of prospering the family. With Mama as their main focus, Satan would be able to keep the two lovebirds away from each other, long enough for Gina to give up hope.

Satan found something interesting while probing around in the Polk house. Something he could use to his advantage against Gina. With what he found, he could use the Polk family as his personal weapon. He would use what Gina thought was hers against the promise. Use God's own plan against her and make her think God was a liar. Just as he fooled Eve, he could fool this child just as easily.

~~~

Watching from on high, Jesus witnessed everything. He watched Ox work diligently, and He watched Satan plan and scheme. All the details (down to the very second needed) were being established correctly by two created beings. One angel, although misguided, was trying to resolve a problem; and another evil minion was trying to destroy something that God had already established. Only the Holy Spirit could secretly align prophecy, and it was up to Him to play these two angels against each other. The Father and the Son, as well as the Holy Spirit, knew about the mystery. Very soon the Holy Spirit would explain to Ox what he unknowingly accomplished. For within all the works and schemes, and when the time was right, Jesus and His subordinates would be able to show mankind right from wrong once and for all!

~~~

When Ox returned to Gina's side, he was astonished to see a scuffle going on in her bedroom and immediately knew why; he'd failed. The angels he had left to guard Gina were fighting with tormenting demons, not energy suckers. Somehow gremlins infiltrated the situation and were causing havoc. Chaos was rampant! When Ox saw that Adrian was also involved in the battle, he knew that this meant Gina must be bound in a nightmare. Fierce anger rose in his chest; he was angry at himself and knew he needed help. He wanted to blow his trumpet and make a war cry, but before he entered the battle, he motioned for Adrian to protect Gina's hearing. If he used his trumpet, the sound would be too loud for a person's natural hearing, and her ears could be damaged from the close proximity. But the second before he blew the horn, he remembered his torque. Things were different now that he didn't have to alarm heaven. He could call on another yoked angel. Ox quickly thought of Insight who also wore God's torque and could send help. The angels under his command could gain strength in the process.

Since he could no longer bellow, Ox barked loudly for Insight to assist. Instantly, hungry, anxious, but smaller eagle-faced angels arrived. When all the demons were eaten, Ox immediately repented. Calling upon the Holy Spirit, Ox asked for forgiveness; he'd forgotten to follow protocol. In his anticipation of the promise, Ox had left Gina's side and jumped out ahead of schedule. When the Holy Spirit assured him all would work out fine, Ox promised the Lord that he would never again risk exposing his human to torment. He would follow the protocol set for him and wait for orders directly or indirectly from Gina's mind or mouth as she professed God's Word. That way, he could work under God's strength and cover.

When the Holy Spirit was satisfied by Ox's revelation concerning the forgotten protocol, he covered the two of them within a heavenly cloud, out of Satan's earshot and sight. Once assured they were concealed, he began to share with Ox what really happened. Yes, Ox did not follow protocol. Jesus knew how Ox would behave long before his newly regained power would affect his reaction. Because heaven knew, the Lord developed a counterplan long ago to prove every move of Satan wrong.

After making Ox aware, the Holy Spirit also told Ox what Satan did behind his back. The seeds planted because of his misguided thoughts and actions would have to grow, but in the end, Jesus would win. Ox could free his mind from worry because Gina had already been given her prophecy. Nothing in heaven, on earth, or under the earth could stop it from coming. Ox would have to endure Satan's tricks, pokes, and prods intended to sway Gina. Because Ox would, he had already become the burden barrier. Satan's evil would play with Gina's mind, but because she had relinquished the yoke and died to self, Ox was her flesh's protector. He could take Satan's blows. Ox would, if need be, become the beaten bulldog God had shown Gina in her dream because she had taken on his persona. At that time, Ox was a just calf, a young and innocent being. Her prophecy was to be like a calf released from a stall and able to leap for joy. His job was to go before her, to cover her, and help her tread down the wicked under the soles of her feet.

Visualizing Gina's dream again for clarification, Ox remembered how it ended. In the dream, the bulldog withstood harsh attacks only to have Gina (who is now the Ox) talk and tend to the bulldog's bruises. If that was the case, Gina's faith would be strong; meaning she wasn't a calf any longer. He shook his head, weary from trying to understand it all.

Once Ox snapped out of his thoughts to focus, the Holy Spirit told him of some of Satan's tricks from the past and for the present. First, he showed Ox something Satan would be using that was very important. This tool would toy with Gina's heart and mind. When it was revealed, Ox gasped. Mrs. Polk had twin boys, and Satan would try to lure Gina, as he did with Eve, to choose the wrong one. Then the Holy Spirit informed Ox how Satan ruined Gina's many years ago and how these past issues still haunted her mind. Roadblocks had been formed to make Gina insecure. Satan planned to use her dad to try to keep her from believing in the love of the Heavenly Father.

Church

I felt horrible when I finally awoke. Not only did I have awful dreams, but my arms and shoulders ached, and my good ankle throbbed with pain. How would I make it through the day? I had big plans. I was going to sit in a church service.

I wanted to whine and moan, but that wouldn't accomplish anything. I wanted a nurse's aide to come and assist me with a bath and makeup. I wanted the sympathy I received from Mamie every day. I wanted, and I wanted, was just that! But all my wishing wasn't getting me anywhere.

While I washed my face, I revisited my dreams. I realized the nightmares were from being under severe emotional strain that day. But since my journey with Adrian, I didn't forget dreams as quickly. The reason was because Adrian occasionally visited me in dreams. But in this dream, I didn't have an angel visitation. There was nothing in this dream but condemnation.

I let my mind return to the scene in my dream. I was front and center, in a court hearing and being tormented. I had been placed on a chair located in the middle of a room full of witnesses while a man in a dark cloak accused me over and over of being openly free with drugs, alcohol, and sex. To my embarrassment, the jury consisted of Mom, Dad, and all four of my grandparents. When the time came for me to hear their verdict for or against me, Dad rose and gave a thumbs-down sign. I was stunned, and my feelings were hurt, but what I remembered most was the appearance of Dad's face. It was set in stone. The hardness in his eyes terrified me. I pleaded and begged for mercy. I screamed, "I'm your child! I'm your only daughter! I'm your only offspring!" None of those facts mattered to my Dad; he was determined to deny me any rights. He had condemned me to eternal torment; I was no longer his trophy, his only child. I was given over to jailors. I screamed at my mom, "Help me!" But she turned her back. My grandparents were all I had left. They usually spoiled me. I pouted and looked sad in their direction, but they too turned their backs. I was abandoned! I had no family! When my jailors arrived, they tied up my hands and feet then hooded my head and dragged me to a dark and musty dungeon.

My mouth was dry, and my head ached. Something about the dream disturbed me and caused me to worry. Was it a sign? Was it a warning? While standing at the bathroom sink, I ran water in my hand from the tap and drank from it rather than hopping to the kitchen for coffee so I could get a jolt of caffeine. I chided myself, "Focus, Gina! It was a dream. Hope and Brent assured you all was okay."

I finished applying makeup, brushed my hair, and then dressed. I looked good in the lovely blue blouse and skirt Hope had given me. The last step was to put on a ballet flat to cover my good foot. When I hopped to the kitchen, Mom was already dressed for church and had breakfast laid out for me. She wasn't mad at me! My dream was a lie! Clearly, Mom wasn't mad at me. The realization allowed me to eat with gusto and have two cups of coffee before Mamie arrived to take us all to church.

When Mamie was at our house yesterday, Mom and I planned to meet her out in our driveway when she arrived. Last night's call to her about my arms changed everything. Mamie wasn't about to let me walk on crutches; she came fully equipped with a wheelchair and met us at my apartment's backdoor. I started to object, but Mamie stopped me in mid-sentence. "Child, you could damage yourself! Give your arms a rest; otherwise, you may fall on your face. Ole Mamie knows what to do. Give me credit!" she professed. Mom helped me down the two backdoor steps into the wheelchair Mamie held steady. I felt like an invalid and probably looked like one to anyone watching, but I had to admit the wheelchair was a godsend; I'd been dreading the painful maneuvering at a new place.

When we reached Mamie's big car, she was prepared there as well. She had a blanket. I was going to blanket-slide again, and Mom was about to get a lesson. Next time she'd have a blanket for me in her car.

The church was huge and lovely. Hundreds of people were gathered inside. Mamie stationed us in the back, close to one corner of the room so my wheelchair wouldn't be in anyone's way. The spot was made for wheelchair patrons. I wouldn't have to move out of my chair and could stay parked next to Mom at the end of a pew. It wasn't long before we had company. Caylee, Hope, and Brent joined us in the row behind ours. The togetherness felt like one big family.

When the music started, everyone stood, which prevented me from seeing, but I didn't care. The songs were exciting and upbeat, nothing like I'd expected. I was prepared for boring, monotone hymns, but this music rocked, and some of the slower songs truly tugged at my heart.

When I heard a commotion behind me, I turned around to see what was happening. Caylee was giggling, and Brent was exiting out of the pew to allow a huge man in who wanted to sit between Hope and Caylee. The large man was Russ Jackson. By Caylee's reaction, he had surprised her by joining our group. This attention made Caylee very happy. Hope was also smiling, which meant she was aware of Russ and approved. This shared joy brought a pleasant thought to my mind: *I'd have a companion here soon also.*

~~~

Ox cringed! Gina's thought about her companion brought a memory back to his mind. Where were the Polks? Wasn't Wade's family supposed to be here today? Mrs. Polk had agreed. Ox was heartsick at the realization. He had created a problem and led evil to their house where Satan witnessed everything.

~~~

I was very uneasy as everyone was standing except me. To keep from feeling insecure, I closed my eyes during the music. When the music was over and I heard the people sit, I opened my eyes. I was new to a church service, and I wanted to see what was next. Pastor Reed stood to give the morning greeting and prayer, so I bowed my head like everyone else. That was when I heard His joyful voice again.

"Wake up, bulldog! You're about to be fed. Listen and enjoy the meat of My Words. Gather strength for your journey. Use the wisdom to help you through."

~~~

Ox also snapped to attention, straightened his back, and extended his wings. He too was about to hear the words of God through Gina, and he wanted his comrades to experience the joy. It had been a very long time since all four comrades were in a church together, so Ox took advantage and expressed his need to connect with them. Once their wings touched, a circle was made around their people. This connection would allow anything Ox heard go to the next comrade until each heard the word, and it returned to him. The effect would make knowledge turn them like a wheel. Each could experience the other's gifting and be empowered at the same time. The four would truly be made one.

~~~

For a brief moment, I wondered, *how did Whisperer know the new me was a bulldog?* Then I mentally slapped myself. *Duh! He knows everything!*

While the Pastor spoke, I reached into my handbag to retrieve my Bible and notepad so I could follow along and take notes. For my Whisperer to alert me as He did, the lesson must be of great importance. Previous times when I heard the voice, the Lord spoke to me when I asked Him a question or had a questioning thought. This time, I was in a pleasant place, so this wake-up call meant something special. I didn't want to miss anything. I wanted to eat every bite, and I wanted to remember what I ate.

Hope watched and listened to everything very keenly. She had made it a specific point to sit behind Gina so she could study Gina's body language. The Holy Spirit had also forewarned her to pay attention to Pastor Reed's sermons as she watched over Gina. His orders were to use every lesson as a guideline for Gina's growth because her knowledge and understanding would feed her spirit and help the harvesting machine run. When Hope heard the voice of the Holy Spirit speak directly to Gina, she knew what was about to happen and made a mental note of the name the Lord called Gina. Using Gina's new nickname would be useful. Bulldog was a good description of Gina. It was cute but also meant she was very determined and strong-willed.

I opened my notepad and had a pen in hand when Mamie patted my arm and whispered, "Child, put away your writing material. I'll get you a CD made after the service. Pay attention, or you'll miss something important."

I closed my book and was grateful that I didn't have to write things down. It reminded me of school, and I hated taking notes in class.

Pastor Reed had a soothing voice. The passion he had for our Heavenly Father was awesome. He shared how from the beginning of time all God wanted was a family to take care of and love. Jesus has given the people back their right standing with God. It was through Him they get to share the love of God. God is a doting Father. The Heavenly Father wants to freely give everyone all good things to enjoy. He wants people to trust and call on Him. Other than Jesus, no human being on this planet can measure up to His standards of love. No matter what people do, no matter what people feel, God still loves them and will not turn His back on them. God is merciful and forgives all their shortcomings.

I flinched when I heard Pastor Reed say "shortcomings." It brought back the dream from the previous night. My mind replayed the dream. I was remembering the fear I had when my family heard how I lived my life. Afterward, every member of my family, from Dad to Mom and even my grandparents, had turned their backs on me when they knew what I'd done. None of them wanted to listen. None of them gave me a chance. I no longer existed for them.

When my mind returned to the service, I tried focusing on the revelation that God loves me no matter what. This had to be a key point for me to remember, but my mind kept returning to Dad in my dream. Dad would have an issue with my past. The thought bothered me greatly. Dad always had me on a pedestal; it would hurt him to know I was a blob of muck instead of a golden trophy.

I heard Pastor Reed say, "Keep a kingdom mindset or Satan would steal your peace. Know your rights and keep pure thoughts." I didn't know what he meant. By the time I heard that statement, I'd lost most of his message. I tried focusing on a pure thought, but I didn't have any pure thoughts at the moment. I desperately sought for something good and pure to think about, but my thoughts kept going back to my old ways. I couldn't shake it. All my worrying kept me from hearing the rest of Pastor Reed's message.

~~~

Ox was furious! Gina wasn't being fed; thereby he wasn't allowed to eat. His hopes of having his comrades share his satisfaction of the good news were dashed. He was so angry he was shaking. He wanted to act. He wanted to strike the demon that tormented him through Gina but was stopped by the Holy Spirit. "We have this. Intercession will be made, wait and see."

~~~

Something within me rattled; it felt like I was being severely shaken. Panic struck me, and I closed my eyes. I suddenly caught a mental glimpse of my bulldog chasing a toy. He wasn't eating. My spirit did not want to play. This revelation brought my mind back in line. I knew I was being tormented by a supernatural force. I also came to grips with something else: my bulldog had no power to stop playing; it was still a puppy and was being lured away from its food by a toy. I gritted my teeth and focused my mind on the fire around me and tried to sit still.

~~~

Hope was listening intently to Pastor Reed until she heard an evil snicker. Focusing keenly toward the sound, Hope found the culprit. She could see a demon sitting on the back of Gina's wheelchair, and it was playing tricks with Gina's mind and having a good time. Hope knew what the creature was doing inside Gina's mind. The creature was tempting her with doubts and fears. Satan always wanted to cloud the Word, and Hope knew Gina was in a dangerous place mentally, and her body language showed she was struggling. Because of the dangerous path, Gina was being led down, Hope knew she had one rescuer. Breathing in deeply, Hope closed her eyes and quietly interceded. "Lord, Satan is after Gina. Help her please."

~~~

The fire was intense, but I couldn't make my body sit until I heard my Master's voice. His was the familiar voice I loved, and he was loudly exclaiming, *"I am the way, the truth, and the life. No one comes to the Father except by Me."* I ran swiftly to Him and sat obediently at His feet.

~~~

Ox witnessed the demon freeze in place. The Lord's voice proclaimed only one way. Now the lure had no power. The dog would get to eat after all. It wouldn't be like Ox hoped, but the food would come. Then Ox witnessed a brief spat between the demon and Insight. The demon struck Insight in self-defense but quickly lost its life. Ox didn't get to eat in church, but Insight did.

~~~

My eyes flew open. The trance was over, but so was Pastor Reed's message. I was so embarrassed. I hoped no one asked me what I got from the message. My recollection of details would be limited.

Thank God for CDs! At least I could listen to Pastor Reed's message again. Getting a recorded message on CD was like getting a takeout meal.

When all of us were gathered in the lobby, Mamie volunteered to get me a CD. While she waited in line, Mom and I talked with Brent and Hope until a man approached us and politely apologized for having to interrupt our conversation. Brent quickly introduced his brother, Carl, before the two of them began talking. Carl brought bad news. Someone named Wanda had suffered a stroke, and he wanted Brent to go with him to the hospital where they could be with her family. Brent looked at Hope, and his concerned expression spoke volumes. She instantly agreed with Carl and told Brent to go.

~~~

Ox really felt bad. He'd caused Mrs. Polk's attack. He knew why the family wasn't at church. There wasn't anything he could do at this point, so he tried to draw comfort from what the Holy Spirit had shared.

~~~

After Brent left, Hope turned her attention in our direction again and asked if we'd like to have lunch together. Caylee and Russ weren't with us. They'd left earlier, so they could be alone. Mamie was up for the fellowship but left the decision up to Mom and me since we were riding together. When I heard Mom say she wanted to go, I was shocked. Her happy tone made me take notice. Not only was she joyful, her appearance was radiant like she was glowing. I wondered, *Did Pastor Reed's message do that to her?*

The four of us decided to eat at a Mexican restaurant close by where we could sit together around one of their large tables and talk. With me in a wheelchair, we could relax and be waited on by a hostess instead of having to walk around buffet tables gathering our meals. With plans and place in mind, Hope told Mamie she would meet us there as soon as she retrieved Greg.

It was during lunch that Mom understood how much these people cared for us. Mamie and Hope shared with her their plans of getting me around to appointments, church, and eventually back to work, which would free her from having to take off work, thereby losing more money. They were the perfect example of a true church family who looked after one another. Mom and I needed that in our lives.

Also during lunch, I learned Mamie had scheduled an appointment for me to see Shawn Davis at the hospital tomorrow around 3:30 p.m. After I called her last night, Mamie scheduled this appointment and retrieved the wheelchair. Shawn was to see that I was fitted with different crutches. Apparently, Mamie thought my armpit bruising was from poorly fitted crutches.

Hope used the news as a cue. Happily, she blurted, "My treat! I'll pick you up in the morning around 9:00 a.m., so be ready." Hope knew the alone time with Gina would be perfect. They could discuss what happened today, and she could share what happened to her last year. Until then, Hope would have to rely on the Lord's protection for Gina.

Chow Down

I was exhausted and full when Mom and Mamie helped me inside. All I wanted to do now was take a nap until Mamie handed me the CD. I wanted to hear the message badly, so I asked Mom if she had a portable player. That way, I could listen while I rested. If I fell asleep, I could listen to it again.

Mom handed me the perfect little player and said it was one she used while cleaning house. Then I remembered Mom's appearance. Before hopping to my bedroom to undress and lie down, I asked how she liked the church. Tears welled up in my eyes. Her answer thrilled me when she confessed, "Gina, it was amazing! I never knew God had such love for us, and He has plans for us. Every detail of His children's lives has already been arranged so they can enjoy life. Gina, honey, I gave my heart to the Lord today. I truly want this. I think I've found peace at last!" After undressing and putting on a robe, I lay across my bed, puzzled. I'd missed a lot that morning. I didn't recall hearing anything about prearranged lives. Knowing this made me more determined to hear what Pastor Reed said. A prearranged life was something I wanted. I put the CD in the player, but before I turned on the machine, I said a quick prayer. "Lord, help me understand this message. Please don't let my mind be side-tracked this time."

"Gina, close your eyes and listen. I'm aware you didn't hear me this morning. Let me soothe your spirit and feed your soul, allow me to tell you everything Pastor Reed said. With me talking, nothing will interfere," He cooed.

I turned on the player and closed my eyes. At first, I heard Pastor Reed's voice say, "I will be teaching from the book of Ephesians chapter 2 and 1 John chapter 4, amplified version, this morning." Then the tone changed, and I heard my Whisperer's voice take control.

My heart began to beat hard, and warmth spread all through my body as His words infiltrated me. My hearing became keen as if my physical ears were hands grabbing at each syllable.

I listened intently while He spoke of things written in Ephesians.

When I found you, you were dead in your trespasses and sin. You were a dead person following the course of the world, held by the sway of the present age. You were under the control of an evil spirit that still works against people who are careless, rebellious, and unbelieving, who don't believe in me and my plan.

You conducted your life in the passion of your flesh, obeying impulses and the thoughts of the mind and were subject to God's wrath. But your Heavenly Father, who is full of mercy, gave you His intense love and changed everything.

Even when you were dead by shortcomings and trespasses, God made you alive through fellowship with His son, Jesus Christ. God gave you the very life he intended for His son. You now have God's grace, which is His favor and mercy, instead of the wrath you really deserved. You have been delivered from judgment and made partakers of Christ's salvation.

In heaven, God already sees you seated alongside His Son. His plan is to demonstrate to all ages and through all times how much he wants you to share His free grace. God wants you to experience His favor, kindness, and goodness. He wants to show His heart to you as if you were His child.

All of this love came because of what Jesus did for you two thousand years ago.

Through your faith, God will give you free grace. This salvation will not be earned by anything you do. You do not have to strive for God's love; He gives the gift of grace freely. It is not the result of what anyone can possibly do, so no one can pride himself in it or take glory for himself. God wants you to know you are His own creation.

You've been recreated in Jesus so you can do good works He predestined long ago. God wants us to walk in paths He prepared ahead of time so we can live the good life which He prearranged and made ready for us to live.

All you have to do is remember how you used to be before coming to Jesus. Remember how living without Christ Jesus kept you excluded from what God wants for you. You were unable to share in the sacred promises because you didn't know your rights. Now you know Jesus died for you. Plus, you know why He shed His blood for you. He did it so you can live in God's covenants by faith and hope.

Jesus is your peace. He reconciled you back to your Heavenly Father. You are no longer an outsider excluded from rights. You share citizenship within God's kingdom in heaven and on earth. You belong to God.

Then I heard Pastor Reed's voice again, instructing us to follow him through 1 John, and once again, Whisperer took control.

Remember from Ephesians you learned that evil spirits led people astray? Now, listen to this. God warns you not to put faith in every spirit. Test them to discover whether they proceed from God because many false words are going forth in the world.

God has given you a way to recognize the Spirit of God. He will be able to profess Jesus as Lord, coming from God to earth as a man. Every spirit that does not acknowledge and confess that Jesus came in the flesh is not of God. Consider it the antichrist.

You are a child of God. You have already defeated and overcome the agents of the antichrist. God is greater than anything against Him in the world.

Unbelieving spirits live and speak from a worldly view. They have no knowledge of God. You are a child of God. You will get to perceive, recognize, and understand God by observation and experience so you can listen to Him and not be moved by the ways of the world. The Spirit of Truth has set you free from the spirit of error.

You are a child of love, for God is love. Anyone who does not love has not become acquainted with God.

God showed you His love by letting you see why Jesus came and died. He let you see He loved you enough to save you from hell. Jesus's blood was the requirement that purchased your life.

Beloved, if God loved you so very much, you also ought to love others.

God wants to stress to you that He wants you to understand, recognize, and be conscious always of the love He cherishes us with. He wants you to experience it through observations. Being in fellowship with God will allow you to go through life free from the fear and free from dread.

Trusting in God's love through faith will expel every trace of terror. Fear brings thoughts of punishment, but God's love brings joy and happiness. By this, you will love God and come to know He loved you first.

"Wow! No wonder Mom gave her life to You. If you spoke to her like You just did to me, it is a wonder she could breathe. You've taken my breath away. I'm overwhelmed! My heart is full of emotion. I can be happy. I don't have to be afraid. I have paths already prepared for me to walk. I have scripture to refer to when in doubt. Lord, thank you! Thank you!" I exclaimed.

"You are welcome, Gina. Rest, take your nap now that you've been fed," He soothed.

~~~

Ox reveled in the taste of meat, happy that his diet would no longer consist of grass. He wouldn't have to drudge through earth looking for straw any longer. Gina's confessions had given him the happy meal. After she heard the Lord, she agreed with the words, giving Ox the protein he needed to acquire muscle. With each revelation she got, it sank deep within her spirit, and he acquired more strength and power. From one meal, he grew as large as Insight. His mind changed, and he became the Shield of Faith instead of a laborer, and he remembered who he was! He was the Requirer of the Word! The revelation from this word gave him correct understanding at last. No longer would he shake his head wearily or have to worry about getting a job done. He'd never leave Gina again because her words gave him the power to put a demand on natural circumstances, forcing them to line up or be destroyed.

He loved this woman God had given him to protect. She had changed things for him. For until this moment, he thought he'd been reduced to backbreaking work that pulled mankind along. Gina had saddled him so she could ride, leaving the heavy plow of accomplishment behind. He wasn't bound to a team of oxen, nor was he a commander of fifty. Her voice, lined up with God's Word, had millions upon millions of angels under their authority, and his mouth made others work. Through Gina's voice, he could even command evil angels to obey. *Thank you, Jesus; my life's responsibility has been renewed!* His job was to go proudly before Gina, not behind or beside her. He was to make sure her path was smooth.

Then he paused and laughed to himself, remembering Insight's arrogance after he received his torque. Ox had watched him fly and grow as he ate. Now, Ox felt the same. Proud and honored to be Jesus's bond servant, he gladly waited for Gina to receive more revelation. If one of her meals gave him this much power, what could days feeding on meat do?

~~~

From His seat on high, Jesus watched Ox be renewed. The visualization made Jesus exclaim with relief, "Finally! My faith's ability is complete. No longer will man beg me for something and wonder if I want them to have their heart's desire. They will be able to see or hear what I want for them through My Word. My grace will be seen and experienced the way God intended."

~~~

After my nap, I joined Mom in the kitchen and noticed she was busy cooking. Mom made sure she had food ready to eat through the week. Since I was a little girl, she cooked two, and sometimes three, different meats Sunday afternoon along with a dessert. The preplanning helped her keep hearty meals on our table. Side dishes weren't a problem; they were easy and usually quick to prepare. If she was tired from work during the week, she would open a can of vegetables, make boxed macaroni and cheese, or boil rice, and we were set because meat was already cooked.

I hobbled over to the kitchen table so I could sit and noticed she was busy preparing the food but was unaware of my presence. When I peered closer, I noticed why. She had earplugs in her ears, listening to something. At first, I thought she may be listening to one of her books on CD until she spoke out loud, "Yes! Jesus, yes! I want your blessings!" Apparently, she had gathered the CD player from my room and was listening to the CD from this morning's message and was totally transfixed. The picture of my mom enthralled by love was priceless.

When Mom turned around and noticed me sitting at the table, her face turned five shades of red. "How long have you been sitting in here!" she squealed.

"Long enough to know what you are listening to," I informed her while trying not to laugh.

Apologizing, she said, "I sneaked in your room to see if you were finished listening to the CD, and when I found you sleeping, I took the player. I had to hear the message again. Gina, I want another copy of this one. I want to frame it or something. This message changed my life. I don't ever want to be without these words."

"I know, Mom. The words changed me too after I heard we had God's love. It made me sad to think He was with us all this time and we never even acknowledged Him. Things will be different now. You and I will learn what it's like to be loved unconditionally and to love others. I know now that it was this love that caused Caylee to sing all the time and why Hope is so determined I don't go back living like a tramp anymore. Mamie, bless her, she treated me like her child from the first day we met. If living for Jesus makes you want to love people and help some see a different way, I am all for joining the team. I was a mess, but now I am different," I professed.

"I am too," Mom confirmed.

After hearing her agree, I asked, "Would you like to go with me and join their church? We can do it together Wednesday night."

"Let's do it! I need this! We need this!" she replied.

~~~

Satan sat perched on the roof of the Grimes's home, looking down at the two joyful women. All their words of love made him want to hurl. How could they be so confident they weren't grounded in the Word? Why would they think God loved them? Even if they heard something wonderful, he could change their minds easily. Gina was a perfect target. He would purposefully toy with her leg. Hinder its healing. Then he would lure her toward the Polk twin. He knew exactly what to do. Ole Dr. Carter had been his puppet too long; it was time to get another.

~~~

I loved being with Mom. Why hadn't I been more understanding of her needs in the past? Was I caught up in my own pitiful wants and needs not to care? She needed love. No wonder she strove to keep me in her life. No wonder she became obnoxious at times. I was determined not to be hard-hearted any longer.

We talked for hours, sharing how we felt and why we felt the way we had. Both of us had been very insecure. Mom didn't have a father who doted on her. Her dad never had a kind word for her and always made her feel worthless. When she learned about our Heavenly Father, she grasped the Word immediately. I had a dad, but he wasn't around much. Even when he lived with us, he traveled for his job. I knew he cared, but I never felt really appreciated. Yeah, he'd brag about me and make me seem perfect to his friends, but to my face, he wasn't very affectionate. Until Friday night, I didn't think he had kissed me in years. When I learned about true love, I also grabbed it with all my might. I needed it and was determined to have it.

It was when we were eating dinner that my leg began to ache and burn. At first, I thought it was because I'd hadn't had it elevated in a while, but when I stood up, the pain made me gasp, and I had to sit down quickly.

It took a few minutes for me to gather my wits. When I did, Mom helped me to the sofa. Once I had my leg elevated, we immediately began to unfasten the straps to the boot so we could see if there was a problem. Mom thought the boot was strapped too tightly, maybe causing the pain. The condition of my leg frightened both of us when we had the boot unfastened and pulled away from my flesh. Ugly red streaks were formed all around the scar. In some places, pus formed. I'd developed an infection.

Mom called Dr. Carter's office, hoping for help, and fortunately got his answering service who told her that he would return her call shortly.

When Dr. Carter called, Mom was told to lightly sponge the infected area of my leg with peroxide but not to move my leg at all. After the bubbling stopped, she was to pat the area dry and refasten the boot. Then he directed her to have me visit him at the hospital tomorrow. When she informed him I was scheduled to see Shawn at 3:30 p.m., he said seeing him was more important. We were both a little spooked but held our emotions in check.

After all, we shouldn't live in fear.

Mom started making plans to take off work when I reminded her about Hope. I assured her I would be fine, and if I needed her, I'd call. My day had already been prearranged, and I was looking forward to being alone with a mentor. I called Hope to let her know what was going on, and she was more than happy to help. Afterward, I took a pain pill and hopped off to bed.

~~~

Ox witnessed everything. He wasn't worried about the situation because he knew the outcome. In time Gina would profess what she needed, and he would have the opportunity to make it happen.

The Trumpet

Hope didn't waste time. Immediately after disconnecting from Gina, she went inside her prayer closet and closed the door. Inside, she knelt beside the beautiful chair she had set aside as God's seat and poured out her concern. "Father, Sweet Abba, I come to you on behalf of my daughter. Her healing is being hindered. Please intervene!"

"Rest, Hope! Calm your soul and find peace. Gina is about to use her gift. Listen! Soon you'll hear her speak," He soothed.

~~~

After ending the conversation with Hope, I didn't turn on the overhead light in my room. I went straight to bed and tried to get comfortable, but when I tried to sleep, I couldn't because my mind raced. *Something isn't right,* I thought. Pain pills usually had me sleepy within a few minutes, but this wasn't the case tonight. I wanted to sleep so I wouldn't worry about my leg. I wanted sweet oblivion but was refused.

Exasperated, I sat up in bed, turned on my bedside lamp, and reached for my big parallel Bible. If I couldn't sleep, I'd study. My mind had to stay in a pure, truthful, and comforting place, or I'd focus on my problem.

Flipping through scripture, I remembered something that made me ask a question. "Whisperer, did you say I walk in paths prearranged for me?"

"Yes! You will walk if you want," He answered.

"I want to walk and run. Will this infection prevent me from moving forward? Will it cause me problems?" I asked.

"It won't if you don't let it," He replied.

"Huh? What do you mean?" I inquired.

"Look at the page you've turned to in my Word, what do you see?" He instructed.

I immediately looked. The scripture verse of Luke 6 verse 45 was highlighted. It was shining! My Amplified Version screamed at me!

The upright (honorable, intrinsically good) man out of the good treasure [stored] in his heart produces what is upright (honorable and intrinsically good), and the evil man out of the evil storehouse brings forth that which is depraved (wicked and intrinsically evil); for out of the abundance (overflow) of the heart his mouth speaks.

My heart pounded, and I sought clarification. "Lord! Can I do this? Can I produce what you told me this afternoon?"

"Yes! Open your mouth and speak it! You have it in your heart and you believe it, so tell the world!" He encouraged forcefully.

"Do I need to get out of bed and tell Mom? Should I call someone *on my phone? How should I do this?" I asked anxiously.*

"Man, will not listen to you, Gina, but the world will. The evil spiritual system reigning over your flesh must obey my Word. Use what you know against your opposition," He informed.

I understood! My opposition at this moment was the infection and my broken bones. Before I spoke to my own flesh, I threw back the covers and unfastened my boot. Gazing at the ugliness of my opposition, I also placed my hand on it and then used what the good Lord gave me. I opened my mouth and declared, "I am a child of God! He has given me legs to walk with! I will not be denied their strength! I will be able to walk in paths prearranged for me! I will live the good life given to me! I am a citizen of heaven now! I am no longer an outsider excluded from my rights! I have been given all Jesus died to give me!"

~~~

The blast of sound made Satan scream with pain as its power knocked him off the Grimes's roof. Landing hard on pavement, Satan grabbed his ears to prevent further damage to his hearing. Once the sound stopped, he realized Gina's words not only affected him but had frozen every one of his tormenting demons in place. This meant one thing! The woman was a trumpet! She had the power to call on heaven. He had to vacate immediately! The beast would soon be released, and he didn't want a confrontation with it yet.

~~~

Ox's ears were filled with pleasure! The trumpet sound always gave him confidence. He was proud Gina used it knowing the Holy Spirit was behind every note and word. The chime of her voice was beautiful as well as forceful.

Heaven opened, and light brightly filled the night. No evil could stand in the brightness. With this blessing, Ox stood tall and growled and then he began demanding Gina's words to be enforced. Barking orders, he commanded the frozen demons to wake and restore what they spoiled.

Some moved swiftly, moving over Gina's flesh, restoring blood flow, and sweeping away toxins. Others hesitated because they were confused, but their trepidation caused Ox to judge them and open his mouth a second time with fire instead of words, consuming them and leaving nothing but ash.

Ox didn't have to tell the remaining demons anything else; his glare focused on their directions showed them what to do because he straddled the ash of their brothers, proving to them who ruled.

~~~

Immediately, my leg started to feel strange. As if awakening from sleep, every nerve buzzed almost painfully. The sensation caused me to wiggle my toes to make the burn and buzz stop. Once they moved, the pain stopped, and the color of my skin brightened. My flesh didn't look gray with yellow hues any longer. Happy with the results, I fastened the boot and relaxed, but before I tried to rest again, I praised my God. "Thank you, Lord. You've shown me through experience your amazing love. I can rest now, looking forward to a brighter day."

"Sweet sleep, my love," He cooed.

~~~

Miles away, Hope heard Gina's declaration as God promised, and the power behind her words was extreme. Joy flooded Hope's soul. Something amazing was forming because after Gina's words were spoken, heaven resounded with musical trumpets of praise. Heaven was having a party!

Peace-driven, Hope left her prayer room, but before she joined her husband, she revisited the awe of the weekend. Not only had she been given rest from fear and shown her angel's strength, she could hear the power behind her spiritual daughter's voice. God the Father was moving swiftly! In two short days, favor had abounded.

While Brent slept, Hope curiously sought revelation from the Word. She wanted to understand what was happening, knowing everything was preordained and written for review within the Bible.

The word *favor* drove her to study Isaiah 61 verses 1 through 4 in her Amplified Bible. There she learned what her Lord was doing, for it said,

> *The Spirit of the Lord God is upon me, because the Lord has anointed and qualified me to preach the Gospel of good tidings to the meek, the poor, and afflicted; He has sent me to bind up and heal the brokenhearted, to proclaim liberty to the [physical and spiritual] captives and the opening of the prison and of the eyes to those who are bound,*

> *To proclaim the acceptable year of the Lord [the year of His favor] and the day of vengeance of our God, to comfort all who mourn,*

> *To grant [consolation and joy] to those who mourn in Zion—to give them an ornament (a garland or diadem) of beauty instead of ashes, the oil of joy instead of mourning, the garment [expressive] of praise instead of a heavy, burdened, and failing spirit—that they may be called oaks of righteousness [lofty, strong, and magnificent, distinguished for uprightness, justice, and right standing with God], the planting of the Lord, that He may be glorified.*

> *And they shall rebuild the ancient ruins; they shall rise up the former desolations and renew the ruined cities, the devastations of many generations.*

Hope sighed! So, this was what her Lord meant! Change was coming, and they were the forerunners. This news also had to be given to her family. She was about to wake Brent and share when the Lord stopped her. *"It is not time. You are not the anointed. Pastor Reed has been chosen. Through experience, you, Brent, Mamie, Caylee, and Gina will soon be used to guide others. All of you will be glorified and equipped to rebuild, renew, and defend. Ease your mind. Be the example for Gina to follow. Use what she learned yesterday to prove me true. Tomorrow let her see what you have. Show her what spiritual opposition she also has."*

"You want me to share my gift?" Hope inquired.

"Whatever it takes! Now get some sleep!" He commanded.

~~~

Satan visited his old enemy after leaving the Grimes's home, hoping to see her vulnerable, but what he saw was Hope still girded with strength. Sneaking closer to see what had empowered Hope, Satan saw what she was reading and panicked; she was reading from the Bible, and it was the prophecy of his demise. Backing quickly away from this enemy so he could regroup his thoughts, Satan realized his time in this area was short-lived. It was time to reinforce his army. He would not leave this area without doing serious damage first. He needed to call on giants he hadn't used in centuries and take down this family.

~~~

Insight was keenly aware Satan invaded the Arnold home. He was watching when the old serpent suddenly panicked and then left quickly before he had time to confront him. Even though Satan wasn't in the house, Insight still wondered where he went and what he was transpiring. Wanting to investigate, Insight informed heaven and then called several of his underlings and ordered them to report back to him as soon as they heard anything suspicious. Meanwhile, along with Justice, he would stand guard over Hope and her family while they rested.

Revealed

Shortly before dawn, heavenly trumpets sounded, alerting Insight that an underling was returning to him with a message. Greeting the messenger, Insight quickly got to the point and cast aside all formalities. "What news do you have?" he ordered.

"Sir, Satan plans to attack Greg. He has brought back to town the child's birth mother and her brother and has influenced them into thinking the Arnolds stole the child. They are planning to grab the boy from school today," the underling informed.

Squawking loudly, Insight called on heaven and earth to protect the child.

~~~

When I woke from a full and peaceful night of sleep, the first thing I did was unfasten my boot. I had to see my leg. For me, to sleep soundly and without nightmares meant that my leg was much better. I wasn't disappointed. The color was good, and the greenish fluid was almost gone. To someone without knowledge, the sight would give the peroxide credit. However, I knew the truth. With my own eyes, I saw an immediate change after I took authority over the infection's opposition.

Knowing that my day would be extremely busy, I quickly cleaned up and dressed before I hopped to the kitchen for coffee. I was about to exit my room when I sensed an urgency. I paused, not knowing what to do just before I heard Whisperer say, "Seek me."

"What? How?" I asked. "Through my Word," He shared.

"What do you want me to see?" I asked, confused. "Hidden," He answered.

One word. He wanted me to seek Him by looking up one word. Quickly, I flipped through the concordance to find the word *hidden*. I came across many that frustrated me greatly, but before I quit trying, I decided to ask Whisperer for help.

"Lord, which reference? I'm confused," I inquired.

"My statement," He replied.

His answer narrowed down my search quite a bit. Every statement Jesus spoke with the word hidden in it was very enlightening, but only one in the Amplified version of Luke stood out for me. Luke 8:17 read,

> *"For there is nothing hidden that shall not be disclosed, nor anything secret that shall not be known and come out into the open."*

My heart beat powerfully in my chest; I was getting very excited by this word. Was I about to see something? Would I get to see my mate soon?

Before I even asked, I heard a soft, *"You will see something special today. Everything you see will be revealed because the Father has allowed it to be revealed. What you hear and see is private. Unless you are being directed to something by a person, the visions and revelations are for you and me only. Most of mankind is not ready. People will think you're unhinged or over spiritual, and you will lose them. Don't risk losing someone with our secrets. In time, I will reveal all things to all people. The key is for you to be silent unless I release you to share. Heed this advice, Gina. Don't even share with your family or best friends."*

My joy quickly turned to awe. I was going to be shown heavenly secrets today, and I couldn't even tell my mom. This would be hard, but I could not disobey.

I was lost in thoughts when Mom tapped on my bedroom door. She asked, "Gina, are you okay? I have breakfast ready."

"I'm fine, Mom. Time got away from me. I must have gotten lost in my reading. Let me put my Bibles away, and I'll join you," I replied.

It was late. I had only a few minutes to enjoy Mom's company before she had to leave for work.

~~~

At the Arnold house, Hope was having minor irritating problems getting Greg fed and dressed. Hope wanted Greg to eat oatmeal, but he wanted to eat eggs and bacon like Uncle Carl. Hope wanted Greg to wear shorts and a lightweight shirt because the weather was hot, but he wanted to dress like his Uncle Carl and wear jeans and cowboy boots. Rather than fight, Hope relented, cooked his eggs and bacon, and let him dress the way he wanted. After all, Carl was her baby's idol and a very good example to follow. Every week, Carl taught Greg, along with all the other guys at the Boys' Home, games, karate, kickboxing, and wrestling, along with Christian values and principles, so he was a hero in their eyes.

Once Hope dropped Greg off at pre-K, she felt somewhat uneasy but didn't associate the feeling as one of concern for her son. Hope knew her baby was in good hands, so she chalked up the unsettled feeling to having to drag up past horror stories for Gina. She hated bringing up her past to anyone, but when her Lord said to share, she obeyed. Only this time, Hope knew why. Gina would grow and know for certain that God is alive and well and truly able.

~~~

I didn't have to wait for my ride; Hope was prompt. She drove her SUV up Mom's driveway at exactly 9:00 a.m. When I was settled in the backseat of Hope's vehicle, she and I didn't waste any time discussing Pastor Reed's message. She would ask me if I understood and then give me her view. Hope's interpretation on the topic enthralled me. She talked as if she had a personal relationship with God as her Father. When Hope finished, she got quiet, and I noticed she was sweating. At first, I thought she was hot from the extremely warm weather until I noticed her hands shaking.

"Hope, are you okay?" I inquired.

She sighed and then replied, "I'm fine, but I have, to be honest. I'm on a mission. Our Heavenly Father has asked me to testify about Him, and the only way I can is to tell you something I'd rather forget. What I'm about to tell you almost traumatized me, and it is hard to share."

"Why?" I asked.

"Because I almost died, but God the Father intervened. Gina, He wants you to know Him like I do. Honey, he is very real. The Holy Spirit has brought you to us, and now it is the time we reconcile you to a love greater than anything you'll ever know. When Jesus died and returned to heaven, He sent us His Spirit, but the reason for all of it was so we could know the Father. When you have God in your life, you have everything. In order for you to truly believe, He has asked me to tell you how we met."

She backed up her testimonies with details; some wonderful, and others horrible. I listened intently to her explain her firsthand account of grandeur and then how angels ministered to her. Then she shared with me her first experience with the Father. She said she'd denied all the beauty, all the jewels, and all the glamor for Jesus. She didn't desire anything but Him, and when she went to Jesus in her birthday suit, God Himself dressed her in royal attire. That was when my jaw dropped. Then I remembered what Whisperer told me this morning. He said if someone came to me with details too unexplainable, that they were sent because He willed them. Hope's testimonies were sent to me by the Holy Spirit as my personal witness to the hidden secrets.

Then she shared the torture she endured and how Jesus helped her cope. Her final testimony was how God the Father showed up and saved her from death by turning the gun on her ex-husband. Brent and Mamie were the only two who knew the truth; everyone else thought Sam killed himself. Now, I was privy to this truth, and God wanted me to know. I was honored.

When Hope parked her SUV at the hospital, I wanted to cry. The journey hadn't been long enough. I wanted more information. I was enjoying every story she shared. Hope's stories made me feel strange. Others frightened me, but mostly each one gave me a new perspective. We are children of God, and we are supposed to be regal and not act haughty. We are already wealthy even if we don't have a penny in our pocket. We are lovingly protected even if we can't see our protectors.

To my joy, Hope wasn't finished telling me secrets. She planned for us to have a lovely morning in a small park located outside the hospital so we could talk, drink cold drinks, and eat a healthy packed lunch before going into the emergency room to see Dr. Carter. She hadn't planned jumping right into spiritual issues before we left the vehicle, but my enthusiasm made her relax where she could share easily. She was glad I wanted to listen. I was like a thirsty person trapped in a desert, and her stories were like water. They were life-giving! When she told me we had an awesome giant guardian angel following us everywhere, I was elated. That meant Adrian was following me. He wasn't gone! But then Hope told me I had a large creature for my angel, and I almost freaked. Suddenly, I remembered my bulldog dream again. I remembered seeing weird beings in my sleep following Hope, Brent, and Mamie.

Meekly, I asked, "Hope, can you describe my guardian? Until now, I thought Adrian was my guardian angel."

"Gina, Adrian was sent to you first so you wouldn't be frightened. His appearance is human because he represents the healing nature of our Lord Jesus, but even Adrian isn't the main guard. Adrian is a sub guard. He takes orders from the main guard called Healer who follows Mamie everywhere. Your guard represents Jesus's determination and self-sacrifice, and His name is Ox, the angel of faith," Hope enlightened.

I felt my eyes go wide with shock! I'd seen the Ox in my dream. He was glorious, sweet, and loving with the face of a cow. Hope noticed my shock and asked, "You've seen him, haven't you?"

"Yes, in a dream! Whisperer, I mean, the Holy Spirit, shows me things when I sleep or when I focus on Him with my eyes shut," I replied.

"That is wonderful! Would you like to see our angels?" Hope asked.

"Can I? How?" I asked.

"Through God's favor, Gina!" Hope exclaimed. "He told me to give you what you needed to be effective for His kingdom."

Again, I inquired meekly, "You can give me spiritual sight?" "No, silly! I can share my gift with you. While I'm with you,

God will grant you the ability to see spiritual beings and see wonderful things, but I must warn you, not all spiritual beings are good. Some belong to our enemy, Satan," Hope conveyed.

"How will I know the difference?" I asked.

"You'll know immediately because every evil and horrible emotion infiltrate them. They are ugly and intimidating. Some feed off negative emotions, so remember that. We are in the perfect place for you to see both good and evil beings. Hospitals are a feeding ground for evil beings because of fear, so good angels have to stay close by to enable people to cope," she answered.

I was scared. I wasn't in a position where I could run. What if one of the evil things tried to get me? With this thought fixed in my head, I stated, "Hope, we need to wait. I can't get away if one comes after me."

Laughing, Hope stated, "Who do you belong to? Who did we talk about earlier? Honey, nothing evil will stay around when your Heavenly Father is present. We want you to see evil flee from you. You need to know how powerful your new family status is, but before we start, let's get comfortable at one of the tables in the park."

We found a table under a big oak tree out of the sunshine where I could elevate my leg and continue our discussion. Hope soothed my nerves by promising nothing would harm me; then she moved closer to me and said, "I'm going to place my hands on you and pray. Gina, I've only shared my gift with Brent and Mamie. They have told me some of the effects last but never as vivid as when first shared. Mamie hears better now, and Brent can see better, but I can't promise you'll have either ability after today. We can only hope."

"I'm ready," I confessed.

I closed my eyes before Hope laid her hands on each side of my face; then she pressed her forehead on mine and began speaking in a foreign tongue. Instantly, I heard sounds I've never heard before; and after I opened my eyes, I looked at Hope closely. She was lovely! She glowed, and she wore this amazing garment over her clothes.

"What do you see, Gina?" Hope asked.

"You are glowing, and you have a beautiful sheer gown on," I answered.

She giggled and commented, "You see my robe. You have one on. Look down."

I did!

Then Hope said, "Look around and tell me what you see."

I obeyed and almost fell off the bench from shock. Standing behind Hope was a giant creature with the body of a man. It had wings, claws for fingers, and the face of an eagle. "What is it?" I asked.

Hope knew by my question and asked, "Does he have a face like an eagle?"

I nodded and said, "Yeah."

"Gina, meet Insight. He is my guardian angel. Insight has Jesus's power of revelation knowledge. He can see and hear better than anything on earth. Plus, he is the champion who goes before me," Hope introduced him.

"Happy to meet you," I said shyly to Insight.

Then Hope said, "Gina, look beside your right side and meet Ox. He has been waiting patiently for you to know about him."

My head turned quickly to the right, and my eyes fell on a huge reddish-brown chest. Slowly, my eyes moved upward searching for the kind eyes I remembered in my dream. Ox was enormous! His head was four times larger than mine, and he had two huge horns. His arms were massive, and his hands were human. He had legs like a man, but his feet were hooves. Like Insight, he also had wings, but what overwhelmed me the most were his eyes. His big brown eyes were crying.

I tried to stand so I could reach up and touch his face. I wanted him to know I already loved him and was not afraid, but he stopped me from rising by gently placing a hand on my shoulder and then mind-melded his love to me first. This form of communication confused me.

Then I heard Hope say, "Gina, Ox doesn't speak. Neither does Insight. They will mentally share thoughts with you. It will be the same as if they were speaking, so don't be afraid."

"Hope, this is awesome! Show me more!" I exclaimed.

"Okay! Gina, I chose this park to share my gift with you for a reason. I wanted you to see both sides in the spirit realm, and I couldn't think of a better place for you to see the truth. If you will, position yourself where your leg is comfortable so you can watch people as they enter and exit the hospital. Notice their appearance and then look beyond the person to focus on what is following them," Hope said.

After I repositioned myself on the opposite side of the picnic table, I began looking at people like Hope asked. Some people had a glow to their appearance and had lovely angels accompanying them, but to my horror, I noticed a lot of the people who came and went already looked dead. When I peered beyond their physical bodies to see what followed them, I understood why they looked gray and lifeless. They didn't have beautiful angels; they had hideous, controlling demons following them. I asked Hope, "Do these people know something is wrong?"

"No! They are already dead," Hope replied.

I had a startling revelation from her comment. Just a few days ago, I was a dead girl walking. "They aren't saved, are they?" I asked.

"No, Gina they are not," Hope shared.

"There is hope for them, isn't there?" I queried.

"That is where we come into play. Our lights, or should I say, our love and confidence in a merciful Heavenly Father draw people into the kingdom. Don't you remember?" Hope asked.

Here again, I did.

We sat in the cool of the lovely oak tree and people-watched for hours. Then after we ate lunch, we proceeded to venture toward the emergency room. Dr. Carter had informed Mom last night that he would see me there. I was to have the emergency room call his office when I arrived. Since his office was located directly across the street, he wanted to see me at the hospital in case I needed specific treatment that required anesthesia.

When I informed the emergency room's receptionist of Dr. Carter's instructions, she looked at me funny. Then she said, "Dr. Carter won't be able to help you."

"Why?" I asked.

She politely stated, "Ms. Grimes, Dr. Carter was killed in a car accident last evening. His incident has been on the news."

"I'm sorry to hear that. Should I come back, or is there someone else I can see?" I asked.

The lady was very cordial. She told us to have a seat and she would see what could be done. The wait was horrible. Not only did I have weird thoughts, I was still empowered with Hope's gift. I heard people's thoughts and saw what their emotions drew. I hated every second, and the time dragged. We waited for an hour before the receptionist finally had news, and by that time, I was weary.

We were told that Dr. Carter's partner could see me later in the afternoon. I could either wait or return. Since I had an appointment with Shawn Davis in the therapy center at 3:30 p.m., I decided to leave. I didn't think I could stand much more of the moaning and complaining I heard throughout all the waiting area. I gave the lady my thanks and told her of our plans. Then with Hope's help, I hobbled out of the waiting area as quickly as I could on my clumsy crutches.

Once we were outside, Hope told me to slow down. She informed me that the uneasiness I was feeling could be attributed to emotion-eating demons. She also said it would take time, but I would be able to recognize when negativity came to misguide me. In time, I would be able to fight the urges to be unhappy, worried, and fearful. She also assured me if I was aware, quick enough of this lure, demons wouldn't even come close. But I had to give Ox permission to guard me; that way, they couldn't touch me or even try. That was good to know.

Hope drove us back to her place, and we enjoyed normal girl topics until about 2:30 p.m. Our plan was for Hope to see that I made it in the hospital then go get Greg from school at 3:00 p.m., take him to the Boys' Home and wait for my call. That way, she would have her son settled with family and could then take care of me, but our plans drastically changed.

We were in the process of entering the hospital door when Hope got a call on her cell. Still empowered with Hope's gift, I instantly noticed her change of clothes. I wanted to express concern, ask what was happening, but I couldn't. Panic gripped my heart! Hope had transformed from head to toe in a slick, red- leather-looking, skin tight outfit, and I couldn't see her anymore. I knew it was her, but even her voice was hard and serious.

Even though she reminded me of Spider-man, only naked in the red, slick suit, she still helped me inside the waiting area and then calmed my nerves. Composed but serious, she explained, "Gina, I have an emergency! Someone has tried to kidnap Greg from school. I will not be able to come back. Call your Mom and have her come to your aid."

I watched this new Hope and her guardian angel walk away, leaving me to wait in the hospital alone. I had been overwhelmed by how she changed, but at the same time, I was impressed by her ability to stay calm and composed enough to help me under the circumstances. I had a new respect for her. This new Hope wasn't my gentle, mild-mannered, and sweet Hope any longer, she'd become a stern and fierce contender. Whoever she would face was in for a surprise. Hope was no coward; she was righteously angry instead of scared and wanted to fight.

Ounce of Prevention

Satan sat back and surveyed the damage he'd caused. Satan loved the mayhem. He loved causing chaos, and he adored death. In the last few days, he'd had fun giving ole lady Polk a stroke, and he had caused ole Dr. Carter's accident. From the two, he was still having fun toying with the Polk men and trying to frighten and delude the Grimes girl.

Today's fun was the most enjoyable yet. Tormenting Hope Arnold never dulled. Of course, he was well aware their game had changed. Hope's newfound confidence caused him issues. That was why he decided to change things. Having pawns to attempt Greg's kidnapping would bring old memories and dreaded feelings back to Hope and give her pain, as well as fear.

~~~

Wayne Polk had more on his plate than he could handle, and his mind could not focus. With serious family issues and his business partner's death, people were looking to him for answers, and he was about to physically buckle under the strain. The pressure from stress made Wayne's head hurt. His back and shoulders were tight with tension, and when he was told that another patient of Dr. Carter waited for him in the emergency room, he almost became unhinged. Every call from the emergency room meant he had to deal with the old man's sloppy work, again.

Wayne was usually a tolerant man, but today he was being pushed to his limit. Three times today, he had to leave his office, walk over to the hospital in order to fix, or figure out some of Dr. Carter's work. In addition, he had to tend to his own patients, and the stress of it all made him rude, impatient with colleagues, and very unsympathetic to the patients who needed him.

~~~

I sat in the emergency room still under Hope's gift, listening to all kinds of drama, as well as seeing the demons feeding, and almost came unglued. That was until I remembered what Hope said. I could ask Ox to intervene.

I gathered my purse and crutches and quietly moved to a part of the waiting area least occupied to mentally talk with Ox. "Ox, can you hear me?" I inquired.

"Yes, Gina I hear fine," he responded. "Let me see you please," I asked nicely.

Instantly, he blurred into vision, and my heart steadied. "Thanks!" I offered.

"How may I help you, Gina?" he asked.

"Don't leave me and don't let those energy-sucking demons near me," I required.

"Rest assured!" he exclaimed.

Then I heard a soft familiar voice, *"Gina!"*

"Whisperer! You're here!" I softly replied.

He said, *"I'll never leave you. Seek me!"*

I knew what that meant. He wanted me to look inside His Word. Frantically, I looked for a Bible. This hospital had little blue ones everywhere, so there had to be one in their emergency area. When I couldn't find one, I gathered my things and hobbled over to the receptionist's desk.

"Excuse me! Do you have a Bible I can read?" I asked.

The nice lady quickly stood then offered, "Let me see if I can find you one. There are several lying around. Make yourself comfortable, and I'll bring one to you."

Because of her nice gesture, I purposefully examined her closely. She was glowing and had an angel following her. That meant I wasn't alone in this room with evil; I had a sister.

Once I had a Bible in hand, I sat quietly so Whisperer could drop me a hint. When He didn't, I asked, "What am I seeking?"

I didn't hear His voice, but I saw a flash of light before my eyes that said "Psalm 140:1–13." I didn't know if Psalm had 140 chapters, but I obeyed the vision and began searching.

Since the Bible was a King James Version, I knew I may have trouble understanding, so I read slowly. It read,

> *Deliver me, O Lord, from the evil man: preserve me from the violent man;*
>
> *Which imagine mischiefs in their heart; continually are they gathered together for war.*

They have sharpened their tongues like a serpent; adders' poison is under their lips. Selah.

Keep me, O Lord, from the hands of the wicked; preserve me from the violent men; who have purposed to overthrow my goings.

The proud have hid a snare for me, and cords; they have spread a net by the wayside; they have set gins for me. Selah.

I said unto the Lord, Thou art my God: hear the voice of my supplications, O Lord.

O God the Lord, the strength of my salvation, Thou hast covered my head in the day of battle.

Grant not, O Lord, the desires of the wicked: further not his wicked device; lest they exalt themselves. Selah.

As for the head of those that compass me about, let the mischief of their own lips cover them.

Let burning coals fall upon them: let them be cast into the fire; into deep pits that they rise not up again. Let not an evil speaker be established in the earth: evil shall hunt the violent man to overthrow him.

I know that the Lord will maintain the cause of the afflicted, and the right of the poor.

Surely the righteous shall give thanks unto thy name: the upright shall dwell in thy presence.

When I finished, I inquired, "Is this a warning?"
"Prevention!" He enlightened.
"What do I do now?" I asked.
"Break down the verses and confess them. Use them now as preventive measures," He encouraged.

~~~

Ox immediately took notice and stood ready for orders. Gina was about to release God's Word for him to require.

~~~

I looked at each verse and then mentally formed sentences to make as my personal statement. Once I had them right in my mind, I began to quietly declare, "My Lord has delivered me from the evil and violent man. I am delivered from evil tongues and poisonous words. My Lord keeps me out of the hands of wickedness and preserves me from violent men. Any snare formed against me will capture my enemy instead because my God has heard my request. Burning coals will fall on my enemies, and fire will destroy them. Any pit I find myself in, my Lord will raise me out of because I know my Lord will maintain my cause. God is forever by my side, and I will continually praise Him."

~~~

Every word Gina spoke was like a sonic boom in the spiritual realm. Each word was her conception of what Jesus gave her, and the faith she had behind each syllable resonated loudly.

~~~

Ox was overjoyed! He could purposefully defend this human. No matter who or what he had to face, he would make sure she was protected because God had granted this declaration.

~~~

After I finished, I looked around to see if people were watching. When they weren't, I sought further instructions. "Lord, what now?" I whispered softly.

"Do you remember how Hope looked earlier?" He inquired.

"Yes! She was amazing!" I declared quietly.

"The suit was me. Hope was wearing my protection in an evil time," He shared.

"Awesome! Do I get to wear the suit?" I asked softly.

"You are wearing me now. Look at your hands," He encouraged.

My eyes immediately focused on my hands. I wasn't wearing a red leather suit. Astonished, I saw that not only were my hands covered, but my whole body was completely cloaked in fire.

Oh, boy! I thought.

"Gina, you've never left My fire. Since you first accepted me, I've been all around you as well as in you. With Hope's gift, you can see your shield. Never doubt me. I'm always here," He cooed. I was really into our conversation when I heard a nurse call my name. When I got up to follow the nurse, I knew Whisperer and Ox would be with me, so I didn't fret. Whatever lay ahead would be fine. God had me covered.

I was covered from fear and violence, but I was not protected from shock. The doctor who came in to tend to my leg was none other than my soul mate. Instantly, my brain went into overdrive as I feasted on his face with my eyes. Here standing before me was Dr. Wayne Polk, God's gift to me.

I was certain we would fall in love instantly, but when he looked at me; his expression was blank and impersonal. At that point, my heart sank. Before he even approached me, he started saying horrible things about my leg. He said I was damaged. He also stated he wouldn't be surprised if he had to perform corrective surgery. But before I could get worried, I noticed something strange. With my new eyesight, I could see his words as if they were written on air; and before any of the negative things could touch me, I watched Ox breathe fire on them, leaving puffs of smoke in their wake.

When Wayne approached, he ordered me to sit further back on the table with a sharp whip of a command, totally lacking any kindness. I couldn't understand why or what I'd done to invoke such rudeness. He was the man I was going to marry, so why was he so hateful?

Before he even laid a hand on my leg, Ox had straddled the table and wrapped me tightly in his wings so that all I could see were feathers. I struggled mentally with Ox's decision. I wanted to see my mate. I had to get a loving response from Wayne, but Ox stood between us. What was happening?

I felt the air hit my leg, then rough and impassionate hands maneuvered the boot away. It made me want to cry. I'd imagined loving touches from Wayne, gentle caresses, not the rough jerks and prods he was giving me. Then I felt a cold liquid being applied. It had to be peroxide because I felt bubbling. Then I felt pain. Wayne was gouging at my leg. I grabbed the sides of the table, and I gritted my teeth. I would not scream even though every fiber of my being wanted to. When he was finished, he ordered me to relax and then said a nurse would be in to assist me shortly. When I heard a door close, I started to cry. My first experience with my soul mate was horrible. I pounded Ox's back, and I slapped away his wings. I needed a hug, not his smothering feathers. When a nurse came in, I was too sad to look up. It wasn't until I felt a soothing touch and heard a loving voice that I got myself together. Standing before me was Mamie and another lady who attended my wounds and helped get me back into my boot. "What happened, Mamie? The doctor didn't even tell me what he did to me," I cried.

"Sweetie, you had two or three pieces of leftover staples still in your leg. Apparently, Dr. Carter's assistant didn't remove all of them the other day, and they were causing infection. Everything is going to be fine now. I'm here to help you into the therapy center. I'm going to make sure Shawn fits you properly this time with crutches," Mamie explained.

I still was not pacified and had to ask, "Why was the doctor so mean to me?"

"Honey, Dr. Polk is going through a lot. Not only has his partner died, but his mother also had a severe stroke, and he is preoccupied. Don't fret, you had nothing to do with his attitude. He is usually a nice man," Mamie answered.

After I had my boot securely fastened and a prescription for an antibiotic handed to me, Mamie rolled me in a wheelchair to the therapy center.

~~~

Ox followed Gina. He was glad he'd made the decision to block her vision, even if it made her unhappy. She didn't need to focus on Wade's brother touching her, being cold and impersonal. She was being duped and wasn't aware.

Healer

Mamie wanted to watch Shawn fit Gina with crutches. Her motherly instincts couldn't rest until she was assured. She had made special arrangements to come with Gina so she could give Shawn advice, but when it was time for the appointment, the Holy Spirit interrupted her plans.

"Mamie, we need to talk. Find somewhere private," He beckoned.

Mamie quickly excused herself by whispering in Gina's ear, "I need to find a ladies' room. Make sure your new crutches are comfortable."

"Okay, Mamie," Gina replied.

In a private area, Mamie asked, "What is it, Lord?"

"Gina is heartbroken. She needs spiritual healing from you. Stop being so concerned with her body. Use your time with her for me. Let her ask questions. She has many, so be mindful of My Word. Satan interrupted Hope's plans today, so you stand in the gap. With Hope out of the way, Satan played a trick on Gina, and it has made her very sad. You do not need to know what Satan's trick was because I am greater than anything he does. Gina's guardian angel knows of the problem, so rest assured I have everything under control. I have warned Gina not to talk about spiritual things, but you need to know she has been empowered by Hope's gift. For now, she sees and hears in the spirit realm. Be prepared when Gina notices Healer. She will call him by another name. I've asked Healer to be present and for him to side with Ox until Gina gets home. You use this time to talk and make sure she gets home safely. Do not allow Gina's mother to assist at this time. Mrs. Grimes would only slow Gina's spiritual progress down," He enlightened.

~~~

Shawn and I were finished in no time. He knew exactly what I needed. I was now the proud owner of arm-grip crutches instead of the underarm kind. When I stopped at the receptionist's desk, I was also given an appointment slip to see Dr. Polk again in a week. I waited and waited in the lobby, hoping to see Mamie again before I called Mom. I wanted to show her Shawn's selection, but she was taking a long time in the ladies' room. I almost called Mom, but something made me hesitate. I felt like something was wrong. I wondered if my new super senses were trying to tell me something. Without Hope around, I didn't like being supercharged. Every sound and sight in the hospital made me feel strange. I didn't have anyone to talk with who could help me keep from overreacting. Then I thought, *Yes, I did! I had Whisperer and Ox.* Why is it so hard to keep that fact in my head?

"Lord, is Mamie sick?" I asked.

"She'll be back soon. I had her on a mission for me," He replied. With His verbal reassurance, I was able to sit quietly while

I waited for Mamie; and with my new sight, I held on to Ox. The time alone, even in their presence, didn't help. My heart was heavy. Because of the rough incident with Wayne, I needed someone to talk with. I needed to vent, but the Lord warned me not to say a word to anybody. Being a new Christian was hard. I had so many questions.

Even though I was lost in my pity party, my supernatural hearing heard Mamie coming. I could hear her talking with someone in the corridor, along with the swishing sound her hosiery made, long before I saw her face. When the door to the lobby opened, I couldn't believe my eyes. I wanted to shout for joy! The person Mamie was talking with was Adrian. I had someone I could vent to. I could talk with him because he knew everything!

"Adrian! I'm so glad to see you," I blurted.

Mamie giggled. Then she came quickly to my side. "Gina, sweetie, this isn't Adrian. I'd like you to meet my guardian, his name is Healer. The Lord told me you would be confused," Mamie shared.

I looked closer and then I nodded a greeting in Healer's direction. When he smiled at me, I saw Adrian's face and grin. I was definitely confused.

Since Mamie knew, I confessed, "Hope shared her gift with me today. I've been seeing and hearing weird things ever since. Your angel looked familiar to me. I'm sorry I shouted."

"Don't be silly! I've been with the Lord, and he told me to be prepared. He said you would be confused. All the angels under Healer's authority look like him. If you have seen one of Healer's angels, you can rest assured he already knows why you did. Healer won't be offended by your misstep," Mamie soothed.

I was thrilled to know Mamie was part of Adrian's group. Maybe one day we could share everything, but for now, I still had to deal with my problems alone. Trying to regroup, I showed Mamie my crutches because she had been so emphatic about a proper fit earlier. I showed her how the grips were secure enough to keep me balanced and how they made me shift my weight on my hands and wrists instead of my armpits. Mamie was impressed, but she wasn't as worried about me having better crutches as she had been. She had another focus. Apparently, her meeting with the Lord had her turned toward another mission.

I sensed the lack of interest in my crutches as a sign that she needed to attend to her new mission. I needed to call Mom so Mamie could get on with the Lord's business. I proceeded to dig through my purse to retrieve my cell, but once I had it in hand, Mamie patted my leg and said, "Child, don't bother your mama.

Ole Mamie will take you home. I know Hope can't come back. This will give us a chance to talk. God said you had questions."

I was shocked again. I was God's business. The Heavenly Father was covering all the bases for me. Mamie filled a void left by Hope just in time. "Thanks, Mamie. I do have questions," I confessed.

Mamie helped me slide in her car, and once we were on the way, I pondered what to ask. I knew I had to be vague; I had to keep my visions private. But then I remembered Adrian and what Mamie said. If Adrian was subject to Healer, then Healer would know. With quickened energy, I asked, "Can visions given to us by God be misconceived?"

"Honey, Jesus warns us in the book of Matthew chapter 24 to be wary of misleading. The reason Jesus said that is because Satan will use anyone or anything to lead you away from what you need to know," Mamie answered.

Then Mamie asked, "Have you been given a vision from heaven?"

"Yes, ma'am," I replied.

"Don't tell me! Things given to us from heaven are private. When you get home, take out your Bible and study the second chapter of the book of Habakkuk. We are told through scripture to write things down. You'll see where an old prophet was told to make the vision plain. Written visions help us keep focused. Then wait for the vision because in due time it will come to pass. Then I want you to study Proverbs 29. I think it says, 'Without a vision, people perish, but when people trust in God, they are blessed.' Look at the scripture and see if I have it right," Mamie encouraged. I was excited! Mamie was on target. Adrian had encouraged me to write down the vision. I patted my chest. Ever since Friday night, I wore my notes in my bra. I couldn't wait to get home and study them again. I read the scriptures Mamie suggested and sought the Lord at the same time. Maybe I could get some relief from my heavy heart. I knew something wasn't right, but I couldn't put my finger on what. With Whisperer's help and between reading scripture and looking over my notes again, maybe I could feel better. Even if I didn't, I had Whisperer to talk with. He would know what to do.

Today's trip had really taken a toll on me. By the time Mamie and I had talked, I'd stopped to get my antibiotics and arrived home; I was pooped! I was physically and mentally drained, plus very worried about Hope and little Greg. Before Mamie left, I asked her to call to Hope's cell. We were both glad all was well, and Hope and Greg were headed home.

I hugged Mamie hard before she could leave and said, "Thanks for the help and thanks for listening to God and to me. Today has been very eventful. I'm tired and sore in more ways than one, and I'm ready to get comfortable with the Good Book."

I didn't waste any time; I went straight to my bedroom. I turned on my lamp, retrieved all my Bibles then lay across my bed. It was time I got reacquainted with my vision, so I plucked the piece of paper out of my bra. I read and was astounded; nothing seemed to fit. What was on the paper and what happened today did not match.

I read every word slowly one more time before asking Whisperer for help. I thought I'd been deceived, so I sought for the answer. "Lord, everything I saw today was wrong except the name and face. Please help me understand."

"Seek me, Gina. Read the scripture verses. Do not deviate from what you were shown," Whisperer answered.

I turned first to the book of Matthew chapter 24 and read Jesus's warning. Clearly, from understanding the Word, I knew that I was being tricked. Then I looked for Habakkuk and found what Mamie said in chapter 2. My Amplified version read,

> *The Lord answered me and said, Write the vision and engrave it so plainly upon tablets that everyone who passes may [be able to] read [it easily and quickly] as he hastens by.*

For the vision is yet for an appointed time and it hastens to the end [fulfillment]; it will not deceive or disappoint. Though it tarry, wait [earnestly] for it, because it will surely come; it will not be behindhand on its appointed day.

Here again, scripture states a vision will not deceive. So, what I lived and saw today was not what God had shown me. I still had questions.

"Lord, who will make my vision come to pass? Who would want to?" I asked.

"Open your eyes and see. Who do you have with you?" He replied.

I was tired and at home. I thought surely that the supernatural gift Hope had imparted on me was gone, but I obeyed Whisperer's command and looked around my room. Standing no more than six inches from my bed was my lovely Ox. He was the one passing by my secret notes. My Whisperer and my Ox were the ones making it happen. My heart sang with joy.

Acknowledging Ox, I reached out to touch him. "Thanks, friend. You knew something wasn't right today. You tried to shield me, but I mistreated you. I'm sorry, I don't know what happened. All I know is the name and face I saw today was the same given to me in my vision. The timing and place for us to fall in love were incorrect. Plus, in my vision, I was walking. Please help me cope and be patient while I wait. I can now rest knowing you will soon make Wayne fall in love with me," I confessed.

~~~

Ox wanted to tell Gina that Wayne was not the one, but the Holy Spirit stopped him by saying, "All is well, my friend. Gina must grow and come to terms. We'll make sure. Listen to her words. Follow what she confesses."

~~~

Once I had the scriptures in my heart, I knew I had to say them aloud. I began by stating, "My vision will come. I have an appointed time, and it will be fulfilled. I will not be deceived or disappointed."

~~~

From Gina's profession, hell shook, and the earth trembled. God was happy. Ox and all of heaven began to dance and shout for joy.

Soon Gina would see her vision come to pass. Then she will be so convinced the kingdom of God is real, nothing or no one could convince her otherwise.

~~~

After I made my verbal stance, I closed my eyes and rested. A lovely nap would help soothe the body and enable me to enjoy fellowship with Mom later.

No Weapon

The Holy Spirit was on top of Satan's threat against Greg long before Hope or Brent became aware. Intentionally, neither parent was warned because it was time for this family to depend on God's covenant. Way before dawn, Insight had alerted heaven of Satan's threat, and angels were dispatched and ready for anything. They had orders to protect and defend the little boy because plans were put in place before Greg left Hope's care. Even during the attempted abduction, angels intervened so that no physical harm would come to this family because the Holy Spirit had caused confusion for the demons surrounding Amanda and Donald Hines. His confusing influence caused the demons to attack one another, thereby leaving their subordinates helpless. This action rendered Satan's plan weak and without any substantial strength. Donald and Amanda were drugs and alcohol-impaired, and they were clumsy, slow, and unable to catch the quick and scared little boy. When their attempt to abduct Greg failed and teachers were alerted of their actions, the school's principal took authority and placed the call to Brent. Brent alerted the police and then called Hope. The Holy Spirit expected immediate intercession to come from Brent and Hope, and when it began, he instantly covered them within His armor to calm their nerves.

Even in God's armor, Hope was angry with herself and couldn't help mentally beating herself up. Aware she would be upset, the Lord let her vent. She knew something was wrong after leaving Greg at school, a gut feeling or intuition, but something just wasn't right. So, while she drove to the school, she chided herself by thinking, *why didn't I pay closer attention to the spiritual warning I had this morning? I knew the uneasiness meant something was wrong. Why didn't I take the time to inquire of the Lord instead leaning on my own reasoning?*

"Hope, please stop! Trust me! I love you and Greg. Even in the midst of trouble, I will be with the two of you. Even though you are gifted, you are still human and will never be capable of knowing everything. It is time you trust completely in my covenant," He commanded.

By the time Hope arrived, her emotions were calmer. Her anxious heart had settled, but it wasn't until she saw Brent waiting for her outside of the school building that she relaxed. Like a flood, she allowed scripture's interpretation of love between husband and wife to overtake her heart, making her rely on Jesus's love. God's covenant arm was strong and powerful, and there was no need for the boxing match in her head. Once her focus changed, the Lord convinced her that the incident wasn't her fault and that she had done right by Greg. He also encouraged her to trust stronger in His protection for her family.

Greg was being comforted by the principal's secretary when Hope and Brent entered the office, but as soon as his little eyes spotted them, he burst into tears, and Hope's heart broke. Rushing over to her baby, Hope gathered him in her arms and held him tightly while she also cried. Hope knew what Greg was feeling.

In Hope's embrace, Greg hiccupped and whispered in her ear, "You're my mama! That lady is not my mama!"

Hope's eyes grew wide when his words registered. Greg was scared, but he was also feeling the fear of being neglected and abused again. Greg's words were a clue, and they made her think and wonder, *Is Amanda Hines out from prison?*

Verbalizing her revelation, she screamed, "Brent! I think I know who the kidnapper is!"

"Who?" Brent demanded.

Making sure Greg was secure, Hope sat on one of the principal's large and comfortable chairs and placed Greg on her lap. Then she motioned for Brent to kneel to their level where he could hear. Then she asked Greg, "Sweetie, tell Daddy what you told Mama. Daddy needs to know who the person was. He must know everything so he can make sure she doesn't come back. He can take your news to the police waiting outside, and you can stop worrying."

Greg's big eyes grew serious, and in between every sniff and hiccup, he explained the foiled plan in detail, giving Brent everything he needed. He shared that while he was playing hide-and-seek with his friends on the playground, a woman who looked familiar approached him. When she told him she was his real mother and there to take him home, he started crying and refused to go along. His refusal caused the bad man to grab his arm, but he had managed to wiggle free and run away.

A teacher interjected after she heard Greg's interpretation to his parents, and she said that Greg's screams were what alerted all the adults on the playground, but by the time they found Greg, the two people attempting the kidnap had escaped, leaving Greg inconsolable. They had no doubt something had happened, and law enforcement was called.

Brent heard the same clue Hope heard. It was Greg's recollection of Amanda Hines that caused him concern. Instantly, he had his cell phone out, calling the office to verify some pertinent fact before sending the police on a wild-goose chase. The information he received made him sick. The insane child abuser was out of prison?

Sometimes Brent hated his job. If it weren't for his responsibility with the Hines case, he could take his family home and be a dad. He would get his family unit regrouped, but right now, duty called. He had to make sure authorities knew Amanda's probation had been violated. Paperwork demanded his attention, and state agencies had to be alerted because Greg's safety heavily depended on him following through with legal precautions.

Brent couldn't rest until Hope and Greg were safe at home. He gave her explicit instructions that after she arrived home, she was not to answer the door until he got home. After seeing his family in the SUV, Brent quickly interceded, asking God to watch over the ones he couldn't. Then he left for his office to make certain that Amanda's freedom was again taken.

~~~

Satan picked up the pieces of the foiled kidnapping and regrouped his crazy demons. Then he juiced Amanda and Donald Hines again on drugs and alcohol; he wasn't through with Hope Arnold yet. In times past, he would have fallen back and waited, but not today. He had to destroy this Arnold's smug confidence, and he knew the little boy was her weakest link.

~~~

Insight watched every move Satan made as he dispatched controlling demons on the Hines. He also heard Satan's plot. He would be ready. Nothing would be allowed past him.

~~~

Amanda and Donald Hines, both high on drugs and under the influence of Satan's will, watched and waited in their beat-up old truck hoping to see someone leave the school with Greg. Amanda wanted to know where her boy lived, and Donald convinced her they would have a better chance stealing the kid when they were away from so many prying eyes. He also thought it best that they attempt another kidnap soon, not allowing time to lapse since the authorities had been alerted. As soon as they had the boy, they could make a run for the border and live in Mexico, away from the legal US scrutiny.

~~~

Hope sympathized with Brent's feelings. She knew he was worried, so she followed his orders to go home where he could focus better with the authorities. Hope also knew she had motherly duties. She had to reinforce her love to her son. Greg needed to feel secure with her and in his own environment, so her mind was preoccupied with his comfort and worried heart.

Just before leaving the school, Hope's cell rang. It was Mamie, wanting to know if Greg was okay. Instead of elaborating in front of Greg, Hope acted like nothing happened and told her all was well. She would not give Satan any acknowledgment even though she wanted to scream and tell the world that someone tried to steal her son. Instead, Hope said God intervened as always.

~~~

Insight flew overhead while Hope drove home, keeping his eagle eyes fixed on what also followed.

~~~

On the way home, Hope didn't study the environment around her; she used the time to talk with her son. "Honey, you are and forever will be my son. You are Greg Arnold. Daddy and I will make sure you never have to leave us. If someone tries to come between us, I want you to pray and ask Jesus for help. He will make sure someone comes to help you. I want you to rely on Jesus more than anyone else. Then you pray to Jesus and think about me and Daddy. Know we are praying and doing everything we can to make you safe. I always want you to trust that."

"Yes, ma'am," he whimpered.

"Tell Mama who you are," Hope encouraged.

"I am Greg Arnold, and I belong to you and Daddy," Greg replied sweetly.

"Who do you call for help?" Hope asked.

"Jesus!" Greg squeaked.

While Hope drove, she kept reinforcing Greg's identity to him and was unaware they were being followed. She was so engrossed with getting Greg's mindset readjusted, that she didn't see an old truck parked nearby until after she drove into her driveway. Hope and Greg were giggling and happy when they entered their home, and she was more fixed on cuddling with him than worrying about a security system. She didn't want to frighten Greg by giving him mixed signals and being too overly protective, so she focused on getting him comfortable and happy by acting normal. She acted like nothing had happened and sat him on a stool in her kitchen, alongside the center island workstation, and poured his afternoon glass of chocolate milk and got him some cookies.

~~~

In the spirit realm, a battle raged. Insight determinedly fought demons of violence, envy, and insecurity until Donald and Amanda Hines were freed because he meant for no evil force to enter the Arnold household. He didn't resist the people he'd freed from entering the Arnold household uninvited, for he knew they were operating in their own weak strength, and their fleshly power would be no contest for what they were about to face. Rather than move, he sat and feasted on the dead demons.

~~~

Hope had Greg eating and watching television, then she quietly walked away from him so she could set the home security system located by their driveway door entrance. The time she took to give Greg peace also allowed Amanda and Donald the opportunity to quietly sneak inside her home. When she managed to return to her backdoor, Hope was met by a crazy, wild-eyed man holding a gun and a thin, unkempt woman, both obviously high on drugs.

Hope immediately knew who the people were, but the Holy Spirit kept her calm. Instead of resisting and starting a fight, she greeted the intruding woman bitterly by name. "Amanda Hines, isn't it?"

Taken off guard, Amanda responded just as bitterly. "Well, well, you know who I am. Then you know why I'm here."

"You'll have to kill me first," Hope said confidently.

Amanda had been deceived. Her drugged mind still convinced her that she was stronger, but Hope knew the Holy Spirit was in control, and He was her defender. She knew this because He had reinforced

His love and protection in her mind and heart earlier, and it was still giving her supernatural confidence and the ability to articulate and verbally torture Amanda.

Donald couldn't stand two women bickering, so he interrupted their hissing party by waving his gun and giving orders. "Sis, I have the gun. Stop spewing stupidity and look at their place! They live in high cotton. Apparently, they are rich folks! Why don't we help ourselves by stealing some of this loot so we can enjoy ourselves when we leave? We could live the good life and wouldn't have to fret. After we pawn their stuff, we can buy a better ride, get new clothes, and buy better drugs after we relocate."

Amanda stopped her bickering long enough to look closer at the surroundings. They had hidden in a laundry room off the driveway door entrance, but even there, the Arnolds had nice appliances, and the pantry was fully stocked. Then she said, "I see what you mean."

When Donald had Amanda focused again, he shoved Hope with his gunned hand and told her to take them on a tour. Not wanting to frighten Greg, Hope entered the kitchen and said, "Greg, come to Mama."

With eyes wide, Greg obeyed and was grabbed instead by Amanda, who declared loudly, "I'm your mama, Brat. Come to me."

Dragging a moaning and scared little boy, Amanda walked away from Hope and studied the photos hung on the wall in the family room. When recollection took, she screeched, "Don't Look! The man in these pictures with this woman and Greg is the beast who locked me up. He stole my child! I'm not leaving until he is punished. I want payback! I'm going to strip him of everything!" Even while being held tightly with a gun pressed to her head, Hope wasn't scared; she was angry. Anger wanted to overwhelm her, but the Holy Spirit held her together. She would not lose control in front of her son. Taking a deep breath, Hope focused and prayed mentally, *Lord, help us.*

"Hope, I'm way ahead of you. I've had this since this morning," He comforted.

She remembered how Greg fought her earlier in the morning and asked, "Were you preparing Greg this morning?"

"Yes, you were fighting against something I asked him to do," the Lord replied.

She grinned to herself and thanked God. "Lord, I have an idea. Are you with me?"

"Yes!" He answered quickly.

"I'll need Abba's strength for this to work, and once I have His blessing, I'll prompt Greg," she told Jesus.

"Do it now," He demanded!

Hope immediately sought the Father. "Father, give my baby your strength. Give Greg all your power. Help him please be who he really is!"

After Hope finished praying, she focused her gaze on Greg. The sight was beautiful! He had his little eyes closed, and he was mouthing the words, *help me, Jesus,* and Hope got to see with her spiritual sight God's answer for her son. Standing beside him were two mighty angels: one was a smaller eagle like Insight, and the other was a small lion, like Brent's. God had given Greg a double portion. Immediately, Hope knew God the Father was on the scene; He had heard their prayers. Now all she had to do was get Greg's attention. She knew the words that would take away Greg's fear. She would use Greg's own words to both their advantages. She forcibly commanded, "Greg!" And when he looked at his mother, she said, "Carl's ass!"

When the words registered in Greg's memory, an amazing thing happened: he changed from a scared small four-year-old boy into a whirling dervish. He was a Tasmanian devil. The first thing he did was stomp his cowboy-booted foot on Amanda's sandaled instep. Then he bit her hand and twisted her thumb until she let him go. Then he started kicking. He had her screaming in pain from all his Uncle Carl had taught him. Greg was loaded with supernatural confidence and physical agility. Every karate and kickboxing move he knew was used on Amanda in full force and all at once. He had her backing away, begging for him to stop, as he screamed loudly and with every breath, "I am Greg Arnold!" Watching his sister being beaten by a kid he hardly knew, Donald turned his gun toward Greg and fired in Greg's direction. Donald didn't want to kill the kid; all he wanted was for the kid to stop. He couldn't stand seeing Amanda act like such a wimp. His stupid action caused Hope's supernatural reaction. For when the shot rang out, Hope's own anger and strength were released, and she went berserk. She too began using all her body strength against the insane man, and within three seconds, she had him unconscious and held his gun.

Not turning her eyes off Amanda or her brother, Hope calmly told Greg, "Sweetie, get Mama's cell phone and call Daddy. Tell him what has happened and ask him to come home quickly and bring the police. Tell him Mama has their gun."

When Brent received the call, his first emotion was to be worried until Greg said, "Mom and I kicked their asses!"

~~~

Insight was very proud of his human. Not only had Hope won the battle, but now she was standing guard. Hope didn't worry about the battles to be ensued on earth or within the spirit realm. Her trust allowed him to move and be on high alert, enabling him to destroy all the giants and demons controlling the Hines and then destroying Satan's plot.

~~~

Satan hissed and spat because of Insight's gloat! Nothing was working against this enemy. Hope had become an awesome contender in the physical, as well as the spiritual, realm. Even the boy was a chip off the block. *It is time to regroup*, he thought. He wouldn't be able to use Amanda Hines again; her probation was definitely revoked. She and her brother would be going to jail soon. He needed to take the time to think things through. Maybe he could find another way to destroy the Arnold family from within before calling the giants of old.

~~~

After the police hauled Amanda and Donald to jail, and the media circus was gone, Brent had a long talk with his small family. Hope told Brent how God showed her Greg being covered by two angels from Insight and Justice, but he didn't hear. He insisted that they always used wisdom and make sure that the house alarm was always on. He never wanted them to risk their lives again. Even if someone broke into their house, Brent wanted them to hide until help came. The last thing he wanted to hear was Hope having to hold a gun on someone.

Hope wanted to object, but she promised and made Greg promise too. She knew her husband had undergone tremendous stress, and she wanted to soothe Brent's mind and stop his worry. But the one thing she kept in her heart was the main security system she and Greg had used. Jesus and Abba were always around! They had all they needed.

That evening, to soothe their families' worries, Brent and Hope called everyone for a family meeting. Hope's parents, the Joiners, as well as all the Arnolds, came over to their house to eat a meal and discuss what really happened. Media always perverted news, and the family deserved to know from Brent and Hope what really happened.

By the time everyone arrived, pizza had been delivered so they could all talk and enjoy one another. Before eating, Joe Arnold said grace and gave God praise. Then the clan drew strength from one another while they enjoyed their pizza. It was during dinner that Greg had a chance to tell everyone what happened to him.

Uncle Carl was given honor during Greg's tale. The boy's story overwhelmed Carl with pride. Carl's reward was the simple knowledge that all his teachings had paid off and lives had been spared. Not only had Hope listened to his advice, but his four- year-old nephew knew how to take care of himself and his mom in a fight. It was clear that they both could kick ass.

Light bulbs Turn Brighter

Mom's hysterical scream woke me from my nap. "Gina! Get up, something horrible has happened. Hurry! Come here!"

I scrambled out of bed, frightened out of my wits. I didn't bother to get crutches. I hopped quickly to the kitchen, thinking something had happened to Mom. When I didn't find her in the kitchen, I turned the corner and saw her sitting on our living-room sofa, glued to the television safe and unharmed. I immediately wanted to scold her because she had scared me stupid. Then she motioned for me to join her so I could see what had her so upset. Mom and I sat stunned as we watched broadcasters show picture after picture of Hope's home while they told the community about the home invasion and second attempted kidnapping of Greg Arnold. No pictures or interviews with Hope or Brent were telecasted, so Mom sat quietly weeping, but my first reaction was to call Mamie. Something didn't sound right. According to the news broadcast, a horrible struggle had ensued, and the parties involved were injured. Everything was so vague, leaving viewers to their own imaginations.

When Mamie answered her cell, I immediately relaxed. Her calm voice had a way of calming my nerves like nothing else could. I began by asking, "Mamie, have you seen the local news broadcast? Something has happened at Hope's house."

"I know, child, I know," Mamie soothed.

"Do you know if they are hurt?" I questioned.

Mamie answered my question with a question. "Gina, what does your spirit tell you?"

"Huh?" I queried.

"Calm your heart and seek," Mamie encouraged. "Oh!" I replied.

I took a deep breath and mentally asked, *Lord, do I need to worry about Hope and Greg?*

"No. They are fine," Whisperer replied.

Mamie patiently waited for me to speak. I sighed then asked, "Mamie, when will I ever get the hang of this? The Lord is close and always very kind, but I keep forgetting and jump to conclusions and call somebody. Did it take you this long to trust Him?"

"Don't fret yourself! You are way ahead of the game. Most folks don't ever know Him the way you do," Mamie conveyed.

"Why? He is wonderful," I asked emphatically.

"No, they lack faith! People say they believe, but they really don't. Most people believe in spooks more than they believe in God. They act on emotion, which causes them to say things God didn't say, and then they do stupid things. God wants us to believe in Him with our whole hearts, but people will listen to the media or run to others who are usually more misled at the drop of a hat. Listen to ole Mamie. Read the New Testament, especially Paul's teachings. Start reading the first book of Corinthians, chapters 1 and 2 and try to grasp what Paul discerned from Jesus. I think that book of the Bible will help you understand who you are and what your purpose is. Sweetie, you are special. I saw faith in you the very first time I laid eyes on you," Mamie shared.

"How was that? Wasn't I unconscious?" I asked.

"You were, but I saw a glimpse of what was inside your heart and who followed you." Mamie giggled.

A lightbulb went on in my brain! I totally understood! Mamie had seen Ox.

"You saw him, didn't you?" I asked.

"Uh huh!" Mamie declared.

"Mamie, why is my guardian angel an Ox?" I asked.

Mamie said, "There you go again. I'm not the one to answer that question. Go to the Lord, baby! Ask and receive the truth! Give Him all your worries! Do it now! I'll call you tomorrow afternoon after I wake up. Let me go, I need to take a quick nap now so I'm rested for my night's work."

Mamie's request startled me! She gave me strict orders before we disconnected. Her every word had been backed with strong emotion. There was urgency behind her request that prompted me to want to be alone with Whisperer. I needed, no—I wanted to be alone with Whisperer, but I obliged to comfort my mom. She was distraught from the news media. She was staring at me, waiting for me to say something. Her pleading eyes spoke volumes, and I had no choice but to help ease her mind the best way I could without lying. I placed my hands on her shoulders and said, "Mamie has assured me that Hope and Greg are okay, and she has asked that we refrain from anything provided by the news because they do not tell the whole truth."

Mom said, "I knew something didn't ring true, but all I could think about was how afraid that little boy must be. Hope is strong, but Greg is so little. Did Mamie say she would keep us informed?" "Yes, ma'am. I'm sure someone will call if Mamie can't," I responded.

After answering Mom's questions, I needed to be alone. I had to excuse myself from Mom's presence even though she was still stressed, but I didn't want to hurt her feelings. I grit my teeth and took a deep breath, hoping she would understand my need. "Mom! May I be excused for a while? I need to pray. I'll join you shortly."

To my astonishment, she agreed by saying, "I fully understand.

I think I'll pray as I prepare dinner."

I didn't waste any time. I hopped back to my room and locked the bedroom door behind me.

In my room, I wanted to kneel, but that was impossible, so I lay across my bed and put my face in my hands. "Sweet Lord, what is going on? People see something in me that I don't. I am just a nobody. You've blessed me with incredible things. Why? Why do I have Ox? What does having him with me mean? You have all my answers," I pleaded.

"Gina, everything you'll ever need to know is in my Word. Listen to Mamie. All you have to do is seek, for my Word is life to those who find it," He responded.

I quickly turned to the first book of Corinthians in my Amplified Bible and read chapter 1 verses 19–21. I noticed that we were chosen. Then I determined with Paul that we should rely only on God and not rely on man because his writings said,

> *For it is written, I will baffle and render useless and destroy the learning of the learned and the philosophy of the philosophers and the cleverness of the clever and the discernment of the discerning; I will frustrate and nullify [them] and bring [them] to nothing.*
>
> *Where is the wise man (the philosopher)? Where is the scribe (the scholar)? Where is the investigator (the logician, the debater) of this present time and age? Has not God shown up the nonsense and the folly of this world's wisdom?*

> *For when the world with all its earthly wisdom failed to perceive and recognize and know God by means of its own philosophy, God in His wisdom was pleased through the foolishness of preaching [salvation, procured by Christ and to be had through Him], to save those who believed (who clung to and trusted in and relied on Him).*

"Lord, I understand, and I agree, but I'm new to all of this. Will you be patient with me? I am trying," I pleaded.

"The knowledge that you are weak is all that matters. The fact that you are trying is precious to me. In time, trusting in me will be like breathing," He encouraged.

"Lord, why did you pick me? I'm useless. I don't have any training. I'm nothing," I inquired.

"Continue reading!" He commanded.

I set my sight again on the first chapter of 1 Corinthians in my Amplified Bible and read,

> *But to those who are called, whether Jew or Greek (Gentile), Christ [is] the Power of God and the Wisdom of God.*
>
> *[This is] because the foolish thing [that has its source in] God is wiser than men, and the weak thing [that springs] from God is stronger than men.*
>
> *For [simply] consider your own call, brethren; not many [of you were considered to be] wise according to human estimates and standards, not many influential and powerful, not many of high and noble birth.*
>
> *[No] for God selected (deliberately chose) what in the world is foolish to put the wise to shame, and what the world calls weak to put the strong to shame.*
>
> *And God also selected (deliberately chose) what in the world is lowborn and insignificant and branded and treated with contempt, even the things that are nothing, that He might depose and bring to nothing the things that are,*
>
> *So that no mortal man should [have pretense for glorying and] boast in the presence of God.*

"Lord! You chose me because I'm weak?" I asked.

"Yes, I must prove to the world around you that I am," He enlightened.

"Okay, but You are going to have to help me through this," I stated.

"You will never be left to your own devices," He promised.

I also read chapter 2 and noticed how Paul endured. Paul trusted God fully so people's faith could be strong. He let his life be the proof people needed so people could rest in the power of God.

Then I wondered, *what is faith?*

"Lord, I'm going to look up the word faith in my Bible because Mamie said she saw it in me, and I see that Paul used it to show others how to believe in You. Will You help me understand what it means?" I asked.

"Of course, I will! Please, look for the word faith. I will alert you when to stop and read," He urged.

After finding many references in my concordance, I allowed my eyes to be directed. They were drawn to Hebrews chapter 11 verse 1 in my Amplified Bible; it read,

> *Now faith is the assurance (the confirmation, the title deed) of the things [we] hope for, being the proof of things [we] do not see and the conviction of their reality [faith perceiving as real fact what is not revealed to the senses]. For by [faith—trust and holy fervor born of faith] the men of old had divine testimony borne to them and obtained a good report. By faith we understand that the worlds [during the successive ages] were framed (fashioned, put in order, and equipped for their intended purpose) by the word of God, so that what we see was not made out of things which are visible.*

"Lord, you gave me the vision to believe in. Was all this for a specific purpose?" I inquired.

"You were given a vision of your heart's desire. I showed you purposefully what to believe in. It will come even though you do not see it, and yes, you were chosen like Paul to believe in it until it comes for a specific purpose," He answered.

"Why?" I pleaded.

"To prove I am. Remember your past—how nothing worked? You struggled for a destiny. Now all you must do is believe and then speak. Your belief is your work. You have the ability to achieve. I

have planted the vision in you to show the world. Having you believe in my vision until it comes to pass will make you able to encourage others," He conveyed.

After I understood what faith meant and why I was chosen, I wanted to know more about my angel. Relying on the Lord to guide my eyes like He did earlier, I asked, "Who is Ox?"

Again, I flipped through many references. Most referred to oxen, which confused me. I was about to give up when my eyes fell on the word cherubim, which lead me to a commentary about the many faces of Jesus. Then the commentary referred the reader to the book of Ezekiel chapter 1. I read many verses in the Amplified Bible, and the word fire caught my attention in verse 4, and I read through verse 13. It read,

> *As I looked, behold, a stormy wind came out of the north, and a great cloud with a fire enveloping it and flashing continually; a brightness was about it and out of the midst of it there seemed to glow amber metal, out of the midst of the fire.*
>
> *And out of the midst of it came the likeness of four living creatures [or cherubim]. And this was their appearance: they had the likeness of a man,*
>
> *But each one had four faces and each one had four wings.*
>
> *And their legs were straight legs, and the sole of their feet was like the sole of a calf's foot, and they sparkled like burnished bronze.*
>
> *And they had the hands of a man under their wings on their four sides. And the four of them had their faces and their wings thus:*
>
> *Their wings touched one another; they turned not when they went but went every one straight forward.*
>
> *As for the likeness of their faces, they each had the face of a man [in front], and each had the face of a lion on the right side and the face of an ox on the left side; the four also had the face of an eagle [at the back of their heads]*

Such were their faces. And their wings were stretched out upward [each creature had four wings]; two wings of each one were touching the [adjacent] wing of the creatures on either side of it, and [the remaining] two wings of each creature covered its body.

And they went every one straight forward; wherever the spirit would go, they went, and they turned not when they went.

In the midst of the living creatures there was what looked like burning coals of fire, like torches moving to and fro among the living creatures; the fire was bright and out of the fire went forth lightning.

"Lord, I notice the angels in these scriptures, but the words say they are connected in one body. I also see where You are referenced as fire and that You live in the midst of them, but when I really see the angels with my own eyesight, they are separated. Why?" I inquired.

"Gina, they are connected even though they are separate. The people they guard are separate, but in me, they are connected. Don't you feel the camaraderie?" He informed.

I stopped to think. "I was definitely drawn to Mamie and Hope, but who had the fourth?" Again, a lightbulb turned on in my head. Brent! I felt safe and secure when I was around him.

"Why was I given Ox?" I asked. Then I flipped through scripture after scripture references like before until my eyes fell on Proverbs chapter 14 in my Amplified Bible. Verse 4 read,

Where no oxen are, the grain crib is empty, but much increase [of crops] comes by the strength of the ox.

I was still confused. So, I asked, "Lord, what does this mean?"

"It means Ox was given to you for strength. He is there to bring you a good life, one full of crops. He will die for you if necessary. He is your servant," the Lord answered.

"My servant? How does he serve me?" I inquired.

"He serves you by hearing my Word," Whisperer declared.

A brighter lightbulb turned on in my brain! Ox did what I confessed! Ox made my life full by what I said! That was why I'd been declaring what I believed from God's Word. Wow! I'd been giving Ox orders, and I didn't even know it!

A memory from this afternoon came to mind. It was after Whisperer told me to seek, and I spoke against violence. I watched with my own eyes as Ox defended me from evil words. Even though the words came from my soul mate, they weren't God's words of blessings. They were stupid words, so Ox destroyed them. Then I remembered what Mamie said about people saying stupid things out of line with what God said. She also said Wayne was under stress so that must have been why he talked crazy. It was why Ox stood between us. Ox was willing to die rather than have evil words hurt me.

"Lord, do I have my thinking right?" I asked.

"Yes, look up tongue," He suggested.

I finally knew how to seek, and I was truly enjoying our time together. I obeyed because I wanted to know about our tongues and how all this worked for us. Again, I trusted my eyes to Whisperer. I knew he wouldn't fail me now. We were in a zone, so when my eyes fell on a reference about tongues in Isaiah chapter 54 verse 17 of my Amplified Bible, I stopped. It was about tongues formed against us, and it read,

> *But no weapon that is formed against you shall prosper, and every tongue that shall rise against you in judgment you shall show to be in the wrong. This [peace, righteousness, security, triumph over opposition] is the heritage of the servants of the Lord [those in whom the ideal Servant of the Lord is reproduced]; this is the righteousness or the vindication which they obtain from Me [this is that which I impart to them as their justification], says the Lord.*

Awesome! The Lord used Ox today for me to have a triumph over an evil comment.

Suddenly, Mom's tapping on my bedroom door drove me away from my trance-like state. I was back in the present.

"Gina, honey, I have dinner ready. You need to eat," Mom commented.

I was getting fed. I didn't want to leave. Then I heard a soft voice say, *"Go and love your mother. She needs you."*

Set Free

It was the middle of the night, and Brent was awakened by a strange weight on his chest. When he opened his eyes, to his amazement, Greg was sprawled on top of him. The gesture broke Brent's heart. Without saying a word, Greg was showing Brent he needed him.

Brent appreciated the sentiment but, at the same time, knew they both needed rest. But for Greg to slip in his and Hope's bedroom without warning meant something had to be addressed. Greg knew better. His child was taught not to come in the room while it was occupied unless invited, or if something was wrong. Brent whispered, "Buddy, what is the matter? Why didn't you wake me up? Whisper in my ear, Greg, so we don't wake Mama." "Daddy, I asked Jesus to help me sleep, and He said to sleep on my Father. I came in to be with you like Jesus said. Daddy, I love you and Mama, and if I hadn't asked Jesus to help me today, I may not be here. Can I sleep with you until my worry goes away? Jesus said to go to you so I could sleep," Greg informed innocently.

Brent knew Jesus told Greg to seek the Father, not sleep on the father but didn't have the heart to correct the little guy, so he said, "Sure! Tonight is special. All three of us need each other."

Cuddled in Brent's arms, Greg slept. The rest of the night, Brent did not. Brent's mind raced while he reflected on the day's trauma. Greg's worries were heartbreaking. His little man had put on a strong front for his family at the dinner table, but the truth, even though late, was revealed. Brent too came to the realization he was helpless. Insecurity drove Brent to pray, "Father, not only does Greg need you, but I do too. We both must overcome fear. Twice, in a little over a year, I've had to watch Hope face violence alone, and now violence has threatened our son. I can't take this strain. Worry and fear plague me. These evil spirits have to be dealt with."

"We'll deal with both. Let me have them!" the Lord answered.

"How?" Brent asked.

"Open your heart and let me show you. Take a few days to be alone with me. Rest and allow me to guide you," the Lord urged.

"Lord, I can't take off work. I have Gina's hearing on Thursday, and I should prepare. Then there are all the legal issues I should deal with from what happened to my family today," Brent objected.

"You need to release me! You are determined to do everything by your own strength! Unless you seek me and unleash me, your abilities are useless to me!" the Lord strongly rebuked.

While lying in bed, tears streamed down Brent's cheeks. The Lord's rebuke tore his heart. Until this very second, Brent thought he was doing all he could and was being led by his Lord. He endured years of study so he'd be equipped to fight for justice in a court of law. He sought an office so he could protect the innocent instead of siding with bribery and unjust gain. He thought he was putting his abilities to use because he prayed over every one of his cases. With every case, he felt God with him, he felt God help him, but now God was telling him he was useless. He thought he was the Lord's voice in the legal arena.

"Lord, I'm sorry! I thought I was helping. Show me where I've failed you. The last thing I want is to be useless to You," Brent cried.

"Brent! Remember when Hope was abducted, and you were too tired to help? You fell asleep during the midst of the ordeal. For that brief time, you released me fully, and your guardian angel ran free. Once Hope was safe again, you tied up your angel and have kept him leashed securely so you could wage war. Justice needs to run free! You already have what you need. Your knowledge of the law is enough to win for Gina. Plus, you know the truth. Spend time with me. Allow yourself to relax. If you don't, all the knowledge you have is for nothing. All the body strength you try to develop is for nothing," the Lord explained.

Through Hope's gift of sight, Brent was aware of a lion angel that followed him, but he didn't know the reason why until the Lord called the angel Justice; then revelation dawned. Justice for the innocent was his Lord's desire. Justice the angel was sent to him to help the Kingdom of God manifest. Now Brent knew what his ability was. As a small child, he had trusted Jesus. As a young man, he cared for the innocent. As a grown man, he promised to fight and defend, but the only way Jesus wanted him to fight and defend was through Justice. Now he knew why his Lord was upset. He was not allowing his angel to move freely, and it was hindering God's progress.

While holding his son securely next to his side, Brent submitted to the call and gave in. He mentally released the cat. "Lord, have your way. I give you everything. I give you my heart, my mind, my family, and my ability. You are free to run."

Justice felt the golden torque encircle his neck at the same time the chains of Brent's insecurity fell away. No longer did Justice have to crouch like a beast. With strong, sturdy, and straight legs, Justice stood tall. Joy flooded his heart! The instinct to purr was strong because he has happy, but he roared instead, for he was finally released to enjoy righteous anger. It was time for Kingdom rule! Heaven's King deserved honor and glory! Jesus would be given earth's crown as well, or he would rip every evil resistance into shreds and enjoy their bloody meat in the process.

Brent watched the sun rise and felt totally rested even though he had lacked sleep. When Hope woke to find the whole family unit in one bed, Brent had no choice but to share with her what had transpired during the night. Hope's love for Brent swelled. Finally, her gentle giant was free. He'd given his fear for her and Greg's safety over to Jesus. When Brent told her of the Lord's request to spend time with him, she was in full agreement. Brent needed time to relax so he could listen to what God had to say. Hope planned to do the same because their lives had to get balanced again.

When Greg sprang from sleep fully energized, both Hope and Brent looked at each other trying to determine what to do next. Both wanted and needed alone time with the Lord, but prancing on the bed was their bundle of joy, the very reason they needed quiet time.

Hope giggled because she knew what Brent was thinking. Then she said, "We'll flip for the duty. Whatever way the coin turns will determine who gets the honor of the tagalong. Even the apostles flipped coins for answers. This will be fun! We'll pray first and then let Jesus decide."

Quickly, Hope retrieved a quarter from Brent's dresser, and the three of them grabbed hands before praying. Brent prayed, "Lord, it's your decision. Heads for me and tails for Hope."

Brent gave the quarter to Greg and told his son to throw it up in the air. Obediently, Greg threw the coin high. All three backed away so the coin could land uninterrupted on the bed. To their amazement, Jesus wanted Greg and Brent to spend the day with Him.

After a hearty breakfast, Greg asked, "Daddy, are we playing hooky?"

Brent laughed. "In a way, son, I guess we are. We are running away from troubles into a fun-filled day with our Lord. Remember last night when Jesus told you to go to the Father? That is what the two of us are going to do. We are both going to be with Jesus and our Heavenly Father today," Brent explained.

"How?" Greg asked.

"By playing and enjoying life," Brent answered.

"Can we go fishing in the lake at the Boys' Home?" Greg inquired. Brent thought a second. Why not! What better way to get reacquainted with God? "Let's go catch some fish! We'll have a fish fry tonight," Brent whooped.

Hope interjected, "Bake me one, please. I want to keep my girlish figure."

~~~

At the Boys' Home, Joe Arnold was perplexed when he noticed Brent and Greg fishing on a school and work day. Curiosity would not let go. Hiking down to the lake, Joe worried until the Lord stopped him.

"Joe, Brent is with me. Don't fret! Let me use you to encourage. Be obedient and answer Brent's questions through me. Remember the Word and allow me to speak truth through you to your son."

Joe walked up alongside Brent and asked, "Son, are you stressed? Do you need to talk?"

"Yeah! Dad, I've been a jackass. The Lord jerked a knot in me this morning," Brent replied.

"How so?" Joe asked.

To indicate something to his dad, Brent pointed his fishing rod in Greg's direction and then answered, "It took the Lord using Greg last night to wake me up. God made me realize that all the knowledge and strength in the world would never be enough to protect innocence. All my life, I thought I had to work and defend the weak for God. Last night, he showed me all that was vanity. He told me to rest and enjoy life and to let Him free. His justice had to prevail, not mine."

"I see, and you chose fishing to help you see straight," Joe stated.

"No! Greg chose fishing. It has helped, though. Watching my son as he plays has given me a new perspective. Dad, this is how God wants to watch us," Brent replied.

"Yeah, but I think you need to see another side as well," Joe urged.

"What do you mean?" Brent asked, confused.

"Why don't you visit Wade at the VA Hospital? Let God show you what happens sometimes to good men under orders. God highly honors the obedient that follow His plan. Go talk with some who gave up life and limb to protect our nation and see how our good Lord looks after them. Son, we are all in a battle. We can't hide. No one in God's Kingdom is free from facing violence. It is how we face it that matters. God does not want us to be cowards. If God is for us, who or what can come against... don't you ever forget that." Joe enlightened.

Brent thought for a moment. God had shown him two sides of a coin again. First and foremost, the Lord wants us happy and carefree; but secondly, he wants us ready and prepared to fight if need be. The thought of talking with veterans intrigued him, and visiting Wade again would be fun.

Taking the few fish that he and Greg caught and putting them inside the home's refrigerator until later, Brent excited Greg by saying they were going to see Wade.

Wade was notified that he had visitors, and he couldn't believe the news because God had just answered a silent prayer. Many times, he'd thought society had forgotten the warriors of this nation, and it made him sad. To have someone show up minutes after praying encouraged him. He knew the patients would be surprised when someone cared. After visits, they seemed to improve mentally, as well as physically. Appreciation was a marvelous medicine. When he recognized the visitors, Wade was thrilled. Children especially made the old warriors merry.

When Wade approached Brent, he asked, "What brings you guys out?"

"We've come to see what the Lord is doing. Why don't you introduce Greg and me to some of your patients? We'd love to see how the technology you've bragged about has helped," Brent enlightened.

"Sure! My guys love visitors. They feel appreciated and loved when people come to see how they are doing," Wade replied.

Wade loved the interaction. Brent and Greg showed honor and love to every person. Greg's curious questions seemed to brighten the old warriors and gave them a chance to tell their adventures. Brent's heart grew with a deeper respect for the Lord's justice.

Now he knew why Hope's face brightened after she told him about Greg's two angels. She tried to tell him they had fought through God, but he reacted out of fear. They'd honored God and had not hidden or been cowards for a reason. The realization gave him pause and made him proud at the same time. Justice, although a very small angel, was released by Greg and had fought for all of them to have peace.

When the visitation ended, and the three guys were alone, Brent inquired on the health of Wade's mother. Wade was happy to inform Brent that his mom was much better but would need special care for several months. He and Wayne would have to hire around-the-clock caregivers to help with her physical needs, and since he wasn't married, he volunteered to move in the house with her to oversee her bills and care of the home.

Wade went on to tell Brent that he planned to visit them at their church but couldn't promise when that would be since his mother's health and welfare were a priority.

Knowing Wade's love of beautiful women, Brent decided to push an envelope. Hoping Wade would like knowing that lovely single ladies attended the church; Brent playfully used his idea and then teased him. "I know a perfect girl for you. Hope and I have fallen in love with this young woman. Not only is she beautiful, she needs your expertise."

"Get out of here! Don't be crude!" Wade stammered.

"No, seriously! She was in a bad car accident and is on crutches. She needs your help," Brent jibed.

"All in time, my friend. I'm not interested in hooking up yet." Wade laughed.

~~~

The day is very informative, Brent thought. After retrieving their fish and then preparing and eating their meal, the family relaxed. The balance was restored.

Day 2 of Brent's vacation was spent alone with his wife. Greg was taken to school. Back at home, a threefold cord between Jesus, Brent, and Hope was entwined and reinforced. This time, Brent promised Hope and Jesus that he would allow Justice free rein, no matter how small.

Covered Inside and Out

For two days, Satan planned and plotted with Lyle Horne and his attorney. Since schemes failed when he planned direct attacks against Gina, Hope, and Greg, he decided to strengthen those he could use to weaken the enemies. He would poke and prod until his spirits of low self-esteem, torment, and delusion were summoned to assist. Court battles were fun, and he loved ruining reputations. He loved bringing bad behavior into the public light so people could be disgusted and hurt. Since Lyle failed to rape and torture Gina the way he wanted, Satan planned to use him to wreck her image. He also had a trick up his sleeve. He was aware Brent had subpoenaed Angie, and Satan knew he could use her to his advantage. Even if she had, to tell the truth, she could still cause pain. He would use Angie's anger for being called away from work and being put on the spot against Gina's confidence. He would make the girl lash out at Gina before the hearing began to cause grief, mental anguish, and pain. *The more hurt I can cause, the better,* Satan reasoned.

~~~

I thought, *even though I can't see and hear with spiritual gifts any longer, I know who stands beside me. I have my wonderful Whisperer and my awesome guardian angel, Ox.*

I used to think being alone would bother me, but having two days to mentally and spiritually prepare for what lay ahead was rewarding. I enjoyed watching wonderful ministers on television, and I was able to talk to all my friends. Hope called to check on me a few times, as well as Caylee and Mamie. Knowing how we were connected gave me peace. I wasn't even worried when I didn't hear anything from Brent because Whisperer told me not to live in fear.

I took the time to study, learn, and harbor deep in my heart God's Word. Several times, I would purposely speak in line with my belief, knowing God would help Ox bring it forth.

It was the night before my court hearing, and instead of freaking out, I wanted to go to church and rejoice. I wanted to be with my friends so I could draw from the unity and hear what God had to say to me through Pastor Reed. At precisely 6:00 p.m., Caylee came to Mom's and drove the three of us to our Father's house.

I heard Whisperer speak through Pastor Reed. The message was designed specifically for me. He talked about standing before the only judge who mattered. Man's opinions did not matter when Jesus cleaned and sanctified a person. He said people would persecute us because of our beliefs and would try and get us to deny our God is real. Then Pastor Reed said something that made Mom and I look at each other and grasp hands. He said Satan would even use family against us if he could. The point of his message was to confirm one issue. Jesus's opinion of us was all that mattered. Tests and trials came. When they did, we were to rejoice and know our God was about to show off and use us to do it. Never doubt that God won't show up when the world asks, "Where is your God?"

~~~

I slept like a log. When the alarm woke me up, I was ready and eager to get with the program. Mom assured me she would be home at lunch so she could help me get ready. I wanted to look confident, so I asked Mom to curl and pin up my hair. I had a dress and a cute shoe to match. I planned to wear Hope's power dress, the one Brent recommended I wear.

While I waited for Mom to get home, I sat in front of my television with plans to feed on God's Word until my cell rang. My caller was Angie. I immediately thought she was going to wish me well, but I had my peace shattered when she opened our conversation with several four-letter words followed by mean and hurtful accusations. She accused me of trying to ruin her reputation. She said I was just as much of a whore as she was. Then she lashed out and said maybe I deserved what happened.

When I asked why she was being so cruel, she replied, "You had me subpoenaed! Because of you, I have to tell people I smoke pot and sleep around."

"Angie, I didn't ask for this. I didn't know," I informed.

"No matter! I have, to tell the truth, but after today, don't call or reach out to me ever again. We were never friends. Friends don't tell on each other," she fumed.

After we disconnected, I cried. I was hurt to the core. Then I remembered Pastor Reed's message. Trials will come. Satan will use those close to you to make you stumble. When I came to those conclusions, I gritted my teeth and declared, "No weapons formed against me will prosper! Every tongue used to harm will be proven wrong! This is a promise from my Lord. This is my inheritance!"

As soon as I'd finished screaming my last word, the doorbell rang. Now, who is here to attack? I pondered.

It was Hope. Praise God!

"Hi, there! I thought you may like some company," Hope commented.

"Yes! Please!" I replied.

"I want to apologize for leaving you in the lurch the last few days. My family had to regain balance, so we leaned on each other. Today is your day. We will be witnesses of God's marvelous plan," Hope encouraged.

"What do you mean?" I asked.

"Honey, sit back and see. Every time something comes against you, there will be a countermove in your favor," Hope replied.

"How do you know?" I inquired.

"Didn't you hear Pastor Reed's message last night? It was to prepare you. Expect that every time something tries to torment, oppress, or discourage you to fail. Be confident in God's love," Hope answered.

"I had my first attack a few minutes ago. Angie called and informed me she was subpoenaed to testify, and she was furious with me. I didn't know Brent had even talked with her," I said.

"Brent has everything under control. Don't worry. You know we are connected, don't you?" Hope queried.

"Yeah. The Holy Spirit enlightened me Monday night. I know I have spiritual help, but I can't see Ox any longer. I like knowing he is here. Getting to see and hear everything kind of unnerved me," I confessed.

"I'm used to it, but it bothered me too at first. Today would be a good day to see and hear. After last night's prep talk of a message, I'm ready for anything. I can't wait to see God move," Hope professed.

"Would God allow you to give me a second chance? I'd like to see for myself," I asked.

"That is why I'm here, silly. Jesus told me to do whatever it took to help you through. You need the ability to watch Ox, Insight, and Justice, stand up in court. Let's pray first, then I'll share again," Hope instructed.

Again, Hope prayed in an unusual language, and when she finished, she pressed both of her hands over my ears and placed her forehead on mine. When she moved away, the first thing I saw was her guardian, the magnificent eagle.

Seeing my expression, Hope knew I had her gift again. Then she said, "Turn around and look at Ox. He is dressed for battle." I turned quickly, wanting to see my champion. My lovely brown-skinned angel wasn't brown anymore. He was a vivid red.

Ox's eyes were no longer brown. They were golden and flashed like lightning. His horns looked like metal, and his feet were bronze. When he opened his mouth, I expected to see straight, cow-like teeth, but what I saw were sharp daggers. He was awesome!

Stammering, I asked, "What, what has happened to him?" "From the looks of him, he is angry, or he is reacting to something you've said," Hope remarked.

"You may be right! I'd just finished declaring scripture about 'no weapon could prosper' before you arrived. Angie had hurt my feelings, so I was angry, and the verse burst right out of me," I confessed.

Hope laughed and then explained, "When scripture comes from your mouth forcefully, it is not you speaking. It is the Lord speaking through you. Ox thinks someone is attacking the Lord who lives in you. That is why he looks ready to tear something to pieces."

Hope's explanation made me wonder about the way she spoke at times. Curiosity got the better of me, and I asked, "Why do you pray in a foreign language?"

Hope replied, "Ah! You heard! Well, when I was baptized by the Holy Spirit, He gave me His ability to speak. Anytime I allow Him to pray through me using my voice, the words come out in another language. He explained that I didn't need to know what He said. I just needed to trust that anything He said was for my good or for someone else's good. Words are powerful, and our weak minds mixed with human emotions are not always strong enough to speak what is necessary. When I let Him speak, He gets the job done. In your case, the words you spoke are what the Lord wants to be spoken, or Ox wouldn't be charged and ready to fight."

I asked, "Would He pray through me if I let Him?"

Hope answered, "Of course! All you must do is ask for Him to take over your mouth. Then you must relax and begin to speak. It doesn't matter what sound is made, just believe it is Him taking over. After a few tries, it will become natural, and words will flow. To keep people from thinking you are weird, you must remember that His prayers are for you. You don't want to risk the chance of scaring or offending a new believer. Society has taught people out of ignorance that people who pray in different languages or in tongues are devilish. That is far from the truth. Sincere curiosity about this gift like you just experienced is the Lord's way of drawing you in, and it means you are ready to accept His gift. It is an honor to have Him pray through our mouths. It edifies us, and it intercedes for others."

"I want Him speaking for me. Help me ask, okay," I begged.

Quietly, we asked for the Lord's baptism of speaking in tongues. I opened my mouth and began forming unrecognizable words. Knowing who was speaking through me made me cry. Afterward, I heard Whisperer say, *"Thank you! Go in peace. Know anytime you need me, I am here to speak for you."*

The knowledge that I didn't have to memorize scripture or have to look up verses when I was distraught felt great. I would still seek the Lord by studying, but I didn't have to fret over my lack of knowledge any longer because He knew everything.

When Mom arrived, the three of us had a nice salad for lunch. I thought Hope's presence calmed Mom's nerves. When it came time to get ready, I quickly excused myself from the lunch table so I could sponge my body, reapply deodorant, and add makeup. Before putting on the power dress, I allowed Mom to curl and then French-twist my hair in a bun. When she finished, I looked sophisticated, and I felt attractive.

When Mom excused herself so she could primp before going to the courthouse, Hope took the opportunity to inform me of something important.

"Gina, I wore this dress during a hard trial for me. Red makes a statement. But what God wanted me to wear was His armor. Underneath all this glitz, you must count on Him first and foremost. I'm going to leave you alone with Him for a few minutes before we leave. Talk to Him and let Him show you His protection. Walk in it and don't focus on this lovely dress you are wearing. The dress is for people to see. You need to see who covers you," Hope urged.

Hope quietly exited the room and closed the door. I knew what she meant. I'd seen her red Spider-man-like suit, and I'd also seen my fire. She was right, though. I did need to be with Whisperer alone.

"Lord, I'm as ready as I could ever be under the circumstances. You must take over. Hope said I needed to see my protection so I could be confident. Please show me," I prayed.

"Do you remember when we first met?" the Lord asked.

"Yes, Sir," I replied.

"Focus again! See the bubble encircling you. It is your shield. It is me! You are no longer struggling within me because you know me and know that I love you. Even though the bubble resembles a raindrop, fully flexible and clear, you will be able to hear and see everything within its protective shield. Also, notice how your body looks in this spirit realm. It is still on fire, consumed within my spirit. The fire has not gone out. Through me, you are a force to be reckoned with on earth. Trust in me and not in your natural appearance," He taught.

When I exited the bedroom, I was covered inside and out. My whole universe was within the Lord. The love I'd allowed to envelope me was stronger than any force.

No words were spoken during the ride to the courthouse. The quietness was sublime because I was in perfect peace.

Judgment

Before walking into the building, Hope whispered in my ear, "Courthouses are like hospitals. Evil likes to hover here also. Be mindful of negative, emotion-eating demons so you won't get sucked into a false mindset. If negative thoughts come to your mind, speak against them quickly. Ox will protect you."

Dad was patiently waiting for us in the courthouse. Instantly, memories of the tormenting dream of him abandoning me flooded my mind. Hope wasn't kidding! Evil quickly came against me. I took her advice and began whispering, "The dream was a lie. No matter what, love will prevail." When I finished speaking, I heard a heavy snort behind me. I knew what had happened. I remembered what Ox did for me at the hospital. The snort was his way of letting me know the little demon had been toasted.

The courtroom wasn't very large, and few people were inside. After we entered, I watched Hope's guardian position himself at the entrance of the room. Each time a person entered, he watched them closely. If anyone entered with an evil influence, he quickly killed and then devoured the problem before it had a chance to interfere with the hearing.

After Angie walked into the room, I had the pleasure of seeing the beast that followed her killed and shredded before my eyes. I instantly concluded that the ugly beast must have been what was causing her meanness toward me. Knowing this gave me compassion for Angie, and it helped me forgive her. I was sincerely glad she was free from the beast's control.

Mamie entered the room and quickly came to my side. After giving me a hug, she stated, "I've been subpoenaed to testify. I'm on your side, sugar."

When Lyle Horne entered with his attorney by a side-door entrance, my heart lurched. He definitely was my attacker. He still looked greasy with dirty, slicked-back hair, but what I noticed this time was not his appearance but the grotesque demon following him. I was not the only one who saw the evil creature, Insight did as well. I expected to see a bloody mess like I did when Insight devoured Angie's demon, but that didn't happen. All Insight did was look sternly at the demon. I took this sign to mean the demon was on trial with me.

I was standing with Hope waiting for Brent to arrive when a nice-looking woman came in the room with a concerned look on her face. Hope knew her because she excused herself from me and went over and talked with the lady. When Hope returned, she had a wicked grin on her face. Something was happening, and I had to know why she looked so smug.

"What is going on?" I asked.

"Stay focused. Remember Pastor's message. Satan is up to something. Brent has been detained. If he isn't here in ten minutes, his assistant will have to take over," Hope answered.

"Okay," I replied.

I felt my body break out with perspiration. I knew my flesh was acting contrary due to fear, but my mind was stable and fixed because of Pastor's message. I was on guard and prepared for anything at the same time.

Hope snickered then reaffirmed my thoughts. "Gina, I'm taking Brent's absence as a sign that God is about to show out. Everything is pointing at us saying, 'Where is your God?' Satan must think we've put our hopes in Brent. He is in for a big surprise."

Brent's assistant, Mary Lassiter, motioned for me to take the chair next to hers in front of the courtroom. Hope moved away from me and took a seat next to Mamie and my parents. When she did, I noticed that Caylee and Russ were also sitting next to Mamie, supporting me. I may be alone in the front of the room, but I had loving supporters at the back.

The judge entered the room and took his seat. Ms. Lassiter politely asked if she could approach the judge's bench so they could discuss Brent's detainment. After hearing this, the judge granted us five more minutes before proceedings started.

During that time, I watched Ox take his stance to the right of the judge's chair and Healer take his stance on the judge's left. Insight's position was still in the rear of the room, so he could make sure evil didn't enter. Bravely, I looked toward my attacker and was rewarded with my gift of spiritual vision. I witnessed a funny sight. As Lyle talked with his counsel, his demon pushed and shoved his attorney's demon. The evil things were fighting with each other. Then I watched Lyle run his hands through his dirty hair, causing the greasy strains to stand up and out, making him look like a crazy man.

I closed my eyes so I could focus harder on the gift of spiritual hearing. I almost laughed out loud when I heard the attorney say to Lyle, "You think I'm going to believe a lovely woman like Ms. Grimes flirted with you? I'm not crazy, man!"

Then I heard Lyle spit. "You are going to say it because that is what she did!"

Then the attorney remarked, "I don't have to say anything. The judge already has your written statement. He's going to think you and I are idiots!"

With two minutes left, I heard with my spiritual hearing a loud roar coming from outside the room. The sound caused Insight to move away from his appointed position so the large door to the courtroom could open. Entering was a huge lion-like angel followed by Brent. Brent's guardian was in control. He was magnificently beautiful, and with each step, he radiated confidence. Brent took his place next to me and sat down, but the lion-angel didn't stop walking. The floor even shook when he walked passed. He marched up the steps of the platform with profound determination and positioned himself behind the judge's seat.

Once there, he turned and faced Lyle Horne.

As heaven's league was situated, the silence in the room was creepy. The two fighting demons vacated the premises, leaving Lyle and his attorney alone. The judge broke the eeriness by demanding the two counsels come forward and face his bench. He asked if all documents representing his case were present, and Brent responded to the judge by saying, "They are Your Honor."

Lyle's attorney was asked if he had copies of the District Attorney's documentation, and he responded also by saying, "Yes, Your Honor."

I listened closely, waiting for the judge to give the order for testifying arguments, but was surprised when he didn't. Instead, he looked directly at me as if he were judging me on appearance alone. Then he fixed his gaze on Lyle for a long moment before he began reading the documents before him.

The several minutes it took for the judge to read all the documentation, counsel stood quietly and patiently before the bench.

When the judge looked up, I swallowed hard and reminded myself to breathe. Then the judge said firmly, "Counsel, have a seat."

After Brent and the defense attorney returned to their chairs, the judge began to speak to everyone in the room. He said, "Ladies and gentlemen, I have come to the decision that we have no attempted rape case here today. Ms. Grimes's counsel cannot prove by the evidence presented that Mr. Horne attempted this act. All the evidence given is circumstantial. What intrigues me, however, is the opposing counsel's statements. It seems that Mr. Horne thought Ms. Grimes solicited his sexual advances.

With the statements presented by his counsel, I see Mr. Horne admits to being physically aggressive with Ms. Grimes. I do not believe she gave him a reason. Because of my unbelief, I reviewed the district office's documentation again and agree he maligned her. I also read in district's documentation that Mr. Horne has been repeatedly in and out of mental facilities. Therefore, I hereby declare that Lyle Horne is guilty of aggravated assault and will be incarcerated for a year with the possibility of early parole. In addition, I also order Mr. Horne to undergo psychiatric treatment immediately. This hearing is adjourned!"

We all watched as Lyle went totally bonkers. He began cussing at and shoving anyone around him. His attorney backed away quickly from fear of being hurt. Lyle became so irate that jailers had to subdue him before carrying him away. Even though I was overjoyed the hearing was over and fair judgment was served, I still felt pity for this mentally sick man. I'd worked in the local mental health facility for a long time, and I knew people couldn't help their behavior. Now I had a new appreciation for why they had problems.

Lyle was no different. The ugly, grotesque demon that bound him destroyed his mind as well. Maybe in time I could forget the violent attack. I already knew Jesus was helping me forgive the man the demon used to attack me. Compassion for him helped. After the judge exited the room, eight of us had one big group hug. Tears were flowing, and noses were running from the joy.

Dad was so happy, he picked me up and swung me around. My dad's love for me was undeniable.

Standing quietly behind everyone was Angie, her face full of shame. When I looked in her direction, she burst out crying. My heart melted for her. All the hurt she'd caused didn't matter any longer. I excused myself from loving arms to hobble over to my crying friend. I knew she felt horrible for all she said, so I didn't bring it up. I put my arms around her and said, "Thanks for coming. I'll call you soon."

Still ashamed, Angie looked at me and said, "Please do." Then she walked out of the room.

Dad was so happy, he volunteered to buy everyone dinner. He wanted to celebrate, but it was still too early in the afternoon to eat. Caylee and Russ stated they had to go back to work. Mamie said she needed a nap, leaving me with Mom, Dad, Hope, and Brent. We quickly decided to go out for coffee and cake.

In the café, Dad and Brent became close friends. It seemed they had very similar interests. Mom, Hope, and I always enjoyed each other's company, and our conversations stemmed around upcoming church events. Hope had Mom interested in Saturday's Labor Day picnic at the Boys' Home. She said several ladies who loved to help—one was her mother and another was Brent's— thought my Mom would fit nicely into their group.

It was also during our coffee break that Brent made a very serious announcement. One Hope didn't even know about. He confessed why he was late for my hearing. It seemed his boss was angry for the time off he'd taken for family reasons, and he'd been called into the District Attorney's Office for a reprimand. He confessed the jibe made against his integrity and family caused him to make up his mind about something. It was something he had been pondering anyway, so the nudge made it easy to make the decision. He was going to run in the coming election for the District Attorney's Office.

Hope was thrilled! Dad patted Brent on the back and told him to count on his vote. I just smiled. I knew who really would be having the office: my Lord and Brent's big cat.

Learning to be Alone

After the hearing, when I was with my parents, my emotions became confused. I should be extremely happy, but deep down inside, I was sad. I tried to analyze why through reasoning. I determined that I wasn't sad for Lyle Horne. He received a reasonable judgment. I wasn't sad over Angie's actions any longer because she had mentally apologized to me at the courthouse. There was nothing indicating why my heart was heavy. The only way I could describe this feeling of sadness was grief.

No one had died, nor was anyone I cared about sick. This emotion was devastating, and I needed to talk with someone. The ache in my chest was almost painful. I thought I could talk with Mom at the dinner table, but I couldn't get a word in edgewise. Mom and Dad were conversing and flirting with each other so much, I felt non-existent. I started to leave the table so I could call Mamie but remembered she would be resting in preparation for work. I knew Hope and Brent would be unavailable because they had said earlier they wanted to celebrate his decision to run for District Attorney with their families. I could call Caylee, but I feared all she would want to talk about was Russ.

I decided to get by myself and talk with Whisperer. I quickly choked down the meal then politely excused myself. Once in my bedroom, I closed the door behind me and began praying, "Lord, why am I grieving? What is happening? Shouldn't I be happy?"

"What you are experiencing is a healthy transition. It is called the circumcision. Your spiritual life is separating from your fleshly existence. Flesh is crying for recognition because it is not the center of attention any longer. Your flesh knows it no longer has a grip on people's interests. The people you care about are moving away from you and focusing on themselves again. This is a good thing because it is the time set apart for us. You will learn how to be alone with me. I am the only one who can and will soothe your emotional hunger caused by the flesh. The sooner you learn how to fully depend on me, the better," Whisperer explained.

Afraid, I asked, "I don't have friends anymore?"

"Yes! The friends you have now are like family. They love you, but it is time you learn to be independent. Support systems are

dangerous. Flesh is weak. I am the only person equipped to be your foundation. You can lean on me, and I will not break. Gina, I am a jealous God. I will never allow my people to trust in anything or anybody more than me. I allow them to love each other and help each other but never be another's strong tower."

"Mamie, Hope, and Brent are strong, and their angels are strong, but without me, they are nothing. They learned how to depend on me, and they know how to keep you from depending on them. They will honor me by not allowing you to focus on them more than you should. Through Mamie, I gave you spiritual and physical attention. Through Hope, I showed you the truth operating within the spirit realm; and through Brent, I defended your innocence. Now it is time they let you go so I can help you walk with me. Their physical separation will be given to you out of love for me. If you want their company, they will be overjoyed, but when you start to lean on them for support, they will back away. My individual instructions for them will be clear. They will only encourage you after today. They will never turn their backs on you, but at times, it will seem like they have. No one cares for you like I do. Let me love you. Be my betrothed and allow me to show you what it means to be loved," He urged.

"Betrothed? You want to marry me?" I asked, dumbfounded.

"Yes! I want nothing more than our minds to become one," He beckoned.

"What about my promise to get married and have a family?" I inquired.

"I want that for you too, but before the promise comes, you have to give everything to me, and I must give everything to you. Gina, you must experience my total love for you before you can be ready for a human spouse. Your faith in me should be more than what you can do in your own flesh or anybody else's flesh. If you don't trust me more, the physical and mental burden you'll place on a spouse could destroy him quickly. It will be the same for him. He should depend on me more than you, or you won't be able to be His perfect mate. The time with me will be enlightening! You'll honor me by allowing me to take care of you. Let your faith in me prove itself," He pleaded.

Without hesitation, I said, "I'll do it! Your explanation makes sense. I've watched too many marriages fall apart, and I've seen too many people die too soon because you weren't their support system. Will You teach me more?"

He replied, *"Seek me from now on as if I'm your vital necessity. Feast as much as you can on my Word. Let us reason together. I will show you how to discern correctly. I want you to become observant. Watch Mamie, Hope, as well as Caylee, and notice how they conform to me."*

"What about Caylee? Will she have to turn her back on me at work?" I questioned.

"Caylee is you sister in Christ, not a parent. Parents go through the tension of separation for their baby's good. Mamie and Hope are considered your motherly guides. For Caylee to separate herself from you, she would have to quit her job. That is not my plan. I chose her to be an example of my love to guide you. Once you start working again, you will not see her the way you once did. You will see her in a new light. You will perceive my blessings upon her, and you can grow from the experience," He soothed.

Everything Whisperer said made perfect sense, and I began to relax. The ache in my chest was a result of my flesh having a hissy fit. The flesh wasn't in control any longer. Everything was fine. I was growing up and becoming someone the Lord wanted to love. My emotions calmed when I mentally separated my mind from my body. He was right! Nothing else could have cured the spiritual issue. I needed Him. I quickly came to terms and submitted. "Lord, I said earlier that I would marry you. I sincerely pledge my heart to you. I bind my mind with yours. Teach me how to love and be loved."

In return, He pledged, *"Gina, I bind my mind with yours. Everything I have belongs to you. Anything said in, by, and through my Word you possess. I allowed my flesh to die so I could leave you a legacy. You and I now share the same name. Operate in that name. It is the same name given to me by the Heavenly Father. You are now part of a royal priesthood. Welcome to our family."*

~~~

In the background, Ox cried softly. Witnessing the wedding vows filled his heart with joy. When Gina's mind entered his Lord's, they became one mind and one voice forevermore. With Jesus's faith, Gina now held the last will and testament. She was the inheritor of everything Jesus left behind on earth and what she would possess in heaven. His job would have royal authority backing him from now on. Anything Gina focused her mind on through faith would manifest, even if he had to go to hell to get it from Satan. He loved Gina, and with her command, he would rebuild the flesh on the bone. She would become all God wanted Jesus to be on earth. He would protect and defend her with his life.

~~~

After our pledges that evening, we spent hours behind the locked door of my bedroom. He took me through the Word but through His mind's eye. We went through stories in the Old Testament as if we were on safari. The desert experiences of His people were fascinating as I watched them move through His eyes.

He introduced me to Job's journey and showed me how traditions played a part in Job's problems. It showed me in detail how Job counted on offerings instead of fellowship for His family's protection. Then Whisperer showed me how Job depended on his good deeds to receive approval from God instead of depending solely on God's love. All in all, I fully understood how Job's fears came. They came because he relied on self-effort instead of God. When Whisperer was finished explaining Job's experience to me, He guided me into scripture where I could see through reading how Jesus operated while in the flesh. After Jesus's baptism, the Holy Spirit led Him purposely into the desert by Himself to meet with Satan. Jesus endured the lack of water and food for a long time until His flesh was almost dead. It was at His weakest point that Jesus defeated Satan, never once battling with the enemy's flesh because the battle was with Jesus's mind. He used this lesson to show Jesus won because He totally relied on what God said and then spoke God's written Word against Satan's temptations, encouraging me, another reason why He wanted me to start speaking God's Word out loud, especially when things didn't seem right.

His last lesson before He wanted me to sleep was the journey He had with the apostle Paul. Paul was one of Whisperer's first trustees with faith and relationship, and Paul didn't know how to explain what he went through. I noticed his reluctance to boldly say that he went to heaven because he kept referring to himself in the third person when he wrote. His story appealed to me. I sympathized fully because it was hard to tell someone you were actually with an angel.

Whisperer also told me that Paul battled with Satan. Satan tormented him the same way he tempted Jesus three different times. A messenger was sent against Paul's body, and he was about to lose faith, and he started begging God for healing. Then the Lord showed me he had to tell Paul not to fret. Grace to recover would follow a healthy mindset. A weak mind was one that doubted God's Word. The fellowship Paul and the Lord shared helped him regain trust, and Paul began to totally trust in God's Word again, and his body recovered. Never doubt God when the flesh is weak because our weakness opens the door for faith to move. Anytime we come to the conclusion we can't do something, then God can and will. It is when we rely on our own power that we fail.

The lessons were very enlightening. It felt like we'd been on a vacation, but before I turned off my light, I extended my thanks. "Lord, thanks for coming to my rescue and for showing me how you want me to be. Be patient with me. I truly want to be everything you desire."

When my mind drifted off to sleep, my eyes opened into a new realm. The first thing I saw was the sweet face of Jesus. He was magnificent! He was everything I ever wanted in a man. He was patiently attentive and compassionate, as well as loving. We spent every second together. He and I ran through fields, fished in babbling brooks, swam in deep blue oceans, and loved on people. Animals of every kind inhabited the land, and they were not afraid of us. Every creature and person visibly loved Him. It was an honor to be by His side.

Everywhere we went people came up to Him to offer Him presents of appreciation, and each time He shared the gifts with me. I lacked nothing. His palace was amazing. The people who lived in His kingdom also had beautiful homes. I was shown beautiful clothes and shoes and was told I could claim them all. Jewels of every hue and shape were for the taking. I was taken to banquets and told to eat as much as I wanted. We had acres of cars, trucks, airplanes, and boats to use whenever we had a need. Every storehouse only opened when Jesus said they could. Money was not a problem. If I wanted something, all I had to do was ask for it.

Jesus told me that as His bride I had one job, and that was to point any lost adult to Him. He would guide them to me. I was not to judge or reprimand; I just needed to show them love and tell them about the Word made flesh Who willingly died for us and rose again. Jesus and I played games with small tots, but when we approached older children mature enough to learn, He would lovingly direct them to me. Then He would tell them, "Listen to my bride. Learn through her example. She will show you how to find me."

We had one other place to visit before I needed to wake from slumber. Jesus wanted me to meet the Father. Before He opened the large doors to God's temple, He took me aside to help me separate my mind from my body. He wanted me to find rest in His body and look through His eyes to see how God welcomed my body into His presence. At first, I could not wrap my mind around the suggestion. As always, Jesus explained, *"I've given you my body. You gave me yours. Rest in me for a bit while I show you how Abba sees you. When Abba sees my mind in control of your body, it makes Him happy."*

I sat back and watched as Jesus took my body into God's presence. If it had been me trying to go to Him, my knees would have buckled. I would not have been able to stand in God's presence. With Jesus in control of my body, it responded correctly and boldly, entering the throne room of the Lord God Almighty. God was immensely powerful. He rippled with muscle and grandeur. The strength in His hands was hard to describe. No wonder scripture said He held the earth upright; His hands and arms were surely capable of carrying the weight. Behind the scenes in Jesus's body, I watched as God clothed my body in royal garments with His strong hands. As He finished, He gently placed a scepter in my hand. Then He beckoned me to sit at His feet and tell Him my heart's desire.

Father's eyes were pure love. His smile warmed me through and through, and every word from His lips refreshed me as if I had taken a long drink of ice water on a hot summer's day. I never felt happier in my life. I had nothing on earth to compare my joy with. I responded to Abba by saying, "You've provided all I need." I did not want to wake from my dream. I wanted to stay with Jesus forever.

He held me lovingly until it was time for my eyes to reopen into my earthly reality. Once opened, I collected my wits and then I heard Whisperer say, *"One mind and one heart forever. Lean on me in earth as you did in heaven."*

~~~

Satan stood outside of the Grimes's home, and he was very frustrated. An invisible wall would not allow him entrance, and he could not see or hear Gina like he could a short time ago. He wanted to study the girl after the supernatural victory she had in the courtroom that afternoon. When Ox met him on the other side of the barrier, he knew what was happening. At the hospital, Satan thought the barrier was caused by angels. This time he knew better. If Ox confidently faced him, he knew that Gina had Jesus's hedge of protection. That meant the girl lived in Jesus for the time being. Soon the hedge would be removed, and he would have a chance to break her down. He would not fail this time. He had too much information to use against her.

New Driver

It was 8:30 a.m. when I crawled out of bed. When I hopped to the kitchen, I noticed a note attached to the refrigerator that read, "Good morning, sweetie. I didn't have the heart to wake you. I cooked oatmeal just the way you like it, and I also made a few sandwiches and put everything in the fridge. I'll call you later. Love you, Mom"

I spooned some of the oatmeal in a bowl then scooted it across the counter to the microwave. I had everything under control so far. I hated to eat standing up, so when the meal finished heating, I tried to carry the hot dish with one hand as I hopped to the table. Nearly to my seat, the hot sticky goo splashed onto my skin. The pain was incredible, and I tried to quickly lick it from my hand, but when I did, I lost control of the bowl, and it dropped onto the floor, shattering the glass into thousands of pieces.

I wanted to cry. I had a huge mess before me. Sticky slop had spread everywhere, not to mention a minefield of sharp shards of glass, and I was barefoot. I couldn't stand in place until Mom got home. I didn't have a choice; I had to risk hurting myself on glass. There was no way I could clean up the mess unless I leaped over everything to retrieve a shoe and my crutches. I was about to take the leap when I stopped dead in my tracks. "Didn't I learn anything from last night? Didn't Whisperer say without Him I could do nothing?"

Quickly, I said a prayer. "Lord, help me! Prevent me from cutting my good foot! Help me jump over the mess."

I looked around hunting for the spot with the least amount of glass. As I was about to take the leap, I heard Mom scream, "Stop, Gina!"

I hadn't heard the backdoor open, and I didn't see Mom slip inside, so when she hollered, I almost had a heart attack from fright. I screamed back, "For goodness sake, you scared me! Why are you home?"

Mom answered, "I remembered leaving the post-office key in the slacks I had on yesterday. Instead of waiting for lunch to retrieve the key, I decided to get it and do the chore early. It's a good thing I did. You were about to hurt yourself."

"You're right. I knew I was in a jam, but I couldn't stand in the kitchen like a stork all day," I proclaimed.

We both laughed at my analogy. Then Mom went to my bedroom and retrieved my shoe and crutches, so we both cleaned up my mess. I thanked Mom profusely as we swept up the glass and wiped up the goo. Before she left for work again, I hugged her tight. I wanted her to know she meant a lot to me. But I wasn't stupid; I knew who came to my rescue. My God can see my past, present, and future. He knew way before I did that I would need assistance. He encouraged Mom to go home. From the experience, I learned two valuable lessons: keep open communication with Whisperer and always cover my foot. Everything else would work out.

I sat on Mom's sofa until watching television got boring. Then I lay in bed reading my Bibles, hoping I'd get sleepy enough to dream again. I was impatient for the day to end. I could hardly wait for the evening to arrive. It was group night. It would be my first meeting with other Christians my age. I was looking forward to getting involved in the ministry. Hope's description of the Boys' Home and Mamie's involvement at a nursing home intrigued me, but neither one appealed to me. There had to be something I could be actively involved with, so I wanted to dive into service. I just needed to be in the proper environment.

I asked Whisperer if He would tell me what to do, but He said I was getting in too big of a hurry. He told me that I would know which area of ministry was for me when the time came. He wanted me to observe through His eyes.

The statement bothered me, so I asked, "How will I know when I'm seeing things through Your eyes?"

"Our minds have merged. From now on, you will see and hear everything the way I do. Relax so you can remember how it was with me in your dreams. Remember how people came to us. Remember how we found the lost and taught and played with the young. That is the ministry I want for you," He informed.

I pondered over what He said. I adored the way He and I loved on people in my dream. I let my mind play back my visions. He showed me lost adults who needed direction and told me to point the way to Him. He and I played with tiny kids, but when it came time for a child to learn of Him, I was given the job of teaching. I loved every second I spent with Him.

I also remembered something about standing aside and letting Jesus go to the Father in my body. The vision caused me to have serious questions. I didn't have fear around Whisperer any longer, so I stopped worrying if my questions got on His nerves. I needed clarification, so I boldly asked, "Can you explain to me how Your living in me works?"

"Sure! Do you remember when you watched your body lying on a hospital bed? Do you remember how you felt when you realized you'd left your body after the car accident? I let you experience that for a reason. I wanted you to see the real you. Your body is nothing without the spirit operating on the inside. I watched when you tried to get your body to move. I watched you compare yourself with it by looking in a mirror. I sent Adrian so you could see how spiritual beings operate. You can go to the past, visit the present, and see the future. Spiritual beings are not bound by time, nor do they feel pain. You are free from them. That is how a spiritual person lives when their body stops functioning. They are free to live eternally in heaven with Father. The only thing that held you in that room while you were separated from your body was your natural mind.".

"Because I have a plan for your future, I need you in a body. The body must operate within time frames. It will experience pain at times. But with the same mindset, I will get to live with you in the body, and Father can watch over us. Father doesn't like for me to suffer pain anymore. When you hurt, He knows I'm grieving for you. He knows I love all of you. That is why I had you wait outside of your body during the dream. I wanted you to see how Father looks and responds to us as one. No one can go to Father without me."

"Gina, I allowed Satan to watch you play in the spirit realm with Adrian. I taunted him by using you. He is the one who slammed you back inside of your body because he was mad at me. Everything has a purpose. We have a purpose for you. What Satan does not know is that I am now residing in your body too. He will never know, so let the real you sit back, rest, and watch. Allow me control of your body for a while," He enlightened.

"Do I have any say in what I get to do?" I questioned.

Patiently, He answered, *"Remember what I told you. Speak my Word and let it go before us. Ox and all his angels will make the way straight. Then we can walk on a clean path. Life is smooth when God's Word goes first. You still have the voice. Your voice speaking what God wants for you will give orders to Ox. Ox and his angels will prepare the way. They hearken to the voice speaking God's plan. With Ox in charge, hundreds of angels will make our paths level and passable. Our journey will be easy."*

Instantly, I remembered how Ox looked yesterday. He was fierce-looking. Hope said it was because he was protecting the Lord. Something I'd said had set him off. Ox was in battle mode.

"Whisperer, Ox looked ready to kill yesterday. Was he protecting me or you?" I questioned.

"Me. You were hurting, so I guided you to God's Word. Then I helped you believe that the words were for you. You followed my lead and declared them by force. I am the Word, remember? The words you spoke ordered Ox to protect me from any weapon. Then you declared that no tongue would prosper. He was carrying out my commands. I was already operating in you before our minds merged. We both benefited from what you spoke. Hope helped you see how Ox looked. Never forget! Now that we have one mind and our voice is also one, Ox can hardly tell the difference. Plus, he doesn't care. I allowed Ox to watch us join minds. Now he knows where I am," He shared.

My mind felt like one large hard drive. Whisperer downloaded mysteries too complicated for the natural person to comprehend. All I could say was, "I don't want to fail you. Don't stop talking to me."

"Try not to make what I say hard. Be happy I'm here," He returned sweetly.

~~~

Mom knew I had plans for the evening, so we ate a quick meal. Caylee volunteered to pick me up around 6:30 p.m. a few days ago, so when the time came I was ready and waiting. When a large unfamiliar truck pulled up in Mom's drive, it suddenly dawned on me that Caylee was bringing a date, and I would be a third-wheel tagalong. Russ was very welcoming. He and Caylee both helped me get inside his large truck. My independent attempts were futile, so Russ had to lift me onto the seat. I thought Caylee's dad's truck was big, but Russ's made his look puny. I didn't refuse the help because I'd remembered Jesus would be using Russ. When I was seated and strapped in, I bowed my head and quietly said, "Thank you, Lord." When Russ said "you're welcome," I snickered. He apparently didn't hear me end the thank you with Lord. Then again, he may have. Who knew anymore?

Hope and Brent were very glad to see me, but they were very busy getting the popcorn and drinks ready before the movie started. Caylee and Russ made sure I found a comfortable spot to rest until everything was ready. Then they went off by themselves to play a game of darts before the movie started. I was happy for my friend. Russ was a wonderful person.

I was also happy for myself. I was on my mission finally. I didn't care that I was left alone because I really wasn't. I was to observe through the Lord's eyes. He said I would know who needed us because they would be clearly presented.

I let my mind roam while I looked around. I was perfectly content until my eyes fell on a young woman also sitting alone. She looked sad and scared, and her appearance made my heart ache. Instantly I knew why. A few days ago, that could have been me. Here again, I had to appreciate being hospitalized. If things hadn't happened the way they did, I wouldn't have my wonderful friends. I'd be sitting in a corner like this lady, watching Caylee and Russ have fun while feeling lost. The word lost caused me to remember! I was to help the lost find Jesus.

"Whisperer? Do I need to get up and approach the lady? What's your plan?" I asked.

"Stay seated. Just open your mouth. I'll greet her," He guided.

I looked over in her direction, and fortunately, she was looking at me. I obediently opened my mouth and heard myself say, "Hi, is this your first time? Would you like to join me?"

The simple questions worked. The lady came quickly over and sat next to me. She asked, "Hi, I'm Stacy Barnes, are you a regular here? I'm new to the area and don't have any friends."

"Nice to meet you. My name is Gina Grimes. This is my first visit too. See the couple playing darts? The girl is one of my best friends, and she invited me. The group leaders, Hope and Brent Arnold, are also my good friends. The three of them rescued me," I stated.

"Rescued you? How?" Stacy asked.

"They helped me find Jesus. I was literally searching for love in all the wrong places. It took a car accident for me to wake up," I shared.

Stacy's eye grew large. Apparently, my comment struck an interest because she said with a high-pitched voice, "Really! I was wondering why you wore the large boot."

I had her attention hook, line, and sinker. It was time to tell my story. I didn't give spiritual specifics, but I did tell her everything changed after committing my life to Jesus. I was perfectly comfortable telling this stranger about my old ways of immorality, alcohol, and drug use. I could tell her truthfully, I didn't have the guilt and shame that followed days after my overindulgence any longer. When I told her I was thankful for having the accident, I watched her face light up. The drastic change in her appearance told me Jesus had her. My job was over. All I had to do after that was listen to her heart speak.

I listened compassionately to all Stacy had to say. I came to find out a horrible event drove her to search for a nicer environment with wholesome people. She was tired of the nightclubs, and a co-worker recommended our group. After hearing her out, I could introduce her to Hope and Brent who took over and welcomed her warmly. It was good to have a new friend; we had quite a lot in common. In time, maybe I'll be the one to offer the lifeline. For now, I wanted to make her feel safe and wanted. We later sat together and watched the movie. When the movie was over, I invited her to come back. I even told her not to stop with just the group. I asked her to come to church Sunday morning because Pastor Reed's messages were wonderful. I suggested she look for me so she wouldn't be frightened in a strange place. Everything I did and said felt good. So, good, in fact, I wanted reassurance. I quietly asked, "Whisperer, did I do everything, right?"

"Yes, you did! You followed every cue. I'm proud of you," He encouraged.

The Love Treatment

When Hope woke the next morning, she felt ashamed of herself. She'd promised the Lord she would take Gina under her wing to make her girl's first experience in their group wonderful, but instead, Gina had been the one who took in a stranger and made her feel welcome.

While making breakfast for Greg and Brent, Hope felt the need to repent and talked the previous night's events over with the Holy Spirit. "Lord, I failed you. I got caught up with the preparations of making popcorn and getting drinks ready for the movie that I failed to focus my time on Gina. I left her by herself. I'm proud of her though. She made a new friend and showed the girl love. Do you want me to get with Gina and make up for lost time at today's picnic?"

"No! Be her friend and spiritual mother, but give her space. It is her day for me to love on her. Don't you remember when I loved on you? Let me show her what it is like to be cared for properly. You didn't fail me last night. Gina wasn't expecting your attention. I had already prepared her and told her things would be different. She was not alone; she was with me. She and I had fun together last night. We could love on a lost young woman. I think Gina did very well," He answered.

Hope's heart sang. She knew what Gina was about to experience and couldn't wait to watch the events unfold. Gina was in for a treat.

"I remember! You told me not to lift a finger, and I had every need met. I learned a lot that day. I'm going to love watching you work," Hope shared.

"Do not fret if you see Gina working. She must be taught by me how to give and receive love. Gina has not had any training on how to live in my kingdom. When you came to me, your life was out of balance. You knew how to give but could not receive. For now, Gina follows instinct without knowledge. I know who and how to make her understand. In the end, she will grow and know her true calling in ministry."

After the Lord's explanation, Hope cooked breakfast with a smile on her face. In fact, Hope's actions were so energetic, and Brent couldn't help but ask what was going on. "What's got you so happy this morning?"

Hope joyfully replied, "Love is in the air! This is going to be a wonderful day! I'm looking forward to the picnic and spending time with my family."

~~~

At the crack of dawn, I awoke with thoughts of having another fun-filled day. My mom and I were attending a picnic at the Boys' Home, and I could hardly wait to see what Whisperer had planned for the day since we had so much fun the prior evening.

Rather than lie in my bed pondering, I decided to jump right in and talk things over with the Lord. "Whisperer, I had a great time last night. Helping Stacy truly blessed me. Can we help someone else today?"

"Sure! Why not start by showing appreciation to your mother? She needs to see that you are grateful. You can do it, I'm with you," He encouraged.

I enthusiastically inquired, "What would you have me do? I'm a little out of kilter. Should I write her a note? What? Give me a clue?"

"Cook her breakfast. You are not completely disabled. With me, you can do this. We'll have fun, and it will help you to pass the time."

Whisperer was right. My hands weren't crippled, and if I put on a shoe and used my crutches in the kitchen, I'd be able to balance myself nicely. This would be fun, and I'd get some of my independence back.

While making pancakes, Whisperer and I talked. We replayed everything that happened with Stacy last night. I learned that sharing my story with Stacy opened a door for Him to work in her life. Until then, she felt like she didn't belong. It thrilled me to know that uncovering my dirty past helped Stacy to fit in. The revelation showed me that all things, even nasty details, did work together for good.

I had everything laid out on the countertop for a tasty breakfast when Mom entered the kitchen. I even handed her a cup of coffee. She was so overcome; tears ran down her cheeks.

"Why are you crying?" I asked Mother, confused.

"I don't know! I guess shock. Not too many people do things for me," she replied.

Her answer made me sad. It was true; I was guilty of taking her for granted. I ignored her good gestures daily. I learned that through cooking, time and effort were required, and it was a labor of love. Mom was all about taking her own time and effort to create a lovely meal for me. It was time that changed.

We ate, laughed, and really enjoyed each other's company. I was in love with my mom. I held her very preciously in my heart. The one person I used to run from, who I thought was overbearing, was now my closest friend.

When we finished eating, she and I cleaned the dishes together. I refused to wimp out using my brokenness as the excuse. I learned a new trick from the experience. I could let my hands go free from the crutch grips. The arm holders on the crutches kept them in place. I could hop with one crutch and hold plates with the other and still having both crutches for use when needed. The Lord was right again; I wasn't crippled after all.

Mom and I were excited when 3:00 p.m. arrived. We'd heard a lot about the Boys' Home and wanted to see for ourselves how it operated. Both for different reasons: Mom wanted to help with functions, and I wanted to meet the kids. I remembered vividly in my dream how Jesus and I played with the toddlers and taught the older children. I was ready to get started.

On the ride over, I let my mind fuse with Whisperer's and mentally asked, where do you want me to start? Do you want me to center up on the older boys or play with the younger?

"Neither," He answered. *"I want you to sit and observe, let me do all the work. I'll let you know when I have need of you."*

At first, I took His statement as a reprimand. Then I remembered a very important point. He was in the driver's seat of my body. The real me was just the passenger. I'd be everywhere He was observing with my mind while He used my body to help someone.

~~~

The Holy Spirit was very pleased Gina understood, but she was only half right. She thought allowing Him to operate in the earth through her was all He wanted. He must enlighten her before they arrived, so He said, *"Gina, you are only half right. I'll use you to do good for others, but I also want you to receive goodness. Remember your dream. When people gave to me, I immediately shared with you. It works the same way now. When someone hands you something, they are giving to me. I can only receive their gifts by using your hands to take their offering. Don't refuse their blessing. This is one of the ways I'm glorified. It is how I am sustained on earth. You allow me to give as well as receive. I am not abusing your body for my gain. I'm blessing your mind and body. In my kingdom, I work in and through everything at the same time."*

When we entered the large home, I could not believe my eyes. Everything was orderly. Nothing was chaotic like I expected. Hope and her mother, Sue Joiner, along her mother-in-law, Olivia Arnold, all greeted us at the door. Mom fit right into the group of older women. Hope and I talked for a few minutes, but she had duties to attend, so I found a spot inside to sit and observe.

I had hardly sat down when a little fellow, maybe two or three years old, came to me. He wanted a playmate. He said, "I have sniffles, and I can't go outside. Mama Elder wants me to stay cool. Will you play with me?"

He was the cutest thing. I knew immediately he was an orphan because he addressed Mama Elder who was the home's housemother. My heart grew warm. The impulse to hold him tight was overpowering. I knew Whisperer wanted to hold the little boy, so I said, "Why don't you crawl up on the sofa with me and sit on my lap so we can get to know each other?" I answered.

He was on the sofa fast and giving me a hug. Then he sweetly said, "My name is Luke, what is your name?"

"My name is Gina. As you can see, I can't play very well with my broken leg, but I would love to read to you. Would you like that?" I replied.

He scurried down from the sofa to find a book and quickly settled himself back onto my lap. His skin felt very hot. I knew immediately he had a fever, so I prayed. "Lord, this baby needs your attention. Would you send Mamie or one of her angels?"

"You speak healing over him. If you don't know the words, open your mouth and let me pray. Hope showed you how the other day," He conveyed.

Oh, my goodness! I'd totally forgotten that ability. I said, "I'm sorry, Lord. Please pray for Luke. I don't have a clue what to do." I opened my mouth to let air in and out while He whispered with my tongue. The words were foreign to me, but that did not matter.

Luke didn't hear the words because he was too busy turning pages in the Bible storybook. I rested in the fact that one did hear, Ox. I knew he would get busy making Luke comfortable.

I cuddled Luke tightly and read four or five stories until I felt him go limp in my arms. The tot fell into a deep sleep. I asked Whisperer, "Is he okay?"

"He will be fine. All he needs is rest. There is too much excitement going on today, so I calmed him down. Enjoy holding him for me. I want him to feel love," He relayed.

I had the pleasure of holding a big baby. I rocked him slowly back and forth in my arms until an older lady came to take him from me. I willingly relinquished my bundle, knowing he would rest better in a bed. I'd made a new little friend and couldn't wait for my next mission.

I began again by observing my surroundings and became suddenly aware of uneasiness when a young teenage boy slammed the front door of the great house. The young man was not happy. The women in the kitchen noticed but did not stop to question what was wrong; they continued working. I wondered if the boy was my next assignment. I asked Whisperer, "Is this boy our next mission?"

"Yes, but let him come to you. Curiosity about your leg will open the door to conversation. He is very upset with himself. You will soon see why. Help him fit in, teach him what I taught you. He is not handicapped but only momentarily restrained. Let him see how the two of you can work together. Flow with the circumstances presented. You'll fully understand at dinnertime," He instructed.

I pretended to read, knowing the boy would soon ask about my leg. Suddenly, I felt the sofa shift, and I heard a loud creak. He'd flopped hard on the seat next to me, and my head shot up. I braced myself quickly for fear of landing on the floor, but amazingly, the seat remained intact.

I heard him snicker then say, "Sorry! I didn't mean to scare you, but you looked funny just then. What happened to your leg? You can't do anything either, can you?"

There it was! I had the prompt that would start our friendship. "Hi, my name is Gina. To answer your question, I was in a bad car wreck a few weeks ago. I'm just temporarily out of sorts, but I've found I can still do just about everything. I chose not to get in everybody's way. That is why I'm in here. But with a proper attitude and mindset mixed with determination, I'm a force to be reckoned with," I answered.

"I'm Brian. What do you mean, 'attitude'? I'm not the one with an attitude. The guys don't want me around because my arm is broken," he said angrily.

I sincerely asked, "Could be they are afraid you'll hurt yourself if you play. Who told you to come inside?"

"Nobody. Carl thought it best if I watched instead of helping with the gear," he answered hesitantly.

"I've met Carl. He's the coach, right? I know he's looking after your best interest. He's a good guy. When did you get hurt?" I questioned further.

Cradling his broken arm, the boy answered, "Last night. I broke my arm in two places wrestling."

"Brian, Carl knows best. Your body went through a lot of stress. He just meant for you to take things easy today. I know he'll want your help later. Give him a break and be thankful he cares about you. Six to eight weeks will pass in no time. You and I will both look back at our injuries and have war stories to tell. We can say we were struck down but not out!" I professed.

"I hadn't looked at it that way. I thought he was mad at me for getting hurt. I let the team down last night, and I do have a bad attitude. Thanks for helping me see," he said cheerily.

"Anytime! Why don't we play a game?" I suggested.

"Great!" Brian exclaimed. "It will take my mind off the ball game outside. Do you like board games or cards?"

"I'll play whatever you want," I agreed.

We played Battleship a few times then we played a game of War with cards. When it was time for dinner, we helped each other with our meals. He brought the food and drinks to the table, and I cut his meat and opened ketchup for him. He and I had the chance to talk about church while we ate. I found out he didn't really believe. When I asked why he said it was because he didn't have any parents. His viewpoint broke my heart.

Suddenly, my heart burned. The heartburn in my chest felt like a torch. The pain was unbearable! What did I eat? Was it grief or stress over Brian's lack of knowledge? I felt sick! I almost excused myself from the table when Whisperer spoke softly in my ear, *"Gina, the burning is not from heartburn. It is not because of food.*

The fire is from unspoken words. Release the truth! Tell the boy about us!"

The need to explain love to Brian propelled me to quickly tell him about a loving Father who cared deeply. Jesus was his only answer, and if I didn't say something, he wouldn't understand. I began by saying, "Brian, when we believe in Jesus, God becomes our parent. It doesn't matter if we have actual flesh-and-blood people anymore. God takes responsibility for us and gives us what we need. Look around. You have this wonderful place to live in with church people who care about you and your well-being. They made sure your arm received medical attention. You have this food and your clothes. And most of all, you have many brothers who are in the same situation, and now you have me as a big sister. Honey, you are not alone. Let Jesus in your heart. He will never let you ever be alone again."

"You mean it! You're my sister?" He asked soberly.

"Yes, in Jesus, we are all kin, and we have one Daddy. Nobody is an orphan, ever," I choked out.

I watched Brian's face change. I thought my remarks hit a homerun but wasn't sure. Brian stood, gathered our paper plates, and took them to the garbage without saying a word. I hoped it was his way of preventing me from seeing his tears. Then again, I had to make sure he was okay. I softly asked, "Whisperer? How did I do? Is Brian okay?"

"He is great! I'm in his heart now. Thanks," He said gratefully. A few minutes later, Brian returned to our table as if nothing had changed, but he carried a huge bowl of ice cream. It was homemade peach ice cream, my favorite. He said, "A sweet for my sweet sister. Gina, I asked Jesus to come to me. You opened my eyes. Thanks."

Whisperer then said so sweetly, *"Truth unspoken hurts you and the person who needs to hear it. You're learning to give and receive. Your words brought Brian to us, and when he found peace, I asked him to take your favorite ice cream to you."*

Preparing for Forty Days and Forty Nights

God watched everything from His viewpoint in heaven. Satisfied with Gina's progress, He determined it was the time she had the long desert experience. He had to command Jesus to remove all the props and even let Gina hear what Satan sounded like. Without knowing proper care in a desolate position, Gina wouldn't be able to face Satan alone. It was time for a meeting while Gina slept. To allow Ox the chance to attend His meeting, God Himself covered the young woman. She was shielded by a shield.

"Come up here!" God's voice boomed throughout the earthly realm.

Jesus, Insight, Justice, Healer, and Ox, along with every angel in heaven, gathered at the foot of God. Rarely did He order a meeting. He usually let Jesus handle everything. This meeting was serious.

"The faith inside Gina Grimes has developed nicely. She knows how to speak my Word. She understands it is the driving force that Ox uses. Now she knows about the torch of truth and how it operates. I've also been listening to Satan. He is frustrated and getting anxious to destroy this woman. He does not want to give over the territory. When Satan saw Hope's revelations concerning him and realized we had Gina shielded, he got busy forming his own agenda. He knows from past experiences that I'm about to allow him a chance to destroy my teachings. A few times he succeeded where women were involved. We have the advantage this time. He thinks Gina is just as weak as Eve or Sarah, but he doesn't know the Holy Spirit occupies her mind. Satan is aligning his giants of old to come against her. I'm going to allow him to think Gina is fighting alone. He will not be able to hear the Holy Spirit speak inside her."

"It is time for her desert journey. She must see how we provide, protect, and defend when all props are gone. The Holy Spirit is guiding Pastor Reed as we speak to give a message tomorrow in church for Gina. Hope, Brent, and Mamie must be sidelined. Gina can only associate with them during church or church events. Caylee's time has come. She will be Gina's encouraging force. We

are almost at the finish line. Look, I see the fields ripe for harvest. Get excited!" God relayed.

Everyone bowed and agreed it was time. God dismissed the crowd, so He and Jesus could speak alone.

"Son, muster your earthly army and get with Ox. The cherub of faith is ready to connect with him. We are behind You," God shared.

"Yes, Abba, I will. Do we know what evil Satan plans?" Jesus asked.

"He plans to use the same old three. They'll be disguised to appear differently. He thinks we aren't looking because we are focused on Gina. He'll never learn." God laughed.

"I'm ready for our meeting. Call Satan to join us, it is time," Jesus agreed.

"Satan! Come forth immediately!" God commanded loudly.

Without going through proper doors, Satan abruptly landed at the foot of Jesus like he was ordered, but he came hissing and snarling instead of groveling. He hated this. It meant one thing. It was time for a dueling match between him and God's precious Word. What he hated, even more, was that after the meeting with God and Jesus, angels would try and taunt him and poke fun because they knew why he was there. Heaven never sided with him. Every being there was a haughty reminder of his earlier existence. His evil imaginations stopped quickly when he heard Jesus ask, *"Satan, do you see our new pupil? Isn't she lovely? She knows the truth. Hasn't she progressed nicely?"*

"Blah! Blah! Blah! Why don't you get to the point? Yes, I've seen your new toy. I know why I'm here, this isn't my first rodeo. I've watched your army protect her. I know all about the shield," Satan answered disrespectfully.

"Well then, you know what's next. Gina's shield will be thinned. You can tempt her and talk to her, but you will not be allowed to harm her," Jesus stated.

"Can I touch her?" Satan asked.

"You can try," Jesus countered.

"What about her angels? Will I be fighting against them?" Satan questioned.

"You know the answer to that already. Gina has authority over Ox," Jesus answered.

"That shouldn't be a problem then. The girl is untrained, and to my knowledge, she has only attended two church services. Am I correct?" Satan spat.

"You know!" Jesus stated curtly.

"Are we finished? I have temptations to prepare," Satan snarled.

"Be gone! Do your worst," Jesus said haughtily.

~~~

Satan didn't bother going through the temple doors; he went straight through the floor back to the earthly realm. He wouldn't allow the taunts to start. He knew strength behind words, even when they came through his own species.

~~~

Back on earth, Satan unleashed the three giants of old from their slumber. Calling them by name, Satan reveled in the knowledge he had of their power. He wasn't ashamed the newborn would have to undergo torments from Lack, Self-Preservation, and Lust. He wanted her faith destroyed and this duel over with quickly.

He would not give up his territory easily. He had forty days and nights to weaken the woman before he would take everything from her. The three giants rarely failed him when he used them against people, especially inexperienced and uneducated people. Jesus was the only one who ever had victory completely over them, and he was out of the picture, seated with God.

Satan pondered the prize, the victory of winning once again was at hand. He remembered how it felt when Eve failed. The thought pleased him very much. The girl didn't matter; he would take her self-induced dead carcass and flaunt it in the Son of God's face. Who would be the crown bearer then?

~~~

Jesus met with Ox to inform the huge beast of things to come. *"Are you ready, my friend?"* Jesus asked.

Ox answered, "Yes, Sir! I have armies in place."

"No, Ox! Are you ready? This is your time. You must protect, provide, and cover what happens from here on. You may take an extreme beating. Are you ready?" Jesus asked compassionately.

"It doesn't matter, Lord. I'll give my life if necessary. You and Gina are my life," Ox stated soberly.

Jesus hugged the huge beast and said, *"I love you too, my friend. Go now! Go back to Gina. You and Satan will be facing each other soon."*

Doing Without

I was in the bathroom getting ready for church when I heard Dad and Mom talking in the kitchen. Apparently, he was there to attend church with us. The thought warmed my heart. I knew Mom had met Jesus. Hopefully, today would be the day Dad got introduced.

I quickly dressed to join my parents. When we headed out the backdoor, Dad asked Mom if she would drive. I questioned why until I noticed the new sports car parked at the curb. His new toy was a sweet red Camaro, which was a two-door. It was my favorite car in the world, but I wouldn't be able to ride comfortably in it, so it made sense for us to ride in Mom's vehicle. I'd have to wait a little longer before I could ride in Dad's. The thought of joy riding in the Camaro gave me goose bumps. I couldn't wait, but what gave me joy at this moment was Mom's reaction to Dad's request. Without reservation, she relinquished control and threw her keys to Dad. "You drive," she stated.

I watched my dad's expression change. He had a gleam in his eye. He took Mom's statement as a sign of honor. She had submitted and allowed him to have the driver's seat. I knew instantly what happened. It was beautiful. They were connecting again, this time, correctly.

Our group met like before. We sat in the corner out of the way with Hope, Brent, Caylee, Russ, Mamie, and to my unbelieving eyes, Dr. Jones. He sat next to Mamie as if he was her date.

The sight had my curiosity in high gear. I leaned over Mamie's shoulder and softly asked, "You two a couple?"

"We've been friends for years. Don't be so shocked," my old friend shared.

The thought occurred to me. I am the only person in our group without a partner. Hope has Brent, Caylee has Russ, Mom and Dad are back together, and now it seems that Mamie was with Dr. Jones. I closed my eyes, put my hand over my heart where I had my vision written on paper and stuck into my bra, then I said to myself, "It won't be for long. Thank you, Jesus."

Pastor Reed's message gave me something to think about. He talked about support systems. He described what happened in detail when people leaned on things other than God. Pastor Reed was very passionate about the topic. He even went so far as to say when people relied on people, it caused the person being leaned on to wear out faster. I immediately thought of Mom. *Was my neediness wearing her out? Was I killing my mother?*

Then Pastor Reed said people depended on money as their god more than Jesus when he should be their only support. He said that was what caused evil things to happen. Money couldn't buy real happiness, and without the proper mindset, no amount of money would be enough to support a person's needs. Jesus not being the support system of our lives caused money to fail, and our pants' pockets, wallets, and purses would always be full of holes. I hadn't thought about money being a god before. Now I understood why offerings were taken up. People were giving away what could rule their lives. For some, it was an outward sign of how much they revered Jesus.

Then I heard Pastor say we should always ask Jesus to guide us in our giving. All Jesus expected was a tenth of our earnings, but if He wanted us to give more, we should. People needed to hear about Him, and His main way of getting people to hear was through the fivefold ministry gifts offered by the church. Pastors had to be supported, but so did the ministry itself. Money was only the exchange system.

I had my checkbook out, but I had not taken the time to see how much money I had. Whisperer would know; He was the spirit of Jesus. "Lord, the offering plate has already passed me by. I just learned I needed to give. What do I have to give?" I asked.

"Give your check to an usher. He will know what to do. Give $125.00 for me, please," He said.

I quickly wrote my check then tore it from the checkbook and folded it in two so I could focus tentatively again to Pastor's Reed's message. After service, I stopped in front of the usher standing at the closest exit door and asked him to please put my check in the offering. He happily obliged.

On the way home, I pondered what Pastor Reed said. It was time I moved back into my apartment. No way was my need for care going to wear my Mom out before her time. Whisperer has shown me I could do things for myself. It was time I stopped being lazy and learn to face my challenges. Plus, my apartment was closer to Caylee's. When time came for me to go back to work, she wouldn't be inconvenienced. This was the right time to leave. The Lord's prompting was loud and clear through Pastor Reed's message. I had no doubt I would be released for work when I met Wayne again tomorrow. I was scared, but I had to place all my life in Jesus's care. I had to go with His flow.

The ride home was quiet. Mom and Dad didn't even talk. Maybe the message gave them something to consider as well. Seeing them together contented me, and not having to make conversation was just another nudge for me to leave. They needed privacy to build their new relationship.

Mom and I changed out of church clothes while Dad waited in the den. I brought my decision into the light while we prepared lunch. "Mom, when we finish eating lunch, I'm going to pack my things. It's time I move back into my apartment. I must get back into a routine for my life."

"Honey, I don't want you to go. I'll worry about you," Mom argued.

"I'll be fine. We both knew this was coming. Let me go without any fuss. You don't have to worry about me, you can visit as much as you like. Things are different because now I actually want your company. I need you in my life, but if I stay here, I risk losing you," I proclaimed.

"What do you mean? You are not going to lose me! Gina, please!" Mom moaned.

"Mom, you can't be my support system, only Jesus can. Let's trust Him, okay?" I pleaded.

~~~

I have her now! Satan thought. Alone with her thoughts, Lack will win swiftly. He'll make her cry and complain. She'll deny God's love quickly. There is nothing like making people miserable by taking away the means necessary to sustain their lifestyles.

~~~

Dad watched and listened to our whole conversation, and he volunteered to help me move when Mom and I finished talking. He told me later that he knew Mom would need company later, and he didn't want her to go into a deep depression. I wholeheartedly agreed. I knew Dad could give her a new perspective.

It took five large garbage bags, plus my one suitcase, to get all my clothes packed. If nothing else, I prospered in clothes. Mom and Dad carried my belongings inside my apartment and placed everything in my bedroom. Afterward, we stood around and stared at one another until it was uncomfortable. Dad broke the oddness by giving me a quick hug then Mom took her turn, crying the whole time. I soothed her mind by saying, "Mom, I love you dearly. My decision has nothing to do with how you cared for me. I felt like a baby all over again, and I loved it. But that's the point, I'm a grown woman. We both should progress, not digress. Call me in an hour or so, and we'll chat and catch up." "You mean it? You won't mind me meddling?" Mom asked.

"No, I'll welcome your calls every time. I've changed, Mom, I want you to meddle," I urged.

I was alone at last and in my own place. I could talk out loud with Whisperer, and the privacy would allow Him to speak aloud to me as well. I might have to change His name. Whisperer wouldn't apply any longer. Then I heard Him chime in, *"No, I like Whisperer. It fits me. Like I told you earlier, I love the nickname you gave me."*

Hobbling around my apartment was easier. I didn't have as many obstacles. Mom had furniture and decorations everywhere at her place. My lifestyle was simpler, less cluttered. My kitchen was even more accessible to my needs. I had a barstool next to the counter. I wouldn't have to jump from place to place.

I was caught in analyzing my surroundings when I noticed a pile of envelopes on my kitchen counter. Apparently, Mom or Dad left my mail there. Curious to see what the mail contained, I sat on the stool and began opening my letters.

After opening the third demand for payment from the hospital, I heard a deep, raspy voice say, "What are you going to do now? You gave the church all your money. How are you going to eat?"

The voice frightened me. I'd never heard it before, but the questions he posed caused me concern. How much money did I have? I hadn't checked, or I hadn't given it a single thought. Of course, I would have hospital and doctor bills. My apartment wasn't rent-free, and I had other monthly bills. Had I acted crazy by writing the check this morning?

I quickly turned on my laptop so I could check my bank account. It showed my balance was $11.30. I'd written a check to the church for $125.00. Panic hit me like a blow to the gut. The check would bounce! I'd be embarrassed.

I heard the raspy voice laugh before saying, "Foolish girl! Let the error teach you a lesson. Now you'll have to pay overdraft fees with interest. You'll see how it feels to go hungry for a few days." I closed my eyes. I refused to answer the evil voice. It wasn't one I wanted to entertain.

I let my mind reach for Whisperer. "Lord, who is this evil voice? What does he mean I'll be going hungry?"

"The voice belongs to one of Satan's messengers. He was sent to torment you. He can only win if you let him. Do not let him know I'm here. From this point on, don't talk to me out loud. He can't hear our thoughts. Trust me, trust the truth. Let me speak the truth with your mouth! The demon will think it is you," He encouraged.

With Whisperer's encouragement, I began to feel the familiar chest burn. This time, I knew what it meant. So, I released the truth. "Go away! I trust in Jesus! He died so I could live! All my needs are met! I will never be begging for bread!"

~~~

The trumpet blast coming from the mouth of the woman caught Lack off guard. The Word commanded that he leave, but before he had the chance, he felt a hard blow to the head. When he turned around, he faced a very angry Ox. Startled, he gasped then quickly fled. Lack pondered, the girl has the Word, plus she has help. Satan has not warned me. Then again, Satan probably does not know either. With that in mind, Lack knew he had to develop harsher words that could destroy this girl. But first, Ox had to be subdued.

~~~

With fear gone, I began researching my bank account. All my bills were paid. The bank had electronically been drafted. I had two days before payday. I would pay the doctors something then. I would trust Whisperer. He wouldn't have asked me to give if I couldn't have met the obligation.

I went to my refrigerator to see what I had to eat. There was old cheese, eggs that needed to be thrown out, two frozen dinners, and a pack of hamburger meat in the freezer. In my pantry, I had paper towels, potato chips, colas, coffee, Pop-Tarts, and pickles. I had a feast, food enough for two days. With food issues settled, I hobbled to the bathroom. I looked for toilet paper and was rewarded by seeing three rolls. Everything indicated Whisperer knew my conditions before I did. I mentally sent Him a thank-you.

~~~

Lack angrily approached Satan. "You failed to tell me about Ox! Why?" he demanded.

"I thought you'd win without knowing. After all, money is the root of evil, is it not? The girl owes doctors thousands of dollars because of me. She doesn't own a car any longer. Better yet, I have the upper hand," Satan quipped.

"What do you mean, upper hand? Let me in on your secrets, or you can fight Ox alone!" Lack demanded.

"Remember Eve? She ate something that didn't belong to her. I'm baiting Gina into doing the same thing. Jesus has given her a promise. I plan to use His promise to break her heart. Gina thinks the wrong Polk brother is her chosen soul mate. She doesn't know he is already married and expecting a baby. All we have to do is keep the other twin busy and out of sight then use this married man against God's plan." Satan snickered.

Lack perked up and then suggested, "I have a perfect idea! Let me cause her heart to hunger. Allow me to entice her appetite. I'll keep the wrong brother out of reach then encourage her to act out of order. Why not assist her failure by using the lure? It will be too late by the time she finds out what she did. By that time, she will be out of Jesus's good graces and no longer under His protection. Then you can destroy her."

"Good idea! I'll keep the twin busy. You set the stage necessary for your plan. When you are ready, let me know, and I'll send you help. Doubt, Worry, and Fear will keep Ox busy while you bait and torment the woman to act out of order. Jesus has always been one for order. He follows instructions to the tee. When Gina fails to stay in line, he will have no choice but deem her unrighteous then call her cursed. I can't wait!" Satan agreed.

Denied Sight

I had a lot of work to do and no excuse for leaving it undone. Clothes and toiletries had to be put away. With crutches attached to my arms, I stood on one leg and stared into my almost empty closet. The old reminders were gone. I threw hangers on the bed then sat and began putting my new things on them.

~~~

Lack watched until a plan materialized. He would plant seeds of doubt and confusion in Gina's mind. Cause her to worry about her looks. Give her passionate thoughts. Keep her awake worrying about seeing Wayne again and forming a relationship. Then deny fulfillment.

~~~

Ox also watched and was fully aware of Lack's presence, so he moved closer to cover Gina in the shadow of his wings. In place and standing guard, Ox waited. He knew Lack was not alone.

~~~

The Holy Spirit grieved. Gina's mind had disconnected from His.

~~~

As I went through the items Hope gave me, I began thinking about Wayne. Just knowing I'd see him again gave me concern. *What will I wear? What will make him notice me differently? Do I even have something to draw his eye?* I thought.

Everything Hope gave me was beautiful. I wanted to compliment my feminine assets while refusing to show off my cleavage, legs, or hips. With this in mind, I tried choosing something to bring out my peachy skin, red hair, and blue eyes. Jewel-toned clothes lay before me. Hope had a passion for dramatic and bright colors. Bright colors looked good with my complexion, but the clothes were businesslike, nothing flirty.

I finally chose a dark-green skirt and rust-colored blouse. Then I chose jade jewelry to accentuate the ensemble. I knew the look would make me pretty; I only hoped my appearance was enough to get a smile from Wayne. My mind wrestled with this plan. I knew baiting Wayne now was doing something out of our time frame, but

I couldn't live with the thought of him being mean again. I had to change that.

With clothes laid out for tomorrow and the others put away, I allowed my mind to drift into troubling waters. Worrying questions began to plague me: Was Wayne a good lover? Would he want an ex-slut? How would I make him like me? Men brought up in church shunned women like me. I was used goods, too experienced. How could I make him see the new me?

~~~

Ox was furious! His Lord was crying! Ox curled his lips and exposed his teeth in anger. He wanted to lash out at the cruel giant but couldn't. Leaving Gina's side made her more vulnerable to attacks. He was about to move in closer over Gina so she could get her mind right again when he felt a sharp poke in his ribs. Turning his head to see what provoked him, Ox wasn't surprised when he saw three other tormentors. His time had come. Gina's dream was materializing for him. He had to stand his ground and keep the shadow in place. He was well aware the three weren't there for Gina. They were sent to torment him. Everything was going as planned. Jesus's shield had been weakened for a reason. Heaven knew the Holy Spirit was crying.

~~~

My mind was in turmoil, which led me into harsher imaginations and exposed to the raspy voice. "Churchmen want virgins for brides. Churchmen want someone like their mothers. You are far from perfect, but there is a way to have what you want. No man can resist a brazen woman. Flirting will go far. Fondling and cooing entice the weak. Don't you want to know if Wayne is weak? You hate weak men. Better to find out now."

The suggestions the raspy voice gave nauseated me. I was not that person anymore! I tore my thoughts away and tried focusing on good. Through my will, I cried out to goodness, "Whisperer! I need you!"

Without pause, Whisperer gently assured me, *"I never left. Stay with me! Don't talk, just think! The only way you can escape evil is to think about good things. Fix your mind on truth. Let your eyes focus on the lovely and lovable. Now you desire kindness, mercy, and friendship over lust."*

How do I make the horrible voice stop? I pleaded in my mind.

"Remember how I presented you to Father? Profess that loudly! Say what you saw with force! Knock the demon out with the power of your words," He answered.

I made my mind go back into the dream. There, I saw myself washed thoroughly by God's Word. I was clean. Then I was presented to Jesus without spot or wrinkle. He accepted me. I smiled with the imaged realization. Then my chest began to burn. Truth had to be set free. This time I didn't need Whisperer's help. I could loudly scream what I remembered.

"Your words do not scare me, Satan! I know for a fact I am washed thoroughly with God's Word. I am clean inside and out!

I do not have a spot or wrinkle. I know I am clean because I was accepted by Jesus, and He helped me stand before the Father!" I shouted.

~~~

Satan was gagged, and Lack was blown thousands of miles away by the sheer force of Gina's scream. The sound alone deafened the evil minions. Satan thought this opponent is stronger than I thought. Nevertheless, Lack's seed was planted; now he could set the stage. Tomorrow was another day. He would take pleasure seeing her hopes crushed. He and Lack could sit back and enjoy the show.

~~~

The rest of the evening, I watched cartoons. I made myself laugh. Before I went to bed, I watched the funny preacher I enjoyed before, Jesse Dopants. I would not allow evil imaginations back in my head. Afterward, sleep came easily. I was given glimpses of Wayne again, and I got to hear him propose to me at Roe's.

~~~

Satan and Lack began their taunts bright and early before Gina had a chance to focus on good.

~~~

Holy Spirit watched and waited, also knowing the disconnection between Him and Gina would come soon, but He would give her space. This time, when disconnect came, He could rest easier. It was evident Gina had a foundation. She willingly came back yesterday by sheer determination after Satan hit a nerve.

~~~

I was eating a Pop-Tart when something dawned on me. Thoughts began running madly in my mind: *Does Hope know about my doctor's appointment? She wasn't the one who brought me home last time. How am I getting to the appointment? Then again, shouldn't I try getting there on my own? But how? I reasoned, there is the bus service. It runs several times daily, and it is near my apartment. Maybe I should call a cab. Either way, travel costs money, and I don't have cash. I only have $11.00 in the bank. What should I do?*

"Whisperer, what should I do? I'm trying to be independent. Money is a problem," I asked.

"Stop worrying. Hope knows you have this appointment. Call her and let her know where you are. Otherwise, she will go to your mother's house," He answered.

I breathed a sigh of relief. Everything was prepared. All I had to do was notify Hope of my whereabouts. I felt shame. One tiny issue tore me away from trust again. "Lord, please forgive me. Be patient with me, I'm trying," I begged.

"Baby steps, Gina. I know you are trying. Don't quit," He sweetly answered.

Hope wasn't surprised when I called. She knew I'd be taking steps toward independence after hearing Pastor's message. She encouraged me by saying, "Every believer has a wilderness experience when they have to purposefully deny fleshly supports. Some thrive, and others lose hope. You, my dear, are going to blossom!"

~~~

Lack waited for the perfect opportunity to attack again. He knew the tradition of dressing to impress was on his side.

~~~

The Holy Spirit stood back, allowing Lack an opportunity, then braced for His disconnect.

~~~

After talking with Hope, I stayed on course by listening to praise-and-worship music and watching cartoons or Christian television until it was time to focus on getting ready. I washed my hair in the kitchen sink, quickly blow-dried it, bathed off in the bathroom, and then sat at my dressing table to apply makeup. Instantly, my mind went dark as I remembered being fake before my transformation and living in pretense. The last time I sat here and took the time to paint my face was the night of the accident. I wrestled with pretense then.

I chided myself. Hadn't I just heard a wonderful woman of God preach a few minutes earlier on pretension? We were more than clothes or jewels. We were beautiful on the inside. She even gave a scripture reference to back up her point. Before I started with all the makeup, I went to the pastor's references and read them using my Amplified Bible. I did so because I was tired of wrestling with my thoughts. I took Whisperer's advice then spoke from the heart after reading.

~~~

The Holy Spirit was very proud of Gina. She was taking baby steps and trying, but like a baby, she was about to do and say things out of sorts. He saw in her mind before their disconnect that she still planned to doll herself up and work out a relationship with Wayne, even though she wasn't using a sexual lure. Then He faintly heard her profess words that were out of kilter from God's. She was now depending on herself.

~~~

"I will not merely adorn myself. I will not depend solely on my clothes or jewelry. I will let my inward beauty shine. My charm and my gentle, peaceful spirit please God. My heart's desire is to please my Heavenly Father," I professed.

Even though Gina's mind wasn't connected to the Lord's, Ox proudly stayed the course, beaten and bruised from the night before but still in place. He had to focus on the task; he had to cover Gina. He straightened his back, fluffed his wings, and breathed deeply. He was ready for round two.

~~~

Hope's first word when she saw me was wow! Then she explained why she remarked that way. "Gina, you are lovely. I thought you looked beautiful in the red dress last Thursday, but this outfit puts the red dress to shame. Your makeup is gorgeous; it makes your eyes pop! You need to wear it more often. If I didn't know better, I'd think you're baiting. Are you fishing, Gina?"

Not wanting to share my secret, I simply smiled and honestly said, "Maybe. I've seen some cute men at the center."

"Be careful!" Hope suggested. "Remember to let God lead you."
"I am. Trust me! I am," I replied.

We were on time for my appointment but still had to wait in the lobby for an hour before I was called into an examining room. The time had come! I was about to see Wayne again! My heart began to pound, and I heard the blood rush into my ears. The wait was agonizing. I wanted to see his face so badly! "Lord, please help Wayne with his attitude. Let him be nice today. Help us!" I prayed.

I didn't hear a word. Usually, Whisperer would say something. He didn't this time. I almost asked again when I heard a light tap on the door. My heart almost stopped. I took a deep breath because I knew I was about to see the face. Then I was severely let down when a short, dumpy young man entered. He greeted himself as Eric Johnson, physician's assistant. Then he said, "I'll be examining you for Dr. Polk. He can't attend to all the patients. The center is still trying to find a replacement for Dr. Carter."

I felt like a deflated balloon. My heart was screaming! Where is the face?

I knew the time for Wayne and me to fall in love wasn't here yet, but I wanted to see his face. I'd planned on settling by feasting on his face until our time came just to help me cope. I wanted to cry. I must have moaned while Eric examined me because he jumped away and asked if he hurt me during his exam. I assured him that I was fine. I didn't tell him I wanted to cry because my heart was breaking.

I left the center with a medical release form and a note saying I could return to work, but I left feeling empty and unfulfilled. My only hope now was a card that I held in my hand that said, "Return in five weeks to see Dr. Polk." Five weeks! I had to suffer five more weeks! I left the office mad!

Hope knew I was distressed and volunteered to stay with me awhile. I wanted to tell her everything, but I knew I couldn't. I wanted her to stay, but I understood I couldn't lean on her any more than I could lean on Mom. I needed to be alone. I had a bone to pick. Where was the Lord? Where had He been?

~~~

Satan and Lack laughed and laughed after hearing Gina's rant. They'd won the second round! Gina was her own enemy. She was angry with Jesus! She'd called on her God, and He denied her a word or thought. Too bad the girl didn't understand. Jesus couldn't agree with anything other than what God prearranged. He wouldn't even discuss the issue. Gina's desire was to see Wayne's face, which played perfectly into their trap. Wayne's face wasn't God's pick for Gina.

The One Who Knows

The Holy Spirit felt it when Gina willingly but angrily reconnected. It would not be until she questioned His whereabouts that He would answer her. She had to learn. What better way to show her than let her be uncomfortable? Babies learned to put their shoes on correctly after wearing them on the wrong feet, didn't they?

~~~

Gina began drilling complaints. "Whisperer, where were you this afternoon? I needed you, and you didn't say anything. Why did you fail me when I needed you most?"

"Welcome back, Gina! Do not talk to me yet. Come into the living room. Turn on your television. Sit and pretend you are watching a program. You are being watched. Until now, you were in Satan's territory. He heard your every thought. Now that you are back with me, don't let on that you are frustrated. Relax, don't act like you are still angry with me," He soothed.

I did as Whisperer commanded. I turned on the TV and then fixed my eyes on the screen, not caring what the program was. I lay back on the pillows then mentally, I asked, "Welcome back? I thought we were always connected?"

"When you are with me, we will be connected. But you shut me out, and your mind left me behind. You took the driver's seat of your life and left me here waiting. When you were alone with your own thoughts, Satan had access to you and your thoughts. He knew everything you thought about. He even gave you the topics on which to think," He answered sweetly.

"What do you mean? I followed your advice. I read and spoke the Word. I kept my thoughts pure!" I rattled out.

"Your thoughts were pure, but you didn't follow the plan. Satan used your promise as bait. Then you jumped ahead of me and God's promise and tried to bring about your future using your own ideas," He enlightened.

"Why didn't you stop me? You could have warned me. It would have kept me from getting my heart broken again," I countered.

"Gina, I cannot, and I will not get off course. I am bound to God's ways. I will not even discuss an issue until it is time. You chose to jump ahead of us. I refused to help or answer your request because

the time was not right. I didn't do this to punish you, and I didn't refuse you because I was angry. I simply honor and want God's complete plan for you. I will not come into agreement with your impatience and the acts that follow."

I wanted to weep after hearing Whisperer's reason, but I could not divulge my distress. It was true. I was not patient. I thought if I could just see Wayne's face and get him to smile, then I could wait. I needed help. If I didn't amend my heart quickly, I'd become a mental patient instead of a mental-health employee.

"Lord. You are right. I was impatient, and I acted on what I thought I needed. Will You help me cope? I need something to help me through. The wait is hard, my mind is too easily distracted, and I don't ever want to be without You again," I pleaded.

"Stay with me. Focus on others as much as possible. Remember Stacy, Luke, and Brian? You wanted more ministry duties, and the time you had with them wasn't long enough. There is truth to the saying 'Time flies when you are having fun,' so make the time fly," He counseled.

"I can do that! Ministering with you was fun and very rewarding, but I wish I had someone to talk with when I wasn't focused on ministry. I wish I wasn't bound by secrecy and could share my promise with another. It would make it easier if I had another person who understood and could help me through the lonely times," I conveyed.

"You've had one all along. You even told her about the journey. Have you forgotten? Who else did Satan try and kill recently? Who has lived through a waiting period and received a reward? Think!" He urged.

"Caylee!" I blurted.

My mind raced. I continued to ramble on in my thoughts but was able to fix on this one: I told Caylee everything in the hospital before I knew better. She's the one who waited, now she and Russ are together. How could I have been so dense? I thought you meant not to say anything anymore. She was part of this plan all along, and Satan tried to take her out! Is she still in danger? Do I need to warn her?

"Whoa! Your mental rambling is like running with a racehorse. Slow down! There is no need to fear. Caylee is safe because Jesus is protecting her. He removed her from Satan's path. Jesus knew what *baited the old serpent. We've been stringing him along. Luring him to focus on Hope and then showing great love and concern for you. It made him crazy and caused him fear. He tried one other time to ruin Caylee out of sheer spite, but his plan failed. When she wasn't paying you much interest because of Russ, he didn't see a threat any longer. He lost interest and is leaving her alone for now,"* the Lord explained.

I pondered what Whisperer said and was still confused. Caylee hadn't abandoned me. She and Russ together gave me attention. How did Satan think she was out of the picture? We were together several times weekly.

"Whisperer, I'm totally confused. Caylee and Russ have been very kind to me. She hasn't neglected me once," I stated.

"Has she ministered to your spirit lately? Has she asked about your journey? Caylee has been caring for you physically. It is time we awakened her ministering spirit again. Call her and ask for her assistance. Tell her you start to work again tomorrow. Use your time wisely and don't let Satan know what you are doing. Flow with me. Minister to her first by asking her to share every detail of her relationship with Russ, then I'll do the rest."

This interested me, and curiosity sprang forth. "You and Caylee have a relationship also? Do the two of you communicate?" I asked.

"Why, yes! Caylee and I talk all the time. I helped her wait for Russ. She entered my presence with childlike faith. God sees her like a child. You entered my presence through fire and water and died from your old life. God sees you as a woman. After you talk with her about Russ, I'll impress upon her to pray for you. Compassion from Caylee will go far into heaven. She will release her angel to help you. Don't talk about your promise with Caylee, let her talk to me about it. I'll cause her to remember the excitement you had in the hospital. She will desire your happiness and want you to know love. She will be praying from experience," He answered.

"I thought I could share?" I questioned.

"You already did. Enjoy this knowledge," He answered.

I was beginning to enjoy the knowledge when something else piqued my interest. "Caylee has an angel too? What does hers look like?" I questioned.

"He is Ox's twin, only his face is childlike. We call him Cherub," Whisperer answered.

~~~

Satan could not believe his eyes. Gina didn't fight with Jesus. She watched television instead, and the program wasn't anything Christian-related. The girl wasn't disturbed. Lack's plan failed anyway, and they didn't even have the pleasure of beating up Ox.

It was time to confer with Self-Effort. He would make Gina his puppet. Her old life still had lingering strongholds. While away, he would occupy Ox by sending Loneliness with Partier to torment him. Hopefully, they could pry him away from Gina long enough to make the covering shadow disappear. He needed to hear Gina's thoughts, and Ox was in the way.

~~~

I went to my bedroom after the conversation with Whisperer. I undressed and put on comfortable clothes. Then I hobbled to the bathroom and stared at my painted face. I hated it. It was a reminder of my past life. I would learn I didn't need paint. I began scrubbing my face with soap and a washcloth. I was so angry at myself. Then I heard a sweet voice say, *"I loved the way you looked. Your clothes and the jewelry were beautiful, and your lips and eyes were very lovely. They popped out at me! Makeup is not my enemy. Why you used it was. Think about this and dress for me while you wait for your earthly mate."*

I playfully asked, "You want to be my boyfriend?"

He playfully countered, *"I thought we were already past that."*

~~~

Ox giggled to himself. Loneliness and Partying spirits would be useless against him. He wasn't Gina's protector either, but let Satan think his shadowing wings were the barrier. Gina had something stronger. She had love.

When the two evil spirits arrived, Ox dug in and toughened his hide. His stance and insolence would make Satan crazy while Gina and the Lord fell deeper in love.

~~~

Miles away and controlled by alcohol and Immorality again, Angie debated whether to call Gina. Loneliness was using Angie as bait. He convinced her that she was lonely and that her partying nature wasn't happy. Angie was tormented, and she thought her current issues must be bad because not one man approached her at Joe's

Pool Hall the previous weekend. She had a better sex life when Gina was around. Men were attracted to Gina because she was beautiful. When they couldn't get Gina's attention, they settled for her. She didn't mind. She enjoyed playful men. If for no other reason she wanted Gina as a friend. It was time to mend fences.

~~~

The ring of my cell phone brought me out of my playful mood. When it registered with me who had called, I was shocked. At once, I realized by her voice that Angie was not herself. She sounded tipsy, and it was Monday night. She usually drank the heaviest on weekends. Concerned, I listened to her spout nonsense about not having any men in her life. She always had men. There wasn't a weekend I could remember when Angie didn't have a man. When the truth came, I was a bit disgusted. She said I drew men, so she wanted us to party tonight.

"Be kind! She is being manipulated by evil. Just politely tell her you are busy. You won't be lying. You will be with me," Whisperer suggested.

Sweet as sugar, I politely declined and told Angie I had plans. I wished her well then said I hoped one day we could be friends again before closing the conversation.

~~~

Loneliness was so angry, he began striking Ox and screaming, "You can't keep her shielded forever. Give up or die, your choice!" Partier, seeing the fun Loneliness had, also began to kick Ox. Ox held his ground because Gina was contented, and every once in a while, he managed to throw out a punch or kick himself.

No matter what, though, Ox stayed firm while he pretended to shield Gina.

~~~

While I still had the cell phone in my hand, I called Caylee. I hadn't told her of my move, and I wanted to have confirmation of a ride to work. Every time I heard Caylee's voice, I wanted to smile. I didn't think I'd ever heard her angry, depressed, or agitated. She seemed to always be happy, like a child. No wonder she could enter God's presence easily. Children had no worries.

We mainly talked about work. Apparently, in the two weeks I'd been gone, things changed, and it seemed everyone blamed me.

Caylee wanted me to know I might have snide comments and sour grapes thrown my way upon arrival so I could be prepared and not let people hurt my feelings. She promised to be with me and help me cope until the feathers settled.

When Caylee said the word feathers, I thought about Hope's angel. *It'd be nice if he showed up at work tomorrow. He'd handle any ugliness.*

I went through a mental checklist as I ate one of my frozen meals for dinner. I had a way to work. Next, I would prepare a lunch to take with me because I had limited funds. Now I needed to figure out how to carry everything and walk with crutches at the same time. I came across a plastic grocery bag with handles while searching in the pantry. It was perfect. I went ahead and placed my last frozen dinner in the bag and popped it in the freezer. I laid out a napkin, a plastic cup with a lid, and a fork, and then I bagged a few chips and two pickles so I'd have them ready in the morning. Food prep was finished. The last thing was to lay out clothes and a shoe and set the alarm thirty minutes earlier to be absolutely sure I had plenty of time to get ready.

The rest of my evening was spent lazing around watching television and reading a good book, perfectly content.

I'm Back Where It All Began

Satan sat in the shadows very confused as he watched Gina. This girl was content. His targets usually succumbed early in their testing phase. Jesus had removed His shield for the duel to begin, so he reasoned that the shadow was due to Ox's wings. His shadow was now the shield keeping her from being affected. He knew better than approach Ox on his own, and he couldn't risk the death of his three large giants. He had no choice but to keep sending tormenting demons to do the dirty work. In time, they may weaken Ox enough to take him out of the equation. Right now, he couldn't risk having his head bashed in.

Satan realized Lack's plans hadn't been strong enough to crush Gina, so it was time Lack and Self-Effort worked together. When the two large giants of old came forth, they agreed to work with Satan, but they weren't fools. They refused to go forward with their ideas unless Ox was subdued or at least distracted. Both giants made a suggestion to Satan. They wanted him to have Worry, Envy, Jealousy, Strife, and Depression gang together against Ox. If the lesser demons worked together, they could guarantee Gina's destruction.

~~~

Ox felt stab after stab from Worry. Then Envy tried to turn him green. Jealousy only made him angry. But when Strife and Depression showed up, Ox became enraged. Ox wasn't angry at their attempts against him, he was angry they wanted to distract him from his mission. They wanted Jesus to fail. The righteous anger drove his hoofs deeper and grounded him so his wings could spread further and wider over Gina. Ox used his horns to butt and bash, his new teeth to snap and bite, and his claws to scratch and gouge.

~~~

Caylee arrived to pick me up early. She was at my apartment at 7:00 a.m. instead of 7:45 a.m. I was dressed but still hadn't eaten breakfast. I offered Caylee a cup of coffee and remembered what Whisperer suggested. He said to ask Caylee about her social life, and He would prompt her to pray.

I hardly had my question out before she burst into every sorted detail. Russ sounded amazing. He treated her with utmost respect and gentleness. She rambled and rambled until we entered the workplace. Listening to her was very enjoyable. It gave me hope and showed me how fast things moved, for her. Only two weeks ago, Caylee was also waiting for her soul mate.

Caylee parked her truck in a handicapped parking place until I managed to get onto the curb; then she hurriedly found another space, and we walked inside the building together. She was right to tell me that my co-workers were disgruntled. The air felt oppressive, and almost no one spoke to me. Caylee took my lunch to the break room so I could talk with the administration. It was when I went into my supervisor's office that I found out why people were unpleasant. Mrs. Juniper politely told me things had backed up in the file room and in other units because people had to cover my position until I returned. Even though I was back, they would still have to cover because of my mobility issue. No one was happy because the crew needed to function like a Swiss watch, but due to my absence, one of the cogs was broken, causing others to work harder and longer.

After my interview with the supervisor, I hobbled to my desk and proceeded to prepare records for the daily appointment schedules when Whisperer said, *"Observe! Don't look around, just listen. Remember how things were at the hospital with Hope. Don't allow yourself to be tormented. Demons are causing bad emotions to flare so they can feed. If you allow yourself to become a victim of strife, the nasty creatures will try to feed off you. When necessary, speak out against evil like you did at the hospital. You don't have to be loud, Ox will hear you. Let him take care of the infestation. I am with you, and I know what is happening. Stay the course until a ministry opportunity for us opens. You'll know when that door opens."*

~~~

Self-Effort saw his opportunity. He would use Gina's own pride against her. He'd coax her into doing something without help. Maybe if he encouraged her to use her own efforts, he could arrange a way for her personal injury.

~~~

Whisperer's suggestion was right on time, and I was finished with the morning's first batch of charts when it dawned on me that I could not carry them to the nurse's station. I was faced with a dilemma. I was faced with getting the charts inside the other office or call a file clerk for assistance. I didn't want Jennifer mad at me, so I started to lay them on the floor and push them along with my crutch when I heard Whisperer say, *"Call your colleague. Don't risk hurting yourself."* Unpleasantly, Jennifer came and took the charts. Her actions spoke volumes. She gathered the charts with a grouchy and mean demeanor. I didn't hear her say anything until she turned her back. That was when I heard her murmur and complain about the double duty.

Her ugly attitude gave me a start at first. Then compassion rose inside me when I realized the truth; she was a demon's happy meal. I really felt sorry for her then. I refused to participate like Whisperer recommended and began focusing my hearing on others around me. I was shocked! No one was happy. No one but Caylee, that is. She was like a breath of fresh air in a room full of cigarette smoke.

I didn't feel the need to speak out. The words weren't directed at me. Though they were worrisome, I didn't feel attacked, so I prayed instead for my colleague's peace of mind.

~~~

It was payday for Gina, and Lack saw another door open for him. He and Self-Effort could make Gina face life without money again.

~~~

At lunchtime, Caylee met me in the break room. I started for the refrigerator, but she beat me to it and ordered me to sit. "You're going to get tired of helping me. I don't want you murmuring and complaining about me like the others," I commented.

"Come on! You'd do it for me. Didn't I promise to stand by you? You'll be good as new soon. Time will fly. Enjoy being pampered while you can," Caylee soothed.

While we ate, Caylee asked, "Would you like to go grocery shopping with me after work? If I don't buy groceries after I get paid, I'll be hungry before next payday."

I was chewing, so I raised a finger to indicate "give me a second" then I reached in my skirt pocket and pulled out my smartphone. I answered, "Give me a minute. I just gave a check to the church, and I need to make sure it didn't bounce. I also need to do a quick calculation before committing. I have several doctor bills that need paying."

While I researched, Caylee said, "Go with me anyway. I'd love the company."

I remained quiet as I researched my bank account. I breathed a sigh of relief when I saw that the church check had not bounced. Then I quickly did a calculation of all I needed to pay and wanted to cry. If I paid each medical bill, I'd be broke.

Caylee noticed my concerned expression and asked a question, and then she made a wise suggestion. "Gina, didn't you say you gave to the church? If you did, you don't have anything to fear. God promises to rebuke anything that tries to devour our resources. Why don't you buy a few things and then go home and pray before paying the doctor bills? Let God make a way for them to get paid."

"You're right," I agreed.

Once I agreed, I began to feel a deep burn in my chest, which indicated that Whisperer wanted the use of my mouth so He could speak out. I opened it and let Him speak through me. I knew Caylee would understand. He said, *"God provides my seed for sowing and my bread for eating, so I will be provided for and have enough to share."*

My heart swelled with love. Jesus was saying through me that He and God were making a way. I needn't fear. I would have money to give and to eat, plus I'd have enough left over to share and help others.

~~~

Seeing Gina's grateful heart, Ox was immediately energized. Strengthened by the Word, he was able to grab Lack by the throat and beat him senseless. Ox didn't kill Lack, but he beat him within an inch of his life. It showed the old giant he meant business, and he would not tolerate the interference. Self-Effort didn't hang around to help Lack. He fled so he could hide behind Satan.

~~~

Suddenly, the break room door flew open, and Jennie Hall ran inside. Jennie was the Mental Health Center's receptionist. Something had apparently unnerved her because she was crying. Caylee and I both motioned for her to join us so we could help her calm down. Then Caylee asked Jennie what happened.

"I lost a patient! He wouldn't listen to me. He killed himself while I had him on the telephone! I heard the gun go off!" Jennie choked out.

"Lord!" I cried. "Help this woman!"

Caylee soothed Jennie as much as possible, but the woman was too distraught and had to be sent home. Instantly, I began to hear the whispers. Colleagues began their murmurs and complaints because no one wanted Jennie's responsibility. Her job was like being on the front line of battle. She was faced every day with mentally ill people. Some of the ill were violent. Some wanted to hurt themselves, and the regular, day-to-day patients were being managed with strong meds. Jennie's nerves broke today, and she became like a patient. No one but Caylee and I seemed to care.

"I care!" Whisperer proclaimed.

My body began to tremble. I knew what was about to happen. He was driving me to ask for Jennie's position. I couldn't believe it. He wanted to use me so He could help the sick. Jennie's position frightened all of us. No one wanted to face what she faced today. Mentally, I begged not to be the one. Stick me in a corner, I thought. I'd do mindless data entry all day. I'd scrub floors. I'd volunteer to do anything but deal with mentally ill people.

"Gina! Please let me help these people. Give me a chance. I'm the only one who can help them. Allow me to use your body. I'll speak, lay hands on them, and heal. Rest alongside me as you watch and learn. I promise it will be just like it was with Stacy, Luke, and Brian. We'll have fun," He pleaded.

I could not deny Him. His pleading broke my heart. He really did care. He loved everybody. He warned me. He said I would know when my ministry arrived. I never dreamed it'd be hands-on with the sick. Was I ready to do this? Better now than later. I braced myself, and I asked Caylee if she minded bringing my cola so I could go and talk with our supervisor. In truth, I wanted her with me in case I fainted. I was going through with it. I would not chicken out. I was volunteering to take Jennie's place. *"Thank you, Gina. Don't be afraid of this. I'm with you. I'll be the one working, not you. You don't even have to worry about what to say. I'll do the talking. You already know when I want to speak. You've learned to recognize my fire inside you. Let me show you joy. Getting to see people set free will be rewarding,"* He encouraged.

Caylee was quick to follow, but she didn't understand what I was doing. When I told her, she turned white and asked, "Are you sure?"

"Yes! I know I heard the Lord on this," I replied.

Caylee didn't try to stop me. She understood a call. We marched together into my supervisor's office, and she welcomed us. When I volunteered to be the center's receptionist, she was overjoyed. She stated I just solved the office's dilemma. If I took Jennie's place, Jennie could take mine, and our workflow would be smoother. The staff wouldn't be grumpy any longer, and everyone could function properly.

The rest of the afternoon, I answered the office phone, greeted patients, and assisted staff. The job duties weren't fun but necessary, and I enjoyed encouraging the people. I enjoyed shaking hands with the needy. I loved smiling at the patients. I even liked talking with a desperate teenager over the phone who was trying not to purposefully cut her arms. Whisperer was right; allowing Him access to people who needed Him through me was rewarding.

Happy for my Friend

Satan was furious! He loathed it when Self-Effort ran to him, begging for protection. Weakness made him nauseous, and Self-Effort was proving to be weak. When Satan inquired about Lack, he was shocked to hear what happened. He thought for sure Ox would be too tired to fight. His five tormenting demons had fought with him bravely all night. Now Lack's usefulness was over. Lack wouldn't have the strength or sense to work again for another decade.

~~~

When the workday was finished, Caylee and I went to the local grocery store. After she parked the truck, she ordered me to stand next to the truck until she returned. I didn't have a clue why until I saw her coming at me in an automated grocery scooter. She'd taken it on herself to fetch me one rather than have me walk too much on crutches. Caylee was a gem. She loved people through words and actions.

We had the best time. Caylee followed alongside me and helped fill my basket, as well as her own. I didn't need much and wanted to be conservative, so I got the necessities with a few goodies, but Caylee loaded her cart. We were about at the cash out when Caylee's cell phone rang.

I had two choices: stay, or drive my scooter away so she could talk privately. I chose to stay and focus on items rather than Caylee. It didn't last long when I heard her hoop loudly. She was so happy that she took my scooter and spun me around and around. "What in the world are you doing? What is up?" I shouted.

"I have a new car! Russ took Daddy and introduced him to his cousin who works at the Kia dealership, and they found me a slightly used Kia Sorento, within my budget. I can't wait to see it. Russ said it is light blue, and it has four doors so you can ride in it too," she blurted.

"That's great! Hurry and get me home so you can see your new car," I urged.

Caylee hurried to get me home, talking about Russ all the way. Then she helped get all my purchases inside the apartment. It wasn't until after she left when I was putting the things away, that I noticed several bags were hers. I quickly called her cell. When she answered, I informed her. "Caylee, you were so excited, you brought in a lot of your things. I refrigerated the cool things and kept all the rest bagged for you, okay?"

Caylee snickered and then replied, "I didn't make a mistake. Consider the food as my love offering. It made me sad to see you denying yourself food. I prayed about it, and God told me to help you. Then He quickly made the way. I don't have a car payment this month. My new payments start next month. Take the food. I may need your help one day."

She wouldn't let me argue, and she told me to enjoy the goodies. All she would allow me to say was thank you.

Tears ran down my face while I put away my favorite drinks, cookies, frozen dinners, soups, bread, peanut butter, jelly, ice cream, and coffee. I was very grateful for Caylee and Jesus. Learning to live through sharing would be hard. There was a stigma that followed charity takers. I was taught never to take handouts from my parents because we weren't lazy people.

"Gina, I'm bigger than any stigma. My love never fails. Don't allow the enemy access by making you feel lazy. You are far from that," Whisperer informed.

~~~

Satan decided to let Self-Effort gain composure for a few hours before calling him into service again. Envy and Jealousy would have to do for this evening's event. When they arrived for duty, they too were hesitant. They were still tired from the night before, but to please Satan, they agreed to scream and shout in Gina's vicinity. Maybe their suggestions would weave into her dreams.

~~~

After dinner, I watched television until my mind started to drift. I thought about Caylee. She was very fortunate. She had a new car, a soul mate, she had it all! In the back of my mind, I heard my old self say, "Goodie Two-shoes may think she has all she needs. Russ isn't all that! Her car isn't even new!"

When I realized I was in a dark place, I immediately tore my thoughts away. I knew what had happened. I didn't ever want to be disconnected from Whisperer again. Anger welled up inside me. I remembered a scripture verse and instantly agreed with what it said.

I opened my mouth and screamed, "I purposefully throw out every thought that tries to make me disagree with love. I capture my evil thoughts and make them obey my Lord. I love Caylee and Russ. I want every blessing and favor to come their way."

~~~

Ox responded with force. Envy and Jealousy were burned but not completely torched; it allowed Ox to have peace and rest for the remainder of the night. He wouldn't have to fight. He could watch and relax while he stood firm.

~~~

It was 8:00 p.m., and I was tired and ready for bed. The day had been exhausting but rewarding. I'd taken off my makeup and put on my nightgown when my cell phone rang. It was Caylee.

"Look out your window. I'm outside in my new car," she requested.

I pulled the blinds aside and peered out hoping to see the car, but it was too dark. Thinking it would only be Caylee and me, I informed her, "I'll come outside. Give me a minute to put a robe on."

I quickly threw my robe on and tied it around me. I found my slipper and hobbled to the door anxious to see Caylee's car. I was excited for my friend. She deserved the best.

I opened the door and walked a few feet outside when I spotted Caylee and Russ. I was mortified! Caylee motioned for me to come over so I could look inside the car, so I couldn't turn back around. It would be rude. There I stood, barefaced, bare-bottomed, and nothing else on but a nightgown and robe, but neither of my friends cared. They didn't judge. Then I heard Whisperer remark, *"You have on more than you used to wear out to nightclubs. You hid behind your mask, remember?"* His comment made me smile. I did hide behind the face paint, but now I was bare, open and without pretense. I was completely accepted and loved.

The car had the new-car smell, and it was beautiful. It suited Caylee to a tee: light blue with white leather seats. It was cheery and girly just like my friend.

Russ opened the back door for me to sit inside. When I was settled comfortably, he shut the door and went around to the passenger side so Caylee could take us for a spin around the block. The car had a smooth ride. It made me think and wonder, *what kind of car am I going to get when I can drive again?*

Remembering what Caylee said at the grocery store about Russ's cousin, I asked, "Russ, would your cousin look for a car for me? I'd like something similar to this. It doesn't have to be new, just nice."

"I'll call him. How long do you think it will be before you can drive?" Russ asked.

"I have another appointment to see the orthopedist in five weeks. Hopefully, I'll be walking by then," I conveyed.

"Good to know. It will give Fred time to find something good," Russ stated.

After we rode around for a while, Caylee took me home, and it was then I realized I hadn't done a very important task. Days earlier, Whisperer told me to build my dream man. He said to look for character traits I wanted in my mate and begin to write them down. That night, while I lay on my bed, I wrote in my notebook and headed the list as "My Ideal Man" and started my first entry as "I want someone to spoil me rotten. I want to be treated like Russ treats Caylee." My second entry was "I want someone to love me the way Brent loves Hope. I need someone who wants to be faithful to only me." My third entry was "I want someone I can talk to, be honest with, laugh with, and trust like I do with Whisperer."

~~~

Ox laughed. He was very proud of Gina. Gina's evening was composed and free from envy and jealousy. She even turned the tables around and desired what Caylee and Hope have without wanting their men.

~~~

Satan was furious! His time was short, and two of his giants had wimped out. Until Lack and Self-Effort could regain their confidence and strength, Satan knew he had to use another tactic. Satan's own impatience made him call on Panic and Unforgiveness. Satan knew their powers may not be able to destroy Gina, but at least they could stir emotions for a while until he found a way to ruin the woman's belief in Jesus.

Satan also called in Rebellion, Malice, Hate, and Anger to tangle with Ox while he, Panic, and Unforgiveness worked their spells on Gina. With Ox preoccupied, Satan thought they would have a better chance of finding out what made Gina tick. She had to have a weak spot.

Forgive and Forget

Every night for three weeks, Satan sent evil suggestions and horrifying memories into the atmosphere while Gina slept. The evil he sent was so strong, it usually made people toss and turn until the dawning of the day, but it did not faze Gina. It had to be because of Ox. During the day, he watched her closely, hoping to hear her say anything against the Lord. He wanted to accuse her and rub Jesus's face in the technicality. The girl was a mystery, though. She never spoke ill of Jesus. This plagued Satan's mind greatly. Who was this young woman that Jesus magnified and made His so-called righteous one? It was evident she was a weakling. She was damaged goods and unlearned.

For the last three weeks, Satan also watched Panic try everything he could to make Gina afraid at her work. Instead of being afraid or disillusioned, he watched the girl thrive. What infuriated him further was the fact the mentally ill patients he used frequently to do his evil work were getting well during her watch. He hated how she worked. Gina made the weak-minded feel strong and gave them confidence. Every time a patient allowed her to engage them with loving kindness, they were able to find acceptance within themselves and broke away from his yoke of despair. He didn't understand. Here again, this girl wasn't biblically taught. How was she operating as if she'd witnessed Jesus's miracles firsthand?

~~~

Unforgiveness also had problems. He couldn't make Gina hate her coworkers. Mean and malicious words seemed to roll off the girl's back like water off a duck. He was also frustrated and worried Satan watched him. He and Panic would soon be rid of duties, and that usually meant death to those who failed under Satan's rule. He was about to throw in the towel and beg Satan not to be angry when a man walked in the Mental Health Center who caused Gina fear in the past. This man was perfect! The man was the very source of all Gina's problems. He and Panic could work together and make Satan proud.

Lyle Horne, even in chains, would be a huge threat to Gina's sanity. It was time he and Panic amped up their powers against Gina's mind to reinforce bad memories! Most people could forgive, but they couldn't forget. When he went to inform Satan of his new plan, Satan wanted in on the torture. Satan wanted to verbally torment Gina too. The three of them wanted to dance for joy. They thought they'd found Gina's weak spot.

~~~~

Jesus grinned! Satan and his bunch never learned. Gina would be able to face Lyle Horne, and she would forgive. Her simple acts would set him free and help her throw the past into the sea of forgetfulness for them both. Not only did He want to heal both of them, He planned to use Lyle to bless Gina. Lyle was doing everything to fulfill his sentence, but in truth, all of heaven knew he was an innocent victim just like Gina. It was time the record was straightened. It was time to balance the scales. Lyle's mind had been controlled long enough, and Gina's act of kindness under His control would cut the cords of the puppet master.

~~~~

My weeks were full and eventful. Not a day and night went by since I started back to work that I had free and boring time alone.

~~~~

Mom and I helped Hope and Brent with his campaign to run for District Attorney on Monday and Tuesday evenings. We were rushed to get things moving. Brent had entered the race late, and everyone was at a mad rush to promote him. Each Monday and Tuesday night, I fell in bed exhausted from working long, hard hours. Wednesdays, I rode home with Caylee so we could go directly to midweek service. Some Thursdays I spent evenings helping Brent and Hope, but usually, I stayed home to rest. Fridays, Caylee, and Russ or Stacy made sure I attended the group. Saturdays, I tried to clean my apartment and do laundry or read a good book because all day on Sunday I spent with my family.

Mom and Dad had made it a habit to pick me up for church then have lunch together after service. After lunch, Mom and I usually snuck off to visit the Boys' Home. Mom loved working there, and I loved visiting my new friends Luke and Brian. We had fun playing games sharing war stories and encouraging one another. I was amazed to see how fast time was moving, leaving me no time to brood.

During the week, I enjoyed my new job duties. I loved greeting the patients and giving them a smile with encouraging words. Even when faced with drama over the phone, I learned to give my mind and mouth quickly over to Whisperer. When I did, I watched His wisdom mixed with love prevail over darkness and wickedness every time. Whisperer's presence helped me also with my colleagues. I was able to mentally talk with Him and brush off my co-workers' snide remarks then pray they could see past stupidity. On occasions, I even spoke out against evil for them, and so the Word of God would stop the emotion feeders.

My day was moving fast and without a hitch until I spotted Lyle Horne being escorted by sheriff officers inside the Mental Health Center. Even in chains and wearing his prison garb, he gave my heart a fright. Memories flooded my mind, and all I could hear was, "He's here! Run, tell everyone your attacker is here! Kick the man while he is down! Say nasty things to him."

I didn't want to move, and I didn't want to talk with this man. I'd made it a normal routine to greet people with a smile, but I knew I could not smile at Lyle. He was the reason behind my plight. I began to rise from my seat, not to approach him but to leave the reception area. I wanted to make an excuse to leave, take a break, or pretend I was sick to leave my post when Whisperer reprimanded me. He firmly said, *"Gina, don't leave. Remember, Lyle is not who did this to you, Satan did! Lyle was his puppet. I have Lyle here for a reason. I want him to receive my grace and strength to heal. You are my vessel. He has to face you. Before he can be forgiven, he has to face me. Judgment has to stop! Allow him to see me in you."*

Tears welled up in my eyes. This request was hard. Hadn't I learned every day since taking my new post that through Jesus's kindness people recovered? For Jesus's sake, I had to put my hurts aside. Lyle was a victim like me. To do this task, I, on purpose, made my mind go blank from all my memories of Lyle's actions against me. If nothing else, I had to pretend he was just another patient.

I put a smile on my face, took a deep breath to calm my nerves, and then opened the glass partition so I could speak to the officer holding Lyle's chain. I asked, "Sir, would you kindly let me greet Mr. Horne."

I watched the sheriff's face soften then he stepped aside and motioned for Lyle to stand before me. When Lyle's recognition came of who I was, I watched fear cloud his face. I could not believe it. He was afraid of me! The awareness of his fear broke my heart. Standing before me was a broken man. Lyle wasn't a monster. My attitude changed to compassion instead of dread, and I quickly said, "Mr. Horne, it is good to see you. Wait right there." Whisperer suggested, *"Get up now and go to him, don't hesitate, then show him forgiveness. He needs reassuring. He feels unlovable, and he's very confused. He needs my touch. You touch him for me. Too many people treat him like scum. Let me show him acceptance."*

Through my thoughts, I agreed with Whisperer.

~~~

Ox stared Unforgiveness down. He dared the demon to try anything to prevent Gina's progress. Satan couldn't believe his eyes. Gina's actions in facing Lyle were infuriating him. He knew her actions would free the man, and he was not going to allow her to cut the ties that bound him to Lyle. He raised his arm to strike Gina, but when he did, Ox butted him in the side, using all the strength he had, which sent Satan reeling head over heels and out of control. When Satan stood upright again and recovered his composure, it was too late. The deed was done. Lyle's cords of evil lay on the Mental Health Center floor.

~~~

I snatched up my crutches, hobbled out of the reception booth, and stood toe-to-toe with Lyle. The sheriff's officer forbade me until I assured him all was well. Then without hesitation, I reached out and touched Lyle's arm and whispered so no one in the lobby could hear. I said, "Mr. Horne, I forgive you. I know now you were sick that night and weren't in your right mind. To be truthful, if I'd talked to you that night instead of being mean, I would not have provoked you, but you did frighten me. Don't be afraid of me now. I want you well. I will not tell anyone here that it was you who attacked me. The doctors and nurses will not be biased. Allow them to help you. Don't fight it."

As I walked away to go back inside the booth, I heard Whisperer say, *"Thank you, Gina. We set Lyle free!"*

~~~

Satan screamed so loud, it shook the center. He was mortified! Ox's action embarrassed him, and it was done in front of his servants! He could not tolerate one of Jesus's angels touching him. Ox had to die. He was tired of playing games.

~~~

The rest of the day, I carried on normally as if nothing happened. I found peace in my work.

~~~

Lyle confessed to everything he'd done while in therapy, and he submitted to treatment. That afternoon, when back in jail, he received word he had a visitor. When he was chained to the floor in front of a glass partition, he was rewarded with the sight of his mother. During their conversation, he told her everything he did. Her love and acceptance helped him finish healing. Before she left, he asked her to do something for him. Since she was the only person who had keys to his trailer, he asked if she minded doing him a favor. He had to make amends for his deed. He told her to look under his bed until she found an old cigar box. She was to take every dollar he'd saved and place it in an envelope and take the money to a lady by the name of Gina Grimes at the Mental Health Center. Being the loving, Christian mother she was, Martha Horne agreeably began the amends for Lyle.

~~~

I was in the ladies' room preparing to leave for the day when my supervisor called me aside. I was confused at first until I noticed her smiling. She told me privately, "Gina, an old lady came in a few minutes ago. She said her name was Martha Horne, and she was the mother of the man who attacked you. When I told her you were unavailable, she asked if I'd give you this envelope. She said Lyle wanted to help pay your medical expenses."

I didn't know what to say. I asked if Mrs. Horne was still in the lobby but was told she left. With trembling hands, I opened the envelope to find three thousand dollars. It was more than enough to meet my needs after my insurance deductible. I cried and laughed at the same time, but it wasn't until I was alone that I heard Whisperer say, *"Thanks again for your obedient service. You helped me heal a broken man. Plus, you helped me answer a prayer for a mother who prayed for her son daily."*

I asked Caylee to take me immediately to my bank after work, and when I got home, I wrote out checks to pay the hospital bills, Dr. Jones, and even the services provided by Dr. Carter. I felt free; the financial burden was gone.

When Mom came to pick me up, I waited before telling her the good news. I didn't want to repeat myself once we got to the campaign center, and I felt Hope and Brent also needed to hear my news. When the four of us were alone, I said, "Guys, I have good news to share. All my medical bills were paid today. You'll never guess who is responsible for freeing me from worry." Mom and Hope spoke at the same time and demanded, "Who? Don't keep us waiting!"

It was comical to hear them talk as if they were one person.

I took a deep breath and paused because I knew they'd have more questions, and I replied, "Lyle Horne!"

Hope danced and spun around. Brent said, "God made the devil pay!" Mom's eyes grew wide with disbelief.

Of course, once the hoopla stopped, everyone wanted to know details. I wanted to tell them everything but knew I couldn't. I knew I was being watched by Satan. Whisperer did not want to be disclosed, and I refused to take all the credit. What I told them was that I felt in my heart what I did was right, and in return, God blessed me.

Childlike Prayers

The Holy Spirit found the perfect opportunity to remind Caylee about Gina. He would use the stormy night to bring memories to the forefront and awaken Caylee's ministering spirit. Completely out of Satan's focus, he knew Caylee's childlike prayers would get Cherub involved. Once Cherub was involved, then Ox could relax and firmly take his stance. Cherub would be allowed to give Ox help because time was short. In two more weeks, the duel between Jesus and Satan would end, and Gina would have to face Satan alone.

~~~

It was during a stormy Tuesday night during dinner that Caylee and Russ reminisced about how they met. When Gina came into their conversation and how she inadvertently brought them together, Caylee started crying.

Russ, totally dumbfounded by Caylee's sudden emotions, asked, "Honey, what did I say? Why are you crying?"

Caylee started to divulge Gina's journey to Russ, but a warning from Mamie rose in her mind. "Let Gina share at her own speed." Instead of telling Russ about Gina's journey and the angel, she decided to see if he was really interested first. She baited him with a question first by saying, "I'm happy, and Gina isn't."

"What do you mean Gina isn't?" Russ asked.

Russ took the bait, and Caylee reached out and took his big hand in hers and began explaining. She conveyed, "The night of my accident, I was headed to the hospital to see Gina. She really wanted to tell me something important. Remember, it was right after she woke from the coma? What she wanted to tell me was she had a vivid dream. In her dream, she married and was having a baby. Everything was so real that when she woke, she felt her stomach to see if she was still pregnant. The emptiness of not having the family almost drove her over the edge. Russ, I was the only person she wanted to tell this to. She thought I could help her understand since I led her to Christ. She believes the dream was God's way of showing her something good is here for her. It is why she didn't die. I forgot. I've been so happy with you that I haven't been praying for my friend. I'm so ashamed!"

"Why are you ashamed? I don't understand," Russ asked.

"Russ, I have a responsibility to pray, and I have not been doing my job. I've been side-tracked. I should have been asking God to help Gina. I should have been inquiring for her. If her dream is responsible for keeping her alive, then I should be asking God to make it manifest. Gina is a new Christian. She wouldn't know how to ask," Caylee enlightened.

"I'm taking you home. We have all the time in the world. You've convinced me. Pray, Gina's dream into existence. If it hadn't been for her dream, we wouldn't be together," Russ urged. Once Caylee was home, she began to inquire of the Lord.

Having no patience for a concordance, Caylee went to her home computer instead. There she had saved in her Favorites a website that favored every translation of God's Word known to man. All she had to do was access scripture verses by typing one clue word after selecting the version she wanted to read.

Caylee spent hours researching biblical scriptures for Gina. She was used to inquiring for herself. Inquiring for someone else made her uneasy. She looked up every verse on visions, dreams, and journeys so she could rest her mind. She had to make sure what Gina experienced was something God had done with someone else in His Word. God is not a respecter of persons. If he did something for one, he would do it for or with another.

Overjoyed that she found several spiritual journeys written about it in the Bible, Caylee took her request to the Holy Spirit in prayer. She loved to visualize herself crawling onto Jesus's lap like a child to ask questions or tell Him what she needed. Today's prayer would not be any different. She would take Gina to her Lord as if she were a broken doll that only God could repair.

"Lord, my friend is broken physically and spiritually. Satan hurt her body, and now he is stealing her joy. Gina told me about her journey. It was a beautiful story. I should have been in agreement with her days ago so it would come to pass, but I got side-tracked. Please forgive me and help my friend. Bring her the happiness you let her see in the journey. I'm afraid she has lost hope. She has not mentioned her journey in a long time. If there is something you want me to do, please let me know," Caylee prayed.

"Caylee, your prayer has been heard. Don't fear, little one, Gina still believes. She could use your help, though. She is being watched and attacked by Satan. From now on, I need you to watch her

closely. Pray her through situations. You know the Word well enough to know when challenges concerning good from evil arrive. Be my spy. When you see Gina struggle, call me immediately. I will send her help. I also want you to covertly call on your church intercessors to help your friend," the Holy Spirit directed.

"You want me to be your spy? I love the idea! I'll do my best," Caylee agreed.

~~~

The Holy Spirit was very pleased. Caylee was in full agreement with heaven's plan. She eagerly wanted her new position on the frontline of battle. She didn't want to play it safe and hide on Jesus's lap. She wanted to be God's spy and catch Satan in his evil plan. The Holy Spirit determined it was also time Cherub saw his brother's condition. When he did realize Ox needed his help, it would give him the desire to grow. It was time Cherub became a powerful ox for a while. In time, he could return to heaven and play like a child, but he was needed and had to act his age and take part in the war.

Ox was lathered from head to toe in sweat. For hours, he'd been battling. Every muscle in his huge body screamed with pain. He and Gina were in the middle of week four in their wilderness experience, and the nights were growing more and more grueling. Demons came by the droves to hamper him while Satan or one of his giants plagued Gina's sleeping environment. He was tired, lonely, and very frustrated. He would love some help from his earthbound comrades.

To keep his focus, Ox visualized the end result; it was not time to lose control. He knew that time was almost near. Just before dawn, Ox heard his name being called from heaven. Wondering who it was, he inquired, "Who's calling me?"

"Look up, brother! Look up, I'm here! I'll be with you shortly," Cherub declared.

Ox couldn't believe his ears. Then he couldn't believe his eyes.

Cherub was in flight. He was coming to the rescue.

Together again, the two huge beasts hugged tightly. Both overwhelmed by the other. Cherub was overcome by how Ox appeared, and Ox was overcome by Cherub's concern. When they finally found composure, Ox said, "It's good to see you."

Cherub replied, "I couldn't stand by and see you struggle alone. How can I help?"

Ox shared, "We don't have much time. Satan usually regroups with his demons and giants shortly after sunrise. Then he will focus on me again. I need you to do me a favor and trade identities with me. It will confuse Satan, and I can regain my strength."

"What would you have me do?" Cherub asked.

"Increase your size and grow horns so you look like me. Then fluff your wings and cover Gina and me within your shadow. I will decrease my size and become a dog so I can guard Gina under your wings. I know this will be hard, but, brother, we need you desperately. I need to be very strong because Gina must face Satan soon without the Holy Spirit. Give me the time to heal before that time arrives," Ox pleaded.

"Done!" Cherub agreed.

~~~

Satan was growing weary. He was tired of failed strategies. Gina was not breaking down. Night after night, he tormented her; nothing caused her fear or dread. Day after day, he and his giants failed to make Gina's life miserable by using people. Then there was Ox, his dreaded enemy. If only they could kill him. Satan knew his demons were not a match for Ox, but they were all he could spare because his giants were diminishing greatly. There again, he was tired of playing games. It was time to call in Lust. Maybe Self-Effort and Lust could work together. He would give the idea a chance.

After their morning meeting, Satan, Self-Effort, and Lust returned to Gina's surroundings. When Satan spotted Ox, he could not believe his eyes. The beast was larger than before. Ox was larger and stronger-looking. Apparently, his demon attack hadn't fazed him but only empowered the creature more. Then suddenly fury overtook Satan. Fury so strong the air grew hot. When Self-Effort and Lust looked around to see why Satan was angry, they saw Ox was taunting Satan. The beast was smiling and actually motioning for Satan to bring it on!

There was one thing Satan hated, and it was being taunted by another angel. He would not tolerate it. No more games. Ox would die! First, he had to deal with the woman, then Ox would be all his.

Behind the Scenes

It was Wednesday morning and four weeks since my last visit with the orthopedist. I had a week and a day before seeing Wayne. As I prepared for work, I worried about how I would look. I wasn't planning to whitewash the walls like I had the time before; what concerned me was a having hairy leg. I dreaded Wayne seeing my hairy leg. Instantly, a strange sensation came over me, and I began lusting for a bath. Not a shower, but a real sit-down bath. I didn't feel thoroughly clean sponge-bathing every day. My skin felt like it had five weeks of grime buildup. A strange desire came over me. I wondered how I could manage to get in the tub. Maybe I could bag my leg in plastic so it wouldn't get wet then sit down in warm soapy water. I'd have to prop the booted leg on the edge of the tub. There had to be a way. I did research on the Internet while I waited for Caylee, hoping to find ideas.

When Caylee arrived to give me a lift to work, I was still fretting over a bath. I expressed my concern about being clean before my next doctor's appointment. I was hoping she would help me with my research, but Caylee wasn't her usual chatterbox self. She was very quiet.

Concerned something was troubling my friend, I asked, "Why are you so quiet this morning? Has something happened between you and Russ?"

Caylee thought to herself quickly before answering, *Should I tell Gina or remain quiet about my mission?* Deciding to be truthful but vague, she replied, "No! Russ and I are fine. I was praying that's all."

"Sorry. I know how that is. I'll be quiet," I replied.

Caylee called on the Lord. Gina was falling for one of Satan's traps. Praying, she conveyed, "Lord, I think Satan is up to something. Gina is doing research on how to bathe. It is too soon, and I'm afraid she will hurt herself. Doesn't the Word say we shouldn't tempt you or our angels?"

"You are right! Bluntly tell Gina you don't think bathing now is a good idea. Tell her about the scripture verse," the Lord urged.

To keep the conversation flowing, Caylee relayed, "You aren't bothering me, Gina. I talk to God all the time. But I was thinking about what you said, and it caused me to remember a Bible verse. We shouldn't tempt God or our angels. If you try and bathe before you are ready, that would be tempting them. Promise me you'll think about this before doing something rash."

Caylee's suggestion jolted me. I hadn't thought things through, so I replied, "You're right. Doctors see patients like me all the time. Thanks for getting my head straight. I definitely do not want to tempt God or my angel!"

~~~

Cherub felt empowered by Gina's declaration. The mental agreement she had with Caylee gave him strength. A fire began to build inside his chest, and pressure increased in his lungs. When he opened his mouth, flames shot out and charred every evil suggestion Lust and Self-Effort had in the atmosphere.

Ox grinned. Then he nuzzled up against Cherub's leg to show him gratitude. "Feels good, doesn't it, brother?" Ox asked.

~~~

Off and on for the rest of the day, I experienced weird food cravings. I usually worked through a day without snacking, so I didn't know what was wrong with me. One minute I wanted chocolate; the next minute I wanted salted nuts or chips. I could not satisfy my hunger. When I didn't have any more change for the snack machine, I went as far as to ask Caylee when we were on break to loan me fifty cents.

As she searched through her handbag for the money, she asked, "Did you spend time with the Holy Spirit this morning or read your Bible?"

The question took me by surprise, but it made me think. Had I? No! I'd been too busy trying to find a way to bathe. I didn't give Him a single thought. I shamefully replied, "No, I didn't. Do you think that is why I'm so hungry?"

"Could be. Pray about it," Caylee suggested.

Steadily munching on chips, I thought, *my body is acting weird today. Is it because I have not sought You out today? Is it because I ran to the world instead of You for answers?*

"Yes! Your mind is hungry, not your body. My presence is all you need. If you had asked me, I would have helped you understand what was happening. Caylee has helped you see. You now need to take a

minute while you are on break and look up meanings behind hunger and thirst," He enlightened.

When Whisperer recommended I search something, I usually jumped right on the task, but this time, I didn't have my Bible with a concordance with me. It was in Caylee's car. I must have looked troubled because Caylee asked, "What's the matter?"

Because I knew Caylee prayed to the Holy Spirit like I did, I didn't hesitate to say, "The Lord told me to look up hunger and thirst in the Bible, and my Bible is in your car."

"No problem! I have an app on my phone," Caylee squeaked. She pulled out her cell phone and found what I needed. After reading through scriptures for a few minutes, she handed me her phone so I could see one she thought I had to see. It was in Deuteronomy chapter 28 verse 48 in the Amplified Version Bible. It read,

> *Therefore you shall serve your enemies whom the Lord shall send against you, in hunger and thirst, in nakedness and in want of all things; and He will put a yoke of iron upon your neck until He has destroyed you.*

"What does that mean?" I asked.

"It means if we don't put the Lord and His Word first, we will be serving the enemy in hunger and thirst, nakedness, and have a want for all things. God allows it to happen, but He'd much rather we take time for Him. Nothing satisfies us but God. When we place God first, we won't be destroyed," Caylee explained.

I panicked and then asked, "I've been really trying to keep God in the loop, but something side-tracked me this morning. I didn't give Him a thought and went straight to my computer. Heaven forbid! What should I do? I don't want to be destroyed!" "You just did it!" Caylee exclaimed happily. "You read what you needed to stop the insanity then you agreed with what it meant and spoke in line with God's plan."

~~~

Satan was so angry he kicked Lust in the backside. "I'm tired of all of you failing. You can't do anything right! We had her right where we wanted! She was ours! Ox must have told her what to read!" he screamed.

~~~

The rest of the day, cravings for unhealthy food were gone. After work, Caylee and I went to a fast food place before church. I ordered a salad with low-calorie dressing because I had no desire for anything else.

Pastor Reed's Wednesday-night service also addressed the subject of lust and idols. He touched on why people were unfulfilled with their lives by saying they blindly relied on things rather than on God. I had two warnings today. I hope I learned my lesson.

~~~

After the service ended, Pastor Reed announced that Joe Arnold had a request. Everyone sat to listen because Joe usually did not talk at service, so it had to be important. Joe took a deep breath and said, "Hello, everyone. As you know, Olivia and I serve faithfully at the Boys' Home. The boys mean very much to us. They need a school bus. The one they have is very old and has been patched many times. It's time they have a newer one. Please help with this need. Please pray about giving. Thanks."

I thought about Luke and Brian, and my heart ached. Their bus was a necessity, not a luxury. I consulted with my checkbook and saw that I would only have fifty dollars left after tithing. I quickly added forty to my tithe offering. I was closing my wallet when I noticed something sticking out of a side pocket. It was the check from the junkyard that bought my car. I'd totally forgotten about it.

~~~

Lust saw his opportunity. He realized he and Self-Effort had to act fast, so he began begging Satan, "Let us torment the girl. She wants a car. We'll make her choose herself and deny God's help, and when she does, you can bring her shame and deny her a good car."

~~~

I stared in disbelief at the check in my hand. I knew it presented itself solely for the school bus. It was not a coincidence. It seemed like my mind argued, though. I kept hearing, "You need a car. This money was saved for your vehicle. I held it for you."

Then I remembered something wonderful. In my dream with Jesus, I saw acres of cars, trucks, and vehicles of all kinds to use. I quickly closed my eyes and prayed, "Whisperer, did you just show me the dream, or are you telling me to hold on to this check?"

"What does your heart tell you, Gina? What was the first thing you felt after Joe made the request?" He countered.

"I thought about Luke and Brian. They were in need, and I don't have a need yet," I stated.

"Act on love. You'll be provided for when it is time," Whisperer shared.

I immediately turned the check over, signed my name, and wrote "given to the Boys' Home" on the back and then I placed it in the offering along with my tithe and extra-offering check.

~~~

Caylee watched Gina struggle to give over the large sum. She knew it was a sacrifice, so she quickly prayed for her friend. "Lord, your seed time and harvest method usually is not swift. Please make an exception this time. Show Gina how much you care."

~~~

Satan would not quit. He tortured Gina day in and day out about giving so much money to the Boys' Home. He had to make her worry long and hard about the act. Worry eventually captured a person's tongue, and when it did, it spoke against Jesus.

~~~

For the rest of the week, I found myself wondering if I did the right thing about the check. Each time I slipped inside Caylee's new car, I scolded myself. Of course, I'll be receiving an insurance check soon, but it won't be much. The junkyard check would have helped purchase a sweet ride.

Sunday was my birthday, and I expected Mom and Dad to pick me up together as usual for church. I was puzzled when Mom came alone, so I asked, "Where is Dad? I thought we were celebrating my birthday after church."

"We are! We haven't forgotten about you. Dad's coming later. He told me he had something pressing and would see us at church," Mom answered.

~~~

All my friends made it a point to wish me a happy birthday when they saw me at church. I didn't recall ever having so many well-wishers. My day was starting off wonderfully. Dad did arrive moments before service began and slipped in beside me and gave me a bear hug before whispering, "Happy birthday, Honey."

I rode with Mom to my favorite restaurant when service was over, and Dad followed. I felt something was off when our waitress motioned for us to follow instead of allowing us to find a regular seat. She took us to a small room sectioned away from the crowd. When the door opened, I was startled to hear, "Surprise!" The whole young-adults group including Hope, Brent, Mamie, and Dr. Jones were there. I was overcome.

"Who did this?" I blurted. "Caylee," Mom answered.

Everyone had a gift. There was even cake and ice cream. I felt like a kid again. I was almost finished opening gifts when Dad came up to me and said, "Open mine last."

I looked at him confused. He didn't like being in the spotlight.

Why would he want his gift to stand out special?

The small box he handed me clearly said by the size that it was a piece of jewelry. I just knew it was a lovely watch or necklace. When I opened it, I saw a key. When I looked closer, I noticed it was a car key with a Chevrolet insignia. "What is this?" I asked, confused.

With a shaking voice, Dad said, "I'm giving you my car. I don't need a sports car any longer. I bought a pickup truck."

"Dad! You shouldn't have," I whispered, overjoyed. "Yes, I should. There is more," he conveyed. "More! I don't need anything else," I stated.

I watched Mom rise from her seat so she could stand next to Dad. Then he said, "Everyone, Pam and I are getting married again."

I was already choked and holding back tears, but Dad's news broke the dam. Tears flooded my face. I was so overcome with joy! It was the best birthday I'd ever had. God blessed me with a new car, and it was my favorite. Mom and Dad were Christians, and now they were getting married again. It was too much to take in. I was loved too much. I gratefully whispered, "Lord, you are too much. Your presents are wonderful. I love you!"

~~~

Jesus grinned, but Satan stomped and screamed, "Self-Effort, you are fired!"

Preparing for Darkness

The Holy Spirit worked feverishly to set the stage before His time to leave. He had until midnight Tuesday to have everything in place then it would be up to Gina to bring the promise to fruition. All His heavenly troops were prepped and ready. He had to have Caylee start intercession, and Brent had to encourage Wade not to leave town before he could tell Gina about His journey.

~~~

All day Monday, Caylee and I couldn't stop talking about the birthday party, the new car, and my parents getting remarried. It was when we were on the way home that afternoon that I made the remark, "I'm so happy. I only have one thing left, and my life will be perfect."

"What's that?" Caylee asked, already knowing.

"It's having my soul mate, remember? I told you about my journey," I answered.

Caylee stammered, "Of course I remember! I've been praying for you. Trust me, he's coming. God is not a respecter of persons. What he did for me, he will do for you."

Caylee's words gave me hope. It was good to know that she had been praying for me. Whisperer said He would help her wake up, and He proved faithful again.

~~~

Satan overheard Gina's conversation with Caylee and realized the girl was still obsessed with the Polk boy. Since the girl was happy, it was a good time to play an evil trick. He would use the Arnolds' friendship with the Polk's and torment the girl a little.

~~~

As Caylee drove away from Gina's apartment, she sent another request. "Lord, I know you heard Gina. What do you want me to do now? Gina is getting antsy, and I don't know what to say."

"Get intercessory help. Have others pray for Gina's loneliness to end. Tell them Gina wants to settle down," He recommended. His recommendation caused her to immediately think of Hope and Brent. Mentally responding, she said, "You're right! I know two intercessors who will tear the roof off heaven's throne. They want

Gina's happiness. I'll get with them Wednesday night." "Tell Hope and Brent this afternoon while Satan isn't watching you, but still put your written request in the church prayer box Wednesday evening," He urged.

Caylee knew Brent and Hope were very busy with their campaign. Tomorrow was Election Day, and she wondered if they would have time or even want to pray. She also knew better than to question the Holy Spirit's command. With no time to waste, she quickly drove to the center, hoping she could speak with Hope alone.

Brent and Hope were going through the motions. Both knew when Brent decided to run for District Attorney that he had already won before beginning the campaign; they just didn't brag about it. When the District Attorney lashed out at Brent unjustly for taking a few personal days to be with his family, God took it personally and set things right.

When Caylee walked into the center, she saw that Hope wasn't busy at all; she was watching television with Greg. Going over to her quickly, Caylee wanted to share before something interrupted. "Hope, I need you," Caylee anxiously blurted.

"What's wrong?" Hope asked.

"I'm on a mission. The Lord wants you and Brent to pray," Caylee stammered almost breathlessly.

"Sure! For who?" Hope inquired.

"It's Gina! She's extremely lonely. God said to get intercessory help for her quickly," Caylee answered.

"Brent's busy, but I'll do it now. Watch Greg for me while I get alone with the Lord," Hope responded.

"Thank you, Caylee. Don't forget to place your written request in the box on Wednesday," the Holy Spirit requested cheerfully.

Instead of finding a room in the campaign center for privacy, Hope went outside and sat in her SUV. Gina was her spiritual daughter, and this urgency prompted her quickly. Hope would not allow Satan a chance. Gina would not be lured back into the world. So, Hope gave her heart and mind over to her Lord then she released her mouth for His use. Every word she uttered was the Lord Himself giving orders in the earthly realm. Angelic armies were stationed, and cues were given, and watchdogs were placed on guard, for the time of darkness was almost here. Then, when He no longer needed Hope's mouth, He comforted her spirit. *"Hope, Gina will be fine.*

God has a plan for her. Keep praying for her. Soon she'll face a time of extreme darkness. You know what that is like. Express your compassion for Gina as you pray, but do not physically interfere. When the time is right, you and Brent pray together. Take your requests to God. Get Abba involved as Gina needs His help, but until then, I can be her only salvation," He consoled.

Instantly, Hope wanted to cry. She knew what the Lord meant. Her precious Gina had to face Satan. If she could do it for her, she would; but then again, Gina had to come to terms alone with the enemy for her best interest. Just like Greg, Gina had to fight for what is right.

That night, when Gina and her mom came to help at the campaign center, Hope prayed quietly. Every time Hope's eyes fell on Gina, she prayed. The thought of Gina having to face Satan was hard to bear. Knowing she would overcome this confrontation was all that kept her from buckling under and succumbing to panic. Satan did not play fair. He was the inventor of cruelty and murder!

Hope's skin burned from the memories. Her ears rang from the memory of the gunshot. What was Gina about to face? The Lord said to express her compassion with prayer. That evening, at home, when she was alone with Brent, Hope shared her worries with him. Together they entered the closet and took the burden to God and asked that he spare Gina from harm, see to her needs, and intervene on her behalf.

Having Hope and Brent pray gave the Holy Spirit time to do other things. That night, He played Bible stories like they were movies in Gina's dreams. He took her to Proverbs and showed her how a harlot lured an innocent man into sin. Then He showed her God's compassion in Psalms. Afterward, He showed her the story of Mary. He enabled her to see how Mary mentally agreed with His messenger and was covered by Him so she could conceive Jesus. Then He concentrated on making her see how Jesus prayed in the garden of Gethsemane while the disciples slept.

While the dreams played in Gina's sleep, the Holy Spirit and Ox had a long discussion. The Holy Spirit shared His plan with Ox. Soon God would call Satan back into heaven for a discussion, and Cherub would be forced to return. Satan, mistaking Cherub for Ox, would allow Ox to remain in hiding as a dog. The ploy would fool Satan into thinking Gina was all alone and without a guardian. Ox had one duty, to hold steady and guard Gina's seed of faith for three and a half days.

~~~

The Holy Spirit's time in isolated prayer was always hard. He did not like seeing any of His loved ones face Satan without His voice, but the prayer time was always worth the effort. This time He didn't have to fret because Gina was handpicked to battle Satan. He was guaranteed to see creation birthed and watch Satan fail. Gina's victory would indicate the end of an age, and souls by the thousands were about to be harvested. Through her testimony, hundreds, if not thousands, would have strength to face Satan also.

Trappings

It was Election Day, so I woke up at 5:00 a.m. Caylee and I wanted to arrive early at the polls so we could vote before going to work. Being up so early made the day seem extremely long, so by 5:00 p.m., Caylee and I were both exhausted and did not want to go straight to the campaign center. The polls would not close until after 7:00 p.m. that night, so we decided to take time out for a nap at my place then have a good dinner before meeting with friends and family at the center later that evening.

When we arrived at the center, people were everywhere. Well-wishers were lined up in droves, wanting to speak with Brent and Hope so they could give their support. I was making my way to the reception table so I could find a seat at the table and help by filling cups with ice when I saw a very familiar face. Wayne was greeting Brent and Hope. I watched them hug and saw Wayne give Hope a sweet kiss on her cheek. Then Wayne turned and faced me and proceeded toward my table. My heart began to pound, and my hands started shaking. Rationally, I knew he was coming over for a drink, not to socialize with me. However, my nerves were on edge. I wasn't ready to have him so close, and his mere presence made my body act disjointed. My hands would not work correctly. No matter how hard I tried, I couldn't get ice in the cups. Then I tried to pour the cola and spilled it all over the table and myself. I was humiliated, and I wanted to scream. By the time Wayne reached my table, my face flushed a deep scarlet.

I did not want to look him in the face, so I focused on cleaning my skirt and watched him help Mom clean the spilled cola from the table. I wanted him to leave, but instead I was trapped. I heard him snicker before asking, "Do I know you?"

With shaking voice, I replied, "I'm Gina Grimes. You treated my leg a few weeks ago after Dr. Carter died."

"Yes, I remember you now. How are you doing?" Wayne asked sweetly.

I could not believe my eyes. He was smiling at me, and his eyes were twinkling and were even a little flirtatious. I swallowed hard before replying, "I'm doing well. In fact, I have an appointment to see you this Thursday. I hope you'll see fit to remove me from this torturous boot."

"We'll see," he said playfully before walking away.

My heart was singing. I received a smile. For the next hour, I watched Wayne talk with Brent, Carl, and Mr. Arnold. It appeared as if they were old friends. I even watched him leave, hoping to see him on his motorcycle. Instead, I watched him get into a jeep. I had to confess that was a little disappointing.

The time was dragging before the final tallies came, and Brent was growing restless. Seizing the opportunity to remove himself from the crowd, he went into the kitchen for a few minutes so he could get a snack before all the food was gone. When he did, he saw Wade in the kitchen talking with his mother. Going over to speak, he asked, "Why didn't you come in the front door like normal people?"

"Good to see you too, your lordship," Wade countered sarcastically, bowing at the waist and extending his arm.

"Stop that! I'm no lord! I just wanted to know why you are hiding out in the kitchen instead of visiting us in the great room," Brent proclaimed.

~~~

"I didn't want to park my bike around so many cars, so I pulled it in between your BMW and Hope's SUV then I came in the back door. Plus, I'm not stupid. I know where the real action is. It's always in the kitchen," Wade replied, laughing.

"At least take your slickers off and act sociable," Brent replied. The Holy Spirit prompted Brent to remember Gina by whispering, "Wade would be a perfect match for your friend." With the thought firmly in mind, Brent corralled Wade. "Hey, buddy, remember me telling you about a lovely girl at church?

Well, she is here. Let me point her out to you," he urged.

"Naw, man! I don't need to meet anybody now. I've still got Mom to take care of," Wade responded.

"As a favor to me," Brent urged again.

"I'll look at her, but that is all. My life is too busy these days.

Work and Mom take up all my time," Wade replied. "How is your mother?" Brent asked.

"She's doing great. Doctors say she will have most of her motor skills back soon, but until then, I want to see that she is cared for properly. We have a nurse watching her during the day, and I stay with her in the evenings. Here lately, though, all I can think about is getting away for a weekend on my bike to be alone," Wade conveyed.

~~~

Satan could not believe what was happening. Wade was not supposed to see Gina. Hurriedly and without thinking things through, he caused chaos in the great room by attacking Gina's Dad. He didn't care what he did; he had to get Gina out of the way. All he could think about was that Gina shouldn't be anywhere near Wade.

~~~

A woman's scream pierced the air. "Help! Someone, please help! Brady is having a heart attack."

~~~

Brent forgot all about pointing out Gina to Wade and rushed to Brady Grimes's aid. Wade began tearing out of his jumpsuit so he could assist, but by the time he entered the doorway of the great room, Dr. Jones and Mamie had Mr. Grimes well in hand, and Brent was ushering the women out of the building. That was when Wade saw her. The woman on crutches leaving with Doc and Mamie was a vision of loveliness, and his heart began to melt.

Later, at Brent's side, Wade asked, "Was the woman leaving with Mamie and old Doc Jones the one?"

Brent couldn't help but grin. He realized Wade had been dumbstruck. "Yes, my friend, she's the one. Now, don't you want an introduction?" Brent asked.

"Yes! Yes!" the Holy Spirit shouted. The old goat fell for the bait. I have Gina right where I need her to be, back at square one.

~~~

I was sitting in the lobby of the emergency room waiting on news about Dad when I heard and saw on the television that Brent Arnold won the post for District Attorney. I was sad because I could not be there to show my support. I really wanted to be in on the fun, but my dad's well-being was my priority; he was in my heart.

I was alone in the lobby because only one person could be with Dad, and Dr. Jones felt it should be Mom. The room was a dismal place, but being there made me think. The time brought back some unnerving memories and some very happy ones. It was on my last visit to this place that Hope shared her ability to hear and see spiritual beings with me. The experience taught me how to defend myself and helped me understand why people acted differently. That same day, I was introduced to my angel, Ox. I also witnessed how Hope handled alarming situations by wearing God's armor, and when she left me alone with Ox and Whisperer, I was shown my gift. I had the ability to live in flames. I didn't have a suit of red like Hope. I wore fire! The memory amazed me because I hadn't thought about my suit since then.

"Whisperer, why has this happened?" I inquired.

"All things work for good," He replied.

"Will you please explain?" I begged.

"Your father is fine. He should lose weight and change his eating habits, but it will be to his advantage," He shared.

"Thank you, Lord. I couldn't understand why. Everything was going great for us," I conveyed.

"Gina, there is more to this than your father's health. Satan thought he was distracting me, but he fell into my trap. Your father never was in danger. He was shown a life-changing alternative. Having you here has made you remember. It has opened a door for me to empower you through this transition in your life. A change is taking place."

"What are you saying?" I asked.

"It is a time of testing. The time when you must face Satan," He replied.

"We can do this. You haven't let me down yet. What do I have to do?" I said excitedly.

"There will be no we. You must do this without me. Father God must prove Satan wrong through you. He is calling me into isolation. While I'm there, I will be praying for you," He reassured.

"No! I can't do this without you. I'm scared," I blurted.

"Yes, you can! Know who you are! You've been given all you need. You've seen firsthand what Jesus has for you in heaven. Plus, Ox will be with you. All you must do is stay on my course. Help others! Love on people and try not to focus on yourself. I've shown you how. I taught you how to listen and observe. You've heard everything I've said through your lips, and you've watched people change. If you have any doubt, go to the Word, you'll find me there," He encouraged.

"I remember everything. I've been pondering on the last time I was here. But I can't hear Ox, and I don't know how to call on my gift," I exclaimed.

"After I'm gone, you'll hear Ox. He will be hiding in the form of a dog. Try and remember the dream I gave you about the bulldog. Anytime you hear him hassle, it means Ox is pleased. When you hear a bark or growl, it means Ox is upset. Listen to him closely. If he is upset, something is not right, and you must check your spirit for truth, or run to the Word. As for your gift, the flame inside you never goes out. It will come on the outside when you profess your greatest desire," He enlightened.

"I remember, but I still don't like this! When will this happen? How long will you be gone?" I sadly asked.

"I'm leaving in a few minutes. Hold firm for a few days and draw strength from your grit. Remember the good times with Jesus. You are strong," He said while slipping away.

Placed on a Lampstand

The moment Satan touched Brady Grimes, God commanded his presence. God's mere verbal command snatched Satan out of the earthly realm. *"What are you doing, Satan?"* God asked.

Satan grimaced. "I'm tired of playing games. Your Son, Jesus, doesn't play fair."

"Explain!" God ordered.

"Gina was not given to me. Jesus never removed her protection. The beast has hovered over her," Satan conveyed.

"Gina does not need a shadow. Ox is only following his instincts," God countered.

"Then order the beast here. I want a fair fight. She needs to hear and see me. Give me three days, and I'll prove to you man is still weak," Satan suggested.

God referred to Jesus. "Son, what do you think? Is Gina ready?"
"Yes, Father!" Jesus replied.

"What do you wish?" God asked.

"Give her to the Tester. Place her in the open for all to see," Jesus answered.

Satan could not believe his ears, so he said, "I want to see the beast here now! I don't want to see a winged creature anywhere around Gina during my allotted time."

"Done, but under one circumstance," Jesus proclaimed.

"What?" Satan spat.

"After this encounter, do not touch her again!" Jesus ordered.

"Fine!" Satan agreed.

Cherub returned to heaven still disguised as Ox, and the Holy Spirit went inside His prayer closet.

Satan returned to earth soon after being convinced the beast was confined. When he found Gina again, she was sitting in his favorite place, his den of torture, and she was all alone. There wasn't an angel in sight. The only thing she had nearby was the spirit of a dog. The creature must be a dead pet trying to cling to its master, he thought.

~~~

I was aware the second Whisperer left me. The silence was awful. I sat there in the hospital's emergency room lobby amazed by what lay before me. Jesus wanted me to take His place to prove a point. It was up to me to carry on with His mission. I had to take the responsibility seriously because time was an issue. I closed my eyes and drew on my knowledge. I required and placed a demand on everything Jesus showed me in my dreams through His teaching and from studying His Word as if it was vital. His life, living through me, depended on me doing this.

I moved into the driver's seat of my body, and when I did, I heard Ox's hassle for the first time. After all, I had the mind of Christ. I knew what Jesus wanted to do, and I knew what my body was. It was just the vessel to carry out His job. As long as I separated the real me from what flesh really was, I would be okay. I knew firsthand my body couldn't do His work without Jesus's spirit working with me, so I began to draw from our personal relationship and His Word.

I was lost in thought when I heard a familiar voice. Mamie was with me. "Honey, your dad is doing well. Dr. Jones wants him to stay the night just to be cautious. Go see him for a few minutes then I'll take you home. Your mom wants to stay," Mamie enlightened.

~~~

While I was hobbling to Dad's room, I heard Ox's low growl, which caused my back to stiffen. Satan was near. I was ready for contact, so it didn't surprise me when I heard a deep raspy voice say, "Where was your God? He let your dad down. Now your mom is worried, and your dad is sick. Where is your security blanket?" I knew better than answer his dumb question. I remained silent and just smiled. When I did, I heard Ox's hassle. Then I heard him suddenly snap and growl.

I immediately called on the Lord, "I know you can't speak to me right now, but you didn't say anything about me talking to you. I just heard Ox growl, so I know Satan is near. Watch over me, please. Please know I'm trying."

~~~

Jesus smiled.

~~~

When the dog growled, Satan realized the creature understood what he said to Gina, but what infuriated him was the little beast's smug stance when Gina smiled. He hated the dog instantly and kicked him hard after saying, "I may not be able to touch your master, little dog, but I can hurt you!"

~~~

I left Dad in good care. I loved Dr. Jones, and I trusted him thoroughly. On the way home, Mamie and I didn't have much to stay, and I knew why. We were both tired. I didn't allow my flesh to freak out because it didn't get stroked with loving words. Whisperer had warned me about the times when my flesh would struggle with separation, so I rested in that fact. I knew Mamie cared for me. I didn't need a spiritual discussion or flowered words. Ox hassled again.

I slept fitfully. All night my head played back memories of me spilling cola in front of Wayne and seeing Dad struggle for life.

If I hadn't been forewarned, I would be in a panic. I knew who was behind the wicked trick when the alarm woke me. When I reached over to turn the alarm clock off, I noticed the time. I was awake an hour earlier than normal. I'd forgotten to reset the time last night. Yesterday, I intentionally wanted to get up early. Not wanting to return to my tormenting dreams, I decided to torment my tormentor. I took care of my bodily needs then crawled back in bed and opened the Good Book. Instead of fretting about spilled cola and Dad's health, I revisited stories Whisperer and I read together. With each verse, I replayed our sweet time together again in my head. I was walking spiritually down memory lane. Hearing Ox's hassle and smacking his jaws made me laugh. It made me picture a bulldog drooling and constantly lapping his lips in anticipation of food. The mental picture gave me a revelation. Ox wanted to hear the Word, so I started reading to him and sharing Jesus's Word.

~~~

Jesus laughed so hard, His side hurt. Gina's understanding was amazing. The funny thing was getting to see Satan squirm, hiss, and spit while she read His Word aloud.

~~~

I called Mom's cell before leaving for work with Caylee. Dad was doing well. Mom said Dr. Jones would be releasing him before lunch. I laughed when I thought about what Mom said because it confirmed what Whisperer had shared with me earlier: Satan's evil would work for Dad's good. I listened to her say that Dr. Jones told

Dad he had lived on fat and sweets for too long. I knew Mom, and this gave her a new mission. She wouldn't quit until Dad was eating right and exercising. Better him than me.

~~~

Gina's laughter grated on Satan's nerves. The thought of her being happy infuriated him. He would make sure her workday wouldn't be so pleasant.

~~~

When Caylee and I arrived at work, the place was in an uproar. Co-workers were extremely unhappy. No one had nice things to say, and Ox was growling loudly. I took a deep breath, realizing it was now or never, and asked myself, "What would Jesus do?" He wouldn't tolerate the evil influence. He'd forbid the demon imps from being in the room.

I didn't know what to say to make them leave, but I did have a weapon. I knew just what to do. I'd read in God's Word to clap my hands and then say something, but I couldn't remember what. It was a good thing Caylee had installed a Bible-search app on my cell phone. I quickly hobbled into the ladies' room and shut the door. I programmed my app and looked up the word clap. The verse I needed to be said, "Clap your hands and shout for victory."

I went back into my workspace and laid my crutches down. I stood straight on my one good leg, clapped my hands together, and said, "Praise God! We don't have to tolerate evil in our space."

~~~

Satan grabbed his ears! "No way!" He spat. He thought the girl wasn't trained. She hadn't been through years and years of study. How did she know what to do? He had to leave her personal space, but he didn't have to leave the room. On his way to the corner of the room, he kicked the dog in his ribs. He hated the creature that stuck so close by.

~~~

The rest of the day, I dealt with issues on the job as usual. I greeted people kindly and encouraged them. Once, I had to say something I remembered Whisperer saying through me, and it worked. The lady responded to the words. We were preparing to close for the day when Lyle Horne was escorted into the building, and I heard Ox growl. I knew instantly Satan was riding on Lyle's shoulders. Lyle's stare was creepy. My flesh wanted to run, but my duty held me firm. I closed my eyes for a few seconds. I drew from memory and required Jesus's love out of vital need. "Lord, you love Lyle. You wouldn't look at his stare. You would be focusing on why he is staring so hatefully. Something is wrong."

~~~

Satan said to himself, "I have her now. Lyle's hateful stare will make her buckle. I'll use him to make her skin crawl then I'll make her remember what he did to her."

~~~

I didn't run, even when I heard the raspy evil voice say, "Where is your god now? This is the man who hurt you! He still wants to cause you pain!" Instead, I purposefully smiled at Lyle and thought about him.

Then I said, "Hi, Mr. Horne. What has gotten you so upset?" Then I waited.

I watched Lyle's face change. It softened. Then he blurted, "Men in the jail are calling me names. I hit one, and the cops blamed me for the fight, so they brought me in to see the nurse." "I'm sorry.

Do you feel okay other than having your feelings hurt?" I asked.

"Yeah!" he answered curtly.

"Let me call you a nurse. Tell her what you told me," I suggested.

Then I remembered Lyle's mother was a praying woman. She must have had him in church, so I called him to my receptionist window and whispered, "Next time anyone calls you names, quote scripture by saying this to yourself, 'No tongue formed against me can prosper, and any word will be proven wrong.'"

I watched Lyle smile, and I heard Ox hassle.

Plots and Plans

Satan had to stop and regroup. Gina wasn't an easy target. Everything he threw at her didn't work. He needed help, and he thought about using Lust, Lack, and Self-Effort again. He wondered what would happen if they all joined forces at the same time against Gina now that Ox was gone.

~~~

Caylee planned to get to church before Gina and her parents that night. She had to covertly slip a prayer request into the intercessory prayer box on Gina's behalf before intercession began. This was part of the Holy Spirit's plan. He wanted the church praying for Gina's happiness, but He also wanted it to lure Satan into doing something stupid.

~~~

Lust arrived first when Satan called. While he and Satan were alone, Lust suggested. "Why don't we use Gina's past against her? She has issues that have not been dealt with," he informed.

"What issues?" Satan demanded.

"Old hurts and wounds from men," Lust replied.

"Of course! I'll enter her memories and search out the worst man in her past and then we'll weave him back into the mix. She will not know what hit her." Satan laughed.

"When will you do this?" Lust asked.

"I'll do it now. So, I can dig deep before church service starts. Then we can have fun while she is trying to listen to the pastor. There is nothing like lighting a fleshly desire within a body."

When Lack arrived, he decided to go ahead of the others and scope out the church. While he was there, he heard Gina's name mentioned in the intercessory room. Curiously, he went inside to see why and saw the prayer request. It read, "Pray for Gina's happiness. She is lonely. Call in her soul mate."

With this knowledge, he quickly left so he could find Satan. When he found him, he said breathlessly, "Sir, the church is praying for Gina!"

"What? Why?" Satan demanded.

"Someone has asked them to call in her soul mate. A prayer request stated that she is lonely," Lack informed.

"This can't happen! I have everything arranged to fail. Go and deter Wade. Convince him to leave town. By the time he gets back, Gina's testing will be over, and Jesus's plans will be ruined," Satan ordered.

"What do you want me to do?" Lack inquired.

"You and Self-Effort convince the man he needs to get alone. Entice him with the free feeling he gets from joyrides. Beckon him with something he hasn't had in a while and then report back to me," Satan urged.

"We can do that," Lack and Self-Effort stated.

"Lust and I will find another distraction. I already know how to use Wayne, but I'm after someone who will bring back lust just before breaking her heart again. This girl must never feel loved. If I have my way, she will only know disappointment." Satan laughed.

~~~

The three of us, Mom, Dad, and I, while on the way to church, discussed wedding plans. We were having fun talking about what to serve at their wedding reception when I suddenly felt a surge of loneliness, and my thoughts went dark. It had been a long time since I was with a man. I remembered one. Although the sex was great, the emotional pain was the most hurtful experience I ever lived through. The thought made me crave Wayne more. I remembered my journey and how he was very tender to me. I started desiring his warmth and body and a deeper sexual commitment. A familiar ache began to burn in the lower pit of my belly. Fleshly desire was torturing me. My mind was grasping for pictures of passionate entanglements, but before I dove deeper into the fantasy, I heard Ox growl deeply, and I heard his teeth snap several times. The sound woke me up! I suddenly knew Satan was near and that I was in trouble.

I yanked my mind free from the sexual thoughts and closed my eyes. "Think on pure thoughts," I commanded myself. I thought about Luke and how much he loved to play. I thought about Caylee and her sweet, funny disposition. Then I thought about Dr. Jones and his love for sweets. That memory did it! It changed everything because it made me laugh. I was able to free myself by remembering what Dr. Jones said to Dad and thought he was funny. Wasn't he the pot calling the kettle black? He needed to heed his own advice.

"What's so funny, Gina?" I heard Mom ask.

"I just remembered something really funny. Do you remember how Dr. Jones wanted two pieces of cake when I was in the hospital? Remembering his desire for cake caused me to laugh. I thought it extremely funny since he told Dad that he needed to lay off sweets and fat," I answered, still giggling.

~~~

Satan came out of Gina's memories smiling to himself. He'd also had a little fun with the memories.

Lust asked, "Did you get the information?"

"Yes, and more! Now all we must do is locate a man named Marshall Dunlap. Gina was crazy for this man. She wanted to marry him, but he didn't love her. She gave him her body and heart, but he used her for sex and kicked her to the curb when she got clingy," Satan divulged.

~~~

A few minutes before church started, Hope rushed in the church building. Quickly she slipped into the seat between Gina and Caylee. After praise and worship, when they were seated again, Caylee leaned closer toward Hope and said, "I placed a request in the intercessory box tonight. I asked for prayer on Gina's behalf."

"You did? I didn't get to pray with the group tonight. Brent and I were held in meetings all afternoon," Hope shared.

"Then who in your group would pray for Gina?" Caylee asked. "Martha Dunlap is a sweet lady. She has a soft spot for young lonely girls. She'll know what to do. Don't worry, Brent and I have really been praying," Hope replied.

~~~

Satan could not believe his ears. He heard Hope say the last name, Dunlap. There was only one way to find out if this woman was related to Marshall. He sought the woman out and then delved into her memories in search of family connections. Overjoyed when he found his victim, he immediately began to plant seeds inside Martha's mind. He knew just what to suggest. He'd use Brent's campaign success as bait and make suggestions for Martha to ponder.

~~~

Under Satan's control, Martha Dunlap suddenly thought about Brent Arnold and wondered if Marshall knew about Brent's campaign victory. She thought *Marshall needs to congratulate Brent. They were good friends growing up. I'm going to suggest he attend Brent's Friday night young-adult group since he is still single.*

Then she thought about the evening's prayer and of Gina Grimes. The girl would be a perfect match for her son, and she went to every group meeting. She thought, *If I manage to get Marshall to the group meeting, then he could kill two birds with one stone. He could wish his friend well and meet Gina too.*

~~~

I sat in the church service bombarded by hateful, lustful, worrisome thoughts and kept hearing Ox's snapping, barking, and growling as well. The noise was so bad; I wanted to stick fingers in my ears to escape the insanity. Oh, how I longed to hear Whisperer's sweet voice.

To rid myself of evil, I clapped my hands together softly and muttered quietly for demons to leave but was abruptly informed he wasn't a demon and didn't have to leave. He also told me that I forgot the magic words. I also heard laughter before he said, "There were too many people in church who unknowingly welcomed my presence."

I knew this to be true. Hope told me once that she saw hundreds of demons in the church sanctuary tormenting, unknowing victims. Then I remembered! This was Satan, and he definitely wasn't a demon.

Rather than sit and listen to Satan speak, I closed my eyes and began communicating mentally with Jesus. "Lord, this is crazy. I don't have time to look up scripture to see what I did wrong, and I'm tired of Satan's evil voice. He won't let me listen to Pastor Reed in peace. I am thankful Father has allowed me to revisit our time together whenever I need. I can go there in my mind while I'm sitting here and remember a good noise. I recall it was noisy in your heavenly temple too. Only the noise there was lovely. I remember the music and the angels singing."

~~~

Satan groaned! How did she do that? She has completely shut me out! he thought.

~~~

The next thing I knew, Caylee was shaking me, asking, "Gina, are you sleeping?"

"Far from it!" I answered.

"Well, it's time to leave." Caylee giggled.

Hope followed me out to my mom's car and invited us to the victory party she and Brent were hosting on Saturday afternoon at the Boys' Home. Because I was tired, I listened while Hope and my mom discussed items to bring. Then Hope said, "I'll see you tomorrow."

It wasn't until arriving at my apartment that I realized why Hope said what she did; she was taking me to the doctor. As I got out of my mom's backseat, it also dawned on me that I wouldn't have to sit in a backseat anymore. I would be able to drive my new car tomorrow afternoon. That reminder made my head swim, and not in a good way. It also meant I'd be facing Wayne alone without Whisperer during my testing period. How was I going to face this man without Whisperer in my head? How would I keep from focusing on my fleshly need? What could I do to keep myself in check? I was already experiencing desire. Who could I focus on instead?

"Lord, help!" I begged. I heard Ox's hassle and knew what to do. Whisperer specifically told me to focus on my angel, Ox and read God's Word.

I recognized Ox's presence and said, "Hi there, old friend. It's me and you for a few days. Please don't let me forget who I serve and why. I've been appointed to represent Him. Let's not fail Him, okay."

As tired as my body was, I could not rest. Instead, I repeated what I did that morning. I read to Ox from God's Holy Word.

The Struggle

Satan wondered, *what is it about this woman? And why did she read God's Word aloud? She is not a dry twig that is easily broken, that is for sure.*

While Satan pondered, Lack and Self-Effort returned to give their report. "Master, we have sorrowful news," they stated.

"What do you mean?" Satan snapped.

"We could not gain entrance to Wade. Ox-like creatures were stationed everywhere. We tried several times to see the man but couldn't. We weren't even allowed to hear any of his conversations," Lack informed.

"Blast!" Satan screamed.

"I fell through a loophole! I forgot to demand that Ox's regiments be forbidden on earth as well. They are protecting the man. There is nothing we can do about it. We must focus on making Wayne our puppet until the time runs out," Satan conveyed.

"Sir," Self-Effort interrupted.

"What?" Satan demanded.

"We checked Wayne also. He is also surrounded," Self- Effort shared.

Satan stomped and ranted. "Then we'll have to warp Wayne's words somehow. Maybe we can use other props to confuse Gina.

We only have a short time. Go, help Lust find Marshall Dunlap. Convince that man to do our bidding," Satan ordered.

~~~

The next morning, Hope called to inform me that she could not take me to the doctor but that she would send Brent. When I asked if everything was all right, she told me she was sick and had been vomiting since daybreak.

I was disappointed, and I wanted her help. I was hoping she would grant me a portion of her gift again today. I wanted to see Ox, not just hear him. I thought if I could fix my eyes on him, I wouldn't be lured into the lustful fantasy of sex with Wayne.

Since I wouldn't be able to see Ox spiritually, I decided to do a childish thing after my sponge bath. I would draw a stick-figured dog in the palm of my hand so I could look at it instead. I had to look at something because I feared falling into Wayne's amazing green eyes or melting from his smooth voice. I also positioned the drawing where I could also dig my nails into it if I had too. That way, I could focus on gripping Ox so Wayne's touch wouldn't become too much for me to bear. My physical pain would keep my attention. I would hear Ox's hassle or warning growls and snaps if I weren't mesmerized by lust.

~~~

Satan watched as Gina scribbled something in her hand and was totally confused. Then he walked with her to her closet and had a great idea. He would bait her into dressing alluringly.

"Wear the red dress. It is sexy and powerful. Wayne may like powerful women. Then there is the green-and-rust outfit you wore last time. Hope loved how it looked on you," Satan suggested.

~~~

I heard the raspy voice loud and clear. It was not the voice I'd ever wanted to follow. The voice I wanted, loved both recommended outfits. He also loved when I wore makeup for Him. "That is what I'll do." I was determined. I would look good for Jesus and let the chips fall where they may. Satan would not have to know the real reason for my dressing up. Let him think I took his bait.

I chose the red dress. I applied makeup and curled my hair. I also splashed perfume on my neck and wrists. It made me feel special. I would be Jesus's bride today. I would proudly walk in that realization. I could also look at my red dress and remember who I was during this lustful trial with Wayne. I mentally said, Thanks, Lord, for helping me remember who I am. Thanks for reminding me how you liked to see me at my best.

~~~

"My suggestion worked. I have her back. She's trying to lure Wayne's eye again, and she'll fail." Satan scoffed to himself.

~~~

Brent arrived on time, and I asked how Hope was doing. He said she was weak from vomiting, but he thought it was from all the pressure they'd been under the last few weeks. Then Brent complimented my appearance as he assisted me in the back of Hope's SUV. "You look nice today. Why the power suit?" he asked. "I'm wearing it to give me confidence in who I am. I'm praying for a victory today," I answered.

"You look and smell great. I'm proud of you. It is always good to have the proper attitude knowing you belong to God," he remarked.

Brent left me at the doctor's office and went back home to check on Hope. He instructed before leaving to call when I needed a ride, and he would chauffeur me home. I sat in the waiting room and read a few articles on health and tried not to think about who I would face in a few minutes. When my name was called, I took a deep breath and followed the nurse into the examining room. She took my vital signs, handed me a hospital gown, and then asked me to remove my clothes. I was stunned. "Why?" I asked.

"The doctor wants a full leg x-ray before he determines whether you are healed," she explained.

"Do I have to remove my undergarments?" I asked.

"Yes, Ms. Grimes. It is always best that we don't have anything hampering our photographs," she answered politely.

"Will the doctor be taking the pictures?" I asked nervously.

"No, ma'am. One of our techs will," she explained.

I sighed with relief. I was taken off guard. I would have been very exposed. I looked at my hand and mentally said to Ox, Boy, that was close! I heard him hassle.

I removed everything and threw on the hospital gown and tied it on as securely as I could; then I sat down on a small chair while I waited for the tech. I was comfortable and unafraid until I heard a rap on the door. Assuming it was the x-ray tech, I sat up straight and prepared for my boot to be removed; but instead of a tech entering the room, it was Wayne and the nurse. My heart lurched.

I quickly looked at my hand. "Help!" I pleaded. Instantly, I heard growls. I knew immediately they weren't the only ones who entered the room. The thought of Satan being in the room made me angry. I looked at my hand again. Thanks for the warning, I thought toward Ox.

"Hello, Ms. Grimes," Wayne greeted.

"Call me Gina, please," I replied.

"Let me help you on the table. I want to examine your leg before they take you to x-ray," Wayne offered.

I heard the ugly raspy voice say, "He's going to touch you. He will see your nakedness. You will certainly grab his attention this time. Where's your protector now?"

Ox snapped and growled. Then I heard him yelp loudly, and it caused a fury to blaze inside me.

~~~

Wayne had me on the table so fast, I didn't have time to think about modesty, but I didn't care. I was too angry that Satan hurt Ox. I kept focusing on my hand and mentally trying to soothe Ox while the nurse and Wayne examined my leg. Scripture came to mind, and I thanked Jesus for taking my reproach, and I asked Him to keep watching over us. In my heart, I knew Ox was sent by Jesus. He was to watch over me, so when I heard him yelp, I knew he was trying to stop Satan from talking to me. His obedience to Jesus was amazing, and it helped me focus on my mission. Because of my worry over Ox, Wayne's touch did not faze me, and his voice was barely audible. I managed to hear him well enough to nod yes or no to some of his questions, but I hardly heard anything else during the examination. I kept my nails planted deeply in my palm. I tried to keep my grip on Ox. All I wanted to know was if he was okay; nothing else mattered. I kept my ears tuned to the spirit realm. I needed to hear a hassle. Minutes flew before I heard Ox. When I did, it was a reassuring loud hassle. He was back! My joy was profound, and what I had feared was over. Wayne's touch hadn't sexually disturbed me, nor had his voice bewitched me. I was almost free. I had one more hurdle: his eyes.

The x-ray table was freezing, and the discomfort kept me focused. I was not a fool; I still knew Satan was near and would try something.

A few minutes later, I was dressed all but the boot and waiting for the verdict. When the nurse entered my room, I jumped because she did not tap on the door. *Just another one of Satan's tricks,* I thought. The nurse didn't mean to frighten me. Satan wanted me frazzled with nervous fear, not her.

The nurse said, "Good! You are already dressed. Gather your crutches and follow me."

"Do I walk with or without the crutches?" I asked.

"Right now, use them. The doctor will explain," she informed.

~~~

Satan's raspy voice spat in my ears. "You're still crippled. You'll never be right! You will never wear high heels or be able to run again!"

Ox started growling and snapping again. Not only did I hear Ox yelp a few times, I heard the thuds of Satan's blows as he kicked or hit Ox's body. I wanted to scream! I wanted to hit at something, but I could not make a scene because the nurse was waiting for me to follow her.

Again, I would face Wayne in anger. I was not angry at him but at what was happening. Satan was determined to trip me up and make me lose my cool. That realization changed the course. I purposefully smiled.

We were in Wayne's office. He motioned for me to have a seat. Then he proceeded to give me my report. "Gina, your leg has healed nicely. The bones have knit well, and all the infection is gone. I want you to use at least one of your crutches until you are steady. In a few days, I want you to start physical therapy. You should be back to normal by New Year's Day," he explained.

"You mean it! I'll be able to ride bikes and play ball again?" I asked.

"Sure! I don't see why not. Everything is fine. All you have is a scar, and in time, that will fade," he said cheerfully.

"Wonderful! I'm looking forward to playing with a few of my friends at the Boys' Home," I shared.

"Are you going to Brent's campaign party at the Boys' Home this weekend?" Wayne asked.

"Yeah!" I answered, shocked by his question.

Satan rasped, "He's flirting with you! Flirt back! Throw yourself at him! He's waiting. After all, he is your soul mate."

Ox snapped and snapped as if he were insane.

Hearing Ox go crazy frightened me. Out of panic, I opened my palm so I could focus on him, but something else caught my eye. It was two pictures on the corner of Wayne's desk. A large one was of him with another woman. My heart broke, and I swallowed hard to fight back tears.

~~~

Satan said to his giants, "I've got her attention now. I'll throw her a curve."

~~~

Behind me, I heard Satan's raspy voice speak as if he was trying to soothe me. He said, "Don't pay any attention to her. She's not his love. You are! Look at the other picture."

I couldn't help myself. My eyes swung to the other photograph. In the smaller frame was a picture of Wayne seated on a motorcycle and holding a black helmet. I studied the picture harder. The helmet had the symbol of a flame painted on it. My heart pounded. Wayne was my soul mate! The girl really meant nothing. God doesn't lie. I just had to wait.

~~~

"**S**he took the bait, guys! Saturday, we are going to crush her and her God!" Satan cheered.

~~~

"**G**ina! Here are your release papers. I've stated on them that you can return to work without limits in three weeks. I'll see you at the party Saturday. You have a good day." Wayne dismissed me.

My heart sang. I smiled at him and said, "Thank you. You have a good day also."

I checked out and immediately called Hope because I didn't have Brent's number. While I waited for my ride outside on a bench, I talked with Ox. "Old friend, we did it. You literally saved my bacon today. I'm sorry you took a beating for me, but if you hadn't fought, I would not have been able to cope. Whisperer knew what He was doing when He assigned you to me. We make a good team." I consoled. I heard Ox hassle.

When I got home, I changed into jeans, a T-shirt, and tennis shoes then spent the rest of the day driving around in my new car. I visited Mom and Dad at their jobs. Afterward, when I was certain school was over, I drove out to the Boys' Home. I wanted to see Brian so I could encourage him. The victory was sweet. I could walk, and I knew Wayne was mine.

That night, Caylee, Russ, and I went for joyrides, and the big boy sat in the back.

No Contest

The next day on Friday morning, Satan ranted. He was furious! He was failing because of a dog. Every time he tried to woo or trick the girl, the stupid dog barked, growled, or snapped at him. Something had to be done. He needed help, so he called a quick meeting.

"We are going to have to do something to that damnable dog!" Satan hissed. "I can't get anywhere near Gina without the stupid thing snapping at me. I have big plans for tonight, and I will need complete access to Gina. Tonight, Marshall Dunlap will be added into torment. If there's a man who can lure desire back into Gina's body, he can. But I can't add my twist to the mental and physical torture as long as that dog is near. I need help. Who will volunteer to distract the mutt?" Satan asked.

The three giants, Lust, Lack, and Self-Effort, looked at one another. They thought distracting the dog would be easy. Animals were lured away easily, and if this animal didn't take the bait, they could beat it senseless. Satan was focused on the girl, and it was far better to take their frustration out on the mutt than have Satan take his out on them, so all three volunteered.

~~~

I woke again an hour earlier than I normally would, simply for the sake of tormenting my tormentor. God's Word was my weapon. It was also my mental stability.

After yesterday's experiences, I wanted to know more about the subject of rage. It was my rage that kept me from folding like a cheap chair. I looked up several of my concordance's references on the subject and found my answer. Rage was like a fire. Instantly, the revelation lightbulb came on in my mind. Rage was part of my gift. It was the spark that set things in motion for me, depending on where it was focused.

Next, I decided to look up the word fire. I found a reference that intrigued me in the book of Exodus chapter 13 verse 21 of the Amplified version. It read,

> *The Lord went before them by day in a pillar of cloud to lead them along the way and by night in a pillar of fire to give them light, that they might travel by day and by night.*

The light bulb went on again! The vision was my first introduction with the Holy Spirit. The water bubble and the flame came flooding back into memory. It explained why I lived in water and fire. The Lord goes before us. In the good times, he stands like a cloud. Clouds are full of water. His life is always refreshing, and He wants that for us. He also goes before us in the dark times like fire. He stands as an all-consuming fire against anything denying us a good life. This was awesome information. I wanted to run this by Whisperer, but He wasn't around. I did hear the comforting sound of Ox's hassle.

Today, I took a long shower and basked in the downpour of water on my flesh. As the water covered me, I thanked the Lord. "Thank you for giving me your good life!"

Around the apartment, I hardly used the crutch. It was easier to brace myself on furniture or walls when I walked along. When I stood in front of my dresser to choose undergarments, I realized I didn't have to wear my snap-on panties anymore. I could wear my dainty, barely-there thongs or even my granny panties if I wanted. I snickered mischievously and said to myself, "Let the old viper think I'm trying to impress a man." Then I mentally said to Jesus, Lord, I'm dressing to please you. You love my body. Then I put on the thongs.

Before I put on outer garments, I continued with one ritual. I placed the notes of Wayne and our journey together, which I had written in folded paper, inside my bra. I refused to let this go. Wearing a pantsuit was freeing; I could move and not fear exposure. I still wore flat shoes but only because my leg wasn't strong enough for heels yet. When I arrived at work, I fully expected to be placed back on my old job duties but was pleasantly surprised. Apparently, the administration recognized a change with me at the reception helm and gave my old job to Jennie Hall. All day I greeted people with a smile on my face and had the pleasure of hearing Ox's lovely hassle.

It wasn't until I was changing clothes to go to the Friday-night group that I heard Ox growl. The sound of his growl was all I needed to react wisely. I knew Satan was somewhere, but I didn't hear him until I was in my car headed out.

The raspy voice said, "Free at last! You are free to move. You can help and not sit on the sidelines. It's your turn to make sure the popcorn is popped and the drinks are cool. Let someone else sit with slackers."

Satan didn't know it, but when he said the word slackers, I got angry. Stacy was not a slacker! She needed companionship, and I was available. I took a second or two and thought about what else he said. *It was deception! He wanted me busy doing menial tasks and not helping people. Bah! I would show him! I could do both!* When I entered the church social hall, Ox began growling and snapping loudly, and it caused my own hackles to rise. Satan was out to kill, steal, or destroy, and it made me mad. I concentrated on my anger. The anger saved me yesterday. That thought blurred my mind. It made me hesitate a minute. I thought, *for weeks I have dreamed of the day I'd see Wayne again. I wanted to gaze on his face, but yesterday his face is the last thing I wanted to see.*

~~~

Satan saw Gina's hesitation and took it for a sign of fear.

~~~

The timing was off, that was all. If Whisperer hadn't been warned of my testing period, I'd be trapped in desire and lost. My test was to live a few days for Jesus. Just a few days were all, so I had to be wise, and being caught under Wayne's spell was not wise. "Thank you, God, for sending me Ox."

I gritted my teeth and proceeded to the room. I hated Satan and his tricks. I was determined to love on everybody and serve them at the same time. I set out to find Hope or Brent and was stopped instantly in my tracks. Before me was my worst nightmare, the person who caused me to change from an innocent girl into a slut. Marshall Dunlap was a vision.

Ox went insane. I heard growls and snaps then I heard blows and yelps. Again, more barks and snaps and more yelps. The sound was awful! My heart broke for my poor Ox! The focus on Ox caused me to breathe rapidly. My lungs felt like billows stoking a fire. I was very angry. I turned away from what faced me. Marshall was not my problem at that moment. Ox's tormentors were. With my face turned away from a visual threat, I concentrated on the evil spirit instead and commanded, "Stop trying to kill, steal, and destroy in the name of Jesus!"

~~~

The three giants grabbed their ears. They left before being consumed. Fire was coming from the woman's mouth. Satan stood stupefied. He managed to remain on only one technicality: Gina hadn't mentioned him by name.

Satan saw that his three giants managed to hurt the dog, though. The dog was down, so he slid over the creature and placed his foot on the ugly dog's throat and dared it to make a sound.

~~~

Ox was down, but he was not out. He knew all he had to do was a whimper, and heaven would come running, so he chose to lie there proudly. Gina was strong. Ox knew his human was on a roll.

~~~

I couldn't hear Ox, but in my heart, I knew he was not dead. I imagined him chasing the evil away instead. I knew he would return. Even though Ox was off somewhere, I couldn't stand in the middle of the room like a statue. I had to keep on track, Marshall or not. I walked up to Brent. I greeted him and said hi to Marshall, then I asked Brent, "Where's Hope?"

"I think she's in the ladies' room," Brent replied.

"Thanks!" I countered before walking in the ladies' room direction.

In the beautifully decorated ladies' restroom, I sought Hope out. "Hope, are you in here?"

"Yeah! I'll be out in a jiff," Hope answered.

When she emerged, her face looked pale. I had my focus! I was to minister to my mentor! "Are you okay?" I asked.

I watched Hope grope the sink to get her stability. Then I watched as she rinsed out her mouth before answering, "I'm fine. It's good news really. Brent and I were hoping to share our news tomorrow at the party, but I don't think my appearance will allow that to happen. People like you know when something is off. Gina, I'm not ill, I'm pregnant."

I had an 180-degree emotional turnaround. I went from rage to sheer joy! "That's great!" I shouted.

Hope and I walked back into the room. Joy was now my strength. The joy of knowing true love kept me grounded, so when Marshall sauntered over to flirt, I was ready. I was also ready for Satan's tricks.

~~~

Satan suggested, "Spit in his face! Better yet, unbutton your shirt a little and let him see what he missed."

Then Marshall drawled, "Hi, Gina! Good to see you again. I didn't expect to see you in a place like this. It's really not my style."

Satan baited. "He looks good, doesn't he? He always dressed in high fashion. He liked nice things, and he's really built well. Remember how he was under the sheets?"

Yes, I remembered everything. That was the issue, so I answered Marshall, saying, "Why don't you give it a try? We help people." Marshall looked me up and down. It made me feel funny.

When he did, I realized he was sizing me up and looking at my body. Come to think about it, I was doing the same: sizing him up, but I wasn't looking at his body. I was reading his thoughts by looking at his actions. I came to realize he was no different than Lyle Horne. He was a sick puppy. The only difference was that he was a handsome sick puppy with money and power.

When he began to flirt with me, my stomach flipped. It literally made me sick. That experience brought to mind, true love. Hope and Brent's true love bound in matrimony.

"Why don't we help each other?" Marshall suggested.

"Go with him! It will relieve your sexual tension and then you can face Wayne tomorrow and not worry about raping him," the raspy voice suggested.

That did it! I didn't need to hear Ox's growl. I was livid! Instead of lashing out at Marshall or buckling under the sexual pressure, I did the opposite. I sweetly said, "I'll help you, Marshall, by saying no to your invitation. I'm not the same person I was a few years ago. We both need what Hope and Brent have, which is a stable and loving relationship. Just not with each other. You don't want me. You never did, but it is nice to know you think my lovemaking is good. Why else would you want seconds? I'll take that as a compliment."

~~~

Satan felt like he'd been hit by a truck. The girl was infuriating! He looked down at the dog under his foot and realized that the animal was not his problem. That didn't matter. Problem or not, the mutt made a good punching bag, so he took his anger out on Ox.

~~~

Jesus was very proud of Ox. Ox was the part of His team that represented His sacrificial nature, always willing to take a beating and keep on defending by dying to fleshly things.

Showtime

I thought about the night's events when I got home. I didn't run in the face of fear. What happened amazed me. Instead of being ugly and hateful to the man who ruined my self-image, I was nice and polite. We enjoyed fellowship after his perverted suggestion was dealt with. We listened to music together and played a few rounds of darts. He got to see the real me instead of my body.

After I got home later that night, the paper fell out of my bra as I undressed. It bugged me. I was missing a piece of the puzzle. The paper was very fragile now due to me wearing it tucked in my bra for days, so I unfolded it slowly and gently. I determinedly read my own writing. Many times I referenced Adrian, and a thought occurred to me. I had two references to Wayne, Adrian, and Whisperer. I had written down my journey with Adrian, but I didn't have anything written down about Wayne's helmet of fire. *How did Satan know?* I thought. Then I realized he didn't! He was watching Adrian and me, so he knew about the motorcycle. He knew everything about the journey; that was why I was shoved back inside my body so hard. Something wasn't right.

I listened for Ox's hassle. Nothing! Come to think of it, I hadn't heard him since first seeing Marshall. "Ox, ole friend! Where are you? Please make a noise! Do something so I can hear you!" I pleaded.

I listened very intently. I closed my eyes and sat very still. Then I heard a soft and low moan. "Ox! Are you all right?" I blurted. He hassled very softly and low.

~~~

Satan called his wimpy giants back to the forefront. "Fellows, here is your chance. Redeem yourselves! We only have one more day, so when Gina goes to sleep tonight, wreak havoc in her dreams. If she wakes before dawn, then vanish."

~~~

I was very tired, but the thought of Ox being hurt bothered me until I remembered how strong he got from hearing God's Word. "Ox, I'm going to read to you. God's Word is our best medicine. I'm going to need you tomorrow, so relax and receive your healing," I soothed him.

I took an ink pen and drew another stick-figured dog, but this time on my leg. I lay on my bed and read God's Word out loud, but I also rubbed my hand up and down on my leg over the drawing. It was my way of seeing Ox being consoled. I read for at least an hour before I heard a healthy hassle. Soon after hearing Ox's hassle, I fell sound asleep with God's Word open on my chest.

I dreamed horrible dreams. I dreamed Marshall wanted to kill me, and Wayne was trying to run me down with his bike. I also saw Ox, the angel, dead. Even Lyle Horne was chasing me. No one wanted me alive. No one had a good thing to say about me. I thrashed and thrashed in bed until I heard something go whomp! On the floor! It woke me up!

~~~

Lust, Lack, and Self-Effort fled quickly.

~~~

Dazed and my head still reeling from the nightmare, I slowly turned and reached for my lamp. With light filling the room, I could see what made the noise. My Bible had fallen on the floor. I reached to pick it up, and my eyes fell on a sentence. The word chase got my attention. The complete sentence read, "And you shall chase your enemies, and they shall fall before you by the sword." Because I was still traumatized from my dream of being chased, I quickly grabbed the book to see the verse up close. I wondered if God was trying to tell me something. "Why else would my eyes find this one particular verse?"

I took the sign to mean something of vital importance. I sat up, and I read the verse several more times out loud to get the meaning deep inside my heart. When I was certain I had it planted securely, I let my breath go and said, "I am not the chased. I am the chaser! All my enemies will fall before God's Word!" Ox hassled loudly!

~~~

"No! It cannot be!" Satan screamed. Then he thought, *my time is not up! I refuse! This girl will not be the one to ruin my system of things. Not a child! Not one who is unlearned and weak! But can she be? Is she the hunter that God prophesied about? I refuse to worry! I still have one more day to get her off course. I still have a chance.*

~~~

With the knowledge of Hope's pregnancy, I decided to get an early start and head over to the Boys' Home because Hope may not feel like caring for dozens of people. I was free to move now and wanted to do my part. When I arrived, I saw Brent's BMW but not Hope's SUV; it worried me. Surely, she would be here. She wouldn't miss Brent's party. I had been determined to make her sit for a change and let me do the work.

Inside the large kitchen of the main house, I found Brent talking with his dad, and I interrupted by asking again, "Where is Hope?" He pointed to the living area. She was lying on a sofa. She was still pale as a ghost, but I wasn't the only one there to fret over her. Mamie was sitting beside her. Hope was in fantastic care. "What can I do? Is the sickness an attack from Satan?" I asked Mamie.

"No, child! It is hormonal. Her body is preparing itself for the baby. Hope will be fine. All we need to do is keep her hydrated. Look in the refrigerator. If they have a cola in there, bring some over," Mamie suggested.

I almost ran to the kitchen. I hated seeing my mentor weak and pale. When I reached the room, Brent looked at me but didn't say anything. Apparently, he knew what I was doing. Just before reaching for the refrigerator, my vision blurred, and I almost gasped. For an instant, I saw Brent's huge lion standing behind him. I calmed down instantly; I knew all was well.

I found some cola and took it to Hope. My vision blurred again, and I saw Hope's large eagle, but before I lost my spiritual sight, I turned my eyes toward Mamie. Sure enough, there was a very large Adrian. *Why am I seeing all this?* I thought. Then it occurred to me. If I could see their angels, I could see Ox. I looked frantically. Nothing! To keep from alarming my friends, I walked out of the room and called, "Ox, where are you?"

My eyes blurred, and I got excited until I saw my friend. He was a bruised and broken mess. He was hassling, though. My heart hurt. I started breathing heavily and felt the fire inside me. I knew what it was. My rage had been ignited. "You were hiding from me, weren't you?" I asked. Ox didn't answer, even with a hassle, but I did see him nod and blip out of my sight again. He didn't want me to see how he looked. He wanted me to focus on his hassle. I understood the meaning behind his gesture, but I didn't like it. I wanted to console my friend. I wasn't going to pity him.

I walked back into the living area, and I focused my eyes on Adrian. I looked at Mamie's angel straight in the eyes and said out loud and without shame, "Heal Ox. Take away his pain."

"You talking to me, child?" Mamie asked.

"No, ma'am. I'm talking to your angel," I countered. "I just asked him to help my angel."

Mamie nodded, and I watched her angel blip out of sight.

~~~

All Hope did was moan as she prayed. She knew what was happening, and compassion filled her heart.

~~~

With my drama under control, I set my sights on getting the party preparations ready. I made tea and helped get the ice-cream churns ready. I also helped some of the boys cover the outdoor tables with pretty tablecloths.

Brent and Mr. Arnold were cooking hotdogs and hamburgers while Mamie, Caylee, and Mrs. Arnold made side platters to go with the main course. Hope continued to lie on the living-room sofa with her eyes closed. I could tell she wasn't asleep though because her mouth moved some.

By 1:30 p.m., all the food was ready, and people started coming. I ran to the restroom to brush my hair. I didn't want to look as if I'd slaved all day. I wanted to look fresh and pretty.

While I was brushing my hair, I heard a familiar voice. "Trying to look pretty for Wayne? He'll be here shortly. Why don't you unbutton your shirt and roll it up and then tie off the ends to show off your flat stomach and round breast? Men like to see flesh, you know," Satan suggested.

I heard Ox hassle when I ignored Satan's comment. Then I heard Ox yelp again. That was it! I had had enough of my angel being beaten. I glared into the mirror and said, "Leave us alone!"

~~~

I found Mamie sitting at one of the outdoor tables and went over to join her. Before I sat, I noticed a Jeep coming up the drive. Wayne was here. We were here at the Boys' Home together. It was autumn; the time my journey suggested. Was this our day? All indicators pointed to that fact. With my left hand, I touched my breast, feeling for my paper. "Surely, this is the day," I prayed.

Finale

Satan, Lust, Lack, and Self-Effort gathered around Gina. Their plan was ready to spring. With bated breath, they waited for Gina's heartbreak. If they played all cards correctly, she would stop fighting for Jesus and begin hating him.

~~~

I didn't want to stare at Wayne's vehicle as it came up the drive, but I couldn't help myself. I just kept praying he wouldn't see me staring. My intent gaze caused me to notice that he had two passengers with him. I didn't want to think about who they were. I didn't want to think about the woman in the picture on his desk. Fear made me turn and face Mamie. I took a deep breath and asked, "Mamie, do you know the people with Dr. Polk?"

I studied Mamie's face and watched her grin. I braced myself for her answer. My heart wanted to refuse anything but good news. My ears were keen to hear anything but what I feared. My gaze was fixed on Mamie's mouth while I held my breath. Then she uttered the unthinkable. She said, "Oh, that's his mother and Amy, his wife."

Wife! No, Lord! Please tell me what Mamie said is not true! I screamed mentally.

I heard raspy laughter and then I heard Ox go insane again. In the midst of complete and mind-blowing heartache, I realized my Ox wasn't happy. He was beyond crazy. Then I heard blows and kicks that made Ox yelp and whine loudly. I turned my back to Mamie and also away from all the people. I wanted to lash out at our hidden tormentor, but I couldn't. If I could punch something, I'd be pacified, but if I did, I'd be locked in a hospital room for the insane. So instead of reacting to my fury, I sat and steamed. The tears on my face stung as if they came from boiling water.

~~~

Jesus heard Ox's whine and saw Gina's reaction. Ox's whine was his and heaven's cue to move. Happily, Jesus flew to their rescue on Cherub's back. Jesus knew only moments were left before Gina would make the decision. He wanted to be the one to show her truth again before she said the next word aloud, but instead of landing on the ground when He arrived on earth, Jesus purposely hid in the lake, and there He waited.

~~~

It felt like bands of death were surrounding and squeezing my heart. My heart was literally being crushed, and with each beat left in it, I heard Satan say, "Where is your God? Where is the liar? Where is the one you put hope in? I don't see Him! Tell me, where is your strength now!"

I closed my eyes, and I tried to focus on Ox but kept hearing him whine. It sounded like he was dying and didn't have long to live. In my distress, when it seemed like death had us both pinned, I cried out to God. "Whisperer, Jesus, Abba, I really need you! I can't do this! Please take me home! I want to be with you," I pleaded.

I felt the earth tremble under my feet. It startled me, and my eyes flew open. I thought, *can it be? Is my prayer heard?* Since my face was turned away from Mamie and the crowd, the first thing I saw after opening my eyes was the lake. Its shimmer beckoned me. I needed God's peace. I remembered how he loved to refresh. I needed to be in the water bubble where I didn't have to struggle. I desired to have a moment of peace with Jesus again. It drove me swiftly to the lake, and I forgot to pick up my crutch. My weak leg didn't prevent me from jogging to the water's edge. There I heard the lapping of the water against the land as the breeze pushed it forward.

There in the peaceful place, I closed my eyes and began to talk with Jesus. Lord, I come to you. You are my hiding place. Somehow, Satan has played a foul trick on me. He destroyed the promise you gave me. I've failed you. One thing I know for sure though is that you are my love and comfort. You stood by me when I had nothing. You brought my family back together and gave them new life. You gave me friends who are more like sisters and brothers, plus you gave me a purpose. I've never been happier. Since I never got to experience the other, it doesn't matter anymore. I know you'll find another way for me to be loved here on earth, I mentally said as tears flowed down my cheeks.

~~~

Satan screamed! Lust, Lack, and Self-Effort scurried away and tried to hide.

~~~

"Open your eyes, little one. I'm here," Jesus said.

I heard my Lord's sweet voice. He was back! He'd heard my prayer. I opened my eyes, expecting to see my own reflection in the pool of water but was pleasantly surprised. In the water was Jesus's face, not mine. My throat tightened. I had trouble speaking, so I settled for studying the face that meant everything to me. I reached out to touch His face and saw His hand move at the same time. Then I noticed His right hand over His bosom; it was where my left hand was. I turned my head side to side and noticed Jesus did the same. We were in perfect sync with each other, moving as one. I smiled and Jesus smiled.

Jesus thought, *I've got her attention. She's beginning to understand.*

Satan realized what was happening and yelled louder, "Gina! He is a liar. He told you a lie! Don't be fooled by His trick!"

I looked to my right when I heard Satan's evil comments, and Jesus moved His head to the left at the same time. We saw the evil beast at the same time there in the water's reflection. Furious rage began to build in my chest as I kept my gaze locked on evil. My lungs heaved and then billowed over the flame inside me. I remembered Ox's rage and how unbeatable and ferocious he looked when he was defending Jesus, and I realized I felt the same way. Standing before Jesus and I was the one who came against everything I held dear. Satan was no longer hidden; I could see him for what he was. He was nothing but foul air and a hateful attitude. Rage's pressure mounted on my chest, and I could not control my tongue any longer, and I didn't care who heard what I had to say.

Since arriving at the water's edge, I'd only communicated mentally, but now I shouted at the top of my voice, "You evil and vile creature. How dare you come against the Word of God. Your words and threats no longer affect me. You will never hurt me again."

Then we, Jesus and I both as one, reached for Satan's throat, and once we had him in our grasp, we threw him to the ground and stomped on his neck. Then my next words came out just as hateful and demanding, "There! Stay under my feet where you belong."

~~~

Lightning came from everywhere! Lack, Lust, and Self-Effort's evil plans were destroyed, and they were placed in eternal chains. Even Satan was bound for a while. He would soon have a court date in heaven to attend.

That was when I noticed my own foot. It was engulfed in fire. I was standing at the edge of the water, and my body was on fire at the same time. I was in the thing I desired most: Jesus! I was operating within the pillar of fire, Jesus's wrath. I looked at my Lord within the water, and He was smiling. Then He said, "Your desire is showing for all of heaven, things on earth, and under the earth to see!"

That was when I witnessed a miracle. Abba was standing behind Jesus, and He was looking at me. He was smiling at me. Me! Not Jesus in me, but me, standing by myself covered in Jesus's fury. The joy was overwhelming until I noticed a small clump within the reflection of Jesus's eyes. It was Ox lying at my feet that Jesus's eyes showed me. Ox was motionless. My heart melted. My friend had taken such a beating to warn me. I looked up into Jesus's eyes and pleaded, "Help him before he dies! Restore him please!"

Instantly, Ox returned to his huge self, wings and all. I reached for his image disclosed inside the water and heard the water sizzle. My hand was still on fire. I looked at Jesus and Abba in astonishment. I wondered why I was still engulfed when I was no longer in a rage. Then it occurred to me. *I was my true self. A fire to expel darkness!*

~~~

Then something else occurred to me. Abba, the Creator of all things, was present. My promise was not lost; it could rise from the dead. I grabbed my shirt and removed the paper to only have it burst into flame. My plan was to drop it in the water where Abba was, but when my eyes looked at the paper, it ignited and quickly turned to ash. I wanted to cry, and my eyes flew to Jesus for help.

That was when I saw it, the piece of paper. Jesus had my written notes in His hand. My eyes filled with tears, but this time, they didn't burn. They were tears of pure joy running down my face because I knew what was about to come next. Jesus, my Comforter, my Giver of all good was allowing me to ask Abba for my blessing. I watched Him hand Abba the small piece of paper then I heard His request. *"Father, I promised this to Gina right after she was reborn, and Satan used it against her. He did his best to prevent my wish for her to happen. It is evident to Gina that You are the only one who can recreate. Please show her we never lie."*

My eyes gaped as I watched Abba look at what Jesus handed him. Gently, He opened the folded paper. My heart pounded, and blood rushed into my ears. Abba was saying something, but a sound behind me prevented me from hearing what He was saying. At first, I thought the noise was my own heart beating hard, making a sound of rumbling in my ears, but when the noise stopped, I realized it wasn't anything coming from my physical body.

For a moment, there was no sound. Nothing! We were in total silence. I kept my eyes focused on Abba. He wadded the paper and threw it in the air. I watched it glide down and touch Jesus's face. I gasped in surprise, for at that moment Jesus disappeared, something hit me hard in the back of the head. I reached up to feel the spot when I heard, "Are you all right?"

I wanted to shout! I knew that voice! I turned around quickly to see the face that had previously haunted but excited my dreams. His lovely face! I knew this man was mine because he still held a helmet painted with flames. It dawned on me that the sound I took for my own heart's beating was noise coming from his motorcycle.

"Hello, I'm Wade Polk," he said.

"Wade! Your name is Wade?" I asked, stunned. "Yes! And your name is?" he asked.

"I'm Gina Grimes," I replied. But I thought to myself, *I'm going to be Gina Polk very soon.*

Epilogue

In time, we would see that Gina and Wade were true soul mates. In turn, they shared their stories of testing and saw similarities.

Wade would explain how his call came while he was on active duty in the marines. He told how he was chosen to search out evil within the broken-bodied by dedicating his life to mending the crippled spirit. He would go on to explain why he wasn't interested in women when Brent insisted he meets a girl. He was waiting for his soul mate. Jesus told him that his bride-to-be would be found working for justice and her walk bound in a cast. Gina was the one. He knew this because Brent stood for justice, and this girl was helping his campaign. So, when Wade's eyes fell on Gina's cast and then on her lovely face, he was determined to see her again.

Gina, on the other hand, promised to use her gift to search out evil within people's minds. Now with Wade, they were like the blood of their Lord Jesus. His blood oozed into every crevice, searching for Satan's touch for the sheer purpose of setting things right again. They were a team, and Satan knew this. They were Jesus's hunters.

Jesus was happy. The harvesting machine was complete. Now He had fishermen like Caylee and Russ and hunters like Gina and Wade. They inquired and required of Him on a moment's notice. Spiritually, Insight, Justice, and Healer with Ox would assist the Lord's vehicle, helping them gather souls. Gina had been the last and vital part. Her fury was needed to ignite the vehicle's engine, and her faith in her Lord made Ox and his regiment propel the machine forward.

Jesus was ready to give His pastor God's commission. Pastor Reed would be equipped to give a message of grace that would start the engine moving and gathering souls, but one more thing had to occur. All-out war had to emerge in the spirit realm, and the earth's support systems had to collapse so people would have nowhere else to turn and would be willing to listen to His pastor. Soon, Pastor Reed would glorify Jesus to thousands and hopefully millions.

Get ready for a journey. It is time for the church to take back what the enemy has stolen and for Jesus to reward His faithful.

Bibliography

Bible Zondervan Publishing

Amplified version references: John 10: 10; 1 Peter 5:8; John 17:15; Luke 6:45; Isaiah 61:1-4; Psalm 140:1-13; Habakkuk 2:2-3; 1 Corinthians 1:19-21; Hebrews 11:1; Ezekiel 1; Proverbs 14:4; Isaiah 54:17; Deuteronomy 28:45.

Biography

Raven H. Price, retired from government service in 2014 and plans to devote her time providing Christian entertainment. Using romance, fantasy, and drama full of intrigue, she will uncover tidbits of the Good News.

Please consider leaving a review on Amazon by clicking here thank you.